I0652463

THE RENT MAN

Iponymous Edition
First edition published 2014
By Iponymous publishing Limited
Swansea United Kingdom SA6 6BP

All rights reserved
© Mike Adlam, 2014
Moral rights asserted

The rights of Mike Adlam to be identified as author of this work has
been asserted in accordance with Section 77 of the Copyright, Designs
and Patents Act 1988. This book is sold subject to the condition that
it shall not, by way of trade or otherwise, be lent, resold, hired out or
otherwise circulated without the publisher's prior consent in any form
of binding or cover other than that in which it is published and without
a similar condition including this condition being imposed on the
subsequent purchaser

A CIP record for this book
Is available from the British Library

Cover photograph © Andrew Davies
www.andrewdaviesphotography.com

Design and typesetting: GMID
www.gmid.co.uk

ISBN (print) 978-1-908773-47-0
ISBN (ebook) 978-1-908773-46-3

www.iponymous.com

MIKE ADLAM

I am a 55-year-old British author and I have written four novels and a collection of short stories. The Rent Man is a down-the-line hard hitting thriller about an ex-special forces man, Charlie Llewellyn who comes to Swansea in Wales in pursuit of the international criminal behind The Rent Man gang, a drugs and male prostitution vice ring. Although it is contemporary and British, sharp eyed readers might spot that it is modelled on the classic spaghetti western High Plains Drifter: a stranger drifts into a community in the grip of a lawless gang and turns out to be more ruthless and violent than them, though ultimately in the cause of justice.

I am just about to start Out of Practice the third and final book in the Stamford trilogy. By now he has carved his way through the Middle Eastern political chaos as a phony Médecins Sans Frontières surgeon after his release from prison thanks to crimes dating back to Malpractice. Got it? Don't worry, it's all explained in the books. By the way, ten per cent of all proceeds from the Stamford trilogy are being donated to the Queen Elizabeth Hospital Charity to thank them for saving my life. This will go directly into their liver research unit whose work on diseases like cancer and hepatitis makes it a world leader in the field.

1

The boy backed away, shaking with terror. The stuff he had just taken and the feeble yellow lights on the top landing of the Swansea tower block were distorting the features of the shaven-headed giant grotesquely. Not even the brown he had shot up earlier could numb the dread that was overwhelming him. He'd heard what the rent man gang did to kids who fucked up. He tried to wipe away his tears with his bare forearm, but he only succeeded in smearing his make-up.

'Please, mister, I never knew...' he whispered, hopelessly. The landing railings dug into his back, making him jerk around in panic. The stuff was piling violent hallucinations and waves of paranoia on top of the horror of the situation. He had blindly followed the fugitive's instinctive urge to climb and now there was nowhere else to go. He cringed as the dog that the skinny one was holding began barking again. It was huge and it reared up, almost dragging its handler forward in its desire to attack. There was blood and spittle around its snarling jaws where he had wrenched his arm away before he ran. The drugs suddenly turned the blood into a black stream, which poured down onto the concrete and crept in a dark pool towards him.

A door opened and a man's head peered out.

'What's all the fuckin' row about then, you twats? People are tryin' to sleep by ere...'

The giant stepped forward and smashed a huge fist in his face.

'Mind your own fuckin' business,' he growled and used

the letterbox to slam the door closed again. He turned to the cowering youth.

'So you fancied a night on the town, did you? Thought you'd get ripped to the tits instead of workin', eh? So how much money have you been spendin' on gear, instead of 'andin' it over to the boys then, you thievin' little wanker?'

'None, mister. This was the only time, I swear. Honest to God!'

The giant leered, enjoying his victim's terror.

'Funny how you lying little faggots all start swearing to God when we catch you at it, but it don't make no difference 'cos we're still goin' to top you, see. Once a lyin' little prick, always a lyin' little prick – that's what I says.' As he spoke, he crouched slightly and moved forward.

Despite the distortion of the drugs, the boy moved in sheer desperation as his persecutor let out a bellow of wildly echoing laughter. He dropped low and tried to dart past the giant on his left-hand side. The move was quicker than expected and the man scrabbled at him without getting a proper grip, but it made no difference. The boy froze with the Doberman's bared fangs in his face.

The giant seized him with one hand by his long, flowing hair. He grabbed an emaciated leg with the other. He picked the youth up like a baby and heaved him up to chest level. With a grunt he pushed him up into the air, extending his arms like a weight lifter, and stepped over to the eight-foot high railings. With another grunt, he flexed and straightened his knees and hurled his victim over the high metal barrier. The boy let out a last, despairing scream as, arms thrashing for something to grab hold of, he disappeared from sight.

The giant and the dog handler emerged from the stairs of the tower block into the unlit car park at the rear of the building. Only the lights from the windows of the flats illuminated the scene. A squat thug in ex-army fatigues was standing waiting for them in the warm drizzle that was falling steadily. As the men gathered around the twisted body, the door of a battered, old Volvo, which was parked under some nearby trees, opened, and another giant emerged. This man, however, was a giant by virtue of his thirty stone bulk. What little light there was glinted on the heavy gold sovereigns that clustered on his knuckles. He waddled over to join the group.

'Tiny, Rake.' He pulled a bundle of notes from his pocket and handed some money to the giant and the dog handler in turn. He turned to the squat one.

'What happened to youz, ya fuckin' quair?' he demanded in a strong Irish accent.

'Shit, Duke, you knows I don't like 'eights,' muttered the thug.

'I don't give a fuck what ya like...' The fat man was about to continue when there was a faint groan from the ground.

'Jesus Christ, boys,' whispered the skinny one, 'e's not fuckin' dead!'

'Planky, come here!' ordered the Irishman. The squat thug stepped forward. The Irishman plonked a fat paw on his head and slowly lifted an enormous leg. He placed his foot on the boy's skinny chest and, using Planky to balance himself, shifted his full weight onto that leg. There was a crack as the boy's sternum gave way and the Irishman's thirty stone bulk crushed his heart.

'He fuckin' is now,' replied Duke O'Leary callously, as he steadied himself again on Planky and stepped off the corpse. He peeled some notes off the wad and handed them to the thug.

'That'll teach 'im, boss...'replied the skinny one, nervously.

'He's dead ya stupid cunt,' replied the Irishman dispassionately.

'It won't teach him nuthin'. Burn his clothes then smash his face a bit and take a few snaps to scare the others. Then feed him to the eels in Coffin Pond. Now sod off the lot of yez.'

He waddled off back across the car park and squeezed in behind the wheel of the battered old Volvo.

*

Al Sullivan manoeuvred his Audi into the only available space in the car park of the old Cardiff Infirmary. He glanced at his watch. He'd made good time from Bristol, despite the rush hour traffic over the bridge. He flicked open his briefcase and checked the sheet of notes on top. Fine, he was due to meet a man called Dyer from Swansea Drug Squad at half nine. Together they had a meeting with a Home Office Pathologist at ten. He closed his case, and glanced up at the rear-view mirror. Out of force of habit he pulled a comb out of his breast pocket and passed it absently though his crinkly, thinning hair. There had been a lot more of it when this bloody case began and none of it had been flecked with grey either. Still, another meeting, another possible lead to bottle-feed to his ravenous boss Maddocks – he grinned at the vision of his pushy, young, fast-streamer boss as a mewling, infant. He grabbed his raincoat off the passenger seat, got out of the car and locked it. The weather had perked up and the rather grim, gothic building looked a little less ominous in the sunshine. He hurried up the steps and approached the window of the caretaker's lodge. He coughed and a woman came forward.

'Can I help you?'

'Yes, I'm due to meet a D.S Dyer here for a ten o'clock meeting with Dr Meredith...' He got no further as a voice behind him spoke:

'Sullivan?'

Sullivan turned. The man, dressed in scruffy clothes, had been standing in shadow a little way down the corridor. He certainly looked the part of an undercover cop. He stepped forward now and extended his hand.

'Arnie Dyer, Swansea Drugs Squad,' he said to complete the introduction. He nodded to the women at the window.

'I know where Meredith's office is. Is there somewhere we can go for a chat first?'

'Do you need a room, or just somewhere quiet, luv?'

'Somewhere quiet'll do.'

'Come with me then.'

She led them down a high, echoing corridor and up a broad Victorian staircase to the first floor. There were a couple of chairs on the landing. The place was deserted.

'How's this?'

'Fine, ta. His office is just along there, isn't it?'

The woman nodded.

'That's right, luv. I'll buzz through to let him know you're on your way.' She headed back down the stairs.

Sullivan leant against the heavy, wooded banister as Dyer sat down and delved into his briefcase. He produced a document.

'Analyst's report from Birmingham,' he said, tapping the cover self-importantly. He handed it over to Sullivan who scanned through it. After a few minutes Sullivan spoke.

'Okay, so it looks like the shipment we took off that trawler last month is pretty much the same stuff you boys found on the kid?'

Dyer shrugged.

'Look's that way. 'Heroin's heroin, so it's never easy to be a hundred percent certain, but both samples look to be cut to about forty percent purity with caffeine so it would be a hell of a coincidence if they were cut by different people. Trouble is you boys captured kilos of the stuff – the kid only had a used wrap in his pocket. It's hard to get an accurate percentage from such a tiny sample.'

Sullivan nodded sympathetically.

'Sure. Got any ID on the kid yet?'

Dyer shook his head.

'Don't ask,' he replied, wearily.

'There's not a trace on him anywhere. We're pretty certain he was working as a prostitute, but we can't find an address for him. We've had posters up and the boys in blue have even done a door-to-door of the area, but it's rough as fuck around there. They don't like us coppers. Anyhow, let's face it, the people most likely to recognise him are his customers and they're not going to come forward, are they?'

'Hardly. Anything coming up on dental records?'

'Not so far. The trouble is we have no way of limiting the search. He could have been from anywhere in Wales, or Britain for that matter. He had no fillings despite the shit state of his teeth, so he might not even have dental records. It's like looking for the proverbial needle in the haystack.'

Sullivan nodded sympathetically.

'Hmm. Looks like another Rent Man killing. I've been chasing shadows for nearly two years on this one. Drives you bloody mad, doesn't it? Still, it's the first time we've even connected a shipment directly to an end-user, so that's something I suppose.'

'Yeah. It'll help if this Dr Meredith cries foul play. We're trying to get something out on next month's Crimewatch and a murder enquiry would strengthen our hand a lot.'

'Sure. Well, shall we go and see what he has to say for himself?'

Dyer nodded and rose. The two men headed down the corridor towards the doctor's office.

*

'Come in, gentleman! Come in! Grab a pew if you can find one.' The doctor gestured to a couple of armchairs piled high with files and reports. 'Shove that crap on the floor and make yourselves at home. Now I gather you want to see me about that p.m. I did on the male prostitute last week?'

Dyer was the first to clear a space on which to perch.

'That's right, sir. We indicated to you before the post mortem that we thought he was probably a male prostitute, did your findings bear that out?'

'I hope so for his sake, given the state of his arse. That or he played for Newport Firsts!'

'What do you mean?'

'Stretched to buggery, if you'll excuse the pun. Severely dilated as we say in the business. No traces of semen found, mind you.'

'Right.'

Both men were finding it hard to adjust to the pathologist's hearty bluntness. He was built like a second-row forward and he obviously had a second-row's delicacy of touch.

'Besides,' he continued, 'he had all the usual give-aways – make-up, dyed hair, earrings, tattoos and so on. Definitely played for Newport Firsts!' He threw his head back and snorted with laughter at this second blow against his favourite opposition.

Sullivan had managed to get seated and now took up the interview.

'The police found a used heroin wrap in his pocket. What were your conclusions regarding his drugs use, other of course, than he played for Newport Firsts?'

The doctor glanced at him, and then began snorting again.

'What more proof d'you need, eh? Case closed in my book. Here, let me see.'

He opened a slim file on the desk in front of him. 'Hmm, track marks on the arms, neck and feet; collapsed veins all over the shop. Blood tests showed heavy use and his liver was taking a caning. There were significant traces of heroin found on his body and in his system. He was probably still feeling the effects when he died. No sign of AIDS or hepatitis.'

'Does that affect the male prostitute theory?'

'Not really. The lack of semen suggests he used a jonny and there isn't much of a disease problem in that neck of the woods.'

'Cause of death?'

Meredith paused and frowned. The heartiness was gone.

'I would like to say bouncing on concrete from a great height and save you fellas a lot of work, but that doesn't quite cut the mustard.'

'What do you mean?'

'Well, at first I thought, what with the heroin, perhaps he'd thought he was Peter Pan and tried to fly. But then I found a couple of things that made me wonder so I popped down to Swansea for a look at the scene. For that theory to hold water, he would have to have shinned over an eight foot high barrier whilst off his trolley on hard drugs; didn't seem so likely somehow.'

'What were the couple of things that made you wonder?'

'There were dog bites on his arm and traces of his blood on the landing. These were serious lacerations. Sort of thing you would expect from an attack dog of some sort. The blood on the landing suggests that he was injured before he fell. If you're trying to escape a savage dog, you might try to climb the barrier to escape and fall in the process, but Peter Pan and Wendy would be the last thing on your mind.'

'So you think he died trying to escape a savage dog?'

'Perhaps, but there was more to it than that...'

'What d'you mean?'

'Well dogs rarely roam around attacking people at random, even in Swansea. Besides, I've never seen a dog in size nine shoes kick someone's chest in.'

The two men stared at him blankly, so he continued.

'He'd obviously sustained multiple injuries in the fall, which is why I nearly missed it. One of his worst injuries was a crushed sternum and heart. A fall like that can cause all sorts of weird and wonderful damage, but this was a compression injury, as if he had fallen onto something like a car, where a corner of the roof might have caved his chest in. According to the reports of the death scene, there was nothing like that in the vicinity. When I looked closer the bruising on his chest had a familiar shape, so I took a gander at his T-shirt. It had faded as it dried and the dust was shaken off, but there was still the outline of a muddy footprint when you examined it closely; matched the bruise perfectly.'

'So someone delivered a fatal injury with a kick?'

Meredith frowned and nodded.

'Something like that, but kicks are usually delivered with the toe of the foot. It would have to have been a real Bruce Lee number. The ribs are springy and much of the force from a kick is absorbed as the fella on the receiving end is knocked backwards.'

'So what are you saying?'

'Well this is a bit of a flight of fantasy, but imagine if the kid is up top being attacked by the dog and its owners. He climbs the railings in an attempt to get away and either slips and falls, or is pushed. Somehow, he survives the fall and someone finishes him off by jumping or stamping on his chest as he lies on the ground.'

'That's quite a flight of fantasy.'

'True, but it's the only theory I've come up with that fits all the facts.'

Sullivan glanced at Dyer and then back at Meredith.

'So in your judgement we're looking at murder?'

'Well, I wouldn't bet my bollocks on it, but that's the direction I'd be coming from unless someone gave me a bloody good reason to think otherwise.'

*

The clock on the wall in the offices of Customs and Excise's National Intelligence Service department in Bristol showed it was gone one o'clock, but no one was thinking about lunch. Sullivan finished speaking and a tense silence descended on the group of people seated around the conference table. His boss, Maddocks, was seated at the top of the table and everyone was waiting for his reaction. He had swivelled his chair around and was studying an abstract space on the blank wall. At last he spoke.

'So we have a dead male prostitute and the pathologist is crying foul, but Swansea police can't even tie a name tag on his toe?'

'In fairness, sir, they're turning over all the stones and D.S. Dyer was confident that the murder angle would get them a slot on TV.'

Maddocks turned from the wall and stared at his number two with unconcealed scepticism.

'Most encouraging Al. Unfortunately, I do not share the widespread belief that television is an indispensable weapon in the investigator's arsenal. When you're dealing with ruthless, professional criminals of this sort, telling them that they are wanted for murder is an invitation for them to tighten their security even further.'

'Surely it's better than nothing, sir and at least we now know the sort of people that this gang are supplying the drugs to.'

'Maybe, but I think the leads you and your team have picked up on this Chief Inspector Ringer and his chum Preece are far more interesting.' He addressed the whole gathering. 'In Hull and Dover, our only two successes to-date, a senior member of this gang has recruited a senior Police officer to ensure people are looking the other way when deals are going down. Tony has been working his computer magic,' he nodded at a geeky looking individual in the corner, 'and it has spat out these two. Both are members of the same lodge and they have met a few times outside of lodge meetings, though that could be coincidence.

'In case anyone hasn't heard, Al took a trip to Kent last week and it turns out Preece is a lot flakier than he initially appeared. Dabbled in intelligence work in his younger days and failed to impress his bosses big-time. There's a very real prospect that he could turn out to be a serious wobbler, so if you meet him in the field handle with caution. His personnel file suggests a paranoid personality with violent tendencies. We think he might be very nasty indeed.'

There was a visible brightening amongst the men and women of the investigating team. Maddocks went on. 'I know it's only trawling and profiling at this stage and it's all highly speculative, but if Ringer connects to Preece and they are our bad guys, we stand a chance of nailing the real brains behind this thing. Nine times out of ten we make a big bust and end up capturing the foot-soldiers not the generals and, frankly, that pisses me off no end.'

There were general nods and mutterings of agreement from around the table. The Customs investigators all had tales of 'the one that got away'.

'The question is,' Maddocks continued, 'how to get in close enough to establish that they are in cahoots and up to no good. Ideas anyone?'

Bailey cleared her throat.

'We don't seem, to be progressing much further with basic surveillance. Could we get someone in under cover?'

Maddocks was his usual dismissive self. He was rumoured to have once remarked that the best plain clothes outfit for a woman was a pinny and a mop.

'Fine, if you can show me the point of penetration. We're drawing a blank at the distribution end and Preece's law practice is a three-man operation with secrecy stamped all over it. I doubt if Chief Inspector Ringer sits in his office issuing compromising orders all day, either.'

Bailey reddened and stared down at her notepad.

Sullivan cut in.

'Even if we got someone in place, Sir, I get the feeling they could take forever to gain trust. These people have secrecy as their middle name. However, Joe here has come up with a lead that might be usable.'

All eyes swung to Joe Prosser, who looked blank. Sullivan continued.

'It was on that memo you sent me on Wednesday, Joe. You mentioned that Preece is rumoured to be having a fling with his secretary. A woman called Juliet Llewellyn.'

Prosser nodded, without looking any the wiser. Sullivan turned to speak directly to Maddocks.

'I know that this is against current best practice, department protocol and all that, but I wondered if it might not be worth our while making a discreet approach to her husband. You know; the green eyed monster and all that. I know you're not fond of outsiders, but perhaps a new recruit might make the difference?'

Maddocks swung back around to stare at the wall. He picked up a biro and weighed it between his fingers, like a dart that he was about to throw at an imaginary dartboard.

'You're too damn right I don't like outsiders. They usually turn out to be nutters or rip-off artists, or both. We've got expert surveillance units, highly trained undercover officers and your own, hand-picked, ops squad. What makes you think that this Llewellyn character is likely to prove useful, or even reliable?'

'He may not be, sir. I've no way of knowing till I talk to him. But I would say the odds are better than on some of the outsiders we've backed in the past. I've done a quick check, and it just so happens that this might be the same Charlie Llewellyn who saved my life in the Gulf.

2

Charlie Llewellyn awoke to the thunder of Jacs' twins racing to the bathroom. He pictured the tussle to be first to the loo, and then Megan yelled, in her best tearful voice:

'I'm telling Charlie on you poo-face!'

'And I'm telling on you for saying poo-face!' retorted her defiant sister.

Charlie pulled the duvet cover over his head to shut them out, knowing as he did so that it was a hopeless task. In some ways they had adopted him as a father more thoroughly than their mother had adopted him as a lover! He heard the bathroom door open and braced himself as Bethan leapt on top of him.

'What horrible brat did that?' he growled.

'Me, Charlie, me,' she sang gleefully. 'Get out of bed sleepy-head. We want breakfast!'

He pulled down the duvet and opened one eye at her grudgingly.

'Okay, okay, I'll be down in a minute. Go and watch cartoons or something.'

He sat up tentatively as Bethan went skipping through the door and disappeared downstairs. His head felt alright, but he was dying for a cup of tea. He groped for his dressing gown and fumbled his way into it as he made his way to the bathroom. While he ran hot water into the sink for a shave, he inspected the face that stared back at him from the mirror. The eyes were a little bleary, but not too bad; certainly not bloodshot. He scooped up some water and splashed it on his chin as memories of the night before pieced themselves together.

He had gone down to the Railway with Jacs and Eric while Eric's missus, Gwen, kept an eye on the twins. She was good like that, but then she never did like pubs much, and, of course, not having kids of her own, the twins could do no wrong. He spread shaving foam along his jaw with the brush. There had been a quiz on organised by the P.T.A at the twins school which he'd forgotten about, so they'd joined up with Jenks and a couple of boys in the front bar to form a team. He had a hazy memory of coming last, or was it second to last? There seemed to be a lot of questions involving soap operas, film stars and pop music.

He tried a couple of experimental scrapes with his razor... Hardly specialist subjects for two builders, a scaffolder and a struggling sculptor he decided... Shit! He hardly felt any pain, but he knew that was going to bleed. He watched to assess the damage as blood welled from his top lip. A large drop formed and fell into his shaving water as he groped for a piece of toilet paper. Damn, it was deep!

When he got downstairs with a wad of tissue hanging from his lip and the taste of blood in his mouth, the twins had already made themselves breakfast. Charlie began resignedly to clean up the mess.

'Charlie. I'm bored of Rice Crispies,' complained Bethan, 'can we have Chocolate Nesquicks next time?'

'If I remember when I'm shopping,' he replied, hedging his bets, and smiling ruefully at the careful arrangement of coffee, mug and spoon from the night before. That was a sure sign he'd had a skinful. Whenever he returned home hammered he became convinced that he was going to benefit in the morning from a cup of strong black coffee and prepared accordingly. As always, he reached for the teabags.

'That's it, I've got diarrhoea!' announced Megan, abruptly. 'No I haven't!' she contradicted herself, bursting into mad laughter. 'I've got a runny nose!'

'Make your mind up lovely,' replied Charlie, drily. 'You've either got green stuff running out of your face or brown stuff running out of your bottom. Which is it to be?' The word 'bottom' sent the pair of them into fits of giggles and Megan's attempt to negotiate a day off school passed unsuccessfully as usual.

Gwen had bathed them the night before so he gave their faces a quick swipe over with the flannel and picked up the cup of tea he had made for Gareth, his nineteen year old son from his first marriage. He headed upstairs to collect the uniforms Gwen had put out for them. He knocked Gareth's door, paused for the sake of decency and looked in. The place was a tip as usual and there was a heap lying on the bed. It could be his nineteen year old son, he reflected, but his nineteen year old son plus duvet normally made a bigger heap than that. He picked his way carefully through the clothes, CDs and assorted magazines, with which Gareth liked to, decorate his bedroom floor, and confirmed his suspicion that the bed was empty. Empty of his nineteen year old son at any rate.

He collected the twins' uniforms and headed back downstairs, trying not to spill the unwanted cup of tea. He was annoyed about the tea. Gareth was old enough to stay out if he wished, but as long as he officially resided at home, he could damn well have the courtesy to keep him informed of his movements. Before he swelled with too much righteous indignation, however, a guilty voice in his head reminded him of a remark about staying over in Bishopston, thrown over a nineteen year old shoulder, which was only now swimming back into his muzzy memory.

He washed their cereal bowls, gave their shoes a less-than-vigorous brushing and shoved a bundle of dark washing into the machine. He was just adding powder when he heard Megan shout out 'Letters!', then he heard her scrabbling at the latch as she stretched to reach it. They had begun fighting over who was delivering what before they were out of the porch. It was developing into a tug-of-war over a piece of junk mail about replacement windows. We'll be needing some, if one of them suddenly lets go, thought Charlie, as he used his second strongest 'Oi! Pack it in!' to cut through the din. Megan dissolved into recriminatory tears.

'It's not fair! I never get to do the letters on my own!' she wailed in abject misery, as her sister bounced up and down with excitement.

'Charlie, Charlie, this one's got a picture on the front!' she yelled waving a postcard above her head.

Charlie crouched down by Megan and hugged her, as he held out his hand for the card.

'There, there, lovely, don't you worry about the letters. You do lots of busy jobs for me. Now what've you got here?' She was still clutching the twisted remains of the mail shot from a double glazing centre in the Hafod. 'Would you like to open it for me?' The misery cleared almost instantly from her face, as she attacked the wrong end of the envelope.

He rose and accepted the rest of the mail from Bethan, who was gazing at the postcard trying to work out how to pronounce Tenerife, a 'welcome to' was splashed across a picture of Mount Teide set against a sumptuously blue sky. He flicked through a fistful of bills and decided to deal with them later.

'Can I see that, Beth?' he asked, holding out his hand.

'Ten-er-if' she pronounced haltingly.

'Nearly, darling,' he encouraged. 'If you are Spanish, like the people who live there, you say Ten-er-ree-fay. Other people say Ten-er-reef.'

'Ten-er-ree-fay' she said slowly. The she repeated it twice, more fluently. 'Tenereefay' she announced firmly, 'I'm going to say it properly, like the Spanish,' she declared with the sudden, stubborn determination that reminded him so much of her mother, Jacs.

He'd brought a hairbrush from the kitchen and with unthinking opportunism he began pulling it through her mop while he had her in reach.

'Ouch! You're hurting me!' she exclaimed, plaintively.

'I'm sorry, my love, the pug fairy really got to you last night. Now can I see that card please?' She had already turned it over and was doing her best to read it as he attempted to pull the brush painlessly through the knots and tangles.

He snatched the card from her more abruptly than he'd meant to.

'Hey! I was reading that!' she exclaimed indignantly.

'What does it say Charlie? What does it say?' demanded

Megan, who had finished picking apart the mail shot and had discarded the 'Unbeatable, Unrepeatable Autumn Double-Glazing Offers!' on the floor. Charlie looked at his watch. There was a quarter of an hour before they needed to leave for school and the girls were more-or-less ready.

'I'll tell you in a minute, lovely,' he replied. 'Just get your bags and practise reading, while I get your shoes, okay?' The twins nodded and hurried about their new task as Charlie headed back into the kitchen and shut the door behind him. He sat down at the table. Whatever she had to say, there was a lot of it, crammed onto the available space in her small, spiky handwriting. He absently noted the Spanish stamp and Tenerife postmark, then began to read:

Dear Charles,
I am writing to let you know I want a divorce. You may deny it, but I know you have been having an affair and I am also sick of you using my money to bail out your rotten business, while you drink the profits. Gareth is a total liability and is going to land himself in serious trouble any day now. I am staying out here until Friday. Hywel has agreed to act for me and I will be talking to him regarding the above when I get back.
– Juliet.

He reread it, and then slipped it into his trouser pocket safe from young, prying eyes. It was hardly surprising that Preece was to act as her solicitor, but why the trip to Tenerife. To the best of his knowledge she was ensconced chez Councillor Preece in Derwen Fawr, not sunning herself in the Canaries.

Along with his recovery from the nightmare of Baghdad had come the realisation that they were incompatible and now in the cold light of divorce there were aspects of her behaviour that were downright inexplicable.

The postcard itself was a stroke of genius. It didn't stand a hope in hell of making it past the local gossips and she knew it. She couldn't have attacked him more publicly if she'd taken out a page in the Evening Post.

*

The van coasted along the line of parked cars in search of a space. It was always a nightmare trying to park outside the school, particularly if you were running late. Fortunately, Charlie was so late that the punctual parents were already leaving. This was out of character for him, but then a postcard like that did not drop through the letter box every day. He spotted Jane Gorman pulling out in her posh new four-by-four and prepared to nip into the vacant space.

'Right you 'orrible lot,' he barked in his best Sergeant-Major's voice, as he hauled on the hand brake and stuck the van in gear for good measure,

'prepare to move out on the count of three; three!'

He noticed he was relying on his regular routines to help him ignore the tightness in his chest. There was the usual commotion as they struggled out of their seat belts and fought over whose bag was whose. By the time he had got out and walked around to the pavement, they were spilling out of the back. As a true measure of their lateness, he spotted the Jenkins boys ahead hitting lumps out of each other as they fought their way to school. They lived nearer than anyone and they were always last.

'Quick,' he exclaimed, 'Luke and Josh are ahead of us!' The twins went flying off in pursuit and Charlie lengthened his stride.

Again, he found himself wondering how quickly news of the postcard would spread. Still, this was Upper Killay so he was kidding himself if he thought his affair with Jacs wasn't already common knowledge. He nodded good morning to Denise Perkins as she hurried across the road to her car. She didn't see him. Or was she ignoring him? For Christ's sake man, get a grip; he'd only had the postcard for half-an-hour!

'Morning Charlie!'

He turned to the voice. It was Jacs. When she wasn't his lover she was the school's lollipop lady and made a point of treating him like the other parents. It was all a bit silly because the whole village knew the Twins were hers and that she and Charlie were an item; it just seemed a bit unnecessary to flaunt it.

'You alright babes?' she enquired. He realised he was frowning fiercely and tried to relax his expression.

'Sure, just something on my mind luv. Juliet is demanding a divorce and she doesn't care who knows. Hey, are we out to play this evening?'

'Spect so. I think my mum's having the twins for me.

'Great, I'll see you down the pub when Johnny and I are finished at the chapel.'

He heard the bell ring and hurried across the playground,

nodding to various parents heading in the opposite direction. Jacs was an old friend and a new lover. They had grown up together on the estate at the top of the village and, for a while, had exchanged some early teenage fumblings. That ended when Jacs was enticed away by one of the bikers who used to hang around outside the Railway in those days. At fifteen, Charlie was philosophical about losing out to an older teenager with a Kawasaki. The disapproval of the local gossips became deafening when it became common knowledge that she had started smoking exotic cigarettes and stopped wearing knickers.

Fortunately for Jacs, she was not riding pillion when her biker hit a sheep as he tried to break the land speed record across Fairwood Common one night. Unlike the sheep, he survived, but he broke both his legs and his pelvis which rather curtailed his sex drive for a while. Unfortunately for him, Jacs had no desire to start wearing knickers again and rapidly moved on to a sailor. He was a tidy bloke as Charlie recalled. He bought her an engagement ring and promised to buy her a wedding ring on his return from the Gulf. Whether Jacs could have contained her urges that long was academic, because the poor bastard was clipped by an RAF Jaguar taxiing on-board ship after the Mina Saud engagement.

She seemed to take this as a warning to stay away from tidy blokes, or perhaps she was just unlucky. Either way she developed a knack of picking shits and idiots. That lasted throughout her twenties, then, shortly after her thirtieth birthday, at the New Year's fancy dress party in the Railway, she arrived dressed as a schoolgirl, collared Terry Humphries behind the toilets in the garden and married him in the spring before the bump began to show. They seemed happy enough and the twins came along. Then she brought them to school one morning wearing sunglasses. It was a rainy day.

Charlie and Jenks hung the bastard upside down over the railings on the bridge by the Railway one night and had a chat with him about hitting women, and the beatings stopped. Instead he took up with a barmaid from Gorseinon. Finally, Jacs kicked him out, so he got his accountant to show the garage was making a loss, and when the CSA wouldn't fall for that, he sold the business for cash to a bloke he met in the Spinning Wheel and buggered off to America. Jacs was left with the twins and a mortgage she had no chance of maintaining. Now she was back renting a house on the estate where she had grown up.

She deserved better, Charlie thought, but was he the one to provide it? His marriage to Juliet had broken down quite rapidly as he recovered from his experiences in the Gulf and Jacs had more than filled the gap that Juliet's disappearance into the arms of Preece had left, but was it fair to lead her on? Feelings aside he had business to attend to and if the relationship continued on its current heading he could only see her getting hurt. Should he end it while he still could? Christ knows! With a mental shrug he followed the Twins into the playground.

*

'Jesus, butty,' grunted Johnny, 'there's some weight in this fuckin' thing, mun. They look like poxy little chickens when they're up.'

The two men were manhandling the chapel's new 'cockerel' weathervane out of the back of Charlie's van.

'That's from fifty feet away, mate,' gasped Charlie, as they struggled up the path with the iron casting and its legend: 'God Tempers the Wind'. 'This one's made for the greater glory of God and Minister Hughes, though probably not in that order. It's got to be bigger than anyone else's. They reached the front wall of the chapel and carefully lowered the casting to the ground. Johnny stood back and inspected it thoughtfully.

'If God tempers the wind, why don't 'e do somethin' about your arse?' he enquired. 'I was scared to light a fag in the van, in case you took my eyebrows off!'

'That's bloody good coming from you, you toxic twat!' retorted Charlie. 'Stop chopsing and get on the end of that rope!' He grabbed the end of the rope that hung from the block and tackle they had erected on the chapel roof, and threaded it through the letters of the casting. He tied it off and gingerly tested the weight. Satisfied he finished the rig and handed Johnny the line.

'Right,' he instructed, 'I'll get up top, you pull on this. He clambered up the ladder and climbed over the parapet on which the casting was to sit. He grabbed the rope, pulled it tight and shouted 'Ready!' The block and tackle creaked and groaned as Johnny hauled on the rope. Charlie peered over the parapet and saw the casting rise slowly towards him. Gradually it crept higher. He put his weight on the line to maintain the tension between each of Johnny's efforts. It was a bright day and the view out to the Gower from the chapel roof was magnificent. He automatically followed the line of houses as they ran up the hill from the Railway to Fairwood Common. Halfway up he spotted his own house and frowned. What was that pick-up doing parked on his drive? He squinted and made out two men lifting something off the back of it. As it came upright, he recognised the unmistakeable red of a Dawlishes' For Sale sign. One of the men produced a sledge hammer and began knocking it into his lawn.

'Hang on there, mate,' he instructed Johnny as he slid down the ladder and sprinted for his van. 'I'll be back in a minute!'

He pulled up outside the house just as the men were standing back admiring their handiwork. He parked across the drive to block them in and jumped out of the van.

'You can't stop there mate,' called one of the men, 'we're just leaving.'

'No you're bloody not!' retorted Charlie. 'Not until you've explained what the hell you think you are doing planting that bloody thing in my lawn!'

The man eyed him warily, weighing up the likelihood of violence.

'Just doing my job mate,' he replied coolly. 'Here,' he reached through the window of the pick-up, pulled out a clipboard, and stepped towards Charlie, holding it out. 'Right address isn't it?'

Charlie glanced down the list to where he was pointing.

'Yes,' he agreed, 'it is.'

The man sensed that he had taken the initial steam out of the situation and decided to keep it that way.

'Geraint,' he called to his partner, who was collecting up their tools to throw in the back of the pick-up, 'this gentleman doesn't think we should be putting up a sign outside his house.

Get on the blower to Susie at Dawlishes and find out what's going on will you.' Geraint straightened up and fished out his mobile. He pressed a programmed number and held it to his ear. He spoke for a moment, and then turned to Charlie.

'They say there's no mistake. They 'ad the instruction in this mornin'.

Charlie's voice rose again.

'Look, this is my bloody house!' he began, and then made a visible effort to steady himself. 'Can I talk to them,' he requested more calmly.

'Sure, mate, her name's Susie.' The man handed Charlie the phone. He took it and put it to his ear. 'Hello, hello,' he said.

'Can I help you?' replied a voice at the other end.

'Yes, my name is Llewellyn, and I want to know why your men have just put a For Sale sign outside my house without my instructions.'

'Well we were told to put the property on the market this morning.'

'Who told you to?'

'I'm not sure I can give out that sort of information, sir.'

'Well, if you don't, I'm instructing my solicitor to sue Dawlishes immediately for trespass.'

'Hang on a tick.' The line went dead as she consulted a superior. A moment later a man came on the line.

'Mr, er, Llewellyn, we appear to have a problem?'

'Too right we do. Some joker has told you to stick a board up outside my house and I want to know who.'

'I see, sir, understandably. Well, we wouldn't normally divulge such information, but, under the circumstances, would it help if I told you the person was a Mrs Juliet Llewellyn? We were instructed this morning by her solicitors, Semple Tucker and Preece.'

Charlie paused – this wasn't on the agenda.

'She can't do that!' He blurted finally.

'If you say so, sir, but please bear in mind that we have only acted in good faith. If there's a problem, perhaps you should contact your wife...'

'Don't you worry mate, I bloody well will! In the meantime, tell your blokes to get this damn sign off my lawn, or you'll be hearing from my solicitor.' Charlie handed the mobile back to Geraint. I'll move the van, you move that thing!' he ordered. He sat and watched, as they pulled up the sign and headed back down the Gower Road towards town.

When Charlie arrived back at the chapel, he found a granite headstone in the shape of a cross dangling halfway up the wall as a counter balance to his iron cockerel. Johnny had obviously chosen an inadequate anchor point when the weight became too much to bear. He grinned at the unintentional inscription on the headstone: 'Nearer My God to Thee' – well nearer by a good fifteen feet if that made any difference. It would take both of them to get the damn thing down. He headed for the Railway in search of his AWOL assistant.

3

The lean figure of Councillor Hywel Preece climbed into the back seat of his metallic black Range Rover Autobiography. He was carrying a large, black leather, solicitor's briefcase. The car crept out of the car park at County Hall and purred of quietly towards the city centre. Preece leant forward and ordered the driver to drop him off at the bottom of Wind Street. They agreed to meet at the same place in exactly one hour.

He strode up the road then turned sharply into Salubrious Passage. He paused to study his reflection in a shop window and looked back to see if anyone came hurrying around the corner after him. No one did, so he pushed open the door of the Gallery Upstairs. He emerged into the silence of the first floor and coughed to indicate his arrival. The owner came bustling out.

'Ah, Councillor Preece, how nice to see you again; let me take your coat please, sir. Thank you. Now, it's a private viewing today, I believe, is it not? The councillor nodded, turning towards the cluttered walls of the main showroom, as the man brushed an imaginary speck of dust off the shoulder of his Barbour, before placing it carefully on a hanger and whisking it off to the coat rack. As always, the place was deserted.

'I'm expecting a guest,' stated Preece, flatly

'Certainly, Councillor, and I am sure he, or she, shares your appreciation of the work of our finest local artists. You may be interested to note a couple of quite exciting new Bannings' in the display...'

'How much is this one? Asked the councillor, indifferently.

'Fifty pounds,' came the instant reply. The councillor produced his wallet and handed over the money.

'Stick one of the usual "Donated bys" on it and give it to Singleton Hospital,' he ordered

'Very good, sir,' he continued. 'I'll let him in, then be off to lunch. Please let yourselves out, and close the door behind you. I'll turn the sign around, so you won't be disturbed.' In the absence of any response, he turned and bustled out.

Preece was inspecting the artwork, with a jaundiced expression, when his guest arrived.

'Come in, Ringer,' was his only greeting. 'What have you got for me?'

Chief Inspector Ringer reached inside his jacket and produced some typed sheets, as he walked forward.

'Not a lot at the moment, Hywel,' he confessed. 'This is a transcript of D.S. Evans' interview with Gareth Llewellyn. He's been trying to get a confession out of him all morning, but he's not having it. He seems quite a tough nut to crack, for a youngster.'

'Hmm', agreed Preece, as he flicked through the pages. 'Like his father. Not easily bullied by all accounts. Still, confessions are deniable, are they not? What we need is evidence, witnesses. Send Evans around to this address,' he handed Ringer a slip of typed paper. 'The kid's been well paid to confess to being young Llewellyn's accomplice. They were thick as thieves at school, so there's a plausible connection. They fell out over a girl and this one got into drugs.'

Inspector Ringer pulled a sour face.

'I can't see a barrister taking long to punch holes in that,' he remarked.

'I doubt if a barrister will get the chance. I don't particularly want young Llewellyn convicted of anything. I just want to make sure that, if his father wants to dispute Juliet's divorce proceedings, as far as the world is concerned, his teenage son from another marriage is a hell raising delinquent.'

Ringer glanced at him for a moment, and then shook his head in a gesture of bewildered admiration.

'Christ you're a devious bastard Hywel. 'Piranha Preece' we used to call you at school and you haven't changed. Shame you were always too clever for the Force. Anyhow, what about the arrangements for tonight?'

The two men went over the instructions to be given to Evans, and then Ringer let himself out. Preece continued his examination of the artwork. He turned with a start. The man was almost beside him before he sensed his presence. Like many big men he was surprisingly light on his feet. Preece eyed his sovereigns with distaste as he held out a briefcase identical to Preece's.

'You're early O'Leary,' he remarked as the two men made the exchange. 'Good week?'

'Aye, not bad. There's over seventy grand in there and that with wages and money for the next shipment taken out.'

'Fine, I'll get Semple to start laundering it.'

'What was Ringer doin' here?'

Preece suddenly found himself feeling uncomfortable under the fat man's cold gaze; he didn't like being questioned by a subordinate, but he knew the bloody man had O'Connell's ear.

'Oh, he called around with some bits and pieces for me.'

'I said what was Ringer doin' here.'

'It's Juliet, you know, my secretary...'

'Your mistress.'

'Yes, well, that as well.'

'What about her?'

'She wants a divorce from her husband. I said I'd help stitch him up. You know, make sure she gets the family home...'

'This stinks!'

'I beg your pardon?'

'I said this fuckin' stinks! How much does she know about the business?'

'Not much. I don't know. I mean she's not stupid. She knows money doesn't grow on trees, but then I'm a solicitor and a city councillor so she'd expect me to be well off.'

'What if she's a plant?'

'For Christ sake, O'Leary, she works for County Hall! I've had her checked out. She's been in local government since she left school.

'And you don't think work records can be faked?'

'Oh come on man, you're being paranoid...'

'And you're letting your bollocks rule your brains! We've put a lot of time and money into settin' this thing up and you're willin' to risk it all for some bint who's short on knicker elastic. Do you realise how long you'll spend at Her Majesty's Pleasure if this goes tits up?'

'It's not like that. I'm not taking any chances. Besides, I'm the public face of the operation. It's important that I'm seen leading a normal life, which in this day and age includes the possibility of having an affair. This is no big deal. Just a bit of insurance to make sure this Llewellyn bloke buggers off without causing a row.'

The fat man's gaze was steadier and colder than ever. His tone was menacing when he spoke.

'To be frank my friend, I don't quite see why the business needs a 'public face' anymore.'

'What d'you mean?'

'Just that. All the PR stuff is history now. The system runs itself the more unpublic it is the better.

'What are you saying?'

O'Leary shrugged.

'I dunno. Perhaps it's time we reviewed our business structure. Maybe you'd like to let go of the reins a bit. Take your new lady friend off to spend some of that cash we've all been makin'...'

'What, and leave you to take over a sixty million pound business in my absence? You must think I'm fucking simple!'

'Calm down, man. I'm just sayin' things move on and we need to move with them. If the pack needs reshufflin', it's up to us to make sure it cuts to our advantage. As to this Llewellyn fella, why drag Ringer into it? Why not let me and the boys top him? A quick hit and run when he's walking home from the pub and it's all done and dusted.'

'And murdering him isn't going to attract the slightest attention, eh?'

'Not if it looks like a genuine accident.'

'Look, Ringer's got his work cut out containing the fall-out from the death of the kid you and the boys chucked off that tower block. Fair enough, the boy had to be made an example of, but Llewellyn is nothing to do with the business and we have no reason to kill him. This is just a personal thing I'm sorting out for Juliet and you won't hear anymore about it.'

The fat man eyed him for a moment longer, and then his face broke into a grin not much warmer than his stare.

'Not much stomach for the rough stuff, have ya Hywel?' he remarked dryly.

Preece shrugged.

'It's got its place, but I'm a brains over brawn man, frankly. We can always call on the boys as a last resort.'

The pale eyes grew hard again.

'Fair enough. Do it your way, but I'm warning you now, if things go pear shaped and I have to straighten them out, I'm going to be talkin' to O'Connell about it and, if he has to make a special visit, someone's gonna get hurt. D'you follow me?'

'Of course, O'Leary, I'm not a bloody fool you know.'

His colleague eyed him for a moment longer, as if to suggest that he wasn't entirely convinced, and then he turned and departed as abruptly as he had arrived.

*

As he made his way back down Wind St, Preece reviewed his arrangements satisfying himself that all the angles had been covered. He wasn't too convinced as to Detective Sergeant Evan's abilities, but Ringer seemed confident enough that he was the man for the job. He shrugged. As a successful solicitor, he was bound to view the likes of Chief Inspector Ringer and Detective Sergeant Evans with a certain contempt.

More importantly, he didn't like the sound of O'Leary's latest proposal one little bit, He'd put money and a successful business into this operation, as well as a lot of time and effort. He wasn't about to let the cod-eyed bastard lever him out! O'Leary was getting a bit too fond of cracking the whip lately and he seemed to think violence was the solution to everything. It was about time the fat thug realised that there was still room for the subtle approach and tucking up this Llewellyn character was the ideal opportunity for Preece to make the point.

*

The assembled company in the front bar of the Railway was unanimously in favour of Jacs' offer to take Charlie home. No one dreamed it was likely to lead to anything. I mean, Jesus, He could hardly say bread. Then again, there's no telling the hidden reserves a man can call on when it's offered to him on a plate, and there's no doubting Jacs knows a trick or two in the bedroom department. Hell of a girl, mind.

According to the landlord, Johnny came in about lunchtime, and then Charlie turned up because he needed him to finish a job on the chapel roof. They buggered off in the Van for a couple of hours or more. Meantime, of course, "Wing Commander" bloody Morgan comes in, shooting his big mouth off about this postcard his missus has heard about. Charlie's missus has dumped him he says. Fucked off to Tenerife in high dudgeon, because our Charlie's been playing away and generally not keeping her in the style she's accustomed to. To hear Morgan tell it, our Charlie Boy's a worse husband than Henry the

Eighth, when everyone knows he busted his arse to keep her happy.

Anyhow, the long and short of it is, when he comes in about five, everyone's heard about the postcard and, well, what do you say, really? In he walks and everyone shuts up and stares at their pints, like a bunch of mammy's dull boys. You could have heard a pin drop. Well, Christ, he was bound to sense an atmosphere

'What's wrong with you lot?' he asks, 'Taken a vow of silence have we?'

Still no one looks up. 'Oh don't tell me, Johnny's put magic mushrooms in the beer again and you're all too stoned to talk.' At last Jones Bach speaks up.

'Sorry mate, no one's stoned, it's just there's been stories going around and well Christ mun, you know what it's like... here, let me get that...' he tries to grin as if to say no offence, like, but Charlie wasn't having any of it. He'd gone dead pale and his face was hard, like it was the night he dropped that twat who was threatening Nicola. No one wanted to know when the bloody nutter smashed that glass on the bar, except Charlie. That hard look, then bang and the bloke was out on the deck with a busted jaw.

'It's alright,' he said quietly, 'I'll stay on my own' He picked up the pint Nicola had poured for him, turned on his heel and walked around to the other bar. He sat on the stool in there on his own, just staring at the wall and drinking, until some of the boys went in to play darts about eight. Even then, they stayed down the far end by the dartboard, so as not to bother him.

Jacs came in, with a couple of girls, about half-past. Normally,

36

that got him going and Christ, there's been some nights with Charlie and Jacs on form, but not this time. She sat and chatted to him for a while, then gave up and talked to her mates. Meanwhile Charlie just kept pouring it down his neck like he'd got hollow legs.

Jenks went out to strain his 'taters just before last orders and whispered when he got back that Charlie appeared to have hit the wall. He was slumped on the bar and his eyes had gone west. Suddenly, everyone wanted to help. Guilty, see. A quid here, a quid there and lo and behold, there was the taxi fare to destination unknown. Somehow Jacs gets involved, and says the twins are staying over at a friend's house for the night so she could take him home to hers. Next thing Nicola announces he is making a gurgling noise in his sleep, and one of Jacs mates, who is a receptionist at the Medical Centre in the square, says what if he chokes on his vomit?

Well fair dos, drinks had been taken, so that was it. No way was our butty going home on his own in a state like that to drown in his own puke. Don't worry says Jacs. She'll take him home and he can crash the night on her sofa. His missus is in Tenerife, so where's the harm? Well, of course we all knew what was going on, but good luck to her. No one said it, be we all thought our mate was better off with Jacs than he'd ever been with that snotty bitch of a wife of his.

Next thing the cab's outside beeping his horn. Charlie's carted out with Jacs holding his hand, and off they go up the hill, with her waving out the back window, like a bloody honeymoon couple.

*

Detective Sergeant Evans pulled his camouflage jacket tighter around himself and shivered slightly. There was a definite chill in the autumn air, now night had fallen. He looked out from his vintage point at the city lights, and the arc they prescribed around Swansea Bay. He peered at his watch for the umpteenth time. It was ten-past-eleven. Not long to wait now he thought hopefully. The bright lights in the distance seemed to make the darkness in his immediate vicinity all the more intense. He could hear the occasional dog barking, but not nearby. He congratulated himself on having had the foresight to spend fifteen minutes lobbing doped sausages into the local back gardens. Shame they weren't poisoned he thought nastily. He bloody hated dogs.

His thoughts drifted back to the afternoon. Things had picked up after that little wanker Gareth Llewellyn cheeking him all morning, mainly thanks to that junkie kid Ringer had tipped him off to. God knows how the Chief had come up with that one – a grass he reckoned. Anyhow, the skinny little toe-rag was singing louder than the Morriston Male Voice Choir...

Something was happening. He heard a car pull up at the front of the building and then doors slamming. He shifted about on the branch of the tree he was sitting in, to make sure he was well balanced and steady, then pulled a camera out of the bag he had slung around his neck. His fingers felt for the settings in the dark, removing the lens cover, checking the flash was off, running over all the details he had run over a hundred times already that evening. There was a long pause. So long that he began wondering if the car had stopped at another house. Then, bingo! The upstairs window, outside which he was hiding, lit up like the Mumbles lighthouse. A woman walked in, followed by a man who was none too steady on his feet, Evans felt his pulse quicken with excitement.

The woman stripped down to her underwear as Evan's checked the focus on his old SLR. He zoomed in and out on his victims deciding on the balance between detail and overall perspective. The woman knelt down and undid Llewellyn's trousers. She pulled them down to half-mast, pants and all. In the detective's estimation, she had her work cut out. She was not so pessimistic. She leant forward and barely a minute later, Evan's whispered, 'Jesus Christ!' and pressed the shutter release. As the excitement mounted he clicked more and more rapidly. Saints alive! This was better than that video he'd bought off that spotty twat in Vice! He pressed the button again. God, she was taking off her pants. The woman appeared to sit down then lay back out of sight beneath the line of the windowsill. He heard Ringer's voice in his head: "Make sure you catch them on the job. I don't want any Clinton-style bullshit about what amounts to the real thing, thank you very much!"

He reached for the branch above his head and pulled himself into a standing position. The couple swung back into view. Jesus he was on top of her now and giving her a right good seeing to. Despite the chilly night air, Evan's was perspiring freely as he raised the camera higher and fired off a dozen more frames. He shifted for an even better angle. To his horror he heard the branch beneath him crack. He froze, but it cracked again. He grabbed for a branch above his head, but too late.

When he awoke, he was lying at the bottom of the tree in agony. He wondered if he'd broken his back. He managed to lift his head a few inches, but that was all. A light had come on next door. He heard a man's voice exclaim: 'Jesus! What was that? Don't tell me cats!' Then the back door was flung open and torchlight probed the darkness. He tried to move his arms, but the pain made him gasp out loud. The beam swung towards him and he squinted as it hit him in the eyes. Then a voice said: 'Jesus, Betty, come and look at this! I think we've caught a peeping bloody tom! From the looks of 'im you'd better call an ambulance.'

*

Barry Naylor was sitting in his battered white Nissan, flicking between the police and ambulance frequencies with one hand, shoving the remains of the kebab he'd picked up in Uplands into his rat-like mouth with the other. It had been dead all night, and he had the feeling that he would soon be employing some of the more creative writing skills he frequently fell back on as a freelance hack.

As he turned the scanner towards the ambulance wavelength he picked up a faint call. Thank fuck, some business at last! He twiddled the knob skilfully as he grabbed a biro and prepared to write on the kebab wrapper. Reading you loud and clear, mate, and on my way, he thought, as he jammed the car in gear and accelerated off up the Gower Road.

There was no sign of the ambulance as he coasted to a halt outside the address he had scribbled down. He noticed the lights were on next door. As far as he could make out from the radio, a man had been found by a neighbour, injured in the back garden, possible having fallen out of a tree. It wasn't clear if the injured party was the homeowner, in which case, what was he doing up a tree in his back garden in the middle of the night? More likely a snooper, or a Peeping Tom, he decided. He grabbed his phone and set it to video. He tucked it into one of the side pockets in his jacket.

There was a gate that led down the side of the house. Naylor tried the latch and it opened. As he walked down the path into the back garden, he made out a prone figure. Naylor stepped forward into the pool of light cast by next door's kitchen window. He looked down at the figure lying on the ground.

'My, my,' he gloated unpleasantly, 'if it isn't Detective Sergeant Evans. Now what would you be doing lying injured in someone's back garden in the middle of the night?' He pressed the record button on his phone as he surreptitiously angled it at the injured copper. This was more than just a Peeping Tom story! Evans' reply was less than friendly:

'Fuck off Naylor!' he snarled, unaware of the phone in the journalist's hand. This is secret surveillance work for the top brass, so if you try to print it in any of those rags you write for, I'll 'ave your bollocks for bed knobs!'

'Don't talk crap.' What the hell would you be doing secret surveillance work around here for? Hardly the corridors of power, is it? I reckon you took a tumble while you were up that tree twanging your wire, you dirty sod. That, or you're on a hobble, doing a bit of private divorce work, eh?'

'Mind your own bloody business! And get out of my sight

before I nicks you for burglary!'

'I'm not burgling anything!'

'Then why are you 'anging around respectable back gardens in the middle of the night?'

'I'm talking to you.'

'Right, and if you don't stop talking to me and get out of my sight in the next five seconds, you'll be 'elpin' me with my enquiries. Now piss off!' Evans groaned and turned his back on the journalist.

Naylor shrugged and turned on his heel. The bent bastard was in a worst mood than usual and there was no point getting himself nicked. Besides, what he'd got on his phone had the makings of a most intriguing story, particularly in his creative hands.

*

The ambulance men arrived and stretchered the injured detective away, unaware that they were being watched from an upstairs window. As they disappeared, Jacs turned and looked down at the slumbering form of Charlie Llewellyn. The sickening sense of guilt flooded over her again. Maybe the bloody pervert fell before he got anything embarrassing she thought hopefully; but she knew that was wishful thinking. She had played her role too well.

There again, what choice did she have? Her thoughts turned for the hundredth time to her odious visitor of the afternoon. She was just giving the kids their tea, when someone knocked the door. It was Dai Shit, as he was known on the estate. What the hell did he want with her? She always steered well clear of his sort. It was rumoured he was a Rent Man and everyone knew someone who had a story to tell about those bastards. It seemed only the Police were oblivious to their activities. Once in a while a mutilated body would turn up and a frightened silence would descend on the city like a poisonous cloud. People would mutter nervously and knowingly in the pubs and clubs, but they never mentioned names. It was simply down to the Rent Man Gang. The man held out an envelope.

'What is it?' she asked.

'Eviction notice,' he said with a sly grin. 'You got a week to get out.'

'This place belongs to the Council...'

'Yeah, shitty wirin'. They burn like candles,' he sneered pocketing the envelope.

'Why?' she asked, stunned, but feeling rising panic at the thought of being homeless with the twins.

'Why not?' he said, with that dirty grin showing off his tobacco teeth. 'Unless, of course, you're willing to do certain parties a little favour.'

'Like what?'

'Like layin' on a little private photo session. There's someone they want catchin' with 'is pants down, see. Someone you're pretty matey with, like. Someone you usually see down the Railway Tuesday nights. The word is you're coppin' off with 'im anyway, so 'ows about one for the camera, eh babes?'

She told him to sling his hook, but he just leered at her and told her to do it in the upstairs, back bedroom.

'Just make sure you leave the lights on and forget to close

the curtains, or else...'

'Or else what?'

He'd leaned forward with his stinking breath. His hand snaked out and grabbed her right breast. He laughed as she pulled back shocked. She should wise up, sharpish, he said. He was all for kickin' her and her brats out on the street if she didn't cooperate, but it wasn't his decision, see. There were other parties involved who weren't so sympathetic. Real fuckin' headers, in fact. Torch the place as soon as look at it, with 'er and the kids inside. So it was up to 'er, really. A nice little jump with Mr Charlie Llewellyn, watch the birdie, or, well, the alternative didn't bear thinkin' about really, did it?

It didn't. The thought of her children being burned alive was unbearable. Panicked by the horrific thought and the man's intimidating presence, she had agreed. She spent the rest of the day trying to justify the decision to herself. She guessed that Charlie's wife was behind this. They were recently separated and Charlie had told her more than once that Juliet was having an affair. Presumably she wanted him caught with his pants down to even up the score in a divorce battle. He had also told her that his wife's new bloke was a nasty piece of work – rich and powerful with all the connections. If he was involved there was all the more reason to take Dai Shit's threats seriously.

But then there was Charlie. Whatever the justification, she knew in her heart of hearts that she would be betraying him and the guilt washed away her self-defence like a sandcastle hit by the tide. He had always stood by her like a rock when she had needed him. So why had she assumed he would not stand up for her now? If anyone could stand up to the likes of

Dai Shit, it was Charlie. He wouldn't panic. He could look after himself, and her too if needs be.

Perhaps, but the twins were all she really had in the world and there was no way she would let any harm come to them. If it was only her at stake, she would have told the pig to sod off and left Charlie to sort him out, but the threat to the girls altered everything. The thought of them trapped in a burning building almost unhinged her.

Her thoughts turned to the present. She sighed and lay down on the bed next to Charlie. Oh well, if this was a set-up by his wife Juliet, perhaps it was no bad thing. It would end the marriage once and for all. She reached out and ran her hand gently down his cheek. You never knew, perhaps one day... She brushed the thought aside. Pull yourself together, you silly mare. When Charlie sees those pictures he's going to know you set him up and that's a fine way to repay his affection. She sighed again and closed her eyes.

4

Charlie stirred, thanks to the pressure of a full bladder. He half awoke, stumbled out of bed, and groped his way to the door. Things didn't feel quite right, but, a quick wee was no reason to unnecessarily disturb his slumbers too much. He opened the bathroom door and headed for the loo, which he could just make out through half-closed eyes. He took aim and fired just as the light went on.

'Why are you pissin' in the twins' bin, Charlie?' asked a drowsy voice behind him. The light and the voice half woke him up. He controlled himself with an effort.

'What you doin' here?' he mumbled.

'You're in my house, you dopy sod. Don't you remember? You crashed here last night.'

'Shit! Sorry, love. I thought I was in the bathroom at home...'

'No you're in the twins' bedroom, but don't worry, there's a liner in the bin; I'll empty it now.'

Charlie nodded drowsily and headed in the direction of the toilet. Now he was awake he was feeling rough. He remembered arriving at the Railway and those soft bastards in the back bar treating him like a leper. But he still didn't remember much after that, like how he came to be urinating in the bin in Jacs' kids' bedroom, for example!

He found a towel on the rail by the bath and wrapped it around his waist, then headed back towards the bedroom he had woken up in. The light was on and she was sitting up in bed. She grinned at the towel.

'It's a bit late to go all shy on me now, babes,' she remarked matter-of-factly.

'What you mean we, er...'

'We certainly did. Don't tell me you've forgotten, you drunken bugger!'

'Well, I...'

'Typical bloody man! Whop it in, whip it out and wipe it on the duvet. That's all us girls mean to men like you, isn't it?'

'No, honest Jacs. It's just well, God help, you know what state I was in last night. How the hell did I ever get it up?'

'Come here and I'll show you if you like.'

Charlie grinned.

'Hell Jacs, I'm a married man. It may not be worth calling a marriage...

'You're right there, now come here you philanderin' bastard.'

Charlie paused again, and then shrugged.

'If you say so. If I'm being done for adultery I might as well get my money's worth.'

He walked forward and climbed onto the bed.

*

When he awoke again, Jacs was gone and the radio alarm clock told him it was nearly nine. There was a note on the pillow next to him. He picked it up drowsily and read:

Dear Charlie,
You look like you could do with a lie-in this morning so I'm off to work. Taking twins to school with me. See you later. Feel free

to make yourself a cuppa.
Love, Jacs.

Charlie read it through again, pausing on the word 'love'. Christ, boyo, you'd better be sure about what you're getting into here, he thought. He was very fond of Jacs, but, since the teenage fumblings had finished, he had seen their relationship as brother and sister. Now, with the split from Juliet, they were lovers! Of course he didn't know what Jacs felt about it. For all he knew she was just out for a quick fling; she had a sex drive too, after all. But, somehow, experience told him otherwise. That little four-letter word spoke volumes and it could only lead to her getting hurt.

He reached over and clicked on the local radio station, Swansea Sound. Good, the news was due on in a minute. His thoughts drifted back to Jacs. Was there anything that amounted to a future between them? Hell, how was he supposed to know? He needed to talk to her; find out how she really felt. One thing was certain, he didn't need any commitments right now; he still had unfinished business of his own to sort out first.

A news item on the radio caught his attention.

'...and there have been calls for a public enquiry following newspaper allegation of misuse of Police resources in South Wales. It appears a police Detective Sergeant was injured last night whilst conducting an unauthorised surveillance operation in the Swansea area. It is claimed the officer may have been bribed to collect evidence in a private divorce action. Swansea M.P, Mr Jack Pritchard, is demanding to know if such moonlighting is commonplace while rumours of the notorious

Rent Man gang still abound and Police are complaining of lack of manpower. Meanwhile attempts to interview the officer are being thwarted by staff at Morriston Hospital where he has undergone emergency surgery. We will be keeping you updated on this story as it breaks. And now...'

Charlie grinned. Britain's scandal-ridden MPs had more reasons than most to worry about unauthorised surveillance operations if recent history was anything to go by! He climbed out of bed, dressed and headed downstairs to put the kettle on.

*

Charlie wrapped Jacs' waterproof more tightly around himself as he strode across the field that ran down the hill from the rear of the Close to his back garden. He had borrowed the hooded jacket to conceal his identity as he walked quickly down Jacs' path and shinned over the fence. Now he was glad of it as another squall of rain drove up the hill into his face. It was only October, but this was Wales, and the heavy cloud blotted out the sun, giving the rain a chillier bite than he would have liked. Even as he tried to console himself with the thought that it would blow away the cobwebs of his hangover, he felt the peculiar discomfort of cold, wet jeans beginning to cling to his thighs below the hem of the undersized waterproof.

To add to the physical discomfort, he found his mind drifting back to that news bulletin. Jacs had got back from her morning shift as he was making the tea. He had tried to bring up the question of how she felt about their relationship, but she had seemed distracted, troubled even, and they had simply agreed to be discreet until his divorce was sorted out. They had parted with a peck on the cheek and a vague agreement that Charlie would call her later. He had not had a chance to listen to the news for any new developments.

The mention of the injury to the police officer came back to him. Preece would probably have the connections to use police officers for a private surveillance operation but, if this was a set-up, what was Jacs' involvement? He didn't want to think that she would knowingly betray him, but then he knew he was up against an extremely ruthless man in Preece; a man who got his way at any cost. Jacs had the twins which meant she could be got at. He remembered her mood when she returned from work. Why so tense? It had to be guilt.

He paused on top of the gate that led into the next field. Through the rain he could just make out the pair of sloe trees that marked the gap leading into his back garden. Alright, just suppose he had been set up. What did it mean? What did it amount to in reality? The more he thought about it, the more it looked like the gloves were finally coming off; the time for action had arrived.

The question was, was he up to it? Had he gone soft, living in a dangerous limbo somewhere between ordinary, married life and his commitment to Detachment 8? Who could say? Things were undoubtedly hotting up and threatening to take on complications he could never have foreseen at the start of the mission. His thoughts turned to his out-of-the-blue contact with Al Sullivan the previous week.

He had been polishing Minister Hughes' cockerel with his angle grinder in his workshop – Charlie grinned and made a mental note of the double entendre – when the call from Al forced its way into his consciousness above the din. They hadn't spoken for years. How are you keeping mate? Good to hear from you! What have you been up to?

They had become good pals for a short while during the Gulf War after Charlie had fetched Al out of a bad situation when he got caught up in a rearguard action by Hussein's Republican Guard. Al was a regular trooper, Charlie was on other business, but he had taken time out to pull the injured soldier out of trouble. They had met to swap stories after the war over a couple of pints, but had soon taken different career paths.

When Al phoned to suggest a reunion, Charlie was pleasantly surprised to hear from his old mate. When Al explained that he was now working for Customs and Excise, the surprise diminished a little. It diminished even more when Al mentioned that he just happened to be visiting Swansea in a few days' time.

They met at the Commercial in Killay Square and a couple of pints later Al got around to the real reason for the reunion. He was working on a smuggling operation and they were now pretty certain that Swansea was one of the ports involved. Drugs were coming in by boat and Swansea had the honour of representing South Wales as an entry point. Liverpool was being used to cover North Wales and North-West England, Glasgow supplied Scotland, and Hull and London supplied the east of the country. The whole thing appeared to be connected to a male prostitution ring involving youngsters. Everything about it made your flesh crawl. Worst still this Rent Man gang was highly organised and ruled by terror. Security was tight as a drum.

Charlie sympathised and wondered how Al and his team hoped to tackle the problem. Al explained that he was just coming to that. A little bird had told them that a local lawyer called Preece could be involved. It was as thin as a whore's drawers, but another little bird had told him that Preece's secretary was Charlie's missus. He was just wondering whether Charlie may have heard something that might have a bearing on his investigation, no matter how thin it was.

Charlie had commiserated, but had been unable to help. He and Juliet were splitting up thanks to Preece so he was hardly in their confidence – sorry. The two men had reminisced a bit more, then finished their pints, shaken hands and parted.

Charlie had watched Al drive out of the pub's car park then picked up his phone and dialled a number. He got an answer phone inviting a message. He spoke briefly:

'This is Charlie Alpha Tango to Det. Eight reporting interested contact with an Alan Sullivan of H.M. Customs and Excise. Please check credentials and background. Out,' was all he said.

*

Charlie climbed off the gate and headed for the sloe trees. What Al had told him was useful and he wished he could have been more helpful in return, but, right now, he had bigger fish to fry.

He let himself in through the back door. Perhaps because of his recent imaginings he half expected things to be different, but the only change was that the 'messages' light on his phone was lit. He walked through the kitchen into the lounge to play them back. The first caller hung up without leaving a message.

The second sounded frightened:

'Dad, it's Gareth; are you there? Listen, I'm in Swansea nick, I haven't done anything wrong, honest to God, but they're trying to fit me up for some robbery. It's bloody mad. I thought it was some kind of wind-up at first, but they've kept me in all night and they keep saying they've got witnesses and everything. Look, I know you're busy, but I think they're serious. They're talking about charging me with taking and driving away, and robbing an off-licence, for starters. I dunno, but I think maybe I need a solicitor to sort this out. Anyhow, I don't know if this counts as the one phone call I'm allowed, but please try and get here if you can.'

Charlie sat down on the sofa to think. Gareth, under arrest, being charged with, what had he said? Stealing a car and robbing an off-licence? Christ this was serious, but it wasn't Gareth. He knew his son better than that. This needed thinking about. He listened automatically to the next message.

'Ahem, Mr Llewellyn, it's Ivor Semple here, of Semple, Tucker and Preece. I'm calling on behalf of Mr Preece who has instructed me to contact you regarding your wife and children, in particular, your son, who is currently in serious trouble with the police. Mr Preece has a proposal he wishes me to put to you regarding an out-of-court divorce settlement and, in the interest of everyone, particularly young Gareth, I would suggest you meet me at your very earliest convenience. I have kept my diary open all day, so there is no need to make an appointment.'

The voicemail informed him that there were no more messages. Charlie clicked the machine to rewind, then set it back to record.

So, this was Semple, Preece's legal lapdog. According to Al Sullivan, he had made the papers in the Sixties as Swansea's leading student radical and he had made himself sufficiently unpopular with the establishment of the day to ensure his flat was raided six times in a week by the Drug Squad. When it was discovered that the only fingerprints on the bag of amphetamine tablets were those of the arresting officer, all charges were dropped, but, from an employment point of view, the legal profession saw him as soiled goods. Things looked bleak until Hywel Preece took him on, and even put him first on the letterhead, but the word was that he got by on a none-too-generous salary and the question of a partnership never arose.

Anyhow, Semple's problems were of no concern to Charlie right now. His first instinct was to get to Gareth, but Semple's message made him pause. They knew Gareth was in trouble and Semple seemed to imply that Preece's proposal would in some way get him out of it. It was no doubt unpleasant for Gareth, but an extra hour or two in custody wouldn't make much difference. It was time to take a closer look at the enemy's position.

He went upstairs for a quick shave and a change of clothes and came down feeling more able to face the onset of war; he didn't expect this proposal to be distilled from the milk of human kindness. As he came back down, he noticed an envelope sticking through the letterbox. He pulled it out, allowing the draught excluder to swing back with a snap.

'He's in there boy's!' Yelled an excited, male voice.

'Mr Llewellyn this is Simon Wiggins of the Evening Post. Would you like to step outside so we can have a word with you, sir?'

Charlie dodged back into the living room and pulled back the curtain of the front window. Through the nets he made out a heaving scrum of what were clearly reporters and camera crews. There were vans parked on his drive and men wearing headphones were waving sausage-shaped microphones in the air. He stared for a moment in horror. What on earth was the press doing camped on his lawn?

Move! Move! Get out of here! They obviously hadn't found how to get around the back of the house yet, but, if he didn't open the front door, they soon would. He stuffed the envelope into his pocket and grabbed his parka. It was sturdier than Jacs' waterproof. He quickly transferred his wallet and keys into the inside pocket and raced back through the kitchen. He locked the back door behind him and ran up the garden to the gap in the hedge. There was nobody in sight as he squeezed through then headed up the field towards the woods. From the cover of the trees he looked back and saw some dark figures scrambling over a hedge a few doors down from his house. He'd cut it fine. He turned on his heel and made his way through the trees and down the hill to where he hoped his van was still waiting in the car park of the Railway Inn.

5

Annette Preece was a very lonely woman. She had given up her acting career in London, aged twenty-five, when she finally realised that she didn't have the staying power to make it on the stage. She'd run home to Swansea, and met Hywel Preece at a ladies' night at her father's lodge. Preece lacked London polish, but he was good looking, had plenty of Swansea money, and a big future in front of him. He was already a City Councillor in his early thirties and her father made it clear that he had the right connections. By Swansea standards, his family were old money. She sold out for a big house and cushy existence.

From the outset her new husband seemed to discourage her from developing a social life and he was noticeably cold to the few visitors she invited around. It gradually dawned on her that she had married a very possessive man and, initially, she found the idea quite flattering. Then it became apparent that, if she was not welcome to make friends of her own, nor was she going to get to know his. She did not even know if he had any. He lived for his work, and the house in Derwen Fawr was testament to his success, not his popularity.

Boredom and loneliness started her drinking and, with that, the few acquaintances that might have survived his frostiness fell away. She was left to dwell on her failure as an actress. The relinquishing of her lifelong ambition had left her desperately unfilled. She wanted children, but Hywel didn't. When she tried to force the issue, he moved into one of the spare rooms and withdrew what little physical affection he still showed her.

Then she knocked little Ryan Kelly down and he was paralysed for life. He came dashing out from between two parked cars in Tesco's car park as she was looking for a place to pull in. She hit him with a sickening thud, even though she was only crawling along. The police arrived with an ambulance and she failed the breathalyser. Hywel turned up at the police station and pulled every string possible, but she had already given a blood sample and she was three times over the limit. It was a first offence, but the injury to the child guaranteed her a banner headline in the Evening Post and total hostility from the magistrates. Mrs Kelly spat in her face and tried to push her under a bus as she left court.

Worse by far, however, was the guilt. She had recurrent nightmares about the child's face as she hit him. The way the little boy looked at her in horror as, for a split second, he realised his mistake. The way his body lay twisted in the gutter as she stared down at him. A woman began screaming and a man began shouting for someone to phone an ambulance. In her dreams, she realised she was the woman. Had it been like that in reality?

Hywel got the dangerous driving charge reduced to careless driving so she escaped prison, but she paid a heavy price. When they got home he went berserk. He dragged her around by the hair, slapping and kicking her, and calling her a useless drunken bitch. Then he left the house without a word.

She took a very large gin into the bath and tried to tell herself it was a one off. How could she expect him to react? She had landed him with a lot of trouble and expense. No doubt he was worried sick about the effect of all this terrible publicity on his career. By the time the gin was gone, it was all her fault and she deserved it for what she had done to that poor little boy.

That episode established a pattern. When something happened to upset him, his anger became directed at her and, thanks to her misguided guilt, this became acceptable. Drink blurred the issue and he made sure her addiction was liberally supplied, while using it as another weapon to attack her with. How could a man get on with a hopeless sot like her holding him back? It became all the easier to justify cutting her off from the outside world.

She had threatened to leave him on countless occasions, usually when her courage was fortified by gin, but the drink blurred any real resolve. Trying to focus on a genuine plan of action through an alcoholic haze was hopeless. She was chained to an environment in which her drinking habits could be indulged in at will and her self-esteem was so low that, in Hywel's case she had developed the dependence of a prisoner on her jailer.

Lacking her husband's cruelty, she was baffled by his treatment of her. Why had he married her in the first place? Image was certainly something to do with it. Successful Swansea solicitors have showcase wives and, before the drinking took its toll, she was a good-looking woman. Her failure as an actress had come largely from the inability of casting directors to see past her looks.

Why did he stay married to her now? She was overweight and raddled. That was hardly good for his image, but then she never saw anyone of importance to him anymore, so that hardly mattered. She was like a professional qualification; she had to be possessed, but never produced.

Perhaps it was money. He was undoubtedly the most avaricious person she had ever met. He measured success entirely in terms of personal wealth and despised people who didn't do likewise. She was no doubt cheap to run compared to the cost of a divorce settlement.

She often groped back through her befuddled memory in search of a defining moment, something she had said or done which had so turned him against her, but, apart from the accident, there was nothing. After that first beating, all she could remember was a descent into hopeless degradation. She had come to the conclusion that he simply enjoyed watching her gradual disintegration.

Now, she was standing in front of her eighteenth century dressing table. She opened one of the beautifully inlaid walnut drawers and rummaged around in the lipsticks and powder compacts. She pulled out a miniature of Booths Gin, unscrewed the cap, and drained the bottle in one. A shudder ran through her as the near spirit hit her empty stomach. She looked at herself in the mirror again and, despite the puffiness around her eyes where she had been crying, she thought she could see an improvement.

She picked the burning cigarette up from the ashtray and took a heavy pull on it. Her hands were still shaking badly, despite the drink. She took another drag and dropped it back in the ashtray. She toyed with the idea of going downstairs to the bar for more drink, but resisted it. Instead, she pulled her nightdress up over her head and dropped it on the floor, then turned to inspect her body in the mirror. The injuries from the slaps and punches were livid against her white skin, and she could also make out darker bruises developing where he had kicked her.

She had been on the phone talking to the hairdresser when he returned. She happened to be facing the window as the green Range Rover turned into the drive and crunched across the gravel to the front door. By the time it pulled up she had abruptly terminated her conversation and replaced the receiver. Already she was sick with dread. He rarely returned during the day, unless something had happened to make him angry, and, when it did, he returned to take his anger out on her. However, this time, it hadn't been quite like that. This time he'd arrived home to deliver the ultimate humiliation and, this time, albeit briefly, she had fought back.

She had sat rigid with anticipation in the front room. She heard him come in and walk down the hall. He walked past the door and into the kitchen. Normally, he would be straight onto the attack, hurling accusations and insults until he had stroked his anger into violence. But not today. She heard him open the fridge door, then he appeared in the doorway holding a glass of orange juice. There was no sign of anger about him. He was feigning carelessness, but his eyes were watchful for her reaction.

'Something's come up, dear,' he began casually. 'Bit of a nuisance really. It looks like we'll be looking after Juliet for a while when she gets back from Tenerife.'

'Why?' asked Annette, numbly? She had a terrible premonition of what was coming.

'She's left her husband. I've said she can stay here for a

couple of weeks until she gets sorted.'

Annette stared at him in disbelief. Drunk or not, she was a woman. Did he seriously think she didn't know what was going on? From the look on his face, he knew well enough. There was a smug triumphalism about him. He was proposing to move his whore into the house, confident that she would not dare oppose him! To her disgust she felt her face crumple into tears. Why did she give him the satisfaction?

'You bastard, you cheap fucking bastard!' she sobbed. 'What have I ever done to deserve this?'

'Deserve what, dear?' he asked, with a mock innocence. 'It'll only be for a couple of weeks.'

'I'm not having that slut in my house for a couple of minutes let alone weeks, you pig!'

Preece strolled over to the drinks cabinet. His tone was patronisingly casual as he opened the glass doors.

'I'm not sure I know what you're driving at, dear. Here, let me pour you a nice gin and tonic to steady your nerves. You've obviously been imagining things...'

'What? Like your clothes smelling of perfume? The contempt that slut treats me with when I call your office? I'm not blind you know! You can screw the bitch till your balls drop off, but you're not doing it under my roof and that's final!'

Her husband turned to face her. He was holding out a drink.

'Well, well', he murmured, feigning surprise.

'My house, my roof, now, is it? Mistress of the house now, are we? What makes you think I'd allow a useless, drunken cow like you to occupy such a responsible position?'

She lashed out, accidentally catching the glass that he was still holding. The drink hit him in the face as if she had deliberately thrown it. He raised his hand slowly to his face to wipe it away, obviously surprised by her unexpected rebelliousness. Then he hit her. He attacked her with a flurry of blows and when she fell to the floor he began kicking her with his hard leather brogues. When he got tired of that he knelt down and grabbed her by the throat. Through the tears she could make out the blurred outline of his face inches from her.

'You understand this, and understand it right,' he hissed.

'You are nobody around here; you are worth less than the fucking furniture as far as I'm concerned. You are here because it suits me and it would take very little for it to stop suiting me. Come the day that happens, all I need to do is upend a bottle of gin down your throat and watch your liver go bang. Do you understand now?'

'Yes Hywel,' she whispered, as he relaxed his grip on her throat enough for her to talk. 'I understand.'

6

Barry Naylor awoke late that morning and headed straight for the newsagents. A grin of satisfaction twisted his rat-like features as he scanned the page bearing his story. He bought a bag of crisps for breakfast and pointed his car in the direction he had followed the night before.

He was heading up the Gower Rd towards the turn-off for the Close when he spotted the crowd of hacks outside the house. He pulled in and got out. He strolled back to the entrance of the drive noting the number of the house. He recognised Arwel Jones from the Llanelli Star.

'So whose place is this then, Arwel?' He called out above the general babble.

'Find out for yourself you thieving cunt!' came the less-than-friendly reply. Naylor remembered scooping young Arwel on a story the reporter had been naive enough to share with him over a pint in the Tav. He obviously hadn't found it in his heart to forgive and forget as yet. He shrugged and made his way over to an outside broadcast unit. A heavily made-up piece with big hair was just getting ready for her next bulletin. She raised the microphone and spoke to camera:

'Thank you Glyn. I'm standing outside the home of Mr Charles Llewellyn, the man named in today's shocking revelations regarding misuse of Police resources in Swansea. We are hoping to talk to Mr Llewellyn shortly to see if he can shed some light on the events of last night.'

Fine. That was all he needed. He'd got the man's name. He

headed back to the Orion. No-one in his right mind was going to turn up with those twats camped outside his front door. They could sit there all day on someone else's payroll. Naylor had to get results to earn a living. He sat in the car and thought for a moment. A house with a drive but no vehicle on it; a well-to-do area and a pathetic bus service; so where was the car? Nobody relied on public transport in Swansea if they could help it. Naylor opened his laptop and Googled the name and address. He found a website advertising Charlie Llewellyn as an Architectural Mason and Sculptor. From the look of the double garage at the top of the drive he ran the business from home. He knew Evans had photographed the bloke sometime after closing time and there was no car outside the Close. So he'd walked there or got a cab. It was common enough to leave your car outside a pub if you were over the limit.

Naylor knew that the majority of affairs happen amongst friends and acquaintances – work colleagues, old friends, brides and best men, bridegrooms and bridesmaids; Naylor's mind turned to some interesting DVDs he had seen on the subject. These were two local people. It was possible, even likely, that the local pub was their common ground. He started the car and drove off looking for a place to turn, then headed down the hill and pulled into the car park of the Railway Inn. It was just after ten.

He parked in a corner and looked around. There were three vehicles that looked like they had spent the night there. On closer inspection, the first looked like it had spent the last six months there. It was covered in that mixture of guano, leaves, grime and twigs unique to cars that have stood under trees for a considerable time. He eliminated that. The second was a possibility, as was the third, a white van.

He dug his laptop out again. He got Hotmail up and typed in the registration numbers of both the car and the van. He added a request for details of the owners' driving licenses. He typed in the address of a contact at the Driver and Vehicle Licensing Agency in Morriston and sent it. The screen showed a confirmation. He glanced at his watch. The lazy twat should be in work by now. Still, he'd need a few moments to call up the details and get his mate in the licence section to do a search too. Against his better nature Naylor sat back to wait. A few minutes later he had mail. He opened the message and read:

Hi Barry,
Sorry to nag but you owe for July and August. I'll trust you on this one, but you're getting nothing else until you square me up.
Gary.

Cheeky bastard! Who did he think he was, flogging confidential DVLA info to friends and acquaintances then putting people on stop credit? What a fucking nerve! Naylor ran a brief fantasy about grassing Gary up to his boss, but it was only a fantasy. His access to the DVLA database was too valuable. He made a mental note to pay him something and returned to the email and opened the usual attachment.

Bingo! The white van was registered to a Mr Charles Llewellyn living on the Gower Road. He turned to the details on Llewellyn's driving licence. The man was born on the third of April 1965; that made him...forty-seven. Good, this was real progress. Naylor shut the laptop down again. He fished out his mobile and scrolled down his list of credit vetting agencies. Money Vet was good, but ironically he owed them cash and they were getting funny about his habit of contesting every bill they sent him, bastards! He selected Penny Wise. The girl at the other end took the details and ran a check. There was no mortgage on the property and no CCJ's or blacklisting's. According to the electoral register, the subject was married to a Juliet Llewellyn. There was one other resident in the house, a teenage boy called Gareth. Naylor closed the connection and sat back deep in thought.

Okay, so things weren't exactly hunky-dory in the Llewellyn household. The husband was shagging around and the wife wasn't answering the door, or she wasn't there. Gone back to her mother's with the kids? If she'd been in, she'd have called the police to clear that posse of piss artists off her drive. Furthermore, Evans had her old man under surveillance and someone had put him up to it. Who more likely than herself, the injured party? But that begged a bigger question: what was a member of the CID doing involved in a domestic? It could be a personal favour, but Evans had never done anyone a favour in his life as far as Naylor was aware. Had he been ordered to snoop on Llewellyn by someone higher up? He decided to dig further into the husband's background.

He phoned a contact in the Benefits Agency. Ten minutes later she phoned back to say Llewellyn had claimed sickness benefit from 2003 to mid-2007, when he had moved to Swansea. He had left the army in 1991 following an injury in the Gulf War. She read out his National Insurance number.

Naylor agreed to meet her for a drink the following week. She was no oil painting, but then he hadn't had a leg over in ages, so what the hell.

He went back to his laptop and Googled the British Army manning records in Glasgow. He explained to the girl that he was searching for his elder brother. They had lost contact when their parents had split up and Charlie had run off and enlisted. He believed he had joined the Army and seen action in the Gulf. She took his National Insurance number and came back shortly. Yes, a Charles Llewellyn had joined up in 1989 at the age of eighteen. She gave him an army number and a regiment – the Welsh Guards currently based in Aldershot. She even had their phone number.

The records clerk in Aldershot swore it was more than her job was worth to give out information like that, but Naylor pleaded. He was a squaddie himself and he had some leave due. If he could track down his brother after all these years, he could come up to Aldershot in a fortnight's time for a reunion.

Alright, she'd take a little look, but mum's the word, okay? He promised on his word of honour.

She came back puzzled. He was a member of the Guards until August 1991, but he couldn't have seen action in the Gulf – the Guards weren't out there. It was possible he had left for health reasons, but she could shed no more light than that. There was no forwarding address. Naylor thanked her and rang off. This was getting more and more intriguing. There were some odd little gaps in Mr Charlie Llewellyn's military history and peeping through gaps was how he made his living.

He let his thoughts drift back to Juliet Llewellyn and her tame policeman. Who would she know who could pull those sorts of strings in Swansea? There were people with that sort of clout, but how did she connect to them? That was not something he was likely to find out sitting in the car park of the Railway Inn he decided.

*

As he was about to start the engine, a movement caught his eye. A man was emerging from the shade of the trees overhanging the cycle path. He was wearing a green parka with the hood up, which obscured his face. There was something about him which gave him the air of a fugitive. Naylor was not surprised when he made straight for the van. Had he found Mr Charlie Llewellyn? The man got in and started the engine. He reversed and drove up the hill to the entrance of the car park. Only then did the journalist start the engine of his own car.

The van turned right onto the Gower road and headed towards town. Naylor let him get well ahead before following. By the time they reached Killay Square he was three cars behind. The van was an easy target, so he maintained this distance until he reached the Uplands. The van turned left into St James' Crescent and suddenly pulled into a parking space. Naylor glanced around hurriedly for somewhere to stop. His luck was out, so he watched Llewellyn park in the only available space and walk up the steps of an imposing Georgian building, then he drove up the hill to Ffynone Road, found a space and walked back.

The brass plaque on the wall announced that these were

the offices of Semple, Tucker and Preece, Solicitors. It seemed he couldn't put a foot wrong this morning. If he was looking for someone with real clout to connect to Juliet Llewellyn, he couldn't have chosen a better address.

He recalled more optimistic days some fifteen years ago. He was making a name for himself on the Post and needed one big story to send him up the M4 to Fleet Street.

He had followed up a piece about an unmarried mother in Clase who had had her front door removed by a rent collector in the middle of winter because she was a month behind with her payments. He tailed the man and began to pick up reports of intimidation from other tenants. Some people were too afraid to talk and all were very nervous. He set about tracking down the landlord and, according to the Land Registry these properties were in the name of a solicitor called Ivor Semple who worked for the firm of Semple, Tucker and Preece. The word was that Semple was a yes-man and that Preece was the real force to be reckoned with. And boy, did he turn out to be a real force.

Naylor recalled the naiveté with which he had handed in his copy to his editor. When nothing appeared the following day, or the day after, he knocked on his office door and demanded to know why. He was invited to sit down and calm down. Given the seriousness of the implications and the risk of a libel action, Mr Preece had been phoned personally by the editor and asked to comment on Naylor's allegations.

Preece acknowledged that his partner owned some property from which he derived rental income, and yes, as far as he was aware, Mr Semple employed the services of a professional collection agency. However, he was quite sure that his colleague would never countenance abuse or intimidation of his tenants. He would bring the matter to Mr Semple's attention immediately and he was sure that it would be looked into without delay. In the meanwhile would he thank Mr, er?

Mr Naylor.

Yes, would he thank Mr Naylor for bringing this to their attention?

The police stopped him eight times that week. They did him for a bald tyre, speeding and running a red light. They went over his car with a magnifying glass. They were so thorough that it sailed through its MOT two months later. He blew into a breathalyser so often that he began to get dizzy spells. He was getting panicky and sent a memo to his editor complaining that he was being harassed. Something was done because the police backed off, but the story stayed spiked and no-one seemed interested in taking up the cudgels on his behalf. And that was that.

Now he had fifteen years of cobbling together shite stories to look back on and his dreams of Fleet Street in tatters, simply because he'd got on the wrong side of Councillor Preece. Barry Naylor had tasted Preece's displeasure and the taste lingered.

Now, either it was an extraordinary coincidence, or it would appear Preece was somehow involved in this business, presumably on the wife's side. Perhaps Llewellyn was intending to thrash out some sort of private agreement. Having experienced a taste of Preece's methods, Naylor did not envy him. He noticed a man from the apartments in the middle of the Crescent was about to drive off, so he hurried back up the hill to collect the Orion.

*

The imposing portraits of some of Swansea's greatest legal minds gazed down from the oak-panelled walls of the waiting room. For generations these people had devoted their energies to helping Swansea's richest residents get richer. The City was still cleaning up the pollution and landscaping the slagheaps created by contracts and deeds that these great minds had drafted. From each portrait dark, soulless eyes gazed down on him contemptuously.

Charlie was beginning to find the wait irritating when a woman's voice interrupted his reverie.

'Mr Semple will see you now Mr Llewellyn,' the severe features of the company's receptionist were peering around the door at him. 'Up the stairs to the first floor and it's the first door you come to. There's a name plaque on the door.'

'Thank you,' he nodded. He rose, irritated by her supercilious manner. This was not part of the plot. He wasn't interested in being kept waiting while a minion played mind games. He wanted an argument with the organ grinder, not his monkey. Still, with Gareth in trouble, he needed to get on with it. Thoughtfully, he climbed the long Victorian staircases that led to the first floor offices.

*

Charlie had only partly guessed the reason for the delay. Ivor Semple was, in fact, in the process of adjusting to the effects of the generous line of cocaine he had snorted twenty minutes earlier. He had meant to stay clean until after the interview, but that had proved more difficult than he had hoped. It wasn't just the addiction – though Christ knows that was bad enough – it was his overall dependence. Hywel told him to do this; Hywel told him to do that. Hywel told him to do every fucking thing and, if he didn't like it, Hywel would tell him to fuck off or, worse still, let O'Leary have a chat with him. He had no clients, no briefs, and no instructions. He only bothered to carry a briefcase because Hywel told him to. All he did all day was sit around snorting coke, cooking the books and laundering cash while Hywel ran everything with an iron fist. There was the occasional meeting, like today's, when Hywel ordered him to kick some silly fucker's arse for incurring Hywel's wrath. Jesus! Forty-five years of age and this was all he had to show for it.

The coke was beginning to hit when the hatchet-faced hag from reception buzzed through to say Llewellyn had arrived. Typical! Ten minutes earlier and he would still have been struggling with temptation. Now he was coked-up and more likely to fall in love with the bloke than nail his bollocks to the anvil! He couldn't see him in this state; that was for certain. He lit a cigarette to steady himself. He needed time to get used to the hit. He pulled a bottle of sherry from the bottom drawer of his desk. He unscrewed the cap and took a long pull. That steadied him a bit more. The initial rush began to subside after about ten minutes and he suddenly found himself feeling supremely confident. Better sort this business out for Hywel, he decided. After all, he paid the pennies that paid for the powder. He buzzed down to Mrs Lewis to send up his visitor and read over Hywel's instructions again.

*

'Come in Mr Llewellyn, please have a seat.'

Charlie eyed the lawyer with ill concealed suspicion, but he sat down. Bit old for a ponytail and there was something unnaturally bright about his eyes, he decided. He struck him as a weak, amoral man; the sort who would push a child out of a lifeboat to save his own skin. That fact that he wished to appear friendly made Charlie even more suspicious.

'Right, well thank you for calling by,' Semple began. 'I imagine that you have some idea why Mr Preece has asked me to talk to you...'

'Why doesn't he want to talk to me personally?'

'Ah, well that's just Hywel's way, you see. Perhaps he feels that, under the circumstances, a third party might serve to keep matters on a more business-like footing. Silly dragging personalities into a thing like this...'

'Not if you're one of the personalities.'

Semple eyed him for a moment, and then shrugged.

'Mr Llewellyn,' he continued, 'you are aware that your son Gareth is in serious trouble with the police and I am sure you know by now that we have a water tight case against you for adultery. It was never intended that this business should reach the ears of the press. That seems to have been a bizarre blunder by the man who was carrying out the, er, surveillance. However, if you had not been committing adultery, the blunder would not have occurred.'

'Okay, I don't need a lecture from the likes of you. I want to know what you are proposing and what is happening to Gareth.'

Again the stare and then the shrug.

'Nothing will happen to your son if you accept our terms. At present he is being held by the police in connection with an incident on Monday afternoon when a couple of joy riders held up an off-licence. The police have witnesses to say your son was one of the culprits...'

'Yes, well Gareth left a message for me saying he had nothing to do with it and I believe him.'

'I'm sure you do, but the question of his guilt or innocence is not at issue here.'

'What d'you mean?'

'Well, the police need not charge him. Hywel has some powerful connections amongst the top brass and it appears that Gareth could walk out of the police station this afternoon if Hywel was minded to make the right phone call. Obviously, if you intend to fight over your forthcoming divorce settlement, he is unlikely to do that.'

'If Gareth is innocent, a good lawyer will sort it out.'

'Perhaps, but can you afford a good lawyer? I understand that there will be no more contributions into your joint account from your wife's side. Furthermore, mud sticks. Believe me, I know. Even if your son is found not guilty, tongues will still wag and fingers will still be pointed. These allegations could do a young man's career prospects no end of harm. On the other hand, we can get an uncontested divorce hearing into court before the CPS has even begun to draft the outline of a case against Gareth.'

It was Charlie's turn to stare.

'So that's what this is all about,' he muttered, finally. You've set my son up to ensure I don't end up with any of Juliet's money in a divorce settlement?' His voice rose. 'You've deliberately buggered about with a young man's whole future, just to score a few extra points in a battle that has nothing to do with him!' Suddenly, Charlie was on his feet leaning across the desk. His knuckles were white as they pressed down on Semple's blotter. The solicitor glanced around wildly for an escape route, but Charlie was between him and the door.

'Listen,' he babbled, 'I had nothing to do with this. I'm just the messenger boy. Getting aggressive won't alter your position; it'll just make it worse. Look, why don't you sit down and listen to Hywel's proposal. I won't pretend you're going to like it, but at least then you'll know where you stand.'

Charlie hesitated, and then slowly resumed his seat. Semple pulled open the bottom drawer of his desk and pulled out the bottle of sherry again, this time with the two glasses.

'Here, why don't we have a drink and discuss this like gentlemen?'

'You're not a gentleman and I wouldn't accept a drink from you if my mouth was on fire.'

Semple shrugged again.

'Don't mind if I do, do you?'

'It's your office.'

Semple poured himself a glassful and knocked it back in one. After a moment, he resumed.

'Have you seen the paper?' Charlie shook his head. Semple opened another drawer, pulled out a newspaper that had been folded open and pushed it across the desk. As Charlie glanced at it, Semple sat back with a faint leer.

'Let's be frank,' he continued, 'with that sort of publicity, the situation with your son is now a matter of overkill. You'd be lucky to be granted the cost of a cup of tea.'

Charlie glanced at the paper again. The man had a point.

'Alright,' he said, 'what's the deal?'

Semple cleared his throat.

'As I said, you're not going to like it, but given that you are not exactly in the best bargaining...'

'Get on with it!'

'Well, basically, you to fuck off really.'

'What do you mean?'

'Well, just that, you bugger off and don't come back. Go west. Start afresh. Turn over a new leaf, etcetera.'

'But what about my house, my business? I've got commitments!'

'People walk out on their commitments all the time; who gives a shit? Hywel's a rich man and you haven't got a pot to piss in. Obviously, there will be expenses involved if you are going to put any distance between yourself and here. Hywel has authorised me to make you a cash payment of ten thousand pounds to help you on your way.' He withdrew a bulky white envelope from the inside pocket of the jacket slung over the back of his chair.

'That's surprisingly generous.'

Semple ignored the irony.

'Not really. We don't want you back. I hear America's a damn sight better than Swansea on the job front these days...'

'What if I take the money and come back anyway?'

'Then the gloves come back off and stay off. Anyhow, you'd

only agree to go in order to save your son, so you're hardly going to change your mind. You can count the money if you like.'

'No thanks, I'll trust you.' Charlie leant forward and picked up the envelope. His irony seemed lost on the man.

'Before you go...' Semple was holding out a document.

'Oh yes, I forgot. You wouldn't be a lawyer if you didn't have some bullshit document for me to sign. What is it?'

'It's merely a formal agreement whereby you agree not to oppose Mrs Llewellyn's petition for divorce on the grounds of adultery. You also waive rights of access to your son. Here, you ought to read it. Hywel has made financial arrangements for Gareth to finish his studies, so you won't be missed.'

Charlie accepted the sheet of paper.

'Pass me a pen,' he muttered. He signed the document and pushed it back across the table. Without another word he rose, picked up the money, and left the room. He made his way down the long, Victorian stair case that led from the prestigious, first floor offices of Semple, Tucker and Preece, St James Crescent, The Uplands, Swansea.

7

Naylor was parked six cars back from the white van when Llewellyn emerged from the building three quarters of an hour later. He stared in amazement. It was like looking at a different man. There was no quickness in his stride. He made no attempt to pull his hood up, as if it no longer mattered if people recognised him. He looked beaten; utterly dejected and defeated. Naylor eased his camera up over the level of the dash board and fired off a couple of shots as Llewellyn fumbled clumsily with the keys and eventually opened the driver's door. He turned and gazed at Naylor's car for a moment, but his eyes were blank and unseeing. Whatever had taken place in that office had clearly knocked the heart out of him. Naylor wondered what on earth had gone on. He had a fifteen-year-old score to settle with Preece and now, seeing that haunted look and those stooped shoulders, his mind was made up. He wanted to see where this was going to lead.

Again he kept his distance as the van headed further into town. Where was he going? The station? Quite unexpectedly his quarry turned left up Mount Pleasant and headed for Townhill. Soon they were heading down past the soulless, rotting terraces with their boarded-up windows. The house numbers daubed on the front of the buildings in white emulsion. Burst mattresses lay in gardens, broken doors were thrown into the street and cars with no wheels were parked on piles of bricks along the roadside. They turned left onto Gors Avenue, then down to the roundabout. Finally the van pulled up outside a pub on the Llangyfelach Road.

Naylor continued past until he found a place to pull in out of sight of the place. He got out, locked the car and walked back. He was glad that his car looked such a wreck from the outside. This part of town was the car theft capital of Britain.

The van was empty when he got there. Its owner had obviously decided to drown his sorrows. Naylor thought about going in, but decided against it. At this time of day he could be the only other customer in there. He strolled as slowly as possible back up the road and gazed in at the dodgy TV repair shops and less identifiable businesses that chiselled out a living there. It wasn't long before people were gazing at him. They didn't like unfamiliar faces. He wandered back down to the pub, and on past, to check his car. It was the start of a routine patrol. A woman carrying a black, plastic bag went into the pub and that was the only sign of life for an hour.

Finally, Llewellyn emerged and got in the van. He looked none the happier for a drink or two. He headed off towards the Carmarthen Road as Naylor raced for his car. They drove towards town and turned left, then right at the top of High Street. They headed down New Cut and turned right along the Strand past the multi-storey car park, then right again as if they were going to enter it. To Naylor's puzzlement the van carried on past. The road was a dead end. What did he want down there? He pulled in, got out and walked quickly down the road. The van was parked at the very end where there were no double yellow lines and Llewellyn was trudging back towards him. Suddenly he turned right. Shit! The tunnel under the railway which led back up to High Street!

Naylor ran back to his car. He reversed back like a mad man

and went racing into the multi storey. The tyres screamed as the car spiralled up to the top floor. He drove illegally out of the entrance across the bridge to the top level and pulled up outside the Station where the taxis parked. He jumped out and slammed the doors.

'You can't park there, butty!' called one of the drivers.

'Go fuck yourself!' snarled Naylor, as he ran out onto the roadside and gazed frantically up and down the street, His quarry was nowhere to be seen. Think! Think! Where would he have gone? He'd started drinking and he didn't look in the mood to stop. Now he'd ditched the van where it could be left for twenty-four hours or more, so it was reasonable to assume he intended to carry on. But had he turned right or left as he came out of the tunnel?

He made a snap decision and turned right, pushing his way into the first pub he came to. He worked his way through the crowd of lunchtime drinkers from the local offices. He passed the bar and headed into the gents. He took the opportunity to relieve himself, and then made his way back through the scrum.

'This isn't a public toilet!' shouted a red-faced barman as Naylor reached the door without buying a drink.

'Fucking smells like one!' retorted Naylor, nastily, as he squeezed through the doors and back out onto the street. He hesitated. He couldn't leave his car where it was for long; the wardens were like locusts around there. To hell with it! He'd try the Adam and Eve. If he had no luck, he'd collect the car and try the pubs further up.

As he entered the pub he spotted his quarry sitting on his

own in a corner at the top end of the bar. He had a large whiskey in front of him. He was staring blankly into space. A barmaid stepped forward.

'What can I get you, luv?'

He held his hand up.

'Just popped in to see if I left my hat here last night.' He lied.

It'll be up there, if you did,' she replied, nodding at a row of pegs on the wall. He made a pretence of looking, and then shook his head.

'Not there now. Thanks anyway, luv.' He turned on his heel and walked out. He raced back up the road to the station. The traffic warden was putting a parking ticket on his windscreen as he arrived.

'For Chrissakes, I've only been gone five minutes!' he exploded. The warden shrugged.

'It's strictly no parking by 'ere, sir, and you're causin' an obstruction.'

'The fuck I am!' shouted Naylor, beside himself with rage.

'If you use anymore language like that, I'll do yer' for threatnin' be'aviour too.'

'Go on, book the twat!' shouted the cab driver he had exchanged words with earlier. Naylor stormed foward, fists clenched, but found himself confronted with half-a-dozen burly drivers and thought better of it. With an effort he spun around and strode back to his car, snatching the ticket off the windscreen as he got in.

He parked the car in the pay-and-display car park across the road from the station, and bought a ticket for the rest of the afternoon. He made his way back down High Street and staked out the pub. Nearly an hour later, Llewellyn emerged, just as Naylor was beginning to wonder if he should check that he was still in there. It seemed as if an aura of even greater depression clung to him as he crossed the road and disappeared into The King's Arms.

It was mid-afternoon when he left The King's Arms, but this time he headed down High Street and turned right at Castle Gardens. He called in at The Office then headed down to The Quadrant Gate near the market. Naylor tried to decide if he looked a little unsteady on his feet. He wasn't sure, but there was no mistaking his air of deepening gloom. He followed him into The Gate and treated himself to a half of larger and a bag of peanuts.

Some boys had obviously been at it all afternoon and a row broke out near where Llewellyn was sitting gazing at the wall. One bloke went down and took several kicks in the face before a barman got between them and told them to leave. Llewellyn didn't even look around.

It was getting on for six when he drained his glass and walked out. He cut down between the theatre and the bus station and walked under the underpass, still deep in thought. Naylor watched from a distance as he entered The Swansea Jack. He thought about it and decided to wait fifteen minutes before following him in. He was almost a hundred percent sure Llewellyn hadn't clocked him in The Gate, but there was no need to risk it. Instead he scuttled across the dual carriageway and sat down on a bench to review the situation.

It was possible that his quarry was on a monumental piss-up, brought on by that meeting in Uplands. In fact, it was quite probable, but Naylor couldn't help feeling that that wasn't the whole picture. His intuition told him that Llewellyn was killing time. And what was the significance of his choice of pubs, if any? Suddenly the answer came to him. He dismissed it as fanciful at first, but it wouldn't go away. Llewellyn was saying goodbye. Nonsense! He hadn't spoken to any bugger since he'd started drinking. Some farewell that was! But Naylor knew that wasn't the point. These were landmark pubs in Swansea. Places where Llewellyn could have drunk his first pint. Places full of memories.

He glanced at his watch and got back up. Time for a half in The Jack and a check on his man. He scuttled back across the road and into the pub. The only difference was the pub itself. Llewellyn was sitting with a whiskey in front of him staring into the distance. Naylor couldn't help wondering if he'd still be sitting there, or in some other haunt, come closing time. However, as the clock reached half seven, he stirred and beckoned to the woman behind the bar.

'You okay Charlie, luv?' she enquired as she moved nearer. He nodded ponderously.

'I'm alright, Helen, just a bit rat-arsed. Could you be a darlin' and call us a cab?'

'Sure, where you going?'

'Just local, tell 'em.'

She nodded and went to make the call as Naylor knocked back his drink and sidled out of the pub. He pulled out his mobile as he hurried down the road. He stopped about twenty yards away and pressed a pre-programmed button. A voice at the other end answered:

'Rapid Cabs?'

'Barry Naylor here, Evening Post. I'm outside The Jack and I need to follow someone who's just called a cab. Have you got anyone local?'

'Hang on a second Barry, I'll 'ave a word.' Naylor could hear the controller radioing the drivers. He came back on line.

'I've got someone droppin' at The Brunswick right now. He'll be with you in a few minutes.'

'Thanks pal, I owe you one. Stick it on account will you?'

'Okay. Ta ta now.'

'Cheerio.' Naylor broke the connection with a grin. He always got a tingle of satisfaction when he got a free ride because some dozy sod in The Post's accounts department still had him down as an employee.

*

'Keep your distance!' ordered Naylor as his driver followed Llewellyn's cab out onto the docks. As they proceeded further their destination became clear. They were headed for the Swansea-Cork Ferry. The ship was already loading and Naylor could see Llewellyn's tall frame some way ahead as they queued for tickets, then shuffled up the gangway. Naylor made a snap decision and joined the queue. He was not surprised when his quarry headed for Paddy Murphy's bar. Another large scotch from the look of it. Christ, this bloke could put it away! His face was bleak and set hard as he made his way over to an empty table. He looked a little less steady on his feet.

A bunch of rugby boys came bursting in. They crowded into

the tables next to Llewellyn.

'For fuck's sake Bear, mun, get 'em in! We wanna be wankered by the time this thing leaves!' yelled one. Up went the chant: 'Get 'em in, get 'em in, get 'em in... .' from the rest. The aptly named Bear lumbered off to the bar, while the others fooled around.

By the time the ship sailed at nine they had achieved their objective and the singing was getting louder and the songs bawdier. The Bar Manager went over and asked them to turn it down and mind their language.

'Whaddaya mean mind our fucking language?' slurred a hefty looking forward.

'What's wrong with our fucking language, you twat?' demanded another.

'Listen to yourself and you'll work it out.' Replied the manager evenly.

'We're not hurting anyone, having a sing-song you miserable bastard!' protested a third, swaying with more than the motion of the ship.

'No, but you're drowning out the music and no one does that in my bar.'

'Stick your music up your arse, mun. I can't stand that diddly-dee crap, anyway.' Suddenly the mood had turned nasty. The boys were getting to their feet, sensing trouble. Then a new voice cut across the tension.

'I'd do as he says if I were you.' They turned to stare at the man they had crowded in on. He too had risen unsteadily to his feet. Naylor slid across a couple of seats to watch what was happening. The one called Bear stepped forward.

'What the fuck's it got to do with you?'

'You're pissing me off. That's what it's got to do with me.'

'Go on Bear, deck the fucker!' encouraged one of his mates.

Bear hesitated. This bloke was taller and broader than he'd looked sitting down. He looked dead mean.

'For Chrissakes, butty, batter the wanker!' added another, who was not on the receiving end of the man's hard stare. Bear was trapped. He couldn't back down. He swung a fist.

The next thing he knew he was laying on the floor, puking up beer and doubled up in agony. He hadn't even seen the man move, but it felt like he'd been hit in the solar plexus with an iron bar. The bar manager broke the silence.

'Now why don't you lads take your mate out on the deck for a breath of fresh air? You can all sing to the seagulls if you're still in the mood.'

A couple of boys bent down and helped Bear to a crouching position. They got him semi-upright and steered him out of the bar. The man sat down and continued staring at his drink. The manager nodded.

'Thanks pal, I was feelin' a bit lonely there for a minute. What would you be drinkin'?'

But Charlie had sunk back into his thoughts. He made no reply. The manager shrugged.

'I'll get a mop,' he muttered and headed back to the bar.

*

They had been at sea for an hour and the rugby boys had obviously found somewhere else for their revelry. Llewellyn hadn't moved. He hadn't even bothered to renew his drink. He had simply sat and stared at the floor in front of him. Suddenly he stood up as if he'd reached a decision. He straightened his shoulders like he was defying a firing squad, then headed for the exit. Naylor slipped out of his seat and followed him. He had to move surprisingly quickly to keep up.

Llewellyn made his way to the upper deck and crossed to the starboard side. Naylor could see the lights of the Pembroke coast twinkling in the distance. Soon they would be out of sight. Was this the final farewell? A last chance to say goodbye to Wales before moving on to start a new life.

Could Naylor's article in the paper have had such enormous ramifications? Naylor shrugged. Hardly. The man was obviously being set up for adultery. Perhaps he wouldn't have had to leave Swansea without Naylor's contribution, but so what. He was a reporter, an observer, a passive participant in the drama.

Llewellyn had moved up the front of the ship. From the shadows, Naylor could see him silhouetted clearly against the clear night sky. Hang on a second! What the fuck was he doing? Jesus wept! Naylor started forward as his quarry stepped over the railing, paused for a moment, then jumped. He reached the side in time to see him hit the water and vanish into the dark, swirling waters of the Bristol Channel.

He opened his mouth to shout for help, then shut it again. Who was he to interfere if the bloke wanted to top himself? Besides, in Barry Naylor's line of business, a successful suicide was news, a failed one wasn't. He watched to see if Llewellyn surfaced, he didn't. He glanced at his watch and decided to wait ten minutes before raising the alarm. By then any potential rescuers would be searching in quite the wrong place.

8

'Wing Commander' bloody Morgan couldn't have made it worse if he'd pissed in the beer, the stupid gobshite.

The darts were just finished and most of the boys had wandered back through to the other bar. Jenks was chatting to Nobby and Jones Bach was trying to convince the Landlord's missus that they used to treat crabs with Parazone in the army, crazy bugger; her, a qualified nurse and all.

Then in he comes; smug as fuck and bursting with bad news. Full up to the bollocks with messenger boy importance.

Had we heard?

Had we heard what?

Had we heard the news on Swansea Sound?

Oh, that news! Of course we'd heard the news on Swansea Sound. What else did we come to the pub for except to listen to the news on Swansea fucking Sound?

He got all huffy then. Sod the lot of us. If we weren't interested in what had happened to Charlie, what did he care – wankers?

He'd got our attention mind.

What had happened to Charlie? Come on man, out with it!

Topped himself, he announces with that know-it-all smirk of his. Chucked himself off the Swansea-Cork ferry pissed out of his skull like as not; depressed about that piece in the paper, no doubt. Still he should have thought of that before he...

For a moment we thought Jenks would give him a slap, but he just growled at him to shut the fuck up. The landlord went upstairs and came back down with a ghetto blaster he'd bought off Dai Scrap for a fiver. To everyone's surprise it bloody worked too! He fiddled around until he found Swansea Sound. Some journalist called Naylor was chatting to one of the blokes who read the news.

*

Simon Thomas, news editor of Swansea Sound, was wrestling with a tricky, personnel management problem. What were his chances of a leg-over with his nubile new assistant tonight? He finished pouring the wine and raised his glass.

'Well, er, Liz, I think this calls for congratulations. Excited?'

'Excited? I'm wettin' myself! I never thought I'd end up actually on the radio, like interviewin' real people.'

'Why not? You're a fun person. You get people talking. You're outgoing...'

Simon was acutely aware that it was not just her personality that was outgoing. He was struggling unsuccessfully to tear his eyeballs away from his protégé's sumptuous cleavage. Apparently unaware of this, Liz raised her fists and jiggled her shoulders in triumph, which produced a positively seismic upheaval beneath her skimpy top.

'Let me at 'em babes!' she crowed.

Hear! Hear! Thought Simon, fervently. He wondered if it was possible for his eyeballs to sweat. In an attempt to re-focus his errant eyes, he moved on to practicalities.

'We haven't even talked money yet...'

'Oh, I'm sure that'll be fine,' she interrupted with a trusting smile, which made his mouth go so dry that he needed another quick swig of wine in order to carry on talking.

'Yes, I'm sure you'll be pleased...'

His mobile rang. Shit! He toyed with the idea of letting it ring off, but it was already attracting hostile stares from other diners. He took the call. It was Ceri on the news desk.

'Simon, mate, there's some bloke called Naylor on the phone; says he's got a real monster story for you.' Thomas frowned. Not that slime ball Naylor. Trust him to interrupt such a promising wage negotiation! Fuck, he'd better take it.

'Okay, hold the line,' he commanded. 'Sorry luv,' he muttered to his curvaceous new assistant, 'duty calls. Back in a minute.' He walked quickly through the restaurant, pausing only for a quick word with the manager:

'Haresh, can you do us a favour, mate. Sort out the bill for me; I'm gonna have to fly. I've got a tab open with Raj in the bar, by the way; he's got my Visa card.'

He hurried out to the patio at the front of the restaurant and put his mobile to his ear again.

'Okay, Ceri, are you there?'

'Yeah, boss.'

'What did he say exactly?'

'Something about a follow up to the story about that bloke from Upper Killay in the Post this morning. Demanded to speak to you personally – sounded a bit of a twat actually.'

Thomas unconsciously nodded his agreement. He'd known Naylor for years and loathed the sight of him. Unfortunately, he was so devious that he tended to scoop some spectacularly true stories amongst the ones he invented.

'Got a number for him?'

'Sure it's a mobile. He said he was calling from the Swansea-Cork ferry.'

'Right.' Thomas took the number, then hurried back to collect his assistant.

'You drive,' he said, passing her the keys. As they raced towards the radio station he dialled the number Ceri had given him. The phone was answered immediately.

'Naylor.'

'Hi, Barry, it's Simon. How you doing, mate?'

As always Naylor ignored any attempt at civility.

'I've got a shit-hot story for you. Interested?'

'Go on...'

'Charlie Llewellyn. The bloke in the Post this morning, has thrown himself of the ferry after a heavyweight meeting with Councillor Hywel Preece earlier on today.'

'How much?'

'A grand plus expenses.'

'You must be bloody joking!'

'I'm offering it to you as an exclusive and you can't afford to miss it. I can get that from the Nationals standing on my head.'

'Why don't you then?'

'I want it out like yesterday and radio's quickest, but it'll wait if you can't afford it.'

'What's to stop me putting a member of staff on it?'

'I am the only witness.'

'Oh yeah? Wouldn't be one of your Jackanory specials would it?'

'Phone the fucking coastguard if you don't believe me.'

'I will. Tell you what; I'll give you five hundred for it.'

'Bollocks. I've been on this story for two days solid. Tell you what, I'll invoice it as four days' work so it doesn't look so steep. What could be fairer than that?'

Thomas hesitated. He was sticking his neck out agreeing to that, but this was a major local story, particularly with Councillor Preece involved.

'Alright,' he snapped,' but if this turns out to be a flanker, I'll shove your invoice where the sun doesn't shine, understand?'

'Yeah, yeah...'

'Wait there. I'll call you from the studio and do it as a live interview, okay?'

He cut the connection and called Ceri back.

'I'm on my way,' he announced dramatically as the reporter answered. 'Get a studio set up for me and have someone ready to let us in. Then phone Swansea Ferries and ask them for confirmation of a man overboard. See if you can get a comment on the possibility of a suicide. Call the Coastguard and find out what they're doing about it. We're just coming through Dunvant now; see you in a minute.

*

Thomas took his cue from the DJ and spoke into the microphone.

'Okay, I have on the line freelance, investigative reporter Barry Naylor, live from the Super Ferry. Barry, you were responsible for the allegations of corruption in the South Wales Police earlier today. Can you bring us up-to-date on the most recent developments?'

'Certainly, Simon; as you know the allegations concerned the alleged improper use of a police detective in a private divorce case. The man at the centre of the case, a Mr Charles Llewellyn, appears to have committed suicide this evening by throwing himself off the Swansea-Cork ferry.'

'What reasons do you have for suggesting that it was suicide?'

'I have been tailing the man all day and he was showing signs of severe depression following a meeting at the offices of Semple, Tucker and Preece, who I believe to be his wife's solicitors.'

'What do you mean by signs of severe depression?'

'Apart from his body language, he embarked on a ten hour drinking session in a number of Swansea pubs.'

'Ten hours!'

'Indeed, and throughout that period he mainly sat drinking and staring into space as if in shock of some sort.'

'And can you describe his behaviour on board the ship?'

'Certainly; he continued drinking in a bar called Paddy Murphy's. At one point he became involved in a fracas and assaulted a young rugby player. This incident had to be dealt with by the bar manager. Half an hour later he went up onto the upper deck.'

'And you followed him?'

'Indeed, though I kept my distance following the assault in the bar.'

'What happened then?'

'Before I could try to stop him, he stepped over the rails and jumped.'

'There was no way he toppled or slipped – you say he was very drunk?'

'Not in my opinion. He paused for a moment before he launched himself as if plucking up the courage.'

'Has a body been found?'

'Not as yet, but the emergency services are severely hampered by the dark. The Captain tells me he could already been carried several miles by the current. Alternatively, he could even be caught on one of the ship's underwater stabilisers.'

'Okay, thank you Barry, I'm sure you will keep us up-dated on any further developments.' Thomas cued back to the main presenter and sat back deep in thought. If Naylor dug deeper and stuck to his promise to give them first bite of the cherry, this could be the best thousand pounds he'd spent in a long time. He made a mental note to call 'Blagger' Jevons the stations ad director first thing. If they kept an 'on-going developments' story rolling for days they could make a fortune flogging ads around it!

*

The landlord leaned forward and clicked off the ghetto blaster. It was like people used to huddle around the radio during the blitz. With the thing off, you could hear a pin drop.

'What's everyone drinking?' he asked quiet like, and it's not every day you get a free pint off his lord and master. As people drained their pints and passed them over the counter for refills, he went out and closed the front door. He started pouring as the assembled sat there, dull, trying to take in the news.

'Well I don't believe it for one,' declared Jenks suddenly. 'Charlie would never cop out like that. Whatever happened between 'im and 'is missus, 'e'd fight to the bitter end.'

'Oh, come on, Jenks mun, you heard the bloke on the radio, 'e saw 'im do it!'

'For fuck's sake Jonesy, just 'cos a bloke on the radio says it, doesn't mean it's true!'

'I know that butty, but 'e saw 'im go over the side. Why would 'e lie about a thing like that? What if 'e was as pissed as 'e was yesterday? 'E didn't know 'is arse from 'is elbow!'

'Well all I know is there's no way 'e'd deliberately top 'imself.'

Jenks jaw was set stubborn and good for him if it made him feel better. He and Charlie were butties and he wanted to remember him right, but most of us believed he was kidding himself.

9

For Jacs, the news of Charlie's death was devastating. Worse still, she was one of the last in the village to know. She had phoned the Council the previous day and resigned from her job as School Crossing Patrol, then phoned the school and told them she wouldn't be in. After that story in the paper there was no way she could face the knowing looks as half the population of the village escorted their kids to school each morning. She had spent the day thinking about leaving Swansea altogether, but, more importantly, she was desperate to see Charlie again. She wanted to explain, to apologise, to beg his forgiveness, to tell him she really loved him.

The following morning she could not even drag herself out of bed. Thankfully her mum agreed to have the kids for a few days. She finally crept out to buy a pint of milk from the corner shop late in the afternoon. The first thing to greet her was the shop's headline board on which Mrs Paltrow, the shop keeper, had written in black marker pen:

SWANSEA FERRY SUICIDE TRADGEDY!

For some strange reason she instantly had the bizarre premonition that it was Charlie. She told herself not to be so stupid. He wasn't the suicidal sort, but then again he was a proud man and the humiliation... Suddenly quite unnerved, she forced herself to go in.

'Mornin' Mrs Richards,' prattled Beryl Paltrow in her gossipy way. 'I'm so sorry to hear about Charlie, I know you two were, er,' she groped for a suitable word, 'friends,' she finished with a smirk.

Jacs did not hear. Her gaze was fixed on the pile of Evening Posts that lay on the counter. Across the front page ran the headline:

INDEPENDENT INQUIRY CALLED FOR
AS SWANSEA SEX-SHAME VICTIM DIES

Charlie's name stood out in the first paragraph. He had thrown himself off the ferry and drowned. Jacs clutched the counter to steady herself as her knees began to buckle. She fought back the rising tide of blackness that was threatening to overwhelm her. She wasn't going to share her grief with that nosy bitch if she could help it. She made it to the door, pulled it open and gulped in fresh air. The milk forgotten, she stumbled off down the road, barely able to see through the tears streaming down her cheeks.

When she got home she collapsed, sobbing, on the sofa. Why? Why had he given in? Surely, if he had come to her they could have faced the humiliation together! Then she remembered that it was probably her he blamed for it all. She had betrayed him she reminded herself, cringing with remorse. Now she would never be able to explain to him why she had done it. The guilt and anguish kept flooding over her.

Then came the self-pity. The first decent man she had stood a chance with. A lifetime spent getting pushed around and cheated on by selfish, bullying bastards, and now the only decent one she had ever known was dead, and thanks to her stupidity! How could she have been so bloody dull? She should have gone to him and explained about Dai Shithead. Of all the people she could have relied on to protect her it was Charlie. In fact, he stood head and shoulders above anyone else. Anguish at her own stupidity ripped through her mind, threatening to unhinge her.

In her mind she saw his poor, drowned, battered body lying washed up on a lonely beach. She fell to her knees beside him, distraught, pleading with him not to be dead. She kissed his cold, lifeless lips, trying to give them warmth. She stroked his wet, black hair again and again. She searched his empty, staring eyes for the spark of humour and zest she loved them for. Now they only accused her. You drove me to this your dull bitch. You murdered me with your stupidity and cowardice, you traitor.

She seized her hair in a frenzy of remorse and ripped out chunks of it. Thoughts of joining him crowded into her mind. That was it! She had pills in the house. She stumbled upstairs to the bathroom and gazed feverishly at the labels on the bottles in the cabinet. Which ones were dangerous? Fuck it! She wasn't a doctor. Take the lot. She hurried downstairs and collected the bottle of vodka she kept on top of the dresser in the kitchen. She returned to the lounge, sat down on the sofa and began swallowing back mouthfuls of pills, washing them down with swigs of vodka.

'I'm coming Charlie, I'm coming my love!' she repeated to herself as she felt the lethal cocktail hit her. The pills and vodka gone, she lay back, her eyelids drooping. She found an image of him smiling at her, warm and loving. She clung to that until her breathing became more and more laboured and she finally slid into unconsciousness.

*

Charlie Llewellyn watched patiently as the coastguard chopper clattered past to the north of him, hugging the coastline, searching for his drowned corpse. As it disappeared from view in the fading light, hopefully for the last time, he dragged himself wearily back onto the St Govan light buoy. He hauled up the waterproof kit bag which contained his belongings and resumed his seat. The air was turning chillier as the night fell and he shivered despite the insulation of his Typhoon Edge wet suit.

He had spent the day jumping on and off his sanctuary to hide in the water as would-be rescuers flew past. In between, he had dried his clothes and eaten the meagre rations he had concealed about his person the previous day. This amounted to packets of peanuts and small bottles of mineral water which he had surreptitiously purchased as he led Barry Naylor on his faked pub crawl around Swansea. Not that he knew it was Naylor. As far as Charlie was concerned the man was probably a private detective hired by Preece. It didn't matter. The more witnesses he had to the little drama he was staging the better.

He had spotted his pursuer before he walked out from the cover of the trees in the Railway inn car park. It was not a place where you went to sit around alone in a car on a weekday morning. To the untrained eye he might have been less obvious, but, to Charlie he stuck out like a sheep dog's balls.

He watched him in his wing mirrors as he led him down to St James' Crescent, and he watched him again as he led him over Townhill.

In fairness the man was pretty good, but he was flying solo and could not drop back out of sight like a member of a rotating team would. That increased Charlie's suspicion that he was a private detective. His presence did, of course, put Charlie under pressure to keep up the appearance of someone getting increasingly drunk and depressed, but then he'd been doing that for the last fortnight, so he was hardly out of practice.

His mind drifted back to hours spent slouching through the rough estates of the Bogside and the Falls Road, looking for all he was worth like just another punter on his way to the bookies. He'd learned these skills on a tough stage. Your opening night could well be your closing night if the Provos decided you didn't look the part.

The pub in Llangyfelach was the riskiest part of the deception, but it was his only chance to obtain the equipment that he needed. This needed some real sleight of hand. Fortunately his pursuer did not follow him in. No doubt he did not want to show himself more than was absolutely necessary. The barman stepped forward to take his order and Charlie leaned forward conspiratorially.

'Listen, mate,' he said quickly and quietly, 'I need a bit of a favour.' The barman raised his eyebrows questioningly, so Charlie continued. 'A woman will be coming in shortly with a bag full of gear for me. She'll hand it over the bar to you.' He slid a white envelope across the bar. 'Can you give her this and keep this for yourself.' He handed the man a twenty.

The man accepted the envelope and the cash.

'Once she's gone, take the bag into the gents and hide it in the lock-up. That's all. Oh, and if anyone asks I just came in for a couple of drinks, okay?'

'Sure.'

He bought himself a ginger ale to pass for a large whisky, and then walked over to a quiet corner of the bar and pulled out his mobile.

'Day's Diving?'

'Hello is that June?'

'It certainly is Charlie. What can I do for you?'

'I need some gear. The only problem is I can't come in and pick it up.'

'Keeping a low profile after that story in the paper are you, you naughty boy?'

Charlie grinned.

'Yeah, something like that. Listen, there's a bad guy following me, though he won't trouble you. I need you to bring the kit in, in a bin liner or such like, and hand it to the barman. I'll be sitting in the corner, but act like you don't know me. The barman will sort you out for cash. Would you do that for me?'

'I suppose so, for you. But don't make a habit of it. I've got a business to run here you smooth talking sod.'

'Thanks babe. Love you forever.'

'If only!'

Charlie began listing his requirements. It was a bit of an ask getting her to drop the kit at the pub, but June would forgive him. They had been friends since his days in Boat Squadron when he was a regular customer. He finished his call and sat back to wait. A while later the door opened and a woman came in with a large plastic bag. She passed it over the bar and left without a glance in his direction. A few minutes later the man finished serving customers and disappeared from behind the bar.

When he returned Charlie headed for the gents. Sure enough the bag was waiting for him in the lock-up. He opened it and emptied out the contents: a full-length wet-suit, a pair of strap-back fins, a diver's knife with a calf-strap and sheath and a waterproof, zip-up kit bag. There was a roll of surgical tape in the bag; fine. He hastily stripped to his briefs, and then pulled the wet suit on up to his waist. He strapped the knife to his calf.

Someone entered the room. Charlie froze. There was the sound of some shuffling then a zip being undone. Whoever it was coughed, farted, and then relieved himself noisily before re-zipping and departing without washing his hands. Charlie breathed a quiet sigh of relief.

Working quickly, he tore off strips of tape and attached one fin to his front and the other, with some difficulty, to his back. Then he ran a single strip twice around his body to make sure.

He struggled into the top half of the wetsuit, then redressed, stuffed the black bag and remaining surgical tape in the pocket of his parka, and inspected himself in the mirror. He'd grown a little, but not so as you'd notice. He headed back to the bar and glanced at his watch as he sat back down in front of his ginger ale; he'd been gone less than three minutes.

The rest of the day had been plain sailing, though he'd developed a hearty dislike of ginger ale and the fins were less than comfortable. Still, those were only temporary inconveniences. Just keep shoulders hunched, eyes dead, and stare at the nearest blank space. He hadn't relished hitting the kid on the boat, but it had got him noticed by everyone in the bar. There would be plenty to testify how drunk he was.

As he walked up on deck he was dragging in lungful's of air to oxygenate his bloodstream. He had to stay under as long as possible. At first he couldn't make out the light buoy. Had he mistimed the jump? Then he picked out the flashes in the distance; six short, one long. He had no way of knowing if the ship's stabilisers were out – it was like a millpond, so hopefully... Oh well, he'd just have to go as deep as possible and pray. He paused to step over the railing, and then paused to check his bearing on the buoy. He took a deep breath and jumped.

It was not much different to the sea jumps he had made from helicopters except that, then, there was no danger of being ploughed down by a ship's stabiliser. As he disappeared from sight he reached up and grabbed his nose. If he hit the water with his nostrils open, it would feel like a grenade had gone off in his sinuses. He kept his feet together and his toes pointed. He kept his left arm pointing straight down his body to keep his parka from ballooning up. As he hit the water he exhaled hard to empty his lungs. He didn't need a natural buoyancy aid forcing him back to the surface until those stabilisers had passed.

He hit at a good angle and sank like a stone. He unzipped his parka to let the air out of it. Good it was getting waterlogged and weighing him down against the buoyancy of the wet suit. He thrust upwards with his arms to drive himself still deeper. He was still worried about a stabiliser in the head.

He had begun counting as he hit the water: one, and two, and three, and four... He reached thirty seconds. Without any air in his lungs, his body was already beginning to crave oxygen. In the darkness a wave of claustrophobia hit him. Forty-three, forty-four, forty-five, forty-six...his lungs were bursting...fifty-five, fifty-six...that'll do! He tore his parka off, let it go and began kicking frantically for the surface. The surface; where was the fucking surface? How deep had he gone for Chrissakes? He had to have air or he'd black out. Above him, suddenly, he could make out a torch light. Why was someone shining a torch on the sea? It grew rapidly. It was a search light. Fuck, how had they got a chopper out that fast?

As Charlie hurtled towards the surface, in desperation he misjudged the last foot and inhaled. He vomited out the lungful of water and gasped in some air before he sank. He rose again and paddled weakly, coughing and spluttering. Above him a gleaning moon shone down where the searchlight would have been. He was alone. The stern of the Super Ferry was pulling steadily away.

He raised his arm in a gesture of silent triumph. He'd done it! He had school teachers, estate agents, solicitors and a national newspaper to confirm his marriage was on the rocks and he was taking it badly. Now he had some sort of detective and a bar full of ferry passengers to witness that, as a result, he had committed suicide in a fit of drunken depression. As far as the ungodly and anyone else was concerned, he was missing presumed dead, and that's exactly how he wanted it.

*

Jacs' stirred and opened her eyes. It was dark and she was surrounded by the stench of vomit. She lifted her hand to her face. Her hair was sticky and wet. Another wave of nausea made her wretch violently, but there was nothing left to bring up. She dry-wretched until the sickness passed. She slipped back into comforting arms of unconsciousness.

In her dream she could hear a bell - a doorbell. Why was she dreaming about doorbells? She wasn't dreaming. It was her front door. She forced herself back to consciousness and sat up feeling like hell. Her hair was matted and it was pitch-dark. God knows what time it was. She brushed the front of her jumper and found herself knocking off the half-dissolved tablets that her stomach had rejected.

Suddenly, despite her confusion her heart was pounding. A man's face was pressed hard against the window, the eyes shaded as he attempted to peer in. The bell rang again, imperiously, demanding response. Who could it be at this time of night? It was her Charlie, come back to her! She groped her way towards the front door. Then reality hit her. Charlie was dead. This could be anyone. Dai Shithead come calling for another 'favour'. She was alone in this house.

Panicking now, she fumbled for the chain. The door was only held by a badly fitting Yale. If the bastard put his shoulder against it, he would be through in a second! With shaking fingers she slipped the chain into place.

'Who is it?' she croaked. It felt like all the fluids had been sucked from her body. Had she been hallucinating? She staggered to the window and peeped out. She could make out a man's figure by the front door. She drew the curtains so he couldn't see in, then felt for the light switch and clicked it on. She returned to the door.

'Who is it?' she croaked again, a little louder.

'It's me, Mrs Richards. You know, Gareth, Charlie's boy. I just wondered if I could come in for a minute.'

'Relief flooded over her.

'Sure, of course; hang on while I get the chain off.' She fumbled it free and opened the door.

He was obviously drunk. He stood there swaying and blinking in the light from the lounge.

'Come in luv,' she croaked. 'I'll put the kettle on.' She guided him into a chair.

'Are you alright Mrs Richards? You don't look very well...'

Christ! What must she look like if a pissed up kid was asking that?

'I'm okay Gareth luv.' She struggled to sound normal, but the lump in her throat hurt and suddenly the tears were pouring down her cheeks again. She stood in front of him shaking with grief.

'It's just, well, it's just the news about your dad. I can't stand it. I just can't stand it! I just took an overdose and I can't even do that right!

Gareth had risen and she could see that there were tears streaming down his face too. He held out his arms and she walked forward blindly to embrace him. They stood locked together in the little lounge, bonded by the agony of the mutual, heart breaking loss.

10

The woman leant forward, providing Tony Cocker with another tantalising glimpse of her cleavage in the rear-view mirror. She was a bit tall for his taste, but fit as you like. He wondered if she was a natural blonde. He wouldn't half fancy the chance to find out!

'Turn right here,' she ordered. It was only the third thing she'd said since he picked her up at Gatwick, the snooty mare. He pulled into the space between the two carriageways. A gap in the traffic appeared and he swung across the road. He made a mental note of the petrol station he had just passed and spotted a road name to back it up; Derwen Fawr Road. What kind of name was that then? Bloody sheep-shaggers! Still, some of them had plenty of dosh from the look of them houses.

'Turn left here where it says Treetops!'

He had to brake and turn quite sharply into the entrance between the high stone walls that flanked the road at this point. He drove up the long drive towards the front of the imposing, mock-Tudor building. He pulled up outside, gazed at the milometer, then at the ceiling, as if performing a complex calculation.

'That'll be two 'undred and eighty quid please darlin'.' He gave her a quick flash of his pearly whites to soften her up.

'I agreed a price of two hundred pounds with your controller.' She sounded distant, bored even.

'Yeah, luv, 'e always forgets to charge more for this car; it's classed as a limo, see. Then of course there's me waitin' time 'cos we 'ad to stop at the services...'

'No, you had to stop at the services, and anyway, the price was all inclusive.'

Cocker's sovereign-laden fists clenched the steering wheel.

'Look lady, I don't do this bleedin' lark for charity, so cough up before I lose my bleedin' rag alright!'

'Are you threatening me?

'What if I am? We're tucked away nice and secluded ain't we? I could climb over the back and take my payment in kind and no-one would be none the wiser. Long way to come for a shag, but I've 'ad worse days out.'

That did the trick. He could see the tight-arsed cow go rummaging in her handbag.

'Here you are.'

He turned to find himself staring at the nozzle of an aerosol. Before he could move the bitch pressed the fucking button! He cried out in agony and clutched at his eyes. He heard her open the door and get out.

'I'd get moving if I was you,' she said. 'My partner is a very influential man and you're a long way from home. When I get indoors I'm going to call the police and tell them that you just tried to rape me.'

He heard her pull her leather holdall across the back seat, and then the door slammed. Through burning, streaming eyes he saw her blurred figure disappear into the house.

*

Preece gazed out of the study window as he spoke into the phone.

'He's just pulling away now Ringer. No, she doesn't want to press charges. He didn't get to actually do anything and we've got better thingss to do. I just don't want him coming back and putting a brick through my front window... He doesn't know Swansea so he'll retrace his steps... Yes along the Mumbles Road, then Fabian Way to the M4... Well, perhaps you could spare a couple of boys to pull him over and check his tyres. You know, make him feel unwelcome, see him off the premises... As far as Port Talbot? Yes that would be fine if you can spare the troops... It's a white Granada Scorpio with a big spoiler on the back. The registration number is Charlie, Echo, Ten, Charlie, Echo, Bravo, yes, fine...thanks a lot now, bye.'

He replaced the receiver and turned to face Juliet Llewellyn. 'There, I don't think we'll be hearing from him again. I'm sorry I had to call you back from Tenerife for a conference of war.'

'So am I. Still, I suppose some things are more important than a tan. So, do you think he's really dead?'

'I'll think he's really dead when I see the body. I was trained to rely on hard evidence. However, the circumstantial evidence certainly suggests he is. Semple tells me he gave it to him with both barrels and he went down without a fight. Apparently he looked a mess, unshaven, hungover, and very depressed. Then there's this business of the binge he went on after the meeting. This journalist, Naylor, has zero integrity, but he's known for being pretty thorough. I once had to put him in his place myself because he got too close to the business.'

Juliet frowned.

'The trouble is that's exactly how he'd look if he wanted us to think he was beaten.'

'Well you know him better than me, but I did have a word with the man in charge of the rescue operation. He reckoned, what with the impact of the jump, the distance, the current and the temperature of the water at this time of year, the odds were stacked against a fit young swimmer of exceptional ability.'

'Yes, well that was Charlie in his day. He swam the channel twice when he was younger, even though the experts said he didn't have enough body fat. I know he was always messing about in boats and jumping into the sea from helicopters when he was in the guards.'

'Yes, but that was nearly ten years ago and he came out with displaced ribs and a taste for the beer. I know he's ex-army, but that doesn't make him Superman.'

'Have it your way. I guess I'm only playing Devil's advocate; it's hard to imagine that he's really dead. Still, good riddance, I've got you now. I've been missing that hard cock of yours out in Tenerife; those beach bums just aren't the same.'

She reached up and wrapped her arms around his neck, pulling his head down to engage in a lingering kiss. As his hands slid down to clasp her buttocks, her teeth closed hard on his lower lip. He tried to pull away so she bit harder, drawing blood. He grabbed a handful of her hair with his left hand and twisted viciously to make her let go. With his right he yanked up her skirt. She laughed and licked the blood off her lips.

In his haste, he tore at her panties until she pushed him away, pulled them down and stepped out of them. She reached forward, undid his belt and unzipped him. He seized her shoulders and forced her back over the desk. She feigned some resistance which simply drove him wilder. He tore open her blouse and pulled up her bra, squeezing her breasts and sucking her nipples like a savage babe-in-arms. She lay back on the large mahogany desk and opened her legs, dragging him down on top of her and eagerly guiding him in.

As his passion grew she hissed and swore, goading him to ever greater effort, oblivious to the spray of bloody spittle. His eyes grew harder and darker and his face suffused with blood. She began to let out sharp gasps and screams in time with his grunts and thrusts. She clawed at his neck and back as he held her pinioned and fucked her.

Finally, he grunted: 'Yes, yes, yes,' and collapsed on top of her. After a pause to catch her breath, she pushed him away. He bent down and collected her panties from the floor, then used them to wipe himself clean and tossed them in the waste paper basket. She adjusted her skirt and rummaged briefly in her Louis Vuitton clutch bag. She produced a packet of cigarettes and lit one.

'I wish you'd give those bloody things up; they stink the place out.'

'Open the window,' she replied indifferently, then resumed their conversation.

'Are you going to tell O'Connell?'

'I don't know yet. I don't want to tell him Llewellyn's dead until I'm absolutely sure. On the other hand I don't need him coming down to Swansea, telling me how to run my end of things when he should be out in Afghanistan haggling with the wogs. He's been telling me to let O'Leary and the boys sort

Llewellyn out ever since the pair of you split up. There's no need to panic. I'll give it a couple of days for the body to turn up then take the credit for sorting him out myself.'

'You're scared of him, aren't you?'

'Who Llewellyn?'

'No, O'Connell.'

'Who me? Scared of Pat? Don't be silly. It's just I'm not so fond of the rough stuff.'

'I am. I wonder what he's like in bed.'

'I'm sure you do. In the meantime I've had your things brought over from Gower Road so you can stay here.'

'What's Annette going to say about that?

'Nothing if she knows what's good for her. We've already had a little tête à tête and come to an understanding. In the meanwhile I want you to keep an eye on her.'

'Why?'

'I don't know, but she's changed and I want to know why. The last thing we need is her sobering up and throwing a bloody spanner in the works. When she knows what time of day it is, she's a bloody do-gooder and right now I don't need any more complications.'

'Are we going to wash our hands of young Gareth?'

'Well the house is on the market and we have no legal obligation towards him. We can kick him out and he can find a flat like any other student, but there is a question of image to consider here. What if he goes to the press? Swansea Councillor makes bereaved student homeless etcetera.'

'What do you suggest?'

'How much longer has he got in college?'

'A couple of years.'

'Well, if we buy him somewhere for the duration, and sell it when he graduates, we'll make a profit, assuming we can't use it for the business. We'll continue to pay his fees and, when he graduates, he can bugger off into the wide blue yonder and never darken our doorsteps again.'

'You're feeling surprisingly generous.'

Preece shrugged.

'Patrick doesn't like publicity and he thinks this thing has already got out of hand. Besides, if Llewellyn turns out to be pulling the wool, his son may turn out to be a 'useful ally'.

*

Annette Preece rose and hurried across the corridor into the lounge. She felt sick with disgust. She had knelt there and listened to them talk about the death of the bitch's husband as if they wanted it, and then about her as if she was a piece of dirt. Then to crown it all, from the sound of it, they'd fucked each other senseless in her house!

She picked up the glass of gin she had been pouring when the bitch arrived, but, instead of drinking it, she dipped her fingers in it and dabbed some around her neck like perfume. Then she fumbled a cigarette out of its packet and lit it with the gold and onyx lighter on the coffee table. She had been stunned by the cool way the woman was discussing her own husband's death. True, their marriage had broken down, but the death of someone you had lived with for years was surely bound to spark some sort of emotional reaction, even if it was just sentimentality. Apparently not. She had knelt at the keyhole listening to her rival discuss it without a glimmer of feeling. God, she was a cold bitch!

However, it was not the woman's coldness that was making her mind race; it was the bitch's uncertainty about her husband's death. Annette had never met the man, but she'd seen the Swansea-Cork Ferry. He would have had to be something out of the ordinary to survive a fall like that!

Now, the bitch had introduced the possibility that he'd done so, it rekindled the hope of some sort of support in the battle ahead and, truth be told, she needed it. Her thoughts went back to her husband's remark about upending a bottle of gin down her throat. That had sobered her up and, with the help of some tranquillisers, kept her sober. The remark spoke volumes. She could live with the occasional outburst of violence, but now she knew she was in real danger. By his own admission her husband had already considered the best way of killing her.

She had often felt trapped in some sort of macabre experiment. It was as if she was the yardstick by which her husband was measuring the depths of his inhumanity. Now, with the bitch in residence he had upped the stakes. He had made it clear that she was finally redundant. His cruel game of self-discovery was reaching its inevitable climax and she knew instinctively that, unless she seized the initiative, it could only have one outcome.

The trouble was she didn't know where to begin. She paused to reconsider that last thought. Maybe she didn't know where to begin, but she had some pointers. What was all that stuff about his partner disliking publicity? What had a firm of

Swansea solicitors got to hide?

Most importantly, she now knew she was under suspicion and viewed as one of the enemy. If she was a 'do-gooder' then by definition, her husband and the Bitch were up to no good and she was going to find out what. All that she had to bear in mind, given the violence she had already suffered at her husband's hands, was that she was discreet about it. Whatever was going on, the stakes were obviously high and she was increasingly certain that the pair of them would stop at nothing to protect their interests.

She wished she'd been able to record the conversation now. It hadn't provided her with any firm evidence of wrongdoing, but certain things didn't add up. One thing was sure however, her tyrannical husband and his mistress did not relish the thought that Charlie Llewellyn might still be alive.

11

The night watchman of the building in St James Crescent shivered as he squinted into the driving rain along the line of his torch beam. Satisfied that the last of the drunks were home in bed he trudged back towards the warmth of his Portacabin. That was the one o'clock tour done and he could get his head down for a couple of hours. Inside, he picked up the mug of hot chocolate he had made before venturing out into the filthy weather. He used it to warm his hands as he sipped away at the contents. Feeling human again, he stripped off his waterproofs. He checked his alarm was set for four o'clock and he pulled the cushions off the old sofa to form a makeshift bed. He lay down, closed his eyes, and concentrated on the sound of the rain drumming on the cabin roof.

*

Charlie was trying to console himself with the thought that, if he was cold and uncomfortable, at least he wasn't wet. He had swum ashore the previous night and worked his way across country to Carmarthen. He'd borrowed a bone-shaking old Kawasaki 250, without the owner's permission, for the last leg of the journey back to Swansea. Every muscle in his body seemed to consider it a personal duty to remind him of his exertions.

The lump on his ribs where the Iraqi interrogators had broken them was throbbing and his left leg had stiffened up where he'd taken that bullet in the thigh in Crossmaglen. Suddenly, he was back in The Province. He remembered the cold eyes behind the mask as the dicker walked forward and aimed the pistol at his kneecap. He remembered shouting: 'Fuck you!' in his best Bogside brogue, then he'd kicked out at the weapon with his right foot. He got it too, but not before the man fired. The bullet went through his left thigh, chipping the bone on the way, but at least it hadn't crippled him. Then he was kicking, gouging and punching. He had nearly made it too when one of them caught an ankle and dragged him back.

The bloke who had jumped him from behind was standing over him. Too close, mug! Charlie had driven his fist up into his groin and rolled aside as the man collapsed to his knees. The other one was a couple of yards away, as Charlie came up into a crouch. The bastard was going for a gun! The adrenaline was pumping and Charlie felt no pain from the earlier bullet wound. He launched himself into a try-saving tackle that would have brought the house down at the Millennium Stadium. He reached up and grabbed hair with both hands, pulling the man's head back and dragging himself up his body, using his weight to pin him down. He smashed the bloke's face down on the concrete a couple of times to show he meant business then sank his teeth into his ear. He remembered the man screaming then Charlie's ears were ringing as the third boy kicked him in the head. Fortunately his attacker was only wearing trainers, so he inflicted more pain on his colleague, who howled as a chunk of his ear ripped away. Charlie rolled away from his new assailant and into a crouch, ready to launch another tackle. He found himself staring at a teenage kid with fear in his eyes.

He'd got the gun, but it was hanging by his side. He was scared to use it. Charlie grinned, as diabolically as he could, and spat the lump of flesh at the boy. The kid dropped the weapon and fled down the alley.

*

The sound of silence brought Charlie back to reality. He was clammy with sweat despite the cold. The man had stopped moving around above him. He twisted his head around to look at the luminous dial of his watch. It was ten past one. He'd give him till half past and, if there was still no noise, he'd take a peep. He settled down again on the cold, hard ground under the Portacabin. Five minutes later he heard a strange rumble. He frowned trying to identify it, and then a grin spread across his face. It was okay to come out now. The man was snoring.

He crawled out into the pouring rain and reached under the cabin to retrieve his gear. The wait had made his muscles even stiffer. He planted his feet on the ground and spent a few minutes working silently through a series of bends and stretches to warm himself up and chase away the stiffness, and then he picked up his equipment and walked around the cabin to the wheelie bin he had spotted earlier. There was just a carrier bag full of rubbish and old teabags in the bottom, which he ignored. He pulled a pair of washing-up gloves out of his pocket, put them on, and then carefully prised the lid off the Tupperware container he had brought with him. The stench of the mackerel hit him immediately. He carefully tipped the bin over and laid it silently on its back, lowering the lid onto the ground as it fell open. He reached into the bin and placed the container on the floor. He peeled off the gloves and dropped them by the container. He slipped quietly back into the shadows and squatted down. His breathing slowed and he let the stillness and silence enfold him. The only sound was the steady patter of the icy rain.

The first animal to take the bait was a bloody hedgehog. Charlie cursed silently. Then the cat came. It hesitated at first. Where did they get that sixth sense from? It still hesitated, but the lure of the mackerel was too much for it. It crept into the bin. Charlie crept forward, equally silently. In a single movement, he whipped the lid shut and stood the bin upright. The animal went berserk for thirty seconds then calmed down. Thank God! It was probably a domestic cat. He'd soon find out when he opened the lid!

*

He was balanced on the railing of the rear fire-escape of the prestigious, first floor offices of Semple, Tucker and Preece. This enabled him to reach the small, frosted window which, by his reckoning, led into the toilet at the top of the stairs on the first floor. It was a good, old-fashioned casement, so he gave the bottom of the frame a whack with the heel of his hand; nothing. He tried again and this time heard the stay pop up. Without the stay, the window was loose and a strip of flexible plastic slipped through easily to turn the handle. He swung a leg over the sill and squeezed through the gap. It was the toilet alright. He climbed in and reached back out to the fire escape.

He lifted his black, canvas sports bag carefully across the gap. He clicked on a pencil-beam torch, then crossed the room and tried the door. It was locked. He stepped into the corridor.

Instantly, the quiet of the night was split by the maddening jangle of a burglar alarm. Shit! There was a sensor on the landing. He'd have to work quickly. Semple's office was immediately to his left. The jangle of the alarm was ear-splitting. He went back into the toilet and pushed the window wide open, then watched with satisfaction as the wind caught it and swung it against the wall with a bang. Rain came gusting in as the window banged again. He left the toilet door ajar and tried the door to Semple's office. It was unlocked – typical of the careless, over confident fool. The next room had had its name plaque removed and was locked. The third had H.L.Preece on the door. It was also locked.

By the side of the door, stairs led up to the next floor. At the top was a door with wired glass in it. It was fastened with a Yale and a mortise lock. The other rooms were unlocked and disused. Empty packaging boxes and old bits of office furniture had been dumped in them. Charlie wrinkled his nose at the smell of dust and damp. He returned to the locked room, pulled out a set of picks and got to work.

He had just got the door open when he saw the reflection of lights on the front office window. Jesus, that was quick! He clicked off the torch and walked over to one side of the window. Sure enough a squad car had pulled into the Crescent and was cruising around.

Charlie strode back to the stairs and hurried down to the first floor landing where he had left his bag. He unzipped it cautiously. The cat tried to struggle but his black leather gloves were ample protection. He got a good grip on its collar and leaned over the banister to watch the front door. Shadows appeared through the glass, though he could not hear the door being unlocked above the noise of the alarm. He saw it beginning to open and dropped the cat. It landed on all-fours on the parquet floor below and began to meow indignantly as the door swung wider and torchlight probed the darkness.

The alarm went off and the lights came on downstairs. Charlie retreated to the shadows at the foot of the stairs leading up to the second floor.

'Looks like we've found the culprit, sir,' announced a satisfied voice from below.

'You mean I've been dragged out of bed and hauled over here in the pissing rain thanks to a fucking cat?' Charlie recognised the desiccated tones of Ivor Semple. He did not sound pleased.

'Looks that way, sir.'

At that moment the toilet door banged in the wind.

'Did you 'ear that?' asked another voice. 'It came from upstairs; better check it out.'

'Okay, you two go.'

Charlie moved swiftly, but silently, up the stairs to the next floor. He slipped through the door with the wired window. He turned the handle and the Yale lock and held the door slightly ajar, ready to close it silently should the need arise. He could hear footsteps mounting the stairs from the hall, and then the first voice spoke.

'There you are Jed. Someone 'ad a dump and opened the window. Poor bloody moggy was probably lookin' for a bit of shelter on a mingin' night like this. Come on, let's piss off.'

Charlie heard the man pull the window shut and fasten it. He opened the door to hear better as the men's footsteps retreated. He could hear the first man clearly as he addressed Semple.

'No problems, sir. Cat came in through the toilet window to get out of the rain. It's all secure now. D'you want to reset the alarm?'

'You must be bloody joking. There'll be hell to pay with the resident's tomorrow morning as it is. If the thing goes off again tonight, they'll rip my guts out with their bare hands. Besides you can never get a sodding engineer on the phone at this time of night. Let's go; I'll sort it out in the morning.'

Charlie breathed a sigh of relief as he listened to the front door being locked. He was in and undetected, and in the morning no-one would suspect that there had been a break-in. He recalled the words of the ex-CIA spook who lectured on intrusion techniques:

'If they reset the alarm, give them an hour, then trip it again. They believe it was the cat. This time they'll blame the alarm system. They've already convinced themselves they ain't being burgled and who likes bein' dragged out of bed in the middle of the night, for Chrissakes?'

Thanks to Semple's laziness this would not be necessary.

*

The monitor of Preece's computer cast an eerie glow in the pitch-black office. A panel requesting a password popped up.

Charlie pulled out his phone and a USB cable. He connected it to the computer and sat down on the floor to wait as the John the Ripper program hunted for the password. It could take a while, but, thanks to the cat, that was no longer a problem.

Three quarters of an hour the program spat out its solution and to Charlie's relief it worked first time. He was in. He went into My Documents. There were three folders: Deeds, Clients and Corr which Charlie guessed was short for Correspondence. This contained a considerable number of files labelled City and County which no doubt related to his role as a Councillor. He resisted the urge to take a look. Get in, get out and analyse at leisure; that's what the trainers drummed into you.

He plugged in a memory stick and copied everything in sight. For a successful legal practice there wasn't a lot. It would appear that Messrs Semple, Tucker and Preece were very exclusive indeed. Satisfied that he'd got everything, he removed the stick and shut down the computer. He picked the locks on Preece's desk and filing cabinet and checked through his bin without finding anything interesting. He suspected that Preece had little fondness for written records that might require burning.

He gave Semple's office the same treatment, and then turned his attention to the room with no name plaque. It had clearly been used as an office at one time, presumably belonging to the retired partner Tucker; it still contained a desk and chair. However, the thick layer of dust on those items suggested that it no longer served such a function.

In the middle of the room stood a safe. Charlie squatted down to examine it. Thankfully it was a sturdy, fire proof mechanical, not the latest electronic. He sat down and addressed the dial.

This was going to take some time. Drilling or plastic would defeat the object of burgling the place undetected, which only left old-fashioned manipulation. This was not the ten minute job you see in the movies. His best hope was to detect slops in the dial's settings which would allow him to work through the combinations in settings of five. He got to work.

Several hours later he breathed a sigh of relief and the safe's door swung open. It contained two, buff-coloured files. The first was labelled Draymark Holdings International Limited and contained about fifty land certificates and title deeds. He examined about half-a-dozen, pulling them out at random and replacing them carefully in their original order. The second file was labelled Tawe Investment and Redevelopment Trust and contained more certificates and deeds; about twenty in total.

He looked at the safe again. Someone had spent some real money to keep these documents safe from prying eyes. But then again, solicitors hold deeds for clients all the time and having them stolen or burned would be a real headache. He thought he recognised some names from the file he found on Preece's computer, but he couldn't be sure, so he pulled out his phone, and photographed all the names and addresses from both files.

As he finished he glanced at his watch. It was already gone four! Time to join the early birds and shift workers. He closed the safe and spun the dial, then exited the office, relocking the door. Finally, he retraced his steps to the toilet, climbed back through the window and disappeared into the cover of the darkness and rain.

12

The overnight rain had finally drizzled to a halt, leaving the drifts of leaves around the university grounds to be blown about in the stiff, cold wind that now whipped in from Swansea Bay. Gareth Llewellyn trudged miserably down the steps behind the library, heading for the visitors' car park where he had left his battered, old Renault 5. He had moved his gear out of his dad's house on Gower Road the previous day and moved into a mate's flat in Brynmill. His mate's girlfriend had made it clear that she was not impressed with the arrangement. He knew he was on a very short lease there.

He had been to see his tutor who was very understanding about things. Had he considered counselling? Would he like to take a year off from his studies? None of it sank in really. He just wanted his dad back. Sometimes his sense of loss erupted as anger. Why had he done it, the selfish bastard? Sure, he was splitting up with Juliet, but there were other people to think about apart from himself. When he paused to consider these 'other people' he couldn't think of any. His mum had died of cancer years ago when he was a little boy and his dad was still in the army. From Gareth's point of view, he was what Charlie had to live for, and it hurt like hell that his father had not considered him a good enough reason to stay alive.

He crossed the road and walked through the trees into the car park, pausing for a moment to recollect where he had parked. He spotted it standing, dwarfed, beside a large, black Range Rover. It was an unusual looking vehicle for a university car park he decided, as he walked forward, groping for his keys. The driver's window slid silently down.

'Gareth, can I have a word?'

He turned startled. It was his step mother Juliet's boss, Councillor Preece. As far as Gareth was aware, Preece was the cause of the split between Juliet and his father, not that he had ever liked her.

'What do you want?'

'I need to talk to you; get in.'

Gareth was all too conscious of the biting wind and it was a civil enough invitation. He walked around to the passenger's side and climbed in. He turned to face the man. Preece was gazing straight ahead out of the front window as if considering his words carefully.

'I imagine you've been giving your future some thought?' he began matter-of-factly.

Gareth nodded.

'Good, so have Juliet and I and we would like to offer you some practical assistance.'

'What do you mean?'

'Well, this unfortunate business with your father cannot be undone, but we don't want to see you suffer unnecessarily. As you probably know, your father's business was, shall we say, on a precarious footing.'

Gareth shrugged non-committedly.

'Well, take it from me it was. The upshot was that your education was being paid for out of Juliet's savings.' He held up his hand as Gareth opened his mouth. 'Don't get me wrong, that wasn't a problem. She was glad to help you complete your education and she still wants to. She believes you have the character to get through the stress of what has happened, and to help you, we will continue to pay your fees and provide you with an allowance and some decent accommodation.'

'Why doesn't she want to tell me this herself?'

'Why should she? I am acting as her legal representative and I imagine, under the circumstances, she feels a personal meeting could be upsetting for you and her.'

'Do you really think your blood money is going to help me get over the death of my father?'

Suddenly, Gareth found himself looking into Preece's dark eyes.

'We didn't throw your father off that boat. He threw himself off.' He replied coldly. 'I'm here to talk business if you're interested.'

Gareth was stunned by the man's directness.

'Go on.' He replied, uncertainly.

Preece returned to gazing into the distance.

'As I said, Juliet and I are willing to support you through the remainder of your studies on the understanding that, at the end of that period, you will be expected to make your own way in the world.'

'Why bother?' You don't owe me anything.'

'Two reasons. First, I am a public figure. As a city councillor, I have to be aware of my image. I have always stood on a platform in favour of family values. The press would hang me out to dry if I were seen to abandon those principles.'

'So you want me to join the Councillor Preece public relations circus.'

Again the icy stare.

'Don't be so naive. I am interested in influence, not publicity, and specifically not bad publicity. I would prefer it if no one knows of our arrangements, but, if asked, I would simply expect you to tell the truth.'

Gareth was finding this conversation difficult. He wanted to dislike the man but, despite his chilly demeanour, what he was offering was more than reasonable.

'What's the second reason?' He demanded, clinging to his distrust.

Preece had rediscovered the distance. He seemed to be picking his words carefully. Finally he spoke.

'The second reason is that there is a slim possibility, and I emphasise slim, that your father may still be alive. If he is, he needs your help, and as long as you're a student in Swansea he knows where to find you.'

Gareth was stunned. His father, alive? How could he be? His heart was pounding.

'But I saw it on the news...'

'What you saw on the news was a report that your father had jumped off the ferry, which is almost certainly true. But no body has been found. That doesn't mean he survived, but Juliet has made the point that, due to your father's military training he would be unusually well equipped to do so. He may have attempted suicide, then changed his mind, or he may have faked the attempt from the outset.'

'Why would he do that?'

Preece did not reply. Instead, he turned around, picked up a leather briefcase from the back seat and opened it. He fished out a sheet of paper and passed it silently to Gareth. It was a photocopy of a letter.

'Go on, read it,' he prompted.

The letterhead bore a Harley Street address for a Dr Stanley Hartman Ph.D., Consultant Psychiatrist. It was dated August 26th 1996. It read:

Dear Dr Howard,

Thank you for referring your patient Mr Charles Llewellyn to me.

I can confirm that he is suffering from Post-Traumatic Stress Disorder following his military service in the Gulf War. It appears Mr Llewellyn was captured by the enemy and suffered severe mental and physical abuse at the hands of his captors. It is a testament to his strength of character that he survived this ordeal at all. Unfortunately, it has left him with some long-term, if not permanent, psychological scarring.

At present, he suffers from recurrent nightmares and daytime "flashbacks", which he finds intensely distressing. Depending on the subject of the fugue? he may be overcome by feelings of dread and terror. These are accompanied by sweating, severe enough to necessitate a change of bedding or clothing. Such attacks are typically brought on by memories of torture. Alternatively, where the memories are of confinement, he experiences symptoms of depression, withdrawal and even delusional paranoia. It is an indication of how seriously disabling these attacks are, that they can be triggered by the most inconsequential stimuli. These would typically include pictures on television, captor lookalikes, the sound of Arabic being spoken, even the smell of an after shave.

He has also become prone to attacks of claustrophobia in confined spaces since returning from The Gulf.

Unfortunately, like many military people, he has tended to tackle these problems with excessive drinking which, as you are well aware, carries with it its own clinical and psychological complications.

Mr Llewellyn is undoubtedly a strong and courageous man and I believe that, with support and counselling, backed up with a carefully controlled programme of medication, he can be helped to regain a fairly normal life. I would caution, however, that, as with all such problems, he is likely to be left with considerably less resistance to stress than he formerly enjoyed.

If this referral is preliminary to a compensation claim and you wish me to act as an expert witness, I will be happy to oblige. Please make appropriate arrangements with my secretary if necessary.

Yours truly,
Stanley Hartman.

Gareth read the letter through twice before handing it back. 'So what are you trying to tell me? My old man's a nutter?'

Preece shook his head.

'No, not at all, but the letter makes it clear that, under stress, he would be vulnerable to a recurrence of these problems which, of course, include delusional paranoia. I'm sure you know yourself that your father's taken this break-up with Juliet very badly. I understand that he has been drinking heavily and, on the day he apparently killed himself, he visited my offices. Fortunately, I was out and my colleague Ivor Semple was able to diffuse the situation, but I understand your father was brandishing a knife and accusing Juliet and me of conspiring to defraud him...'

'I don't believe you, you bloody liar! That's not my old man...'

'No, you're right. It isn't. It's someone quite different. Someone on the edge of a breakdown, because of the stress he's been under. Someone who needs help.'

'So, what can I do about it?'

'Well, you can hope and pray that Juliet is right and he's alive. If he is and he contacts you, let me know immediately.'

'Why should I let you know? You've hardly got his best interests at heart, have you?'

This time the dark stare was tinged with contempt.

'Juliet told me you were bright. I can't think why. I have explained to you, logically and unsentimentally, why I am willing to help you and your father yet you fail to grasp it. Let me spell it out for you. If your father is alive, he may be a very sick man. I have a business to run. I have already told you I do not want publicity, and I certainly don't want some deluded individual going around accusing me of tucking him up, or, worse still, turning up at my office threatening people with a knife. Your father was a highly trained soldier. If he turns up unhinged and runs amok, there is no knowing what he's capable of.'

'So what makes you think I can't help him?'

'He didn't ask for your help when he decided to throw himself off that ship, did he? More importantly, if he's in a delusional state, he may not believe he needs help. There may be no outward indication that he is ill.'

'So you want me to tip you off, so you can get him safely banged up in Cefn Coed?'

'Grow up sonny. In the unlikely event that your father turns up, I want you to have the common sense and maturity to help me ensure that he is properly looked after and not likely to cause injury to himself or anyone else. Now, are you going to continue behaving like a petulant kid, or are you going to act like an adult in the event that you hear from him?'

Gareth hesitated, he could see no further line of resistance to the man's arguments. He nodded.

'Okay, if I hear from him, how do I contact you?'

Preece took a business card from his breast pocket.

'Try me on any of these numbers during the day and on that one in the evening. If I'm unavailable, leave a message.' Gareth accepted the card as Preece continued: 'When you are ready, you can also call the St James' Crescent number and have a word with Ivor Semple. I've asked him to look out for a couple of flats that might suit you. Now, if you don't mind, I've got a meeting to prepare for.'

Without knowing quite how he got there, Gareth found

himself sitting behind the wheel of his car watching Preece's Range Rover as it pulled silently out of the car park. He felt dazed. Half-an-hour before, he had no vision of his future, not even somewhere he could call home. Now, those problems were gone and, better still, there was some sort of hope that his dad was still alive! Alright, it was a slim hope, perhaps a desperate hope, but it was better than no hope at all. The only thing that troubled him was the source of all this good news. He told himself not to be so soft, but he could not escape the feeling that doing business with Councillor Preece was like forming a latter-day pact with the devil.

*

His tongue slid away from her eager mouth and he lowered his head to her heaving breast. He encircled a nipple with his hot lips and teased it to hardness. His strong, manly hand felt for the junction between her slender legs. He pushed her thighs gently apart and she shuddered with pleasure and excitement as his fingers probed the most intimate regions of her womanhood. She arched her back as he...

'Excuse me...'

Linda Angellini looked up with a guilty start from the pages of Love's Buccaneer, the bodice-ripper she had just bought from Smith's on her lunch break.

Damn, an interruption just as it was getting interesting.

'I'm sorry to trouble you,' continued the man, 'it's just it's my first visit and I'm not sure where to begin...' He gestured somewhat helplessly at the computer monitors that filled the reading area of the Cardiff Information Centre in Companies House.

Linda sat staring at him, gob smacked. Dear God it was him, the man from her book! Sebastian Hart; tall and broad shouldered, tousled blond hair and a sort of, well, piratical air about him. She made a mental note to look up 'tousled'. He was wearing black leathers and carrying a crash helmet under his arm. Jesus, he was lush!

She dog-eared her page and quickly fumbled the book into the top drawer of her desk. She pulled off her glasses. Damn! Why did she have to forget her contacts today of all days? She rose, legs like jelly, what with the book and the vision in front of her.

'Can I help you please?' she enquired as she hurried forward.

'Yes, I'm sure you can. I want to have a look at the records you have on a company called Draymark Holdings International Limited.'

'Certainly, let me just make a note of that.' She picked up a pen and pad from a nearby desk and scribbled the name down. Her handwriting was strangely unsteady.

'Is there a charge for the search?'

'Not for a handsome boy like you.'

She turned and hurried back to her computer, blushing furiously. Where had that come from for God's sake? If a supervisor had heard that she'd have had a written warning and no mistake. Thankfully he'd only grinned.

When she returned she didn't know where to put herself. He must think she was a right slapper. Come to that she would be with him given half a chance!

'Have you ever used one of the monitors?' To her delight he shook his head. 'Just a tick then and I'll show you.' She let herself out from behind the counter and led him down the room. She could feel his eyes behind her weighing up her contours. She knew instinctively he would appreciate the fuller figure.

When she got back to her desk she sat down to steady herself and peered back down the room. She reached in her desk and slipped her glasses back on. That was better. He was staring, deep in concentration at the monitor she had demonstrated to him. She picked up her bag and headed for the ladies. Inside, she had a quick wee while she aimed her body spray under her blouse to freshen up. She hesitated, and then gave the gusset of her panties a quick squirt for luck. Well you never know... In front of the mirror she checked her foundation and touched up her mascara. She made an O with her lips and applied fresh lipstick with a new coat of lip gloss. She paused to admire her handiwork in the mirror; snog-factor ten she decided.

She coaxed a bit of bounce back into her perm with an afro comb. She ummed and ahhed about her choice of perfume and finally gave herself a shot of Dior behind her ears and on her wrists. She undid the second button on her blouse, and then the third. Too tarty? What the hell! Why would he be visiting Companies House if he wasn't interested in assets? She smirked at her little joke as she shot a good blast of Dior down her cleavage. As she returned to her desk she saw him get up and walk back to the counter so she hurried forward to see if she could help again.

Was it possible to take copies of these records, he wanted to know. Again that air of boyish helplessness, coupled with that roguish grin. She led him over to the copier. Did he want a copy of every page? He nodded. If she didn't mind, it was very good of her to help him like this. To be honest, he was a bit of a technophobe. They didn't have kit like this when he was at school!

She bent down to check that the printer had paper in it, coincidentally stretching the material of her blouse further apart. She glanced up to find she had caught his attention. He raised his eyes to hers and smiled in that knowing way, like Clint Eastwood before he drags them off to the barn. Jesus! Did he know what he was doing to her with his thumb hooked in his belt like that?

He asked her for copies of the files of two other companies and protested when she refused to accept payment for the searches. Alright then, if she wouldn't take the money, would she at least let him buy her a drink after work? She accepted the invitation with the reluctance of a bridesmaid diving for the bouquet and they agreed to meet in the pub opposite the castle since he didn't know the area.

*

Over a drink he explained that he was actor/manager for a touring theatre company who were doing something by someone called Acheborn. She remembered from school thinking what funny names people who wrote plays had. She could never get over Shakespeer, particularly when her friend Becky told her it was all about sex. To be honest, she didn't really follow too much of what he was saying, but she didn't care. He could have been speaking Double Dutch as long as those broad shoulders and that promising grin were in front of her.

Then he asked about his hair. What should he do? He was playing a late middle-aged man in the play so he was meant to be grey. He'd bleached it like it said on the packet because he was dark, but he hadn't expected it to go blond and now he looked like a right Susan! She was enjoying herself more and more. He was down-to-earth and a real good laugh, as well as sexy! She explained that she used to work in a hairdresser as a Saturday job, so they went back to her flat and dyed his hair grey. That made him look dead distinguished. God, she fancied him something rotten!

He insisted on buying dinner, so she took him to an Italian, owned by her aunt and uncle, to show him off. He was wonderfully easy to talk to, particularly as the wine flowed. He was actually interested in what she did for a living! When the food was cleared away and the last of the wine was gone, she asked him if he wanted to go clubbing. He shook his head. He had two left feet, and, besides, he had work to do in the morning. Did she know a reasonably priced hotel where he could get a bed for the night? She wouldn't hear of it. What did he want to go wasting money for, when she had room for a guest in her flat? She got her uncle to call a cab and marched him purposefully out of the restaurant.

It was stickier, sweatier and funnier, and more real and wonderful than anything in Love's Buccaneer and, when it was finally over, she pulled his arm over on top of her and cuddled against him.

He cried out in his sleep and woke her. She clicked the bedside lamp. He had thrown off the covers and sweat was rolling off him. His teeth were clenched and the muscles in his cheeks were rippling. His right forearm was thrown across his eyes as if sheltering himself from a blow, or a light. Uncertain what to do, she stretched out a hand and smoothed his hair, then ran it gently down his cheek.

'There, there, it's okay,' she murmured, as if calming a frightened child. Gradually, the terrible tension began to subside and the sweating stopped, leaving his skin gleaming in the lamplight.

The alarm clock told her it was ten-to-four. The wine had worn off and she inspected her new lover more dispassionately. So he was an actor and his name was Steve? Hmm, she was not so sure. What was that strange white scar on his stomach? It looked like some kind of burn. There was a bump on his chest, like there was something wrong with some of his ribs. Then there was that mark on his left thigh. She'd never seen a real bullet wound, but that was what she imagined one would look like. So what? He could have been a soldier before he became an actor, like Dirty Den in Eastenders; he'd been a soldier in real life. Shot some taxi driver in Germany according to the paper. She wondered if he had bad dreams too.

She shrugged to herself, clicked the light off and lay back down. She didn't care who, or what, he was. She knew she couldn't keep him. If he really was an actor, he was a free spirit, a wanderer and she'd sacrificed too much for the security of her job and her flat, just to throw it away for a night of passion. If he wasn't who he said he was, he obviously had his reasons for not wanting her to know. Either way, he'd be moving on. Perhaps he really was Love's Buccaneer, but if he was, she decided, he made a poor pirate – he'd given her much more than he had taken from her. She closed her eyes with a smile.

In the morning, when the alarm clock woke her, he was gone.

*

Farmer Price shook his head and sucked his teeth pensively. He had just finished the milking and was looking forward to his breakfast. He was studying a letter carrying the crest of Cardiff University and explaining that the bearer, Dr Gavin Stewart, was engaged in field research on the Gower Peninsula on behalf of the botany department.

'So 'ow long you thinkin' of stayin'?' he enquired.

'A few weeks maybe. It depends how long it takes me to collect my samples.'

The farmer grunted non-committedly.

'It's just we don't take caravans this time of years see. Season's over, like. Will you want feedin?'

'No, I'll be out all day and working in the evening. I'll probably slip down the pub for my evening meal. I'll be no bother. You'll hardly know I'm here. I just need somewhere to park the caravan where it won't get pinched or broken into.'

Farmer Price cast a jaundiced eye over the battered old Snipe Tourer. Who the fuck would want to pinch that? If someone was robbing caravans, the bloody Gower was sinking into the sea under the weight of gleaming white, state-of-the-art jobs.

Still he'd heard these boffins were usually a couple of bales short of the full haystack. He allowed himself to look a little persuaded.

'No bother, you say?' He stared out across the valley thoughtfully. 'Alright then, an 'undred quid a week and a week up front, inclusive.'

'Inclusive of what?'

'Inclusive of water and electric. You can park in the field by there. There's a socket in the barn and a tidy shithouse next door to it.'

'Where can I get milk and stuff?'

'There's a Spar back up the track in the village.'

The man nodded.

'Fair enough.'

He pulled out his wallet and counted out ten, crisp twenty-pound notes and passed them through the window of Price's ancient Land Rover.

'Can I have a receipt, please? I need it for my expenses.'

Farmer Price grunted his agreement.

'Park the van by there and I'll be back now.'

He turned the Land Rover and drove off back across the field. He hadn't expected the soft bugger to fall for that sort of money! He was welcome to a receipt as long as he didn't mind one from the book that the taxman never saw. Farmer Price rubbed his hands together in anticipation. There was going to be one hell of a piss-up in the Southgate Club tonight!

13

The wheels of the red Mercedes Roadster spun on the gravel as the car shot forward. Annette Preece watched from behind the lounge curtain as the Bitch pulled out of the drive and accelerated away. Annette grinned at her annoyance. She was out of tampons and Annette had decided she couldn't help. Hywel had already left for the morning, so a trip into Mumbles was unavoidable. Annette breathed a sigh of relief. It was the first time since her husband had instructed the Bitch to keep an eye on her that she had had any breathing space.

It was becoming a real strain keeping up the pretence of drinking and Juliet was forever calling out 'Another top up, Annette?' in that phoney, brittle voice of hers. There was only so much whisky you could dispose of by dabbing it around your neck and she wasn't always near a sink or toilet. She wondered how long it would be before the house plants started keeling over with alcohol poisoning.

She extinguished her cigarette and hurried down the corridor to the door of Hywel's study. She tried the handle expecting it to be locked, but to her surprise the door opened. She hesitated, aware that such temerity would undoubtedly earn her a fearful beating if she was caught, then she took a deep breath and slipped inside.

She had walked past the room on a number of occasions when the door was open, but usually under the influence of drink and with no particular curiosity about what was in there. There had always been an unspoken understanding that this was Hywel's territory and that she should keep out. The last thing she wanted to do was to provoke him into violence by disobeying his unwritten rules. The sudden realisation that her actions were setting her on a road from which there could be no turning back hit her with panic-inducing forcefulness. She hadn't felt such sickening tension since she quit acting. She remembered in the old days throwing up in dressing room toilets minutes before the curtain was due up.

She glanced at the plain carriage clock on the mantelpiece. Good. She reckoned she still had at least thirty minutes before Juliet would be back. She began to study her surroundings. They certainly reflected their occupier's personality. The room was dark and Spartan, with mahogany dressers full of leather-bound books around the walls. The books were stacked in monotonous rows behind glass doors as if to deny their ornamental value. Behind the dressers the walls were plain magnolia and the floor was covered with a good quality, but well worn burgundy carpet.

The desk was mahogany too. It looked like an expensive reproduction. Behind it stood a black leather, modern, executive chair. Apart from the clock on the mantelpiece, the only other ornamental thing in the room was a glass cabinet mounted on the wall, which appeared to contain a collection of antique pistols. A brass reading lamp, with a small green shade, stood on the desk. It shared its space with a computer and printer, set to one side of which was a clean blotter with a gold fountain pen on it.

Annette tried the top drawer of the desk and again, to her surprise, it was unlocked. It contained business stationery for Semple, Tucker and Preece and other office paraphernalia such as a stapler and a hole punch. That was all. The second drawer contained household bills filed under each utility and marked PAID. On the spur of the moment Annette selected a gas bill and a water bill from the middle of the files and slipped them into a pocket. Then she replaced the files carefully in the drawer exactly where she had found them. The other drawers contained packets of typing paper and envelopes. Clearly not even Hywel felt secretive about the contents of his desk. There was no other apparent storage space in the room.

The smart, off-white computer squatted silently in the middle of the desk as if challenging her to reach out and switch it on. She sat down in the leather chair and stared at its buttons in bewilderment. She guessed that the big button on the upright box might be the ON button. That was probably also the case with the big button on the little TV set thing but what the other little buttons and lights were for was anyone's guess. She had never used a computer in her life. To her surprise she found herself itching to turn it on, but common sense prevailed. She probably wouldn't be able to turn it off again, or she'd make such a mess of things that her espionage would be instantly detected and God help her then. It was clear that any records of wrong-doing her husband may be keeping were denied to her by her years of blinkered isolation.

As it was sinking in that this little adventure was proving to be utterly unproductive, the phone rang. She nearly leapt out of the seat with fright. She hadn't even noticed the damn thing, which was sitting on a small occasional table in the corner at the far end of the room. She rose and moved towards it. As she did so the answerphone cut in, inviting the caller to leave a message. There was a beep, then a pause as if someone was collecting his or her thoughts, then a man's voice with a well-modulated Irish accent spoke:

'Er, Hywel, this is Patrick. Can you tell Semple to sort out this kid he's got stashed in the extension? He's kept the boy in there over a fortnight now and that's costing us money; he should be well and truly hooked by now. More important I've got another shipment due in there shortly and we're gonna need the space. I don't care what he gets up to in there; just tell him to wind it up. I think he's enjoying this 'training programme' too much. Anyhow, sort it out will you.'

Annette stood motionless as the machine reset itself. So Patrick O'Connell was still on the scene. She thought Hywel had said he had retired; or was that Mr Tucker? It was hard to follow Hywel's occasional remarks through a haze of alcohol. They had only met on one or two occasions and that was years ago, but the voice still had a familiar ring. It was even more unfeeling than she remembered, and he had always struck her as a brutal man. She shuddered at the memory of his eyes. Her husbands were cold, but there was something instantly unnerving about Patrick O'Connell's. She went back over the message in her head. Extraordinary as it seemed, it sounded for all the world as if her husband and his colleagues were keeping a young man prisoner! But what on earth for?

She paused to study the machine. This was technology she was familiar with. Her life as an actress had revolved around dashing into her latest flat to pick up messages on her answerphone on the way to her next audition or rehearsal. She reached out and pressed the button. Again the pause then O'Connell's dry, unemotional tones came again.

Hearing the message again seemed to bear out her initial impression. O'Connell referred to a boy 'stashed' in some sort of 'extension'. It sounded like he was being kept against his will. She had watched enough soaps and police dramas to know that 'hooked' was a slang term for drug addiction. Were they involved in running some sort of drug rehabilitation program? Why should they be? They were solicitors by profession and none of them struck her as having an ounce of the sort of warmth and compassion needed to work in that field. In fact, from her wife-beating control-freak of a husband down, they struck her as the exact opposite of such people.

The unpleasant sneer with which O'Connell had mentioned Semple's "Training Program" came back to her. Semple had always made her flesh crawl with that silly little ponytail and the air of effete debauchery that clung to him. The thought of him as a jailer to a young man made her blood run cold.

She forced herself to pause and think. She mustn't jump to conclusions and she mustn't give herself away. If her suspicions were correct, she needed real proof. This call gave her a lead, but if she blew it she was in deep trouble. She glanced at the clock. Still at least ten minutes before Juliet came back. Good. She spoke out loud in the strongest Swansea accent she could muster.

'Hiya, Sandra, luv is that you.' She repeated it several times until it sounded absolutely authentic, and then she picked up the phone and dialled 1471. The automatic voice at the other end told her the number twice and invited her to return the call by pressing 3. She took a deep breath, reached out a shaking hand and pressed the button. On the third ring it was answered. This time a young woman's voice answered.

'Comfy Discount Furnishing, can I help you?'

'Hiya, Sandra, luv is that you?' replied Annette.

'Er, no... This is Comfy Discount Furnishing Ltd,' came the bored reply.

'Oh, sorry luv, I must've dialled the wrong number. D'you do beds then, 'cos I'm lookin' for something cheap for me mam?'

'Sorry we can't help. This is a trade wholesaler; we don't sell to the public. Try Yellow Pages.'

'Oh, right you are then. I'll try them. Ta very much.' She hung up. She was shaking but exhilarated by her detective work. The actress in her had taken over and she could still function like she used to. More importantly, she was now satisfied that something fishy really was going on. What kind of furniture warehouse had an extension with a kid 'stashed' in it and what could Semple be doing that made him enjoy the kid's 'training programme' too much?

She checked the room to make sure she had left no trace of her visit, and then slipped out closing the door silently behind herself.

*

Annette replaced the receiver on the hall phone.

'I've got an appointment with the hairdresser at two, darling,' she called to the Bitch who was busy in the kitchen. Thanks to her theatrical background, she could slightly slur her words and 'darling' with the best of them, which had now become a necessity in the atmosphere of artificial bonhomie which now existed between the two women. Knowing that her husband's mistress was now appointed as her prison guard in her own house appalled her. What had she ever done to deserve such treatment? Still, there was some satisfaction to be had from spying on the spy.

'Fine,' came the predictable reply. 'I'll run you into town. I've got some shopping I can do while you're in there.'

'No thank you darling, I've phoned for a taxi. I've got a few bits and pieces to pick up from Marks as well, so I'll be a bit longer than usual.' Annette noticed her hands were shaking. This was her first bid for a little freedom and from the Bitch's tone of voice it could easily become a battle of wills.

'There really is no need; I'll run you in now.'

'Don't worry the taxi's already on the way. In fact, here he is now.'

To her relief a car was pulling into the driveway. She picked up her bag and an empty tumbler from beside the phone as the Bitch emerged from the kitchen.

'Be a darling and swill this out for me will you? I'll see you later.' She leant forward to air-kiss the Bitch and give her a whiff of her whisky perfume as she handed her the tumbler, then turned and opened the front door. 'I'll be back before teatime,' she threw over her shoulder as she hurried off down the drive, barely suppressing a grin of triumph. The Bitch's face was as black as thunder. She was clearly accustomed to getting her own way and it was obviously infuriating her that this despised drunk of a woman had suddenly become so hard to control.

*

The cab dropped her off on Belle Vue Way and she hurried into Alfredo's. Joyce was waiting for her.

'Well Mrs Preece, you're looking great!' she exclaimed, with a sincerity which, under other circumstances, would have been most welcome. Now, it only served to remind Annette that, despite her best efforts with the make-up box and whisky perfume, her abstinence was threatening to give her away. She was losing weight rapidly and the puffiness around her face was almost gone. Loose-fitting clothes helped a bit, but they could not disguise the aura of greater physical well-being. She could only hope that these changes were more apparent to someone like Joyce who hadn't seen her for some time.

'Listen Joyce,' she began in a conspiratorial tone, 'I'm in a bit of a rush today, so I wondered if you could perhaps push me through as quickly as possible if you don't mind?'

Joyce shot her the knowing glance of an experienced hairdresser. When a client came in looking like a new woman, asking to cut short a good pampering at the hands of Alfredo's expert staff, it could only mean one thing – a lover. She smiled understandingly.

'Of course Mrs Preece, I'll get one of the girls to shampoo you right away.'

*

Just after three o'clock Annette left Alfredo's with a new shampoo and cut and walked around the corner onto the Kingsway. She crossed the road and headed down to the bank. She'd had an hour to think about her next move and her stomach was knotted with tension. Her changing appearance and the sheer stress of remembering to maintain an air of permanent inebriation were factors that could no longer be ignored. They were driving her towards the moment when she would have to leave Swansea and disappear, or confront her husband with irrefutable proof of serious wrongdoing. She knew she needed solid evidence to challenge Hywel, but the afternoon's main objective was to organise an escape route. For that she needed money.

She had a card which she used for buying clothes and bits and pieces, but she had no idea what was in the account. She knew it was different from an old-fashioned cheque book when you had a few days grace for a cheque to clear. She suspected that Hywel monitored it continuously. He thought nothing of asking her to explain a payment if its purpose was not clear from the statement. That was the limit of her financial freedom. She had no idea what she could withdraw or how to do it. The last ten years of banking innovation had passed her by completely.

She joined the queue and noticed that they now had a system of flashing lights to indicate a free cashier; in the old days they used to call you over. She waited her turn and approached the counter. The woman finished sorting some notes into a drawer and looked up. A badge on her lapel informed Annette that her name was Donna.

'Can I help you?'

'Yes, I'm sure you can. It's just that my husband usually does the banking so I need a bit of advice...'

'Certainly Madam, what is it you need to know?'

'Well, it's rather silly actually, but it's our twelfth anniversary in a couple of days' time and I planned to whisk him off on a surprise trip to the place we went on honeymoon.'

'Ooh, how romantic!'

'Yes, well that's what I thought, but it's a last minute booking and the travel agents across the road said they would need four days for my cheque to clear which isn't enough time. Otherwise, I need to pay by cash or credit card and I never carry a credit card.'

Donna nodded sympathetically.

'I know it's so easy to get carried away with plastic isn't it? I'm hopeless myself.'

That struck Annette as being a bit like being told to give up smoking by a doctor with a cigarette in his mouth, but she found herself warming to Donna. It was all a lot less stuffy than she remembered.

'The trouble is,' she continued, 'I don't know how much money we've got in our current account.'

'Oh, that's no problem, have you got your card there?'

Annette nodded and slipped it under the window. Donna turned to her computer and rattled some keys; it spat out a slip of paper which she passed back. It had £16,743.28cr printed on it.

'Thanks, oh, one other thing; if I take this out today, how long will it take to show up?

'I'm sorry?'

'How long will it take to clear? We're flying out in two days' time and it might ruin the surprise if he notices I've spent that much money.'

Donna resisted the urge to patronise.

'I see, of course, unfortunately it will clear instantly. It's not like an old-fashioned cheque I'm afraid.'

'Oh dear, I don't know what to do now...' Suddenly Annette was gripped by panic. Her plan was unravelling already. She needed to be as far away from Hywel as possible before she risked challenging him.

'Perhaps it would be alright if you only took out what you need immediately,' suggested Donna, with the understanding of a woman who also took a surreptitious hand in the management of her husband's wages. 'Provided a payment doesn't get declined, he might not check his account for days...'

Annette smiled gratefully at the advice. Donna clearly didn't know Councillor Hywel Preece! On the other hand, she had a point. He might not check and, more importantly, once she withdrew anything more than a hundred pounds she was crossing the Rubicon anyway. He would know something was up and there would be no going back. The thought that the withdrawal would take time to clear was just an illusion and she might wait a long time for another opportunity to get to a bank. It was now or never.

'Okay, I'd like to take out five thousand pounds then, please.'

Her hand was surprisingly steady as she passed her card back through to Donna. She probably had the tranquillisers to thank for that because, by rights, she should be shaking like a leaf. Up to now she had done nothing irreversible, but as she handed through the card she knew she was rewriting her life. She also knew that, if her husband discovered the withdrawal before she got out of Swansea, her life would not be worth living.

14

The sweat was running off him and he was blowing a bit, but there was still some spring in his legs as he pushed on up through the bracken towards the summit of Cefn Bryn. In the old days, when he was training for selection, he used to do this run in full kit with a thirty pound Bergen on his back, but then, this wasn't the old days. He'd been ex-SAS for nearly eight years now. He spotted King Arthur's Stone up ahead and pushed himself hard over the last fifty yards.

He checked his watch and grinned. Not bad for an old man, Charlie Boy. He wouldn't be entering any cross-country meetings yet, but it could be worse. He dropped his pack and sat down with his back against one of the large rocks that surrounded the landmark, pausing to get his breath back. He pulled open the small, black, nylon knapsack he was carrying and took out his new, fleece-lined tracksuit. He had rather enjoyed spending some of the money the generous Mr Semple had given him to 'fuck off' the day before. He pulled the bottoms on over the trainers he had bought in Cardiff.

The October sun was beginning to sink and the air was getting chilly. He donned the track suit top as well. Before he lost the light, he pulled out the sheets of notes he had made throughout the afternoon as he pored over the printouts from Preece and Semple's computers and the copies from Companies House.

He grinned again as he looked at the frantic tangle of jottings, underlining and logic sequences that scrambled across the four pages. Pity any poor bastard that took it upon himself to make sense of that lot! He pulled a pen and a fresh sheet of paper out of his bag and settled down to summarise his conclusions.

In all honesty, they were more suspicions and intuitions than conclusions. Preece was obviously not the sort of man to erect a large notice board saying: 'Look at me everybody; I'm a crooked pig and this is how I do it!' Nevertheless, somewhere between wishful thinking and demonstrable fact, Charlie was sure he could hear the whisper of wicked voices.

When Farmer Price had finally returned with the receipt then disappeared in the direction of his farmhouse, Charlie had settled down in front of the new laptop he had bought on his shopping spree in Cardiff. He had already spent some time getting used to it by concocting a Cardiff University letterhead for Farmer Price's benefit using the crest he had found on the University web site. Tucked away in his caravan, in the corner of a field on an out-of-the-way, private farm, he had gone online and visited the address to which he had posted the files he had found on Semple and Preece's computers.

Now, perched high on Cefn Bryn in the fading light, he was trying to make out what those wicked, whispering voices were saying. He reached into his bag again and pulled out another document. It was a map of Swansea. He spread it out on the rock in front of him and studied the crosses he had marked on it that afternoon. Each represented one of the properties listed in the file on Preece's computer. There were thirty-seven addresses in total and there was a land certificate for each in the filing cabinets he had found in the third office. On his second sheet of notes he had scribbled *'LOCATIONS???'* In thick red pen. Now, he looked at the map, a question, if not its answer, was beginning to crystallise in his mind.

The crosses formed clusters, with the biggest concentration running across Townhill and Mayhill down to Cwmbwrla, Dyfatty and Bryn-Melyn. There were clusters around Blaen-y-Maes and Penlan, and out to Gorseinon in the west. Looking east, there were groups in Clase and Llansamlet, Winch Wen and Bon-y-Maen. Looked at individually, it was hard to see any great significance in any particular address. Looked at as a whole, the crosses shaded in a map of the roughest, most run-down and deprived areas of the city.

That did not necessarily prove anything. It had only taken a quick phone call to Taunton to confirm that the Tawe Investment and Redevelopment Trust was registered with the Charities Commission. A copy of the original, 1995 registration application, prepared by Semple, Tucker and Preece, the charity's nominated solicitors was still stored in a file on Preece's computer. The mission statement claimed that the charity's purpose was the rehabilitation of young drug offenders through the provision of drop-in centres, therapy, counselling and good quality housing in depressed and disadvantaged areas of the city.

What set the voices whispering more loudly in Charlie's ear, was that the trustees of the Tawe Investment and Redevelopment Trust were listed as a Mr James Tucker and a Mrs Mary Tucker of 18 Farrell Road, Aberdeen, Scotland. He remembered Juliet telling him that Tucker had left the practice at about that time to return to Scotland to nurse his mother. He also recalled her snide reference to Tucker as 'Queen of the

Scots, so where had the wife come from? Furthermore, why resign from Semple, Tucker and Preece, set up a Swansea-based charity, and then promptly disappear off to Aberdeen? Charlie wondered if Mrs Mary Tucker was the ill mother. It would be handy for someone manipulating the charity if, out of only two trustees, one of them was an elderly, Scottish lady with no interest in the Tawe Investment and Redevelopment Trust whatsoever. Charlie wrote on his clean sheet: *Where is James Tucker???* He underlined it.

*

The light was going fast now, so he slipped his notes back into his bag and settled down to wait. Darkness closed in completely and he tuned into the new sounds as the countryside went nocturnal. Suddenly he spoke.

'Evening Rotty. Park your elephant by that big stone. I take it that's Billy with you?'

'What elephant you cheeky fucker? You're the only thing with bloody big ears around here. I guess it must be quite a strain always listening out for angry husbands, eh?'

Charlie grinned. The big Aussie had obviously been reading the papers.

'How's the scenery?'

'All clear. We've done a three-sixty sweep and there are no nasty people hiding in the shrubbery.'

'Good.' Charlie rose from behind the rock and stepped forward to greet his former comrades. 'Jesus wept!' he exclaimed in disgust. 'You minging bastards! You smell like a couple of septic tanks in summer. What've you been up to?'

'We've been up to our armpits in a fookin' drainage ditch watching gun-totin' rag'eads smugglin' dope while you've been showing off your spotty arse to the tabloid press!' replied Billy, in blunt Mancunian tones which suggested which of the parties had, in his opinion, been having the easier time.

'Hmm,' sympathised Charlie. 'I guess you boys did draw the short straw there, but then I suppose you'll just have to accept that my spotty arse is more photogenic than you two. Still you could have tidied yourselves up a bit – this is meant to be an area of outstanding natural beauty.'

'Stick it up your arse, ya gobby Welsh bastard. We only flew into Brize at lunchtime and we had to call in at Stirling Lines on our way here for a debrief.'

'Why the urgency?'

'There was a contact when we went forward to recce the factory. We got on target alright – and the place is still runnin' just as you described it. We gave it the eyeball for a couple of hours and were just about to do our slippin' away into the inky darkness routine, when a raghead guard comes around the corner, clocks us and starts screamin' like a fuckin' banshee. It was just one of those weird ones. Seconds either way and we'd have missed each other. Anyhow, I gave the bloke a squirt with me M16 from point blank and damn near cut him in half', he spat.

'Soon as it goes noisy every raghead in the area starts loosin' off rounds and the perimeter fence lights up like a fuckin' Christmas tree. Thankfully we'd gone in native style – bedou coats and dish-dashes. Rotty here, twigs that no one knows what they're meant to be firin' at and joins in, dancing, around and loosin' off rounds with the scariest of them. I put my best Correspondence School Arabic to work and start yellin': "They went that way! They went that way!" and the next thing we know we are racin' out of the compound, behind a bunch of howling ragheads, in hot pursuit of ourselves.'

Charlie grinned at the image in the darkness.

'I dunno,' he muttered. 'The lengths you blokes will go to get a curry on a Saturday night. Anyhow, you reckon the plant was still up and running?'

'You betcha. The stuff is coming out of Afghanistan and Iran as morphine base and being brought into Iraq for processin'. We followed a consignment all the way and there was no hassle, not even at the borders, so someone's being well paid. It's turned into smack in the main building and then taken to the other side of the compound for cutting.'

Charlie nodded.

'Sure, they use ether and hydrochloric acid in the refining process. It's so bloody volatile they keep the finished stuff well out of the way. Okay, progress. We know O'Connell's original set up is still in operation, but we don't know if he is still controlling it or even using it as a supplier. Is the stuff being tracked as it leaves Iraq?'

'Yeah, but it's out of our hands. We were exfilled just short of the Iraq/Turkey border. After three weeks in the desert I guess they were worried that Billy's B.O. could be mistaken for an act of biological warfare. Anyhow, we passed the baton to a joint ops set-up that our Int boys reckon is made up of Interpol and a special Customs and Excise unit based in Bristol. The lot your pal Sullivan works for. How soon we hear from them depends on how long the couriers take to move the stuff across Europe.'

Charlie nodded.

'Sure. Could be days or weeks. Set the recorder going and I'll give you the Sit Rep at this end.' He paused as Billy pulled out a hand-held recorder, fiddled with the controls and nodded for him to proceed.

Charlie spoke in the direction of the machine. 'Situation report for Det Eight from Charlie Alpha Tango One.' He waited as Billy rewound and played this back to ensure it was recording, then he continued as Billy cued him back in.

CAT 1 has now gone covert as planned. A recce of the target's HQ was carried out last night and certain material collected. This to be delivered to you in hard copy straight from this RV. CAT 1 believes this is promising material, but needs time for further analysis. Also further observation of target essential. The second player in the gang may no longer be active, but needs further checking. The situation is liable to be more volatile than anticipated and CAT 2 may require rapid exfiltration. Please prepare accordingly. Next RV will be confirmed by word of mouth. This is Charlie Alpha Tango One signing off.' Billy pressed the stop button.

'D'you really think O'Connell could be behind all of this?'

Charlie shrugged.

'It's not beyond him. I'm pretty sure Preece is only running the Swansea end of the operation and they need someone with international connections to oversee the drug smuggling. Given O'Connell's paedo affiliations it wouldn't be hard to see him involved in male prostitution as well.'

15

The moon was sliding in and out behind clumps of heavy rain cloud as Charlie stood outside the caravan gasping for breath. It was gone one in the morning and he had been working since his return from dinner at the King Arthur around nine. To avoid unnecessary attention, he had drawn the curtains carefully and contented himself with working by the light from his laptop. A couple of times he had felt the walls closing in on him and had had to fight to quell the waves of rising panic and the memories they triggered. This time it had come upon him suddenly and the need for space and open air had forced him outside in a rush. He leant weakly against the caravan, dragging the damp sea air into his lungs.

He cautiously allowed himself to relive the memory a little at a time as the Det. psychiatrist had taught him. He recalled the bastards lowering him, cuffed, into that stinking, bloody drain in Baghdad. O'Connell's chief Iraqi interrogator wanted the last word.

'You be safe in there motherfucker. No brainy bomb come get you down there. We take good care of guest.' He banged himself on the chest with mock pride, then threw back his head and laughed uproariously. More than anything he remembered that last glimpse of O'Connell watching with amused curiosity as the guards rolled the cover back into place.

Total darkness and the thick stench of human excrement. Then the rats came, squeaking and scampering over his legs. His bare feet were vulnerable where the guards had stolen his boots. At first, when they bit, he would kick out to scare them off. By the third night he was too exhausted. Finally he learned to sit cross-legged with his bare feet tucked under his thighs for protection and his back against the wall to hide his hands. If he tucked his chin into his chest, sitting upright like that, they seemed unable to attack his face, though it didn't stop them trying.

Soon, it was worse when the rats went away and there were no distractions. Then the pitch blackness came pressing in on him and the panic rose invading his mind like a malignant virus, overwhelming his reason and self-control, and forcing him to gulp in the poisonous, foetid air of the sewer. Twice he had lost it and they had dragged him out snivelling and foetal in the morning. Each time they had injected him and let him sleep, only to send him back down there the next night. Sometimes he prayed for a smart bomb to come snaking down the street and put an end to his torment. Then the thought of being trapped down there under tons of rubble, without even his torturers to pull him out, would drive him to the brink of madness again.

Charlie ran his hand across his face, as if to wipe away the memory. His cheeks were wet with tears. Shit! Was he up to this? Would he have been wiser to stay on the Swansea-Cork Ferry and steam off into the sunset? He straightened up and squared his shoulders. No, he decided, he wasn't the steaming off into the sunset type. What he had to cling to was that the bastards had hurt him and even damaged him, but they hadn't broken him. He had done the hard yards then – he wasn't about to give up now. Besides he had a soft Irish voice to remember and a score to settle. His memories could only be permitted to drive him forward.

*

It was 9.30 the following morning and he was trying to track down the retired partner Tucker, but without success. There was a phone line registered to a J.Tucker at 18, Farrell Road, Aberdeen, but the number was ex-directory and no amount of smooth talking had moved the staff of Directory Enquiries. There were several C. Tuckers listed in the Swansea directory, but one was an elderly woman and neither of the other two had Scottish accents.

Drawing a blank was hardly a big surprise. If O'Connell really was the man behind the Rent Man gang, it was more than possible that Tucker had retired on a more permanent basis than his pension advisors had anticipated. Tucker needed finding, but perhaps he was not the immediate priority. It would be a time consuming, if not hopeless business, and it was already five days since he had jumped off the ferry.

He was now certain he was dealing with people with a lot to hide, and they were possibly not as convinced as the rest of the world about his death, particularly with no corpse turning up. At any time, a chance recognition, or a bit of bad luck, could blow his cover. Time was not on his side.

He went back over the grounds for his growing suspicions. Aside from the mystery of the retired Mr Tucker's disappearance, there was the secrecy surrounding the three companies listed on Preece's computer: Draymark Holdings International Ltd,

Cambrian Aggregates Ltd and Comfy Discount Furnishings
Ltd. According to the print-outs he had brought back from
Companies House, all three had exercised their right, according
to various sections of the Companies Act 1985, to dispense with
annual audits, annual general meetings and the annual laying
of accounts before the company. Linda had assured him, over
dinner in Cardiff, that there was nothing unusual about this.
It had been introduced as a cost saving for companies with a
turnover of less than three hundred and fifty thousand. What
struck Charlie as fishy was that all three were declaring turnovers
just under that amount. Odder still, they were all donating a
substantial slice of their profits to the Tawe Investment and
Redevelopment Trust. Somehow he didn't expect companies
with names like Cambrian Aggregates and Comfy Discount
Furnishings to be motivated by charitable ideals.

Each company only listed one director doubling as company
secretary, and the company reports were models of brevity.
Again, nothing wrong, Linda had assured him, but seen as
a whole, it seemed as if there was a concerted effort by all
involved to reveal as little of their activities as possible.

There were also the links between them. It appeared from
the deeds, and correspondence conducted through Semple,
Tucker and Preece, that Tawe Investment and Redevelopment
Trust had purchased the properties on Preece's list in the mid-
nineties. Then there was the PR campaign, again spearheaded
by Semple, Tucker and Preece, to raise redevelopment funds.
The City Council, the Welsh Development Agency, the EEC,
big business, even the Masons, had all been petitioned for
donations, grants and interest free loans across the decade. As

each redevelopment was financed, parties were thrown and speeches were given, then the building work went to Cambrian Aggregates and the fitting out went to Comfy Discount Furnishing. It was too cosy for words! Finally, after a year or two the redeveloped properties were sold on the Draymark Holdings International who defined themselves briefly as a property management company.

None of that, of course, was proof of any wrongdoing. What seemed more bizarre was that the registered address of the Tawe Investment and Redevelopment Trust was none other than the deserted second floor of the Semple, Tucker and Preece building in St James' Crescent. For such a thriving concern, it now appeared to exist in little more than the cyber space of Preece's computer.

To Charlie's ear, the whispering voices had become considerably more raised, but he still couldn't hear anything clearly. It was the second charm offensive that caused him to lift his head and stare, sightlessly, through the little caravan window, across Farmer Price's fields, to the cold, grey sea beyond.

The letters were addressed to officers in Social Services departments throughout Britain. They began in 1994, outlining the activities of the Trust as a charity concerned with drug rehabilitation amongst young people from underprivileged backgrounds. Its goals were:

– The treatment of young, drug-addicted clients in partnership with the Busch-Gorman Narcotics Dependency Clinic, Boston, Massachusetts. (Corporate profile enc.)

– The social reintegration of ex-addict clients into new surroundings.
– The on-going provision of adequate housing and job opportunities for those clients.

The letters emphasised the need for clients to be housed in areas which reflected their social roots and likely aspirations, citing statistics which indicated the futility of relocating such individuals into unfamiliar social contexts. The letters referred to 'Displacement Syndrome'. They emphasised the importance, however, of the need for a significant change of environment. This was best achieved, according to a number of studies, through the Evacuee Principle, which espoused the rehousing of clients in new towns or cities away from old haunts and influences.

The programme was called 'Roads to Freedom' and it was aimed at youngsters who were just emerging from the care system at sixteen and finding it difficult to settle into a community. Typical clients included youngsters with drink and/or drugs problems and youngsters with a history of absconding.

The Trust, the letters explained, had a number of properties under redevelopment, which would shortly be available for occupancy. If the officers therefore had clients they would like to sponsor for the Road To Freedom programme, would they care to attend an open day (pre-paid reply enclosed) to hear a talk from the Principal of the Busch-Gorman Clinic, Dr Martin Lehrman, and to view the whole rehabilitation programme in action? Food and accommodation would be provided and travel expenses paid.

Not surprisingly, the response was overwhelming and those who attended the open day were enormously impressed. It seemed the charity had identified an urgent need. Letters came flooding back with details of youngsters whom the officers were sure were ideal for the programme. Looked at from their point of view, Charlie understood why it all appealed so much, but from where he was sitting, the most salient fact was that none of the individuals involved in the Tawe Investment and Redevelopment Trust, with the possible exception of the mysterious American, Dr Lehrman, had any training in, or experience of, the care of youngsters, let alone those with severe emotional problems.

Sitting in the little caravan, staring at the grey sea, Charlie decided it was time to take a closer look at the work of the Tawe Investment and Redevelopment Trust. He chose six addresses from his map, pulled on a set of overalls and a donkey jacket, locked the caravan door behind him and climbed into the Land Rover. He drove up the track, and put some distance between himself and the farm, before reaching into the back and picking up the hard hat that completed his disguise as a Council maintenance officer.

He headed for his first objective, a recently renovated terraced house on Townhill. He parked about twenty yards down the road from the house and, very slowly, ate lunch. He got out and, at an equally leisurely pace, made various abstract measurements of the road with an impressively large, winding tape measure. He plausibly managed to watch the building for an hour and a half, but he knew he was being watched too. If your face wasn't known on Townhill, people wanted to know what you were doing there.

He reached a point where he couldn't front it out anymore, so he drove to the next address. He managed a similar surveillance there, and at the next property, but there was continual pressure to move on and gathering material evidence such as photographs was out of the question. He abandoned surveillance for the afternoon and began to scout for a safe house from which to do the job properly.

As he drove from one address to the next, searching for a hidey-hole that would give him the privacy he needed, he listened to the whispering voices and now their message rang clearer. Thanks to his afternoon's work he now suspected that, despite the laudable objectives of the Tawe Investment and Redevelopment Trust's mission statement, and it's equally plausible charm offensive, its properties, so lovingly renovated with generous donations from the great and the good, were now operating as back street brothels. It would seem that the prestigious, first floor offices of Semple, Tucker and Preece, St James Crescent, The Uplands, Swansea were nothing but a front for a prostitution racket staffed by addicts and misfits, unwittingly supplied by British social services officers.

*

It was three o'clock in the morning and he was on the move again. He skirted around Cadle Common and parked the Land Rover out of sight down a track. He emerged from the trees onto the rough ground by Woodford Road just as a huge, white, ghostly figure loomed up in front of him. Jesus wept, it was a bloody horse! Small wonder they called this place the Ponderosa.

He pulled his hood over his head, hunched his shoulders and began to weave his way up Woodford Road. He staggered across the road and headed unsteadily up Blaen-y-maes Drive. These were the streets the Rent Man gang ruled with fear and people closed their curtains when strangers passed in the night.

Down on the rough ground a car was still glowing where the boys had got bored of joyriding and torched it. Next to it a kiddie's bike stood balanced on its stand. As Charlie got nearer, he realised that that too had been set on fire. Talk about starting young.

He turned left and staggered on past dilapidated houses. He reached the house with the Stars and Stripes painted on the concrete frontage and a huge picture of Elvis in the front window. Good, he knew he was only six doors away from the passageway that led between the houses. That led in turn to the narrow alleyway that separated the back gardens of the two terraces. He reached the gap and paused uncertainly, then tottered down the path. If anyone was watching, they would assume he was doing what drunks tend to do in alleys at that time of night. When he didn't emerge, they would think he had simply continued through into the next street.

As he vanished into the shadows, his whole posture altered. His knees flexed and he leant forward to stay beneath the false horizon of the garden fences. Now he was moving in total silence; heel, side-of-foot, toes. Ever forward, each step checking for cans and other rubbish. He could barely hear his own, shallow, breathing.

He turned right into the alley and worked his way along it, trying to picture the obstacles he had encountered that afternoon, when he had recced it in a hard hat and overalls with a clipboard under his arm. Only one woman had challenged him and she'd accepted the answer: 'Routine maintenance, luv,' without further ado. He squeezed around the rusting pram at the back of number twenty-five and stepped over the abandoned Bontempi keyboard at the back of number thirty-one. When he reached number thirty-seven, he felt for the latch, lifted it gently and let himself into the garden.

Closing the gate behind himself, he crept down the path to the house. He was further inland here and the cloud had gathered into a solid mass through which only the faintest glimmer of moonlight occasionally penetrated. There was no street lighting at the back of the houses making the darkness almost impenetrable. At least he couldn't be seen. He reached the back of the house and located the boarded up window by touch. His fingers found the heads of each of the six heavy screws that had been driven through the chipboard into the wooden frame. He pulled up a trouser leg and untapped the electric screwdriver from his shin. He pulled off his parka and wrapped it around the tool to muffle the noise. Here goes! It sounded like a drill to him, but he knew from experience that it was inaudible ten yards away and the only people that close to him would be on the other side of a brick wall.

He left the top, right hand screw till last, and then only loosened it, allowing him to swing the board aside. He stepped through the void where the window pane had once been and felt the broken glass crunch under his foot as he transferred his weight and slipped through the gap. He eased the board back into position and wedged it with the screwdriver. Even in daylight it would take close inspection to discover the break-in. He clicked on his pencil beam torch. He was in a back room. The door was in the far, right-hand corner. It smelt like a zoo. A quick flick of the torch revealed why. There were piles of horseshit on the floor and hay scattered everywhere. There were several bales of hay stacked in the corner. He'd heard all the jokes about Shergar being alive and well and living in Blaen-y-maes, but he'd never been much amused by it; he was now.

He picked his way carefully through to the doorway. To his right was a poky little kitchen, to his left a passageway led to the front door. He followed it. The front room was to his left and a narrow flight of stairs led up the wall to his right. He flashed the torch briefly around the boarded-up front room. The floor was littered with Special Brew cans and White Lightning bottles. The beam picked out a few discarded syringes and empty Rizla packets. The place had obviously been quite a party venue until the Council boarded it up.

Charlie didn't linger. He headed upstairs to the front bedroom. It was much like the front room downstairs in terms of debris, but, unlike the rest of the house, the window wasn't boarded up. Perhaps they had run out of chipboard or, more likely, they had decided that even the most dedicated party animals wouldn't try breaking through an upstairs window in full view of the street. Whatever the reason, it had put this place at the top of Charlie's list of potential observation posts from which to study one of the houses on Preece's list.

A filthy old net curtain still hung in the window. Taking care not to step in front of the window itself, he pulled the left hand side across a couple of inches and watched dust drift down in the light from the street lamp opposite. He squatted down and played the pencil beam across the floor – he didn't fancy finding a discarded syringe sticking in his backside. He couldn't see anything life-threatening, so he sat down to the left-hand side of the window. His eyes were just about level with the sill. He could have done without that bloody street lamp!

He pulled a small telescopic tripod from the inside pocket of his coat. He extended the legs and screwed a Pentax compact onto it. Without the back up of a surveillance team, the emphasis was on small and neat. He lined it up with the gap in the curtains and angled it back down the street at the front door of number twenty-eight. He zoomed in as tightly as possible on the doorway. His main objective was to catch the visitors, but, from that angle, there was a chance that he might catch the person who answered the door as well. He placed a pair of miniature binoculars on the window sill and wiggled around until he was leaning with his back to the wall next to it. He drew his heels up to his backside and rested his forearms on his knees. His watch showed there were still two-and-a-half hours to sunrise. He cushioned his forehead on his arms and closed his eyes. His breathing gradually deepened and he slept.

16

The internal phone buzzed insistently, forcing Ivor Semple awake with a start. It was eleven in the morning, and he had been in work since nine, but he'd had a heavy night and he'd resisted the temptation to wake himself up by powdering his nose. As a result he had nodded off at his desk. In a state of some confusion he answered with a croaky 'Semple'.

'Ivor, its Hywel. Would you pop in here a moment?'

The tone straightened him out like a bucket of cold water in the face.

'Two minutes please Hywel.'

'No, now.'

'Okay, I'll be in right away.'

He replaced the receiver and yanked open the bottom drawer of his desk. Thank God, there was some vodka left! With a bit of luck Hywel wouldn't smell it. He frantically unscrewed the cap and took several long gulps as he racked his brains for what he had done wrong. He couldn't think of anything, but then again, it was rarely the obvious that lit Hywel's fuse. Another couple of swigs and he put the vodka back in the drawer. He knew what to expect and the vodka was not going to blot that out, but even a little Dutch courage and anaesthetic was better than nothing. He braced himself and headed for the door.

'Come!'

Semple opened the door and stepped into Preece's office. His boss was sitting behind his desk, studying a document. As Semple walked forward he dropped it onto the polished surface. It was an itemised phone bill. He didn't look up and, despite the vodka hit he was experiencing, Semple could feel the tension in him. Finally, he spoke. His voice was taut with suppressed fury.

'Remember that call out you attended the other night, Ivor?'

'Yes, Hywel.'

'You reckoned a cat had got in through the toilet window as I recall.'

'Yes, that's right Hywel; we found it downstairs in the hall.'

'So you shut the window and reset the alarms?'

'Yes, that's right.' Shit! He hadn't meant to lie; it just came out that way in the tension of the moment.

'You mean you personally shut the window?'

'Yes...I mean no. Sorry, no, the police shut the window. I was downstairs, but I heard them do it clear as day.'

'And then you reset the alarm?'

'Yes.'

'Don't lie to me.'

'I don't know what you mean...'

'If you had called the engineers to reset the alarm, it would have shown up on this bill. Instead, it appears that during the night someone got into my computer and ran up a quite different bill emailing its contents to a remote website. Rather than exercise the intelligence and caution I pay you for, you chose to accept a cat as a decoy and leave our whole operation exposed to an intruder!'

His voice had barely risen, but it was thick with pent up rage. Semple could feel his knees shaking as his boss finally raised his eyes to stare at him. 'Have you anything to say?'

Semple shook his head, speechlessly.

Preece rose and walked around from behind his desk. He locked his office door, and then he walked to a tall cupboard. Semple tried not to cower, because he knew from experience that that only provoked more sadism. He was visibly shaking with fear as Preece turned to face him. He was holding an old golf club. To the untrained eye it was just a piece of battered, old sports equipment but, with its heavy-edged iron head, to Semple it was an instrument of torture.

He fended off the blows as best he could in the knowledge that too early a submission would only provoke greater aggression. Hywel demanded his satisfaction. When his vision became obscured by blood from a gash on his forehead, he collapsed on the floor and tried hopelessly to cover up. The beating continued for perhaps a minute longer as his tormentor aimed shots at his kidneys and his groin, and then Preece tired of it. He threw the club back in the cupboard as Semple lay cringing on the floor. He turned suddenly as the fury blazed again. He seized his victim by the hair and dragged him violently to his knees to open his defences, then aimed a few more kicks at his groin. One landed squarely in his crotch making him retch and vomit up the drink he had taken minutes before. Preece threw him violently aside in disgust.

He returned to his seat and studied his victim with contempt as he caught his breath. When he finally spoke his voice was steady, almost matter-of-fact.

'How's the replacement for that boy who died the other night coming along?' he asked finally.

Semple struggled to his knees.

'Very well, Hywel,' he gasped, trying to steady his voice. He's injecting now and he's well and truly hooked. As for satisfying his customers, I've been overseeing his training myself...' Despite the recent battering, a faint leer flitted across Semple's face as he made this last remark.

'Hmm, I bet you have. I know your habit of dragging out the 'training' for as long as possible. I suggest you have the boy set up in a flat and earning his keep by tomorrow. As far as I'm concerned, training costs money, and I'm not in business to sponsor your disgusting habits. Do I make myself clear?'

'Yes Hywel,' whispered Semple, all too well aware that another beating was not out of the question.

'Good, then get out!' snarled Preece. 'Get out of my sight and clean yourself up!'

Semple dragged himself to his feet and staggered to the door. Not for the first time, he weaved his way blindly down the landing and into the toilet of the prestigious, first floor offices of Semple, Tucker and Preece.

*

It was eighteen minutes past two in the afternoon when the first man approached the house. He came hurrying down the pavement on Charlie's side and only crossed the road at the last moment. Through the binoculars Charlie saw him press the bell three times. He was admitted quite quickly, but not before the shutter of the Pentax had clicked open and closed half-a-dozen times. From then on a fairly steady trickle of customers arrived. They varied in age and dress, but they were all male and they were all cloaked in an air of furtiveness. By early evening he had photographed four men entering and leaving the building and it was clear, if anything, that trade was picking up.

He found himself wondering what exactly was going on behind those closed doors. He was pretty sure it involved young boys imported through a web of secrecy and deceit from distant parts of Britain. This was the business end of a sickening male prostitution ring where powerful predators held drug-addicted young boys in nightmare isolation, powerless to imagine, let alone exercise, the free will that ordinary people took for granted.

Okay, so how did all this square with his mission? If O'Connell was the man behind the Rent Man gang, there was no problem. In pursuing the gang he would also be pursuing his target. So what was his hypothesis?

An ex-IRA, homosexual psychopath looking to repair his damaged business empire needs a new identity. An embittered former MI6 spook with delusions of grandeur has taken over a law firm with a senior partner, Tucker, looking to retire. A link between O'Connell and Semple is developed via an internet paedophile ring and an introduction to Preece is made. A deal is struck and Tucker retires to Bonnie Scotland with a healthy kickback. Perhaps O'Connell continues to use Tucker's name as a convenient alias when it suits him. Preece and Semple reduce the law firm to an operating front, while O'Connell uses his old Iraqi connections to set up the drugs end of the business. The Rent Man Gang governs the prostitution and drug distribution with an iron fist. With tweaks and local variations, O'Connell clones the idea around other British ports. Perhaps it never even began in Swansea. The hypothesis worked, but was it only wishful thinking?

There was only one way to find out, and that was to force them out into the open, which from what Charlie had already seen, promised to be extremely dangerous. O'Connell's legendary ruthlessness clearly pervaded his whole organisation. Still, that was not the issue. The question was how far should he pursue the Rent Man gang in the hope that it ultimately led him to his personal quarry?

When Detachment Eight had tracked the drugs to Swansea and tasked him to look into how they were being distributed, things had seemed pretty simple and even held out some promise of settling his old score with O'Connell. Now, in the outside world, there were other evil men to confront like Preece and Semple. Regardless of any personal revenge, the Rent Man organisation needed stopping. If this meant extending his brief beyond his original mission, then so be it.

Suddenly he sat upright. A familiar face had just crossed the street and approached the door. He fired off a number of frames as the man knocked the door three times, then he grabbed the binoculars and studied him more closely. It was him alright! He had noticed him at the second surveillance the previous day. It was partly his swagger that set him apart from the other callers, and partly that he had stayed no more than five minutes, when the average stay was more like half-an-hour. Now he was back at another address. What was he up to?

Given the boot sale chic of his grubby tracksuit bottoms and hoodie, and the lack of socks under his cheap trainers, he didn't look like he had the money to support such a sex life, let alone the energy. More importantly, he had a cockiness about him which suggested that he believed he didn't need to pay for it. Perhaps he was some kind of pimp?

It struck Charlie that he was not going to find out sitting there. He knew now that, if he stayed in place, he was guaranteed ever more shots of men sidling up to that door, but that only suggested the use the place was being put to. It was important evidence, but it did not create a link with the really bad guys. For that, he had to get on the inside, and it was just possible that this man could turn out to be just the break he needed. He made a snap decision and began to unscrew the camera from the tripod.

*

Mort sauntered up the steps to the Club Casablanca and pressed the buzzer on the intercom.

'Club Casablanca, can I help you?' intoned a voice from the inside.

'Evenin' Duchess, it's Mort.'

'Come in.' The buzzer sounded and he pushed his way through the door. He sauntered down the dimly lit corridor until he came to the reproduction, leather-topped desk where Queenie O'Leary invariably sat.

'The boss in?'

She nodded.

'Course he is, ya soft shite, its payday ain't it? If you're goin' up, don't go pesterin' me girls, right. They don't need windin' up from a gobshite such as yourself when they're meant to be workin'.'

Mort grinned and swaggered on down the corridor. He paused in front of the fake-gilt mirror at the end of the corridor, whipped out a comb from his back pocket and raked it expertly through his thin, mousy hair. He grinned back at himself in approval, his self-esteem quite undented by the rows of jagged, black teeth the grin revealed. Satisfied with his sex appeal, he carried on into the lounge where several girls were sitting around waiting for clients.

'Hiya, babes,' he greeted them, 'now which of you slappers is up for a free jump this evenin', then?'

'You can go and jump in the docks for free,' suggested one of the girls indifferently.

'Up yours you twat. Tarts like you don't know what a decent shag is.'

'Hark at 'im girls! Thinks 'e's a bit of a stud now!' sneered the object of his affections.

'Smells like 'e's been on a stud farm more like,' commented one of her colleagues. 'He's fuckin' mingin' in that bloody track-suit!'

'Yeah,' added another, 'why don't you get your mam to take you to the charity shop and get you somethin' new, you smelly tosser. We don't want you 'angin' 'round 'ere, stinkin' the place out and puttin' off the customers. Go on, piss off or we'll call the Duchess!'

As usual, Mort's stock of repartee was all too quickly exhausted.

'Fuck you then, bloody lezzies!' he snarled. 'At least I'm not a pro!'

'No, you're a bloody renty, livin' off those poor little kiddies out there, so don't come in 'ere gettin' all chopsy, you smelly twat. Go on, fuck off!'

The girls returned to their nails and magazines, leaving Mort helpless in the face of their contempt. Having only succeeded in winding himself up, he stomped out of the lounge, heading for the back stairs. The girls and their customers used the first and second floors; he was headed for the office built into the third floor attic. This was reached by a flight of wooden stairs with a wobbly banister. He negotiated his way past the boxes which were piled permanently on top of them and knocked three times on the door at the top. After a moment someone peered at him through the door viewer, then the door was opened and he went in.

Some of the boys had made it in before him. They were sitting on the benches around the walls, waiting to cash in their day's takings. He sat down next to Dai Shit. He unzipped his hoodie and pulled up his tee-shirt to get at the money belt he wore underneath.

'For fucks sake Mort, don't you ever wash? You're bloody hangin' mun! I'm only sayin' for your own good, like.'

Mort was already sorting out a fistful of notes.

'It's me glands, Dai.'

'Glands my arse! Glands don't make you smell of piss. You wanna cut back on the pop, butty!'

Mort scowled.

'Will you fuckin' shut it? You just made me lose count.' He slapped the two piles of notes back together and began again.

About ten minutes later Dai went up to pay in his takings. Then it was Mort's turn. He walked up and slipped the wad of notes into the trough beneath the pane of bullet-proof glass. As always, O'Leary's thirty stone bulk was seated, Buddha-like, on the other side. His fat paw, heavy with gold sovereigns, reached out and claimed the money from amongst the empty coke cans, fag packets, and takeaway wrappers that cluttered his desk.

'And what would we be havin' here then, young fella?'

'That's six 'undred and eighty from Missy and Rocco.'

O'Leary licked his thumb, and then counted through it with astonishing speed. Satisfied, he nodded.

'And how much gear are ya wantin'?'

'Missy's askin' for an extra fiver's worth a day.' Mort saw O'Leary's eyebrows raise a fraction, but otherwise his fat features remained impassive.

'Why? The stuff he's gettin' is good as it gets. What would he be needin' that much more for?'

'Says he's depressed, like. Got hit around by a punter the other day.'

'Well what does he think we're here for? Tell him I'll have one of the boys keep an eye for a week and if the bugger comes back we'll sort him out. Up his allowance by a gram a week top end. We don't want the little wanker o.d.ing on us, now do we?'

'Right boss.'

'Oh, and another thing. I had a call from the top brass earlier. Word is there could be a snooper around. Fella by the name of Charlie Llewellyn, but probably not callin' himself that. Keep your eyes open and if you're approached by anyone, don't spook him. Just let me know directly on your mobile. There's your money.'

O'Leary slid an envelope under the glass; his standard form of dismissal. At the bottom of the stairs, Mort stopped and tore it open. He counted out two hundred and thirty quid, which was correct as usual. Brilliant! He had a shed full of beer tokens and an evening out with the boys to look forward to!

*

He had just stopped in for a pint before catching the bus out to the Hafod. He was on his third when the bloke asked him if the stool next to him was free. Funnily enough, the stools on either side of him were. As he sat down, the man knocked the bar with his pint and some of it splashed on Mort's trousers. He was dead sorry. Christ, if he wasn't so skint he'd pay to have them cleaned. Really, could he buy him a pint by way of apology? Fair do's, he bought him a pint and it turned out he'd just come out of Swansea nick. Mort bought him one back, because he'd been there himself, and they got chatting.

He was looking for work, but it wasn't easy with his record.

'What was that, then?'

'Oh, a bit of ABH and possession of an unlicensed shotgun.'

Shit! What was wrong with that? There were bouncers working the clubs who would call that qualifications.

Another pint and it turned out he'd also been caught in that drug raid up the valleys a few years back, which is what he'd just finished doing time for. They solemnly agreed that that was a bit of a more serious blot on the charge sheet. Still, Mort thought he might know someone who could help him out. Did he want him to arrange a meet? The bloke couldn't believe his luck at first and insisted on buying another. Jesus! Fancy bumping into his butty Mort and getting a result like that! Mort called his boss on his mobile and had a word. No problem. His boss would see him tomorrow morning. Eleven o'clock at the Club Casablanca. Ask for Duke. He was a tidy fella and didn't hold things against people.

17

Annette hurried down Derwen Fawr Road, her mind in turmoil. Her trip into town two days before had been stressful, but nothing compared to this! She had obviously done a convincing imitation of someone lapsing into a drunken stupor because the Bitch's voice was brimming with contempt when she said:

'Come on dear, it's bedtime. Do we think we can make it up the stairs?' She never missed an opportunity to express her contempt.

She had allowed herself to be escorted upstairs and had slurred her assurances that she would be quite okay to get undressed herself. She had then waited inside her bedroom door until the Bitch's footsteps had retreated back downstairs and she had heard the lounge door shut. She had then slipped back out of her room and tiptoed down to the hall.

She had eased open the front door and closed it behind her with the faintest of clicks. Then she had retrieved her handbag and a rain mac from the cupboard in the porch where she had hidden them earlier. She had slipped out of the porch door and skirted around the front of the house, hugging the wall to stay out of range of the automatic floodlight. She had been surreptitiously checking these details as she pottered around tidying up the front garden that morning.

Now, as she pushed on through the squalling rain, her mind was overwhelmed by the enormity of her actions. She was leaving her husband. She was walking out on the man to whom she had been married for the last twelve years. The fact that the marriage had been little more than a catalogue of abuse made it all the more daunting. Like so many victims she had become dependent on her torturer.

The previous day had been spent gearing up as much as possible for the flight. She knew it had to be this evening, because Hywel had a lodge meeting, which greatly increased her chances of getting away undetected. Furthermore, she was running out of time if she was to stand any hope of gathering evidence against her husband. The money she had withdrawn would be showing up in the account and the cat would be out of the bag the moment Hywel noticed.

The local phone directory had listed Comfy Discount Furnishings Ltd in its business pages. The address was tucked in her bag along with a brand new copy of the Swansea A-Z and the remains of the money she had withdrawn two days before. She reached the bottom of the road and turned right into the pay-and-display car park, which served that stretch of the sea front. Much to her relief, despite the rain, she could make out the outline of the Volkswagen Polo she had bought from a backstreet garage in Brynmill two days earlier.

It had been advertised in the Evening Post, which she had bought after her visit to the bank. When Juliet had been forced to pop out the following day, she had phoned the number and taken a cab over there. The man had sworn it was a private sale on behalf of his mam, who only ever popped out to the shops in it, like. Hence the mileage. Annette chose to ignore his oily overalls and the fact that he had to get out from beneath another car to explain this. She was taking a gamble anyway. She had neither the time nor expertise to shop around. Moreover her knees were shaking like jelly at the prospect of a test drive. This was the first time she had sat behind a steering wheel since that fateful accident all those years ago.

To her surprise, after a few stalls and fumbles with the indicator switch, the driving came flooding back. The car started first time and seemed fairly nippy. There was no smoke pouring out and she could hear no alarming noises so she paid the man eight hundred and fifty pounds for it. She even knocked him down by fifty pounds, though she had no idea if he was asking a fair price in the first place.

She drove away rejoicing. She could hardly believe she had done it! After years of hopeless dependency on drink and her tyrannical husband, this single act of independence took on enormous significance in her mind. It gave her hope.

Now, as she approached the car, some of that resolve came back. It had collected a parking ticket, but at least it hadn't been stolen! Hywel could deal with the ticket as a little token of her affection. She threw it in the glove compartment and went around to check her boot. The clothes and make-up she had invested in, following the purchase of the car, were still neatly packed in her new holdall. Good. She closed the boot and climbed into the driver's seat.

She started the engine and panicked for a moment trying to remember how to turn on the lights. She got them on, but stalled as she tried to reverse out of her parking space. She took some deep breaths to calm herself and tried again, this time with more success. Despite the overwhelming urge to get away, she took the time to drive a couple of laps of the car park, getting the feel of the gears and steering again, then she pulled out and turned left onto the Mumbles Road, heading towards town.

*

Annette lit another shaky cigarette to steady her nerves. This was the fifth time she had had to stop to consult her A-Z. She had stopped twice on her way to Fforestfach, but that was just to check her bearings- she hadn't been there since before she left home for Drama College in London. Her real problems began when she reached the industrial estate. It was like a maze made more bewildering by the sporadic street lightning and pouring rain. Her headlights picked out large, redbrick, Victorian-looking warehouses selling tiles, discount clothes and furniture from house clearances. She was passing fairly modern buildings, but she couldn't be sure what sort of business they were engaged in. Suddenly her headlights were shining on a sign that said Queensway. That was it! She slowed and turned into another squall of driving rain.

She reached the end of the road. Nothing. She had somehow expected a big building with a jaunty sign across the front. Furniture took up a lot of floor space. Then she reminded herself that the company did not sell to the public, and, besides, it was highly questionable to what degree it was a real furniture store. She remembered a couple of small redbrick buildings about halfway down and set back from the road. Perhaps those were worth a look. She turned the car and cruised slowly back down the way she had come. Before she reached the point from which she reckoned she would be able to see the buildings, she pulled in and killed her lights. She glanced at her watch. It was five-to-ten. The whole area was utterly deserted. Did she lock the car? What car thief would be hanging around in this industrial wilderness in the pouring rain at this time of night? She decided to leave the driver's door unlocked in case she found herself beating a hasty retreat.

She stepped out into the rain, pulling the hood of the rain mac over her head, and closed the car door. Gusts of wind and chilly rain buffeted her from behind as if driving her forward into the unknown. She found herself making an effort to keep her imagination in check. The buildings came into view. The first appeared deserted. By the light of blurry street light, she could make out weeds growing out of cracks in the concrete apron at the front. The windows were boarded up with sheets of plywood.

The second unit was less dilapidated. There were bars on the windows and, although no lights were showing, there was a car parked outside the front door. She walked cautiously down the short approach of the road and began working her way around the perimeter of the parking area keeping as much as possible in the shadow of the untidy shrubs that boarded it. The car was a sporty, red, two-door Toyota. She crept forward and put her hand on the exhaust. It was still quite hot. Someone had arrived in it fairly recently. She tried the front door of the building. It was locked. There was no sign identifying it occupants. A phrase from Tucker's message on the answer phone came back to her:

'...this kid he's got stashed in the extension.'

A flashy sports car didn't prove she had found Comfy

Discounts Furnishings Ltd, but some sort of extension on the building would strengthen her case. She peered down the side of the building. It was pitch black. She began to feel her way along the brick wall. She encountered the odd brick with her foot and a sheet of what felt like corrugated iron with her out-stretched hand. After what seemed like an eternity she reached the end of the building and turned the corner.

At the back of the warehouse, out of the shadow of the building next door, the background glow of the city silhouetted a protruding part of the building against the night sky. It was lower than the main structure. Annette stepped forward and pressed her hand against the wall. Instead of the smooth brickwork she could feel the coarseness of breeze blocks. She traced the line of cement between the blocks to confirm the difference in the building materials. She had found an extension.

She paused to think. What could she do? She probably couldn't break in and, if she did, what might she encounter in there? She wasn't armed and wouldn't know what to do if she were. Tucker wanted the 'kid' moved out of there. Maybe that was happening tonight. If it was, she still had a fighting chance of discovering what was going on. Perhaps she could track down Charlie Llewellyn, if he was still alive and enlist his help. This could be the very lead he was looking for.

Her mind made up, she turned to go, but froze in terror. A dark figure stepped out of the shadows and a glove hand wrapped itself tightly over her mouth as a voice in her ear murmured:

'Now I wonder what Mrs Annette Preece would be doing sneaking around in a place like this, in the pouring rain, in the middle of the night?'

18

It was just coming up to six-forty as Mort hitched his buttock up off the bar stool, broke wind loudly with immense satisfaction, and announced his bus was leaving shortly. He apologised to his butty for having to dip out, like, but he was off out with the boys for the night and had to get home first. The meet with O'Leary? Think nothing of it. Glad to be of service. See you around, mate.

Charlie watched Mort's profile through the frosted glass of the pub window as he disappeared around the corner en route for the bus station. He drained his own glass and left the pub. He strode off in the direction of St James Crescent, weaving his way through the milling shoppers and office workers still bustling around the city centre. He reached the tranquillity of the Crescent in ten minutes flat and was relieved to see Semple's red Toyota standing on its own outside the office. Better still it wasn't directly under a street lamp.

As he walked briskly around the Crescent he pulled a bunch of keys from his pocket and sorted through them until he found the Toyota skeleton key. He reached the back of the car and glanced around. There was no one in sight. He crouched down, slid the key into the lock and probed until he felt it turn. He popped it, partially raised the lid, and squeezed himself into the cramped space as the alarm went berserk.

He lay utterly still, wondering how Semple would react to the second alarm in a week. Under normal circumstances he would see his car wasn't being stolen or broken into and simply turn it off, but, if they had discovered the break-in, he might be unusually suspicious. Still he'd be unlikely to imagine that someone was hiding in the boot. He heard footsteps approaching, and then the noise stopped. The footsteps came nearer. He was walking around the back of the car. Charlie's body tensed and his right fist clenched. Mr "you to fuck off" Semple was in for a nasty shock if he opened that boot. He heard the metallic tap of a signet ring and a dry rubbing noise. Semple was running his hand along the bumper, probably checking to see that he hadn't been nudged by a car from behind as it was pulling out. He was apparently satisfied, because Charlie heard his steps receding.

He forced himself to relax again, despite the claustrophobia he could feel nibbling at the edges of his self-control. The parcel shelf above his head allowed a little grey light to filter into the blackness. A couple of minutes later Semple returned and got into the car. The interruption of the car alarm had obviously persuaded him to finish for the day. Charlie heard the engine start and felt the car get underway. It reached the end of the Crescent and turned right. Good, Semple was heading away from the Marina where, according to his registration at Companies House, he owned or rented a flat. At least he wasn't going straight home for the evening.

Charlie ran his fingers along the back ledge of the boot searching for a catch, but all he encountered was smooth plastic. A wave of real claustrophobia washed over him now. He couldn't get at the lock from inside. He was trapped in the boot! With an effort he steadied himself. No need to flap. He could kick the parcel shelf out if he had to. It was more important to concentrate on matching the car's changes of direction to the map he was holding in his head.

At that moment the opening chords of Child in Time by Deep Purple opened up next to his ear. There were speakers fitted in the boot and Semple clearly liked his music loud. Charlie frowned – it was so loud that it was distorting grotesquely. Suddenly, despite the discomfort of the cramped conditions, he grinned – that wasn't distortion, it was Semple singing. He hoped to God they reached their destination before the wailing bit at the end of the song.

The interruption had broken his concentration. As far as he could tell, they were headed in the direction of Fforestfach. Could that mean Comfy Discount Furnishing? There wasn't much else out there that Charlie could imagine would interest Semple. One thing was certain; he needed to figure a way to get out of the car. If Semple stopped and reset the alarm the ultra sound system would activate if he so much as twitched. There was no way out of the back, so the only other option was to escape through the front. At least the din in the car would cover any noise he made.

He gently lifted the back edge of the parcel shelf. It rose about an inch, tilting on its hinges, before pressing up against the boot lid. He let it drop. Fine, it was a standard design, which meant the hinges on the front edge should unhook to allow for its removal. He worked his fingers in around the leading edge and levered backwards. The shelf slid back and came clear of its hinges. Charlie eased it back into place, but held it in position instead of reinserting the hinges.

The car turned left, then left again and then swung hard left as if pulling into a parking space. The music died as the engine stopped and he heard Semple's door open. He raised the shelf a fraction of an inch and peeped out. He could see lights on the dual carriageway of the Carmarthen Road. They had stopped in the car park of the Marquis Arms. He lowered the shelf as Semple shut the door. Would he set the alarm? On past history, he was careless with security devices, but he had already had one reminder this evening. Charlie cursed under his breath as he heard the device beep.

What was Semple up to? The Marquis Arms was a family pub, not the sort of den he could imagine Semple habituating. It was also a long way off his patch. He might have a meeting there. But why there? This had more of the feel of someone stopping off for a quickie after work on his way to somewhere else. It struck him that Fforestfach was only just down the road. He had the suspicion that Semple's average day was built around drinks breaks of the alcoholic variety. None of that, however, was solving the problem of how to escape from the car. Short of giving his presence away, he was trapped and the prospect of a night in Semple's boot did not appeal. The claustrophobia was beginning to take some holding back.

A few minutes later another set of lights swung into the car park. The car pulled in next to Semple's. Charlie made a decision. It was risky, but it could be his last chance. He waited until the driver slammed his door, and then lifted the shelf a couple of inches. Instantly, the car alarm sprang to life. Charlie watched as the driver spun around in confusion then hurried towards the door of the pub.

He lifted the shelf and dived forward in one movement. His

hand went down beside the driver's seat, scrabbling for the boot release. He found a lever and pressed it. He heard the catch pop. He kicked back with one foot to open the hatchback. He dragged himself backwards and pushed it up. He could hear the dialogue running in his head:

'Anyone in here own a red Toyota?'

'Aye, what's wrong?'

'Sorry, mate. I just pulled in next to you and set off your alarm.'

'Oh, right, the bloody thing's buggering about at the moment, I'll sort it now.'

How long would Semple take? Would he pause to finish his drink? Charlie was out of the car. He straightened the shelf and closed the boot. Still no sign. There was clearly no value to hanging around in the pub car park. At that moment he saw the movement at the rear door of the pub. It was Semple. Charlie slipped back into the shadows at the perimeter of the garden and watched him turn off the alarm.

This time he did check in the boot. He repositioned the shelf on its hinges and shut it, then he walked around to the passenger door, opened it, and leant inside. He emerged suddenly with a powerful flashlight in his hand and flashed it around the car park. Charlie retreated behind a bush just in time. Next he knelt down beside the car, despite the rain, and inspected the underneath of the vehicle. Finally, he released the bonnet and flashed the light over the engine. Apparently satisfied, he climbed into the driver's seat and started the engine. As Semple turned left out of the car park and pulled out onto the Carmarthen Road, Charlie found himself wondering how many Swansea solicitors felt the need to check that their cars had not been tampered with just because their car alarms went off twice in one day.

*

According to his watch it had taken him twenty-five minutes to make his way from the Marquis Arms to the warehouse on the Queensway. It was only a ten minute walk, but Charlie had taken the time to ensure he wasn't seen as he approached the registered office of Comfy Discount Furnishing. He made his way silently down through the shrubs on the embankment in front of the forecourt. He had guessed right. Semple's car was parked outside, even though he could see no lights from within the building. He squatted down on his heels and began to survey the area. What was going on in there? A drugs factory? If he went in, was he walking in on a heavily armed gang, or was Semple in there, on his own, catching up on some paperwork? There was no way of telling. It was certainly a perfect location for a drugs factory – anonymous during the day and deserted at night.

A car cruised past on the road behind him, its headlights distorting in the driving rain. A lookout? Charlie hunkered down in the bushes to wait and see what it did on its return trip – the road was a dead end. A few moments later he caught the faintest purr of an engine. It died abruptly. Did the driver have a vantage point from which he conducted routine patrols? He decided to wait ten minutes, then take a closer look; without someone to mind his back, his only protection was painstaking caution.

He caught the movement on the slope leading down to the parking area. Whoever it was, was moving with distinct furtiveness, bending low and hugging the shadows cast by the bushes. Charlie moved onto his stomach and wriggled back further into the darkness. It was a woman! He could see a skirt flapping around her knees as the wind gusted behind her. She was barely five yards away as she bent and felt the exhaust of Semple's car. She straightened and approached the front of the building. Whatever she was up to, her approach was nearly as clandestine as his own. As she turned back from inspecting the door, the watery glow from the street lamps up on the road illuminated her face. It was Annette Preece!

What in God's name was she doing skulking around a deserted industrial estate in the pouring rain, in the middle of the night? To the best of Charlie's knowledge she should be wandering, sloshed, around her mansion in Derwen Fawr. Charlie had only caught a glimpse in bad light, but from what he could see her face was grim with tension, not flaccid with drink.

He watched as she hesitated then crept off down the side of the building. This was not the behaviour of someone hand-in-glove with the villains. He wondered if he had found a potential ally. He rose and followed her silently. He watched as she rounded the corner. She seemed to be examining the walls. Why was she there? What did she know? There was only one way to find out. As she turned to go, he stepped out of the shadows and clamped a hand firmly over her mouth.

*

She tried to struggle, but it was hopeless. His hand was too big to bite and an arm was around her, pinning her arms to her sides. She connected once with a back-heel to the shin and heard him grunt with pain, but he obviously was not going to release her thanks to that! A voice whispered surprisingly gently in her ear.

'I'm sorry to scare you Mrs Preece,' he whispered hoarsely. 'It's Charlie Llewellyn. Please listen. I'm not going to hurt you!'

She stopped struggling.

'If I let you go, promise you won't scream, because if you do I'll have to knock you out and run. Do you understand?'

She nodded as vigorously as the hand would allow.

'Okay, I'm letting go. I'm sorry to frighten you, but you mustn't make a noise, right?'

She nodded again and felt the grip relax, but not release her altogether.

'Would you mind telling me what you're doing here?'

'I've left my husband,' replied Annette, as if that would explain her presence on a windswept industrial estate in the middle of the night.

'And wealthy Swansea women come here at night when they've left their husbands, do they?'

'No, I've come out here because I believe he and his business partners are involved in some sort of crime.'

'Really, and what makes you think that?'

'I overheard a man called O'Connell on Hywel's voicemail. It gave the impression that they are holding someone here as a prisoner. A young boy mixed up in drugs.'

'Did it indeed?' Charlie paused, and when he spoke again,

his tone was less sceptical. 'If you don't mind my saying, you seem very forthcoming.'

'When that story about you jumping off the boat appeared in the paper, Hywel was so furious he beat me up.'

'Why, it wasn't your fault.'

'He's beaten me for years. It got where I thought it was normal. Then I overheard him and your wife worrying that you weren't dead after all and I began to hope that you might come back. They seemed scared of you. Anyway, I stopped drinking and decided to run away.'

'That must have taken some doing.' Charlie nodded towards the building. 'So what do you think's going on in there?'

Annette related Tucker's voicemail message. Charlie listened carefully and stopped her on a couple of occasions to check details; then he briefly explained his own findings.

'Good God, it's unbelievable,' muttered Annette as he finished. 'What are we going to do?'

'We?'

'Well you can't tackle all this on your own, and I do have my uses you know!'

'Sure, I'm beginning to realise that. You have a car parked up on the road haven't you?'

'Yes.'

'Fine, I mistook you for a lookout at first, but I don't think they have any posted. Given there's only Semple's car here and everything seems so quiet, I reckon they rely on keeping a low profile, but I'd like you outside in your car with the engine running just to be on the safe side. Is that okay?'

'Certainly, what are you planning to do?'

'Well, first off I'll rescue this kid if I can – assuming they haven't moved him. What happens after that I can't say, except that things are likely to start coming to a head very fast and I won't be taking any prisoners.'

'Meaning?'

'I'm not a policeman, I don't have any powers of arrest and these people are very dangerous. If you throw in your lot with me you're risking your life.'

Charlie sensed her nod in the darkness.

'I reckon my life isn't worth a fig as long as my husband's at liberty; I'll get the car shall I?'

*

Charlie slipped the cut-down loyalty card back in his pocket and eased the door open. He was guessing that Semple would have disabled the alarm on entry, but he couldn't be sure how sophisticated the security was in here. He slipped inside and put the Yale lock on the latch. A quick flick around with his pencil torch revealed a standard warehouse trade counter. He lifted his backside gently onto the counter top, swung his legs around and lowered himself down on the other side. He moved over to the inner door that led 'out back'. He eased it open and again slipped through. Still no jangling alarms thank God!

At the far end of the room he could see another door framed by the light filtering through the gaps around it. According to the geography of the building this was the door to the extension. Very slowly, feeling forward with his feet, Charlie began to work his way across the warehouse. He reached the door and paused. Did he kick and charge, or did he kick and step back behind the wall. Given the lack of reaction so far, he had to believe he still had the element of surprise. Without a gun, he needed to get in as close and fast as possible to use his hands and feet. He backed up a few yards, braced himself and charged the door. It flew open as his shoulder hit it and his momentum carried him through. He stopped dead and raised his hands.

A young, teenage boy lay naked on a mattress on the floor. His expression was vacant. Semple had obviously had time to pull on a pair of boxer shorts. He was holding a gun and it was pointing at Charlie. On the desk beside him lay an empty syringe and other bits of drug paraphernalia including a rolled up five pound note and a mirror. Semple's eyes were glittering and he looked extremely jittery. When he spoke his voice cracked with nervous tension.

'Well, if it isn't the f-fucking g-ghost himself!' he stammered. 'Thought you'd p-pop in and surprise me d-did you?'

Charlie had not noticed a stutter when they last met. The man was obviously as high as a kite. He wondered how unstable it might make him.

'Something like that.'

'Yes well we don't like noisy alarms around here,' the slyness of triumphant paranoia played across his face. 'You've been sounding a b-buzzer every step of the way across that room you f-fucking simpleton!'

Charlie shrugged.

'Bad stutter you've got there pal. Too much coke making you jumpy, eh?'

He took a step forward.

'What's it got to do with you? And stay where you are!'

'What's the problem? You've got the gun.'

'You're f-fucking right I have, and if you come any closer, I'll use it!'

'No you won't. It takes nerve to shoot someone. A tosspot like you wouldn't have the bottle.'

Charlie saw Semple's finger whiten on the trigger and swayed aside. The bullet missed him by a foot, but it made him pause. Semple was more dangerous than he'd anticipated.

'There you are,' he continued casually. 'Not as easy as it looks on telly, is it? Shooting at the wall isn't going to scare me. What you've got to do is point the gun so the bullet hits me when you pull the trigger, you chickenshit coward.'

'You're f-fucking mad!'

'No, you're fucking mad. Look at you man! Coked out of your skull; stuttering like an idiot; shaking so much you can't even point that gun straight. I ought to take that off you and shove it up your arse! Charlie's voice had risen to a parade ground shout. Semple was still pointing the gun vaguely in his direction, but he was cowering. Again, he loosed off a shot, but he wasn't even looking where he was aiming. He had his arm raised as if to ward off a blow. Under the pressure Charlie was exerting, the cocaine rush had turned from bravado to paranoia.

'Leave me alone!' he screamed. 'Leave me alone you fucking bastard!'

Charlie stepped in fast, knocking the gun aside with his left hand and slamming his right elbow up under the man's jaw.

Semple staggered back and Charlie's right foot lashed up into his groin. He groaned and doubled over retching as Charlie smashed a fist into his right temple. He slumped to the floor, unconscious.

Charlie walked over to the young man and lifted his emaciated arm.

'Can you hear me?' he asked gently.

'What've ya done to me mate?' asked the youth, dully, in a thick Geordie accent.

'He wasn't your mate, boy,' said Charlie quietly. 'He was a murdering little bastard, controlled by a bigger, murdering bastard. I've come to help you. Have you got any clothes?'

The boy shook his head slowly.

'Nah, they've tooken them away ages ago, like. Ah bin nekkid like this ages noo.'

Charlie remembered being made to strip in front of the Iraqi guards. He understood. It was all part of the humiliation and subjugation intended to break your will.

'Wait there a second,' he said. He walked over to Semple's prone figure and dragged him into the middle of the room; then he bent down and pulled off his boxer shorts. He helped the boy stand up and steadied him while he put them on, then he helped him to dress in the rest of Semple's clothes.

'Come with me,' he said encouragingly. 'There's a lady outside who's going to look after you.' He put an arm around the boy's shoulders and guided him carefully across the floor of the dark warehouse. Annette was waiting outside with the engine running. He beckoned her forward. As she pulled up he opened the door and helped the boy into the passenger seat.

'Have you got a name son?'

'Aye, Bomber.'

'Right, Bomber, this is...'

'Netty,' interrupted Annette, remembering her old nickname from drama school – somehow she didn't think Bomber would get along with 'Annette'.

'Hiya, Netty. Nice to meet ya,' mumbled the boy. 'The man says ya gonna look after us.'

'That's right Bomber, I'll certainly do my best.'

Charlie cut across them.

'Listen, you two get to know each other while I go and tidy up in there. If anyone turns up, drive off and keep going. If they follow you, drive to the nearest Police station and run inside. Explain who you are and demand refuge. I'll be back in a few minutes.' He turned on his heel and disappeared back into the warehouse.

*

Semple was stirring as Charlie walked back into the room. He tried to sit up. Charlie pushed him back down and knelt down on his left arm, trapping his wrist and biceps. He reached over to the desk and picked up the syringe. He held it up in front of his eyes and pulled the plunger out to about two-thirds of its length. He bent forward and grabbed Semple by the hair. He twisted his head to one side.

'What are you doing, man?' croaked the lawyer.

'Giving you an injection.'

'What of?'

'Air.'

'You can't do that! It'll kill me!'

'So what? You just tried to kill me. You didn't seem to see anything wrong in that.'

'So you're going to kill me for trying to defend myself?'

Charlie paused.

'Alright then, if you want to defend yourself, you can start by helping me right now.'

'How?'

'Well you can start by answering a few questions.'

Charlie saw a glimmer of hope spark up in Semple's shifty eyes.

'Such as?'

'Well who is, or was, Tucker?'

'The Old Man? He was the boss before Hywel took over. Originally the firm was Tucker, Carnegie and Co. The two of them moved to Swansea after a fag scandal up in Edinburgh back in the olden days. They set up down here and ran a steady family practice until Carnegie got AIDS and Tucker broke his heart to learn that his partner had been shagging around. Carnegie died and Tucker struggled on until Hywel turned up and paid him a few bob to fuck off back to Scotland. We've never heard from him since.'

Semple was almost babbling in his eagerness to buy a reprieve.

'How did you get involved?'

'Tucker and I were shagging on and off; I was doing it mainly for the scraps of work he threw my way. Anyhow, when Hywel took over he offered me a job. I couldn't believe my luck; he seemed so straight-laced I assumed he hadn't spotted the booze and the charlie and he seemed totally oblivious to my, er, sexual preferences. I fell for that alright!'

'What do you mean?'

'What do I mean? I mean Hywel is way beyond anything I'm into. Okay I've got a weakness for boys, but I'm gay and I like fresh meat. Alright I like to powder my nose and I drink more than I should, but that's self-inflicted damage. Hywel gets off on damaging other people. He's straight, but he's a psycho and that bitch he's fucking is something out of De Sade.'

'So how did you end up doing this?' Charlie nodded at the sordid surroundings.

Semple shrugged.

Hywel's clever. He knew my weaknesses from the outset. It wasn't long before he had enough to blackmail me with and then he began to show his hand. It wasn't exactly hard to reel me in. He had me watched until he'd built up a complete fucking file on me and then gave me a choice of a free diet of young boys, coke and gin, or a diet of old lags, gruel and mail bags. It was a bit of a no-brainer given my predilections.'

'Do you know a man called Patrick O'Connell?'

'No, but Hywel does.'

'How do you know that?'

'Well, blackmail cuts both ways and, besides, us queens love a bit of gossip. I happened to be outside Hywel's door the other morning when I heard him on the phone to a man he called O'Connell at one point; they were talking about you if I'm not mistaken. Hywel seemed quite cross, then he calmed down and called the man Pat from then on. It must have upset him because, when he called me in a bit later, he blamed me for a problem with the building's alarm system and beat the crap out of me; he enjoys that.'

'What else do you know about him?'

'Who?'

'O'Connell.'

'Nothing really; I've never laid eyes on him, but I assume he's the boss, or at least higher up than Hywel. Once he calmed down Hywel seemed keen to keep him happy when they were on the phone, and I've noticed Hywel seems to get wound up if there's a problem with a shipment or any of the kids, like there's pressure from above.'

'What is the Rent Man Gang?'

'It's just the part of the business that runs the prostitution and extortion end of things.'

'Extortion?'

'I believe the punters are caught on hidden camera and blackmailed.'

'Why Rent Man?'

'I dunno. Rent Man, Rent Boys, it has a ring. It's just a gang name that seems to strike fear. Some hack on the Evening Post probably coined it and it stuck. Anyhow, Hywel keeps everything compartmentalised and I'm happy to keep my nose out of that stuff.'

'So that's it. Anything else you'd like to tell me?'

''No, that's it.'

'Fine,' Charlie picked up the syringe and twisted Semple's head back again.

'No wait! What are you doing?' he gasped.

'I don't think you've helped me enough yet. Who's in charge of the Rent Man Gang, for example? I'm sure Preece doesn't get his hands dirty.'

'I dunno...'

Charlie brought the needle up into his line of vision.

'I dunno, but it could be a man called Duke.'

'What makes you think that?'

'There was a bit of a panic about something a couple of months ago and, for once, Hywel left his phone on his desk. I risked a quick peek and that name was top of his Frequent Contacts. I've heard him on the phone to a man called Duke as well, though Hywel cuts it short if he realises I'm about.'

'I see, well thanks for that.'

Charlie moved the syringe up against Semple's neck.

'Stop! You said you wouldn't kill me for defending myself!'

'I'm not. I'm going to kill you for what you've done to Bomber and all the other kids. Count yourself lucky. It'll be quick.'

Charlie inserted the needle in the man's neck. He drew back the plunger a quarter of an inch more and watched blood spurt through. It was in his jugular.

Semple tried to struggle. Veins were standing out on his forehead and his face was puce. There were flecks of white spittle at the corner of his mouth. Charlie pushed home the plunger, pulled out the needle and stood up. Semple froze with realisation, his eyes wide with horror, and then his face twisted into an agonised grimace as the embolism reached his brain. He lay still. Charlie pulled off a glove, reached down and felt his wrist. There was no pulse.

He straightened up and gathered up the items on the desk. At the door he paused to look back. Semple's naked body lay huddled on the concrete floor. For a moment he felt a fleeting glimpse of pity, but it was pity for a sordid end to a worthless life, not pity for the man. Still, it was no doubt more sympathy than his colleagues would feel for him; they would not be pleased to find themselves dealing with Semple's naked corpse in the morning. Charlie pulled the door shut on the squalid scene and headed for the exit.

19

Hywel Preece sipped at his tomato juice and Worcester sauce as he gazed out to sea. He glanced at his watch. It was nearly ten-fifteen. Dark clouds were rolling across the night sky and below him he could hear breakers crashing against the rocks at the foot of the cliff. Behind him in the function room of the hotel he heard a ripple of applause as the assembled masons greeted Chief Inspector Ringer's announcement of another successful fundraising event with bored approval. He hated lodge meetings, but unfortunately they did provide some useful contacts and a chance to talk in real privacy.

'If he's still out there, I'm gonna be fuckin' pissed off with you,' remarked a quiet male voice in a soft Irish accent. Preece glanced around as the man walked through the patio doors and moved forward to join him. As always at such functions, O'Connell was immaculately dressed. From his black, patent leather shoes up to his carefully trimmed moustache and combed grey hair, his appearance was faultless to the point of fastidiousness. His face had a freshly-scrubbed pinkness about it, which in artificial light gave it an almost made-up look.

The fastidiousness of his appearance, however, was offset by his size, in particular his huge hands and head, which gave him an air of raw physical power. He always struck Preece as looking like a successful Tory candidate. His eyes were such a pale blue that the colour was barely discernible. They totally lacked any suggestion of humour or empathy. They were killers' eyes. Preece nodded a perfunctory greeting.

'Evening Patrick.'

'Evening Hywel. Heard anything yet?'

Preece shook his head.

'Not a dickey bird, but the office was definitely broken into and my files downloaded thanks to that idiot Semple.'

'You can't blame him entirely. We should have topped the bastard at the outset like I said. Made it look like an accident or, better still, put the word around it was a Rent Man job.'

'Yes, well it was a personal matter and I didn't want it involving the business.'

'Well it's certainly involvin' the business now.'

'That's as may be, but I control the respectable end of things and that was how I chose to play it.'

'Fine, and I control the whole organisation and I would have it played differently. You'd better sort this out, because if I have to deal with it, there's no tellin' who will get caught in the crossfire.'

'Is that a threat?'

The cold eyes held Preece in their icy gaze for a long moment. O'Connell was clearly in no hurry to issue a denial. Finally, he looked back out to sea and spoke in his usual even tones.

'Not as it stands, but you'd better sort this out before I have to. We have a hand-picked selection of the city's most dangerous criminals on our books, so we don't need to be pussy footin' around with the bastard. He and I go back a long way. He's a dangerous fucker and so is the organisation he works for, so he needs sortin'.'

'You didn't tell me that.'

'I don't tell you everything.'

'What if we can't find him?'

'He'll show. As you said on the phone, he's going to need a lot more evidence than he downloaded, which means he's going to have to get right up close. With everyone looking out for him he doesn't stand a chance.'

Preece's mobile rang. A voice at the other end simply said:

'Are you free to talk?'

'No. This phone's in my name. Wait a minute. We'll call you back on a pay phone.' He broke the connection and knocked back his tomato juice. The two men walked quickly back through the function room to the pay phone in the hotel's reception. Preece picked up the receiver, dialled O'Leary's number, and fed some change into the machine. It was answered almost instantly.

'O'Leary.'

'What have you got?'

'A possible contact.'

'Go on.'

'One of the boys stopped off for a drink on his way home from work. A tallish fella came onto him. Reckoned he'd just been kicked out of Her Majesty's bedsitter on the Oystermouth Road and was lookin' for work. Had the right sort of qualifications.'

'What did our man do?'

'He's fixed up a meet for tomorrow.'

'Fine. See what you think of him and if he fits the bill you can organise a reception committee for him. Make sure you offer him a permanent position.'

'You're sure you want it permanent?'

'Absolutely. Put the best boys you've got on the job.'

'Right you are. I'll sort it straight away.'

Preece hung up and turned to O'Connell. There was an air of triumph about him. When he spoke his voice rang with self-vindication.

'It looks like one of our boys has been approached by a likely candidate and I think I made it quite clear to O'Leary that he's not to pussy foot around with him.'

'Oh, indeed you did,' murmured his business partner dryly. 'Let's hope it's the right fella. You wouldn't want an innocent party on your conscience, would you?'

For a moment uncertainty flickered across Preece's face, then he made a grab for the higher ground.

'Are you sure O'Leary can handle this? From what you say Llewellyn's hardly some doped up kid who's gone off the rails.'

O'Connell shrugged.

'Duke was my head enforcer in the IRA. He can handle it. If Llewellyn's planning to get himself recruited as a Rent Man, I can guarantee you Duke won't pussy foot around. By the way, have you told Semple to sort out that kid yet?'

'Yes. He should be moving him tonight. I tried him on his mobile a few minutes ago, but he's not answering.'

O'Connell raised his eyebrows.

'Is that usual?'

'Not especially; knowing Semple he's probably enjoying a goodbye shag. Really, there's nothing to worry about.'

'How are you off for gear?'

'There's enough to last a few more days then we'll need another shipment.'

'That's cutting it a bit fine isn't it?'

'Liverpool is holding surplus stock they wish to be rid of at the moment. They can run it down here in a day. Don't worry, it's all in hand.'

Preece's mobile phone rang again. He answered it and began to frown as he listened.

'Okay, I'll be back shortly,' he said finally and rang off.

'More trouble?' asked his business partner.

'I don't know,' replied Preece thoughtfully. 'That was Juliet. Apparently she left my wife upstairs in a drunken stupor and, when she checked on her an hour later she had disappeared. Apparently she's searched the house and the grounds and the bloody woman's vanished completely.'

20

'Pull in by ere,' instructed Mort, indicating the entrance to the flats.

'Where shall I park?' asked Charlie as he followed the road around.

'Just keep goin'. We'll leave it around the back be'ind the block. We won't be gone long.'

Charlie did as Mort directed. It was midday and he was now on the payroll of Draymark Holdings International Ltd, following his meeting with the fat Irishman, O'Leary. His malodorous companion Mort had been instructed to show him the ropes. Mort had obviously taken his new-found responsibilities to heart, because he hadn't shut up since they left the club.

Charlie couldn't help admiring the craftiness of hiding the really sordid business by using a sex club as a front. The Rent Men could wander in and out all day and an observer would simply assume they were punters. He guessed the money moved out of the premises pretty quickly and, if there was a raid, well it was all cash and the girls had had a busy day. Beyond that, the system was simple. Each Rent Man collected 'rent', the prostitute's takings, from five or six addresses per day. At the same time they kept them supplied with heroin and provided protection from dodgy customers. The opportunities for blackmailing the punters were endless. There were also babysitters, usually old women, who answered the door and did the shopping and cleaning in return for free food and accommodation. Charlie hoped the voice activated recorder on his mobile had caught all this as Mort rattled on.

The road came to an end behind the tower block and Charlie pulled into the small parking area. He locked the Land Rover and they climbed the stairs. Mort explained that a rent man had been caught in possession when a lift broke down with him in it. Someone had called the fire brigade and the police had turned up with them. They had searched him, for lack of anything better to do, and found the brown.

Mort knocked the door three times and waited. Charlie heard a scraping on the other side and guessed they were being inspected through the fisheye. The door opened six inches and a grey-haired woman with matching skin peered out. She had a roll up stuck to her bottom lip. She nodded at Charlie.

'Who's 'e?' She muttered, suspiciously.

'New rent man, luv. Come on, get the fuckin' kettle on. It's nobblin' out here.'

The woman turned and shuffled off down the corridor. They followed her into the kitchen.

'Wayne up yet?' inquired Mort.

'Money's in the tin on the table,' she said, as she rinsed out some mugs. 'The soddin' perverts were knockin' the door till one o'clock this mornin', so 'e's still in bed, luv 'im.' Mort had warned Charlie that the prostitutes were male. The straight stuff went on in the clubs. Mort had seated himself at the kitchen table and was counting the money.

'If 'e was so busy, how comes there's only two 'undred and forty 'ere?'

'I says it was late, not busy. A couple of 'is reg'lars never turned up, see.'

'Not 'oldin' out on me are you?'

'Never! Honest to God! That's every penny 'e took, I swears it.'

'Well tell 'im to make it up or 'e'll get sixty quid's worth less brown this week.'

As if summoned by the threat, the subject of the conversation appeared, dramatically, in the doorway. He wore nothing but a long, pink, taffeta dressing gown, which he hadn't bothered to do up. Charlie guessed he was about seventeen, but it was hard to judge, because his pallid skin, emaciation and total lack of body hair all served to make him look younger – deliberately, Charlie suspected. He could see track-marks on his feet and shins.

The exaggeratedly youthful body was a marked contrast to his face which was surrounded by a Gothic shock of dyed black shoulder-length hair. He was crying and his attempts to wipe away the tears had reduced last night's make-up to a panda-like smear. The effect, with the remains of his scarlet lipstick was grotesque. He looked like a raddled hag.

'What you saying, man?' he lisped, with a noticeable Midlands accent.

'You fuckin' heard, you thievin' twat. Pay up. You knows the rules.'

'Oh, c'mon man. Give us a break will you?'

'Piss off.'

Wayne walked unsteadily forward and sat down at the kitchen table. He buried his face in his hands and sobbed, his thin shoulders heaving violently with each gasp. The sobbing quietened, gradually, and he groped in the pocket of his dressing gown. He pulled out an old tobacco tin and prised off the lid. Inside Charlie could see a syringe and some foil. This seemed to exhaust Mort's patience. He reached forward and grabbed a handful of dyed hair, twisting his victim's head back.

'I'm not sitting around 'ere while you gets shitfaced, you little wanker. 'Ave you got the money or not?'

'No, honest to God, Mort!'

'Well 'ave it by tomorrow then, or no brown, and if I 'ears of you buyin' it anywhere else, the boys'll be around to give you a right good tunin', understand?'

The grey woman tried to intervene.

'Oh come off it Mort! You can't do that to the kiddie!'

'Watch me. And you can forget the tea, I don't fancy it no more.' He turned to Charlie.

'Come on mate, these twats are pissin' me off. Let's go before he does my fuckin' 'ead in.'

*

The Land Rover's battery turned over again, but the engine wouldn't fire. Charlie reached down by the pedals, feeling around for the bonnet release. Suddenly he heard Mort exclaim: 'It's all yours, butty!' He looked up. In front of the vehicle stood three men.

The one on the right was tall and skinny. He looked mean and vicious, but not particularly powerful, unlike the Doberman he was holding by its studded leather collar. The one on the left was short and squat. He was wearing an Army Surplus combat jacket. His forehead was so low he looked like an ape. Charlie guessed his stunted nervous system gave him a high pain threshold. He was holding a wheel wrench in much the same way his ancestors would have clutched a shinbone.

It was the one in the middle, however, that grabbed the attention. He held nothing but the Land Rover's H.T. lead. On top of a huge, barrel chest was a bull neck supporting a massive, shaven head. He was a giant. He grinned sadistically, as he dangled the lead in the air in front of the car window, then brought his fist crashing down on the bonnet, caving it in. Charlie glimpsed a set of steel knuckles, as the man hurled the lead to one side. Then he turned back to the window and pointed a finger directly at Charlie and beckoned him out of the Land Rover.

Charlie glanced to his left. The passenger door was open. Mort was gone. He threw his own door open and jumped out, rather than be dragged out. These boys were dangerous. He'd obviously been set up and, given the nature of the business he'd uncovered, it was safe to assume they intended to silence him for good. He knew now why Mort had been so talkative; traitor's jitters.

He needed space, but as he moved away from the vehicle, they edged sideways, keeping him trapped in the triangle created by themselves, the Land Rover on his left and the high wall behind him. He'd parked too close to the wall. There was no gap behind the vehicle to try and make a break through. The wall was climbable, but not with that dog sinking his teeth in your leg. The only way out was through them. He studied them surreptitiously, looking for a weak spot. Getting past the dog was out of the question. The short one was holding the wrench in his right hand, so a rolling dive between him and the giant was the best bet. That way he would be following Charlie with the wrench, not striking straight at him.

The man turned to his companion and said something in Arabic. Why was he speaking in Arabic? What had Charlie been thinking of, mistaking an AK47 for a bloody wheel wrench? He could smell the cordite in the air from the last round he had fired off before he ran out of ammo. He felt a sense of paralysing helplessness as the Iraqi soldiers in their combat jackets walked towards him down the narrow wadi. Paddy and Jake lay dead beside him.

Then a rational voice in his head was saying: 'You're having a flashback, Charlie Boy. Get it together, for fuck's sake!' He shook his head to clear it, just as the giant's steel clad knuckles crashed into the side of it. It wasn't a clean blow, but it opened a gash above his left ear. He staggered back and then launched himself forward into the dive. It was like wading through water. Everything was slow motion. A huge leg came across and he found himself flat on his face at the man's feet. He'd seen his chance and simply stood there hallucinating.

The man bent down and lifted him effortlessly up above his head, then slammed him down on the concrete like a rag doll. Charlie just about had the presence of mind to use his arms, judo-style, to lessen the impact, which saved him a bad winding. He needn't have bothered. The giant came crashing down on top of him. He felt his three displaced ribs give way as the breath was crushed out of him. It was agonising, but it focussed him.

One thing was obvious. If it stayed like this, he was a dead man. The second thing that struck him was that the others were spectators. They were probably enjoying the show, but, more importantly, with the giant on top of him, there wasn't much of him showing for them to attack. He hooked his left arm between the giant's legs and held him down. His right arm was by his side. In a single movement, he drew up his right knee, yanked up his trouser leg and pulled the diving knife from the sheath on his calf. He plunged the six-inch blade up to its hilt in the giant's right buttock, then dragged it back, cutting a deep gash across his backside.

The man bellowed with pain and began bucking to try and get free. Charlie wondered if he was going to blackout from the pain in his chest. He ripped the knife out and pushed the man away. With a wound like that, he wouldn't want to play anymore.

Charlie wriggled clear and rolled. He fully expected the skinny one to have released the dog, but luck was with him. He had sensed the ape man was itching to have a crack at him and now the gorilla came trundling forward and swung a boot. He misjudged the distance thanks to the roll. Charlie, still on his back, slashed back at him with the knife. The vicious point of the curved, steel blade met the swinging leg halfway up the shin and stuck like an arrow.

Charlie jumped up still holding onto the handle of the knife, locked in a bizarre pas de deux with this Neanderthal partner, who was consequently trying to balance on one leg. He was right about the man's pain threshold; he seemed more puzzled than disabled by the knife sticking out of his shin. Charlie circled around to keep his opponent between him and the dog, which had the added advantage of exposing the man's groin. Charlie's right foot lashed upwards. This time his dancing partner registered pain alright. As he threw his head back to try to gasp in some air, Charlie stepped forward, fingers bent, knuckles flat and hit him with all his force in the windpipe. He twisted the hilt of the knife and wrenched it out of the man's leg.

The gorilla went down like a dynamited factory chimney, slowly at first, but with gathering momentum. For a short man, he seemed to take an age to hit the ground. His face was blue and he lay ominously still.

The skinny one finally seemed to realise that things were not going to plan. He released the dog's collar.

'Go on, Tyson, fuckin' 'ave 'im!'

The dog hurtled forward. Charlie knew it would go for his right arm and that one held the knife. He twisted and held up his left, to keep his right hand free. The Doberman's weight and momentum bowled him over. He blacked out for a second as he landed heavily on his broken ribs and his head cracked back against the pavement. As his vision cleared he realised he had lost the knife. Pain was shooting through his arm where the dog's jaws were locked onto him and it was beginning to play tug of war. He could feel its teeth lacerating his skin. What with the dog's weight and the injuries he had sustained, he was becoming exhausted.

Ignoring the pain, he pulled back against the animal, provoking the tug of war. His strength was going and he needed a good shot. The dog's weight was fully on its front paws as it pulled against him. Charlie reached across with his right hand, grabbed the dog's right paw and yanked, levering his left arm to turn the dog's head. Losing the support of its right leg, the animal rolled onto its shoulder, exposing its stomach. Charlie twisted on the ground and kicked it. He felt the dog's grip slacken and pulled his arm free. The wretched creature struggled to its feet, staggered drunkenly towards its owner and collapsed, bleeding internally from a ruptured spleen.

Charlie too, struggled to his feet. The skinny one was dazed.

'My dog. You've killed my fuckin' dog!' was all he could say.

'Stay where you are, or I'll kill you too,' ordered Charlie, a lot more confidently than he felt. The man didn't move. Charlie spotted his diving knife a couple of yards away. Without taking his eyes off Skinny he edged sideways and retrieved it. Now, with the tactical as well as psychological advantage, he glanced around. The dog and ape man weren't moving. The giant was crawling across the car park on his elbows. He appeared to be making for a battered, black minibus.

'Go and help your mate,' ordered Charlie. Skinny hurried off in pursuit of the giant.

Charlie struggled over to the Land Rover and climbed into the back. God that hurt his ribs! He tasted blood in his mouth and wondered if his broken ribs had punctured a lung. It could be blood from the gash on the side of his head. He opened his black nylon knapsack and pulled out his tracksuit. He took off his jacket and spread it on the floor. He unscrewed the cap to the spare water bottle and tore a strip of material off the tracksuit bottoms. He soaked it in water. Using the rear-view mirror, he methodically began to mop the blood from his face and matted hair. As each strip of material became blood-soaked, he carefully placed it on his jacket. Finally, he eased his blood-soaked T-shirt over his head, taking care not to reopen the gash. He put on the track suit jacket and zipped it up to the top. He added his T-shirt to the other bloody rages, rolled his jacket into a ball and stuffed it into his knapsack. He was leaving the forensic boys enough DNA samples as it was.

He used the remains of the track suit bottoms to wipe around the interior of the Land Rover, then got out and wiped the door handles. He stuffed the rag into his knapsack, and limped off up the narrow alleyway that led into the rest of the estate as fast as his battered body would allow him.

*

Charlie paused mid-sentence and took another swig of scotch. Even the action of typing was killing him. The throbbing in his chest, arm and head subsided a little, though he knew it was only temporary relief. The trouble was that he needed a clear head to complete the dossier of photographs and memoranda he was compiling and too much liquid pain relief would get in the way. Unfortunately, so would too much pain. It was nearly one in the morning and the caravan was completely blacked out. That way he could burn the small kerosene lamp and avoid the claustrophobia. He couldn't face that right now.

He had called in at the King Arthur on his way back to the caravan and watched the evening news from a corner of the bar. There had been no mention of dead dogs and cavemen being found, so either the ungodly had removed the corpses, or someone powerful was imposing a news blackout. When he got back to the caravan, there was evidence of a visit, but the clumsiness suggested it was Farmer Price snooping around.

He got up painfully and went outside to stretch his legs. Despite the cold, his T-shirt was wet with perspiration. He toyed with the idea of changing it, but didn't fancy the extra pain involved. He went back in, sat back down and began typing again – not much further to go and he could try to patch up his chest a bit.

Three quarters of an hour later he saved his work and left the printer to get on with it. This time he had no choice but to wriggle gingerly out of his T-shirt. He had already disinfected and dressed the dog-bites on his arm. He had also shaved his head and bathed the gash, then closed it up as best he could with butterfly stitches. That was as much self-improvement as he could take in one hit, without overdoing it on the scotch. Now he needed to attend to his ribs.

The cough had started as he left the scene of the fight. The stuff he coughed up was pink and frothy, which meant a punctured lung. It had worried him at first, but he had kept going. He knew blokes in the Regiment who had crossed deserts with worse injuries than that. He also knew blokes that had died of less. All he could do was monitor the situation.

He had made it to The Commercial on Llangyfelach Road. He went in and bought a pint. He borrowed a paper from behind the bar and made the drink last. Gradually a pattern emerged. As long as he stayed still, he only coughed occasionally, bringing up a small amount of pink froth. It suggested the injury was fairly stable. He could only pray it didn't deteriorate. The landlady called a cab for him.

Now, over twelve hours later he was feeling a little more confident – he wasn't dead yet. He gently examined the wound with his fingertips, but he couldn't tell much except that it hurt like hell. The last thing he wanted to do was cause any further damage, so the best he could hope for was to strap it tightly to minimise movement and protect it against knocks. He picked up the bottle of scotch and unscrewed the cap.

He finally reached the end of the sticky, elastic bandage and taped it down to stop it catching on his clothes. He felt like The Mummy, and he was sweating buckets from the pain of trying to wrap the bandage around and around his chest, but he could already feel the benefit of the support. The question was, would it see him through the next few days?

He lowered the flame of the lamp and lay down on the narrow bed, letting the pain and weariness flow out of him into the mattress. One thing was certain, he wouldn't be jumping off ferries or fighting Dobermans now. He needed help. The team from Detachment Eight was waiting in the wings, but he still hadn't made a connection between Preece and O'Connell. They could go in for the final kill if necessary, but things hadn't reached that stage yet. Besides, he didn't want to hand over the reins. He wanted O'Connell for himself.

He wondered about his personal contacts. Johnny and Jenks were both good mates, but this was too dangerous to involve them.

He thought about Gareth. It was a hell of a lot to saddle a kid with, but then, he reminded himself, he was in the army learning to shoot Provos at Gareth's age. Somehow the thought didn't make him feel any better. He decided to keep him as a last resort.

Jacs would help but he knew in his heart that she had set him up for that photograph. She would only have done it under the severest pressure, but still. He wondered how they had got to her, the kids probably. Anyhow, if they could get to her once, they could get to her again.

A fresh fit of coughing took him by surprise. He looked at his palm. Despite all the bandaging the blood was still there. There was no point kidding himself anymore; he was going to need help and from the way his breathing was getting more difficult, he was going to need it soon.

*

By Swansea standards, the funeral cortege was a modest affair – no floral tribute to DAD or SON, no cars full of weeping mourners. The undertaker and his colleagues were aware of the need for a discreet burial and, besides, the apeman, a.k.a. Planky had no surviving relatives, at least none that would be bothered to turn up at his funeral. Of the deceased parties, the Doberman was probably the more popular.

The lead car was a rusty, maroon Volvo Estate driven by Duke O'Leary. The hearse was the black van driven by the skinny dog handler, Rake. The pallbearers were a motley crew of gang members who had been drinking in the Cock and Bull Club in Landore when the bodies arrived. The Boss had obligingly provided a lock-in while the corpses were prepared for their last earthly journey by being weighted and taped up in black bin liners. The lock-in had turned into something of a wake while the mourners waited for the one-thirty a.m. kick off, at which time Preece had arranged with Ringer for police patrols to be elsewhere. As a result, what the occasion lacked in dignity, due to the informality of a 'jeans and trainers' dress-code,' was made up for by a certain drunken solemnity.

There was almost nothing on the roads when the vehicles pulled out of the club's car park and headed for the Carmarthen Road. They reached the Cwmbwrla roundabout, but instead of carrying on they turned sharp left into a small slip road. A steady drizzle was seeping out of the heavy night sky. They killed their lights and followed the road around at a respectfully funereal pace.

"Urry up Rake, mun! It's fuckin' stinkin' back 'ere. These bodies smell worse than fuckin' Mort!' hissed one of the pallbearers, in suitably subdued tones.

'There's nothin' I can do about it,' whispered Rake. 'Duke's in front, an' I can 'ardly see, what with this rain an' no lights.' As if to prove his point, there was a crash, and a lot of muttered swearing, as the van ran up the back of the Volvo and pall bearers found themselves tangling on the floor with the overripe corpses. As Rake got out, O'Leary's huge bulk appeared out of the enveloping darkness.

'For fuck's sake Rake, will ya tell those fuckin' eejits in the back to shut it?' he growled, obviously more concerned about the decorum of the occasion, than the impact of the van on his ageing Volvo. He pulled a half of Jack Daniels out of his jacket pocket and unscrewed the cap as he lumbered around the back to supervise the unloading of the corpses. This was done in something akin to a respectful hush, considering what a heavy little bastard Planky turned out to be with a paving slab tied to his chest.

The weight was to prove an even greater problem as the funeral party attempted to progress up the steep, twenty-foot bank that led up to the railway line. The rain and the cold made fingers numb and the bin liners slippery. Soon the pallbearers were on their arses trying to drag the bodies up the muddy bank. As the story did the whispered rounds of the pubs and clubs over the next few months, it is hardly surprising that Rake was rumoured to have pissed himself when the bin liner ripped open and Planky's grinning corpse carried him fifteen foot down the bank in a clammy embrace.

Eventually, the burial party reached the top of the bank in one piece. They were well away from civilisation now and the language and general demeanour of the pallbearers was tending to deteriorate, particularly as they stumbled across the twin tracks of the railway line with the sodden corpses. They reached the other side and worked their way along, looking for a gap in the spiked iron railings which protected the public from the murky depths of the old steam train reservoir known to the locals as Coffin Pond.

They found a break in the fence and squeezed through onto the bank. They laid out the bodies, and stared out across the black water while O'Leary passed around what was left of the Jack Daniels.

'Does anyone know a prayer?' he enquired. There was a general shaking of heads, so the Duke cleared his throat.

'Holy Father,' he began, solemnly, 'take this man and this dog unto your tender mercies. The fella was not much liked in his time down here, owin' to his violent temperament and cheatin' ways, but hopefully, in your eternal wisdom you'll find some good in the bastard. Amen.'

'Amen,' murmured the rest of the congregation, then they lifted first Tyson, then Planky, and hurled them out unto the tender mercies of the pike, perch and eels that lived in the cold, dark waters of Coffin Pond.

21

Her mam had sounded a bit cat's-arsed on the phone when she asked her to look after the twins for another week. She should have known that getting involved with a married man would lead to no good, and the girls were eating her out of house and home. It was all very well being broken-hearted, but she should have thought of that in the first place! Then she'd popped around with a Chinese takeaway, and tidied around, and taken away a bag of washing. It was her way of showing she was worried.

It was also an effective way of reminding Jacs that life goes on. If she wasn't going to end it, then she had to live it, and besides she wasn't really the suicidal sort. Her failed attempt seemed to be telling her that it wasn't time to go.

She had a hazy memory of Charlie's boy Gareth arriving on the night she took the pills and she'd seen him twice since. Both times he had told her there was a possibility that Charlie was still alive. She knew he was only saying it to be kind, but the glimmer of hope it lit in her heart prevented her from grieving properly. Now, she had decided it was time to accept that, for reasons she would never understand, the man she loved was dead, and when the milkman or the postman knocked the door, she was not going to open it to find her Charlie standing there – not now, not ever.

There was a knock at the door. Her heart leapt despite her good intentions of a second ago. Don't be so stupid, she told herself crossly, though she couldn't think who it could be. She peeped around the curtain in case it was someone after money. There was nobody there. Jesus, she'd started imagining things! As she turned away from the window the knocking came again; weaker this time. She hesitated, but she couldn't let it go. She opened the door. Again there was no one there, then a slight movement caught her eye and she looked down.

Charlie was sitting slumped against the wall beside the door. There was blood around his mouth and all over his front, but he was looking up at her with that old grin of his. Jesus Christ, this was horrendous! She was fucking hallucinating him now! But then she'd heard the knock...she had definitely heard the knock!

As if to dispel the shock he tried to speak, but it only came out as a barely audible whisper. Still, he was alive, her Charlie was alive! How or why, she didn't know or care. She dropped to her knees and grabbed his face, seeking reassurance from the warmth of his skin. Too stunned to think, she began smothering it in kisses, then reality hit. Blood! He was covered in blood! This was no time for kisses she had to do something! She pulled back to inspect him more closely, but he beckoned her closer. She turned her ears to his lips.

'Caravan; get me to caravan,' was all he said.

Caravan, what caravan?

'I'm sorry, love, I don't understand what you mean. I don't know any caravan, but I think you need to go to hospital...'

'No!' weak or not, his voice was determined. He shook his head painfully in emphasis, 'No doctors, no police! Caravan on Gower; help me, please!' He threw his head back and squeezed his eyes shut with the pain of speaking.

Jacs stared at him in turmoil. Charlie was alive but badly injured. My God, this was unbelievable! It was as if someone was trying to drive her around the bend! With an effort she pulled herself together. Charlie was asking for help and she had to make a decision. He said he didn't need a doctor, but he was covered in blood and hardly breathing! But then this was Charlie and he always seemed to know what he was doing. She remembered the last time she had failed to put her faith in him and she wasn't going to make the same mistake again.

She stood up and went back into the house. She grabbed her coat and struggled into it, then picked up her mobile from the table in the living room. She hesitated a moment longer, then shoved it in her pocket. She almost ran out of the front door, yanking it closed behind her.

She squatted down by Charlie and put her lips to his ear.

'Show me where to go, okay?'

'Sure.'

She gently pulled his arm around her shoulders and began to pull him upright. He groaned, but struggled to his feet. Bent almost double they weaved their way over to the car.

*

Jacs started the car and pulled jerkily out of the Close. Then she put her foot down and they went tearing off up the Gower Road and out onto the common. The only thing in the world of any interest to her now was Charlie; her Charlie.

He was sitting in the passenger seat, slumped against the door. His eyes were closed and he was deathly pale. There was more blood around his mouth and down his shirt. He seemed to have stopped breathing. Oh my God, what if he was dead? She reached across and lifted one of his eyelids. She saw the pupil contract. He was alive, at least! He slowly lifted the other eyelid and she saw recognition light up in them. His mouth twisted into a pale imitation of his old grin, but it was so weak it was pitiful. Even that effort clearly hurt.

'Charlie, my love, what's wrong?' she croaked, and realised she was crying. She brushed the tears away, cross with herself for being so weak. She snatched another glance and saw his lips were moving. He was trying to speak. She strained to hear what he was saying. At first it was an unintelligible murmur, and then, painfully, he repeated himself and she caught the barest whisper.

'Slow down. Police...'

She nodded to show she understood and eased off the accelerator. At least he was well enough to criticise her driving! He began coughing violently, his face twisted with pain. Gradually the attack subsided and he closed his eyes again. This was no good; she needed directions!

'Charlie, Charlie, where is this caravan?'

'Take North Gower Rd.' This time his voice was a little clearer, he had only been resting.

North Gower Road! Jesus Christ, it was almost upon them!

She slammed down a gear and swerved right across the junction leaving an oncoming Four-by-Four driver waving a furious fist.

Charlie groaned and began coughing again. Jacs waited for it to pass, and then made her mind up.

'Charlie, my love, I am not going to let you die on me,' she began, much more certainly than she felt, 'but we cannot go any further like this. There is something badly wrong with you and I'm not driving you off into the middle of nowhere for you to go and die on me. Either you tell me here and now what I can do to help you, or I'm taking you to A&E!'

With an effort, Charlie slowly lifted a hand and placed it on the back of hers where it gripped the steering wheel. She glanced around again and he managed a weak smile. How could a man who was so desperately sick be the one who was handing out reassurance?

'Okay,' he whispered, 'take next right and park in woods.'

Park in the woods? What the hell for? Then it hit her. He needed somewhere private, out of sight, which meant he had a plan! God knows what, but he would tell her what to do. She indicated and took a side road signposted Cillibion. A couple of hundred yards on, she spotted a track leading into the woods and pulled in. When she turned to look at Charlie again he was unconscious.

*

She rested her forehead on her arms and shut her eyes. She had to think. Alright, they were off the road and Charlie clearly believed he was treatable; but what with? For the first time she looked around the inside of the car. There was a Lloyd's pharmacy bag on the back seat. She reached back and pulled it over into the front. She opened it and began searching through, looking for anything that might help. She found bandages, several pairs of scissors, a scalpel, tape, a bottle of Dettol, pain killers and a syringe. They simply served to remind her that she didn't know what to do.

But Charlie did! She reached over and shook him gently.

'Arrrgh!' That was more than just a groan. It was a cry of pain. 'Charlie,' she whispered, fighting back a wave of panic, please, tell me what to do!'

Charlie opened his eyes a fraction.

'Listen to me, Charlie,' she insisted. 'You can't go on like this. You're getting worse.'

He nodded and gestured weakly to his chest. He opened his mouth, so she quickly moved forward to listen.

'Cut bandages,' he murmured.

What bandages? Did he mean get bandages out of the first aid kit and cut them? What type of bandages? Oh, for Christ's sake, get real! He had gestured to his chest. She leant forward and unbuttoned his shirt. His chest was swathed in heavy elastic bandage.

'Do you mean these?' He indicated a 'yes' with an almost imperceptible nod. She scrabbled about in the box, coming up with a pair of sharp-pointed scissors. No way was she going to try to use those next to his skin. She found a sturdy pair of round-nosed scissors and turned back to the patient. Painfully, Charlie moved his hand up to his chest. He cautiously probed his ribs on the left-hand side and winced. Immediately he was racked by another fit of coughing and Jacs watched in alarm as more blood sprayed onto the newly exposed bandages. He waited till the coughing subsided and probed again. Then he traced a line from the bottom of the bandage to the point he had identified. He was showing her where to cut.

She had an idea. 'Hold it there, my love.' She threw open her door and ran around to Charlie's side. She opened the door and felt around for the lever that reclined the passenger seat. She found it and carefully lowered the seat back as far as it would go.

She reached across and delved into her handbag coming up with a biro. She marked a cross on the bandage where he was pointing and drew a line down to the bottom, as he had shown. She picked up the scissors and began to cut. At first it was quite easy, but after a couple of inches, the bandages got thicker and thicker and the scissors began to chew at them. It was heavy duty, sticky bandage and he'd put it on like body armour. Her fingers weren't strong enough. Oh God, she was getting nowhere! He'd asked her to help and she couldn't even cut through the fucking bandages!

Charlie's hand closed over hers and gently pulled the scissors away. He licked his dry lips and she realised he wanted to speak again.

'Scalpel,' he whispered, as she craned forwards to listen. Another surge of panic. What the hell was he going to ask her to do with that? Again she forced herself to calm down. She was hardly instilling confidence in the patient at this rate! She went back to the bag and found half-a-dozen steel scalpels in sterile packets. She opened one and Charlie gestured for her to pass it to him. With painful slowness he inverted the blade and showed her how to use it cutting away from the skin.

Twice he stopped her as she worked. Each time the coughing fit twisted his face into a mask of pain. Each time he nodded at her to continue as the attack subsided. Gently, she worked her way up, pulling the sticky bandage up away from the skin with her thumb and forefinger, then slipping the blade underneath and using its sharpness to part the fibres.

At last, she reached the spot she had marked, the bandage was peeled back out of the way, and she could see the lump from his old wound. She dabbed his lips again with a wipe, to clean and moisten them. Then she leaned forward and gently kissed them.

'What next?' she asked.

'Feeling brave?' came the barely audible reply.

She nodded, even as her heart sank. She'd had enough time to wonder what would happen once the bandage was out of the way.

'Biggest syringe.'

Oh no! Please God, not a syringe! She hated needles. It wasn't the pain of the injection. It was the sight of the needle. She was the only one in her year to faint when the school nurse had visited, and she still insisted on gas at the dentist's. Even childbirth had failed to cure the phobia – she'd decided to get by on gas and air when she saw the epidural needle!

Tough. Charlie wasn't about to die because she was scared of bloody needles! Get on with it! She returned to the bag. She had noticed a bottle of smelling salts in her first search. She dug it out and unscrewed the cap to the last thread. If she went woozy, it could be her last resort. She put it on the rear window tray of the toolbox, within easy reach, and began to hunt for a syringe.

She wished to God he hadn't said 'biggest' – she couldn't

explain why it sounded so much worse, but it did. She pulled out all the syringes she could find and held them up to the car window to inspect the size of the needles through the packaging. Her hands were trembling and she realised that sweat was running down her forehead into her eyes. She selected the biggest and dropped the others back in the bag. She pulled out a wipe and, this time, mopped her own brow as she breathed deeply to calm herself. She tore off the wrapping and held out the syringe.

'Will this do?' she asked, fighting to keep her voice natural. He took it and held it up in front of his eyes to inspect it.

'Biggest?' he whispered.

'Yes.'

He pulled out the plunger and handed it back.

'Spit in it.'

'Spit in it?'

'Uh huh.'

She hesitated, and then tried to muster some saliva. God, her mouth was dry! He didn't want her to inject him with spit, did he? She managed a lady-like trickle.

'More.'

She tried again. She held it up for him to inspect. He nodded his approval and began to probe around the old wound again. His forefinger stopped. It was pointing at a spot between two ribs close to the ridge formed by the displacement.

'In there?'

'What right in?'

'Yeah.'

'What about this?' she held up the plunger.

'No need.'

'Okay. Ready?'

He nodded. She dragged her sleeve across her eyes and took another couple of deep breaths. She reached across his chest with her left hand and gripped his left bicep. With the help of this arm to steady her trembling right hand, she guided the needle into position up against his skin. She looked up into his face. His eyes were watching her, unflinching, giving her strength.

'Go on,' he murmured.

She pushed, wondering at the effortlessness with which the needle slid in, just as another bout of coughing seized him. There was nothing she could do as the spasms shook him. She let go of the needle. By the time the fit passed, the syringe was dangling from his chest and the saliva had drained out. She mopped the beads of sweat off his forehead, and the fresh blood from around his mouth. It had failed! After all that it had failed! She looked at him. He seemed even paler than before.

'Charlie, my love. The needle's come out. Charlie, please, help me! What do I do now?'

He opened his eyes and, from somewhere, found a faint grin.

'Put it in again.'

With an effort, she picked up the syringe, which had dropped into his lap. She could barely control her hands as she struggled to tear open a new sachet to get at a wipe. By the time she had got it out and cleaned the needle, Charlie was indicating the insertion point. She dribbled more saliva into the syringe, then leant forward and steadied her arm as before. Her head was reeling and she wondered if she should stop for a whiff of the smelling salts. No. They had lost too much time already. Get a grip!

She moved the point of the needle up into position. Her hands were shaking so much that the tip pierced the skin several times and drops of blood oozed out. A wave of blackness was threatening to overwhelm her, and she couldn't drag her eyes away from the gleaming needle. For what seemed like an eternity, she sat there paralysed, shaking, then she drove the needle into his chest, up to the hilt.

'Take it, Charlie. Take it.' she whispered. Then she was falling back into darkness.

The smelling salts jolted her back to consciousness, unceremoniously. She was sitting squashed up in the floor-well of the rear passenger seat where she had collapsed. Charlie was leaning across holding the bottle. For a moment the significance failed to sink in. Then her heart leapt. He couldn't do that when she fainted!

'Alright, kid?' he enquired with a grin, sitting back. There was colour in his cheeks.

'Sure, if I can get my arse out of here. How 'bout you?' She levered herself, with difficulty, off the floor and onto the rear seat.

'I've been worse and, thanks to you, I'll live. Look.' He opened the hand that had steadied the syringe as he leant forward. The plastic cylinder was now taped in position and she could see air bubbles bursting through the saliva. 'It was whistling out at first,' he explained, 'but now most of the pressure's off.'

*

They attacked the caravan door with a sixteen kilo steel Enforcer ram which smashed it open first time. It was about four in the morning and Jacs was sitting by Charlie's recumbent form, watching his chest steadily rising and falling as he lay sleeping on the caravan's tiny bed. Before she could move she found herself restrained by a man in black body armour. Within seconds she was cuffed and dragged out of the vehicle. A third man was already levelling a Heckler & Koch MP5 at Charlie.

Charlie sat up painfully. He wasn't going to show it, but he was alarmed at the general hostility and tension. These were slick operators, real pros. That spelled Al Sullivan's people, but why the sudden aggression? Something had obviously gone badly wrong. He was sure he had done enough to convince Sullivan he was not a player during their meeting in Killay Square.

He thought about taking the shotgun off his captor, but they had Jacs and, besides, he had no way of knowing how badly his injury might impair him...

He tried making conversation with his captor, but it yielded little.

What did they want?

The boss would explain.

Were they under arrest?

No, but they could be if he wished.

Charlie preferred not to be and the conversation died.

The door to the caravan swung open. A slim man of average height entered the caravan. He selected Jacs' seat uninvited. He wore a black, waterproof jacket over jeans and a checked shirt. His receding hairline emphasised his high forehead which gave a slightly boffinish impression, but his eyes were sharp and hard and there was a toughness about his jawline which offset the initial impression of a college lecturer. He directed those hard eyes at Charlie now and sat, studying him dispassionately. Suddenly, he spoke.

'I take it I am addressing Mr Charles Llewellyn of 571 Gower Road, Swansea?'

'Who are you?'

'My name is Maddocks and I'm a senior investigating officer with Her Majesties Revenue and Customs. Would you answer my question please?'

'Yes, that's my name and address, what do you want?'

'I want some very convincing answers regarding your involvement in the criminal organisation known as the Rent Man Gang. If you fail to convince me, I have a warrant here for your immediate arrest.' The man produced a document which Charlie ignored.

'I have no involvement with any criminal organisation.'

'That's not how it looks from where I'm standing.'

'Meaning?'

'Well, it is a well-documented fact that you jumped of the Swansea-Cork ferry the other day in an apparent suicide attempt. Thanks to the persistence of one of my investigating officers, Alan Sullivan, we did not take this episode at face value and treated it with the scepticism it obviously deserved. Mr Sullivan is apparently a former acquaintance of yours and assured me that, given your military background, it was conceivable that you might have survived such an ordeal. I understand he had an off the record meeting with you the week before, to try to enlist your help with our investigation, at which time you were uncooperative. According to Mr Sullivan you were, and I quote: 'Not the man he used to be.'

'I was in the middle of a messy divorce and I'd been drinking heavily for some time. After I met Al, I had a meeting with my wife's solicitor who stitched me up. I'd had enough.'

'Mr Llewellyn, I am an experienced Customs officer. I have spent my entire career investigating hundreds, if not thousands, of highly imaginative attempts to breach this country's borders. If there is one thing I am certain of, it is that your actions on the night in question were not those of a drunk. It is one thing to convince onlookers that you are getting pissed, it's an entirely different thing to jump forty feet from a moving ship then swim three quarters of a mile in strong currents and successfully arrive at an exact, pre-determined location. Furthermore, stealing and hotwiring a motor bike is beyond the capabilities of most members of the public.'

'The shock of the cold water sobered me up and I used to be a channel swimmer. Sure I borrowed a bike to get back to Swansea, but I left it where it would be found and returned. I'm good for the fine if you want to charge me with that.'

'No Mr Llewellyn, petty theft is not my remit. I want to know why a man fitting your description was seen yesterday by an undercover drug squad officer called Dyer entering a place known as Dyfatty flats in the company of a convicted criminal and suspected member of the Rent Man gang called Mort. The officer subsequently witnessed a fight in the car park adjacent to the flats involving other gang suspects, a dog and your mysterious lookalike who apparently escaped.'

'There are plenty of men in Swansea who fit my description.'

'Yes, but according to the officer, the man in question apparently sustained chest injuries in the brawl and here you are hiding out in a caravan in the middle of nowhere with your chest swathed in bandages.'

'I was hit by the ship's stabiliser; the rest is purely circumstantial.'

Maddocks slammed a clenched fist down on the bed beside Charlie.

'Dammit Llewellyn, cut the crap! I want to know exactly what you know about the Rent Man gang and if you don't want to tell me I'll assume that that is because you are one of them...'

'If I were a member of this outfit, why would I be having a punch up with them?'

'How the fuck do I know? Criminals fight amongst themselves all the time; perhaps they caught you fiddling, who knows? Anyhow Dyer reckons he could pick out the man he saw in an ID parade so it won't take long to put you in the frame. This is your chance to get out from under while you can. We're a spit away from cracking this case and with Dyer's back-up I've got enough evidence to hold you until we do. Help us now, or, when that happens I'll make it my personal mission to hang you out to dry.'

'It sounds to me like you haven't got a pot to piss in. You'd have arrested me by now if you had a case.'

Maddocks sat back abruptly and stared at Charlie thoughtfully. When he finally spoke, his tone had changed.

'Whoever or whatever you are, you are not a foot soldier.'

Charlie raised his eyebrows.

'Thank you,' he replied sardonically. Maddocks continued as if he hadn't heard.

'Your average criminal would be shitting himself right now and you're as cool as a cucumber, so the question is, are you one of the good guys running an investigation we don't know about, or have we stumbled upon someone higher up? Personally, I'm inclined to vote for the latter and lock you up until I'm convinced otherwise. However, there is someone who might talk some sense into you before I do that. Wait there.'

He rose and stalked to the door.

'Send Sullivan in!' he snapped at whoever was standing guard. He turned and stationed himself at the end of the bed as Charlie's erstwhile comrade entered and sat down.

'Hi Charlie,' he began awkwardly.

'Hi.'

'I hope you don't think I've been spying on you...'

'Of course you've been spying on me; it's your job. It seems you're pretty good at it.'

'Well, that's as may be, but believe me mate it's for a bloody good reason. The people we're after are unbelievable. If you have become involved with them, whatever the reason, we need your help to get on the inside. I don't believe you're one of the bad guys, but my boss here doesn't agree, so please give yourself and us a break.'

Charlie smiled to himself at his interrogators' version of the Good Cop, Bad Cop routine, but he had to admit that they were narrowing his options. The last thing he could afford was to get himself arrested right now. At least he'd achieved his first objective and they were now asking for his help, not demanding it. He ignored Maddocks and addressed Sullivan directly – divide and rule.

'Okay, just supposing I was the man your undercover guy spotted, what help do you think I would be able to give you?'

'Well you could start by telling us why they were trying to kill you.'

'Because I was trying to get myself recruited as a Rent Man and they decided that they didn't want my services.'

'Why?'

'Because they had identified me as an enemy.'

'And are you?'

'What do you think?'

'I think we're wasting time here,' interrupted Maddocks, impatiently.

'Then why don't you go and find something else to do?' enquired Charlie, bluntly. 'You have been quick enough to tell me how you see things from your point of view. From my point of view, you have wasted time and resources staging this pantomime in the deluded expectation that I will be shocked or scared into sharing information with you; information which I have invested considerable time and effort in acquiring. If you want my help, you'd better learn to ask politely.' He turned back to Sullivan.

'What is it you really need to know?'

'Well, we are still having problems getting from the foot soldiers to the generals. We could arrest several Rent Man suspects and raid the brothel they appear to operate from, but the drug squad tried that a year and a half ago and it was obvious that there had been a tip off. They ended up with a handful of convictions for possession and soliciting. It was a total waste of time.'

'And you think I may have unearthed something further on this link to Councillor Preece?'

'Well you're obviously taking more than a passing interest.'

Charlie nodded.

'I am, but not quite for the same reasons you are. However, I am willing to share on a limited basis.'

'Meaning?'

'Meaning I am not a policeman or a Customs officer, so I don't have any conventional powers of arrest. I agree with you that the Rent Man gang needs stopping, but it will be up to you lot to put the cuffs on. I'm willing to help you do that if you help me in return.'

Maddocks interrupted a second time.

'What do you mean 'help you in return'? You're a bloody criminal; you're hardly in any position to trade!'

Charlie ignored him and again addressed Sullivan.

'I need some kit and I need it tonight which means it'll be too late if I call it in from outside. Fortunately, any one of your somewhat overdressed officers is wearing what I need, so I'll swap you my assistance for the gear. I'm sure one of them is about my size. I want a concealable, Kevlar vest and a handgun; something like one of those nine mil Browning's would be fine,' he nodded at the armed man standing guard at the door. 'Can you do it?'

Sullivan turned to his boss for help and Charlie watched as Maddocks suddenly found himself torn between his unwillingness to back down and his desire to crack the case. Finally he spoke.

'Okay, if you are not a villain, a policeman or one of us, what do you want a gun for? Ordinary citizens don't carry guns in this country, thank God. I'm not going to be held responsible for arming some sort of vigilante, so, if that's your wish list, you're going to have to explain who you really are.'

Charlie paused; it was decision time. He turned to Sullivan.

'I'm sorry Al, this is above your pay scale; you'll have to give us a minute.'

He waited as Sullivan exchanged glances with his boss then left the caravan taking the guard with him. Charlie turned back to Maddocks.

'I am pursuing a man called O'Connell. He is the head of this Rent Man gang, and a former IRA man who became a freelance arms dealer when that organisation began to talk terms with the British Government. My organisation caught up with him and nearly destroyed his operation some years ago, but he escaped and moved into drug smuggling. He is a very clever man and, as you are discovering, has figured out a way of avoiding the usual pitfalls associated with that trade. As far as my organisation is concerned our remit is to bring him to book for his crimes as a former IRA member and subsequent arms dealer. Furthermore, we are particularly concerned about his choice of end user whatever he's selling. O'Connell doesn't give a shit who he sells to or what he sells them. He's sold guns to Gaddafi and now he's selling heroin to kids. It is believed he may be using the profits to get back into the arms trade flogging hardware to insurgents in Afghanistan. That classifies him as a terrorist and I am therefore governed by the rules regarding the apprehension of such people.'

'And does your organisation have a name?'

'Certainly, Detachment Eight, but you won't find us in the phonebook or on Google.'

'Any other way of checking?'

'Sorry, that's above your pay scale too. You can try calling Number Ten for confirmation, but I doubt if you'll get anyone to talk to you. You'll just have to take my word for it.' Charlie smiled to himself as Maddocks fought to hide his annoyance at being patronised. When he spoke again his voice was level.

'I take it you want the gun in order to kill this man? Without some sort of official endorsement I am not willing to sanction that.'

Damn, the sod didn't respond to Charlie pulling rank and he clearly wasn't handing over a gun without something to ease the insult to his authority.

Charlie shrugged.

'I'm not James Bond so I'm not planning to kill him. I work for the Government and the Government doesn't sanction murder. However, he is an extremely dangerous man with a penchant for violence, so I will need to take all means necessary to protect myself.'

'You don't look in a fit state to protect an orphaned kitten.'

Charlie glanced down at his bandaged chest.

'It's only a punctured lung. I've got a tube in now so it's stable enough. I'll live.' He paused; he needed that gun. 'Look, if it will set your mind at rest, how about I give you a number at Det Eight?'

Maddocks looked slightly mollified and pulled out a mobile. 'Who do I ask for?'

'Ask for Colonel Jarvis, but I warn you, he won't like being woken up.'

Maddocks hesitated then nodded.

'Go ahead.'

Charlie dictated a number then lay back and watched as Maddocks made the call. A minute later he ended the call looking slightly dazed.

'You must have it in for this bloke big time to work for a man like that...'

'Let's just say, I spent some time in Baghdad as O'Connell's personal guest.'

Maddocks nodded thoughtfully.

'Okay, if I give you what you want, what do I get in return?'

'You get the credit for it all. I'll do my best to leave you Preece, O'Leary and the Rent Man Gang to mop up and it'll be up to you to coordinate a swoop on the other ports with your colleagues. Without O'Connell, the supply of drugs will dry up or at least have to find another outlet, because he has always controlled all the overseas supply contacts. All I ask in return is that you give me a couple of days to do the job and leave O'Connell to me.'

Maddocks paused a moment longer, then stuck his hand out.

'Okay, you've got a deal.'

22

It was a piss-miserable morning as Gareth trudged up Glanmor Rd from the shops. It was one of those days when you simply couldn't imagine the rain easing off. It was now a week since his father had disappeared and, thanks to Councillor Preece, he was financially sorted and living in a tidy bedsit. At the risk of being ungrateful, he wished he wasn't. He wished to God that he had never met Preece. Gradually, the fresh hope the man had given him was withering and dying, and the process was worse than when he had no hope at all.

He reached the front door of the old mansion block, put down his shopping and let himself in. He let the door swing closed behind him as he struggled past the pushbikes parked in the corridor. He reached his own front door and just about lifted one of the shopping bags high enough to push the key in the lock. He shoved the door open with his foot and walked in. He stopped dead in amazement.

'Dad!'

Charlie grinned and rose from the arm chair where he had been reading the newspaper.

'Hello, boy, been missing me?'

'I thought you were dead.'

'Dead? Me? Come off it, you know me better than that!' He laughed and suddenly began coughing. He pulled out a handkerchief and wiped his mouth. He held out his arms. 'I'm sorry, I had to disappear. There was no other way. Come here, I'm not a ghost.'

Gareth crossed the room and threw his arms around his old man. He felt him wince. He hugged him more gently, and then stepped back. Close up, his father was haggard and, under his knitted hat, he appeared to be bald. Gareth noticed that he had only embraced him with his right arm.

Christ dad, what've you been up to?'

'It's a long story and it hasn't finished yet, so I'd rather keep explanations to a minimum for the moment. I need to ask you a big favour.'

'Sure, whatever.'

'It could be dangerous?'

Gareth shrugged

'Go on.'

'I need you to deliver this for me.' His father was holding out a memory stick.

'What's on it?'

'A dossier of files containing evidence of Councillor Hywel Preece's criminal activities. Take a look if you want. Go on.'

Gareth hesitated then walked over to his desk and turned on the laptop his dad had given him for getting into uni. His father sat back down in the armchair with an audible sigh of relief. He waited for the computer to boot up then inserted the stick and opened it. He began working his way through files of pictures and text without making any sense of it. Many of the pictures seemed to involve men knocking on doors. Then there was page after page of closely typed script. He couldn't take it in. He hated himself for it, but there was a frantic intensity about the dense text that brought back Preece's remarks about paranoia. He shut down his laptop and handed the stick back to his dad.

'I think I'd need more time to study that properly, why's it dangerous?'

Charlie rose and took Gareth's arm. He led him over to the window.

'See that building over there? There's a man, built like a gorilla, watching you from the right hand window on the third floor. He followed you to the shops and back this morning.'

Gareth stared at the net curtain across the road. It was an eerie feeling being told you were being spied on, although he could see nothing that suggested he was. More paranoia? His dad continued.

'That man works for Preece and he's there because Preece knows I'm alive and wants me dead. He is hoping I will try to contact you. I promise you that they will stop at nothing to get their hands on that stick. I'm not quite ready to retake my place in society, so I need someone to deliver it to the police for me. I'm really sorry to saddle you with this, but please believe me, that information could save a lot of lives and time is critical.'

'What if he tries to stop me?'

'That's why it's dangerous. It's quite possible that he will. That's why I'll be watching your back.'

'A bit like a tethered goat?'

Charlie nodded.

'I'm afraid so, but the tiger doesn't always attack and I promise you, I wouldn't ask you to do this if I couldn't handle it.'

'How did you get in here, if this place is being watched?'

'I came in through the skylight upstairs before it got light and hid in a broom cupboard.'

'How did you know I was going shopping and not straight co college?'

'I didn't. I was going to wait all day if necessary.'

Gareth paused then nodded.

'Okay, I'll deliver it.'

*

His dad was gone and Gareth's head was spinning. His old man was alive, but he was obviously badly injured. He was clearly convinced he had the low down on Preece, but what was the use of that if he died trying to prove it? Gareth walked over to the desk on which his PC sat. He opened the drawer and pulled out Preece's business card. He stared at it thoughtfully for a moment, and then he picked up the phone and dialled Preece's office number. He got put through almost immediately.

'Hywel Preece.'

He remembered that quiet, controlled voice and those cold, dark eyes. Suddenly, he felt sick with nerves.

'It's Gareth Llewellyn.'

'Yes, any news for me?'

'My father contacted me this morning. He has given me a file to give to the police implicating you in some very serious crimes.'

'Has he indeed? So why are you telling me this?'

'Because my father has asked me to pass a message to you.'

'I'm listening.'

'He has told me to advise you to call off that man you've got watching me, and to warn you that, if anything happens to me, he will take you out personally.'

There was a noticeable pause before Preece spoke.

'Why isn't he telling me this personally?'

'That's obvious. He prefers to keep his distance in case you try something stupid.'

'Don't you think this all smacks of the paranoia discussed in that letter I showed you? This is Swansea, not Chicago, you know. If your father wishes to make allegations against me, he is free to do so. Frankly, working as a messenger boy for his silly threats is not the kind of help I suspect he needs from you right now.'

'Let me worry about that.'

There was another pause, and then Preece spoke again.

'You're making a mistake Gareth. Believe me, I do understand the dilemma you're in, but, to be blunt, I'm getting more than a little tired of this whole thing. Your father bears a grudge against me, relating to his separation from Juliet. As far as I'm concerned, the best thing you can do is take this file to the police and let them talk to me about these allegations if they wish. That way, it can all come out in the open, and you and your father will then, hopefully, realise that you are mistaken.'

It was Gareth's turn to pause. The man always sounded so plausible! Preece cut across his thoughts.

'There is one thing I would ask, however.'

'What's that?'

'I don't want a file full of slanderous allegations sitting around on some duty sergeant's desk waiting to be read by any old Tom, Dick or Harry. I want the matter properly investigated, not used as a way to smear me. In fact, you and your father should bear in mind that, if anything you accuse me of enters the public domain, I will have no alternative but to sue to protect my good name.'

'So what do you want me to do?'

'You must hand it, personally, to someone senior.'

'Such as?'

'To be honest, I don't know. Semple, Tucker and Preece don't handle criminal work, so I don't have dealings with the police, but I suggest you need to be thinking in terms of the Chief Inspector. And remember, if anything leaks, you are a party to this defamation and I will have the best libel lawyers money can buy, making sure that you and your father spend a very long time paying me back.'

'You're in no position to threaten anyone Preece,' retorted Gareth, and cut the connection. He noticed his hand was shaking as he replaced the receiver.

*

It was mid-morning when Gareth left the flat. The data stick was under his shirt, next to his skin, and he was wearing a jumper and coat over that. No one was going to snatch it from him. He headed back down the hill towards the shops and the bus stop. As he reached the Uplands Parade, he noticed a burly man in a raincoat peering into the video shop window. There was never much to see in that window. They wanted customers to go inside and browse. As he got nearer, he realised that the man was rather more than burly. His dad had called him a gorilla and he could see why. He was sure he recognised him from his earlier trip to the shops. He remembered his dad's advice.

'Stay among people. If the file's hidden they will have to grab you, and people get in the way. If someone comes at you, look at his eyes. If they are focussed on you and you cannot dodge him, attack before he has a chance to pull a weapon – he'll leave that to the very last moment. Punch or kick whichever you prefer, but don't let him grab you. If you're grabbed from behind, struggle and scream and be prepared to lose your coat to get away. The intention will be to force you into a car. Shout for help, so everybody knows who the bad guys are. I'll sort out the backup in the car. Your attacker will back off sharpish without their support. Remember this is broad daylight, so if it goes down at all, it'll be fast.'

'Wouldn't a cab be safer?'

'No, they only need to get a car in front, and one behind, and you're going nowhere. Before you know it, you're surrounded, with only a frightened driver as a witness. He's not going to say much once someone's had a word with him.'

It had all seemed so easy, talked about over a cup of coffee in the flat, but now he had to walk past a potential attacker without batting an eyelid. He managed it, but the man was now behind him. He felt the hair on the back of his neck actually standing up. He glanced at the shop window beside him out of the corner of his eye. As far as he could tell, no one was poised to jump on his back. Then he was at the bus stop and mingling with a handful of elderly shoppers. The man had carried on past and was inspecting the list of guest bands appearing at the Uplands Tavern. Somehow, he did not look like a candidate for karaoke at the Tav's open mic night.

To Gareth's relief a number twenty-two came sweeping around the bend and pulled in. He boarded it and walked down to the back, which was empty. He sat down in the last vacant double seat. A couple of passengers later the man got on. He came down the bus and Gareth felt him swing into the back seat behind him, as Charlie had predicted. Passengers were still loading and settling into seats ahead of them as the man leant forward and spoke quietly.

'There's two ways we can play this, see, mate. The first is where you use a bit of common and 'and over what you're carryin' to me, nice and easy, like. The second is where I follows you off the bus and sticks the knife that I am carryin' in your back. Then my mates chuck you in a car and take what you're carryin' off you anyway. I'm easy, see. It's up to you really.'

Gareth sat motionless, gazing straight ahead. It was the casual matter-of-factness about the announcement that unnerved him. And where the hell was his father? The bus doors began to hiss closed then, suddenly, there was Charlie, running up gesturing for the driver to let him on. The doors hissed open again, and Gareth watched his father pay, then come shuffling down the bus towards him, coughing and wiping his mouth. A couple of passengers turned away in distaste, the rest were engrossed in conversation. As he drew level with Gareth's seat, he was stuffing his handkerchief back into the side pocket of his coat, and then he lurched, apparently with the motion of the bus. There was a single, dull crack.

'Sorry, mate.' Gareth heard him say, quietly. No one was paying attention, so Gareth glanced back. His dad was slipping something back into the pocket that he had stuffed his handkerchief into a moment before. The man was slumped against the window, apparently fast asleep. There was an ugly, dark smudge on his temple.

A few minutes later the bus turned right into Craddock Street. Gareth stayed seated as his father walked forward and followed a handful of passengers off the bus. Alone again, he continued on his way to the bus station in the Quadrant Shopping Centre. He got off and walked quickly through the glass doors into the mall. According to his dad, the villains would assume the gorilla still had him in his sights. But then his dad had grinned and added that that was only a theory. He ought to assume they would pick him up again pretty quickly. He should cut up through the market to avoid the taxi rank which would make good cover for a snatch vehicle. From there he should follow the pedestrian precinct up to the Kingsway.

Charlie would monitor him all the way, but he reckoned that if they were going to try anything it would be away from the shoppers, which meant Orchard Street or Alexandra Road. The police station sat at the apex of the two streets, which left them very little margin for error. If trouble started there, he was to make a run for it and leave Charlie to fight the rearguard action. They debated which of the two roads to approach from and settled on Orchard Street as the busier of the two.

As he came out of the market entrance, he noticed a scruffy-looking bloke in his twenties reading the Evening Post. He looked at Gareth hard and closed his paper. Gareth kept going quickly, without looking back. Again, his dad had explained that it was psychologically difficult to attack a rapidly receding target from behind. Aggressors liked eye contact, and without it would often keep putting off the moment. Gareth found himself wondering where his dad got all this stuff from; anyhow, he certainly seemed to know what he was doing if the gorilla on the bus was anything to go by.

He reached the top of the pedestrianised area and walked a few yards down the Kingsway. As always, cars were streaming around the corner and he had no choice but to wait for a break in the traffic. He glanced back as the scruffy one came sauntering around the corner talking into a mobile. He saw Gareth and stopped. He cut the connection, turned, and strolled back a couple of paces. He was obviously just a tracker, but he was none too discreet about it. Gareth had the feeling that he was being shepherded into a trap.

A gap appeared in the traffic and he darted across to the central reservation. More traffic. He glanced back again. He was just in time to see his dad approach the man. He was gesturing as if asking for directions. Suddenly, the scruffy one doubled up. A bus got in the way. In the split second it took to accelerate off down the bus lane, the man had lain down on a bench and Charlie was walking around to follow him across the road.

He negotiated the other half of the road, and then crossed Bellevue Way. He began the walk up Orchard Street. The rain had stopped, but it was still a chilly day. Nevertheless he could feel sweat running down his back. He had been afraid before, but this was something else. He was so wired that it felt as if his eyes were out on stalks and everything appeared to be moving in slow motion.

Then he saw them. A car was pulled in at the bus stop, which narrowed the pavement down considerably. There was a man leaning against the wall opposite the back door of the car, which narrowed the gap still further. There was one man in the back of the car and two in front. He toyed with the idea of running into the road, but he knew the driver and the man in the back would be waiting for that. As he reached the bus stop, the man on the pavement stepped in front of him. He was of medium height, but broad and fit-looking. There was no apparent avenue for flight, so it had to be fight. Gareth launched himself forward, swinging a fist. The man swayed back out of range and, as Gareth's momentum carried him onwards, butted him in the face.

As he went down on all fours, with the sound of his breaking nose still ringing in his ears, he saw the rear door of the car swing open. Then he saw nothing as tears welled up and blotted out his vision. He could taste warm blood running into his mouth. The man grabbed him and then let him go. Gareth heard the same dull crack he had heard on the bus, and then his assailant was down on the floor beside him. He dragged his sleeve across his eyes to clear the tears, just in time to see his father throw some sort of canister into the car and slam the door. Then he felt himself being yanked to his feet.

'Let me look at your face, son.' He felt strong fingers grip his throbbing nose, then another crunching sensation in his head. To his amazement, his eyes were no longer streaming, and he could smell acrid fumes as the three men stumbled out of the vehicle. He was glad to see their eyes were streaming more than his had. They were also coughing and gasping for breath, and in no condition to pursue matters further.

'Pretty again?' he asked, more bravely than he felt.

'As a picture,' as he spoke, Charlie began coughing. He

groped for his handkerchief, but the fit was far more violent than anything Gareth had seen before. As he straightened up his face was grey, and contorted with pain, and Gareth could see pink froth flecked around his mouth. His eyes were watering as he dabbed at his lips with the handkerchief.

'For Chrissakes, Dad, you need to see a doctor...'

Charlie grinned weakly.

'Don't worry about me. Just get that file to the police. Now come on, get going before any more heroes turn up.'

Gareth hesitated, but he knew there was no point arguing with his father. He turned and raced up the road towards Swansea's main police station.

*

Constable Watts was feeling extremely irritable. She always did at this time of the month. She was stuck on the front desk with another thirty-five minutes before lunch, which was her next chance to get another couple of paracetamols down her neck. Why was it that every jerk and misfit in Swansea chose to call in with some petty complaint requiring endless paperwork when she was feeling like this? Jesus, look out! What was this coming in?

The object of her curiosity was a young man of about twenty. Student type from the way he dressed. He'd obviously been up to something naughty because there was blood on the front of his shirt; quite fresh from the look of it. He was looking about, uncertainly.

'Can I 'elp you? She enquired. There was something not

quite run-of-the-mill about him that piqued her curiosity. He registered her and walked forward.

'Yes, I'm sure you can. I wish to see a Chief Inspector.'

She was slightly affronted by the calm authority with which he made the request.

'Oh do you indeed? 'Ave you got an appointment?'

'No, I'm afraid not.'

Normally she would have found him pleasant and even rather dishy, but today, she decided, he fancied himself too much.

'Well, it's not usual for people to just walk in 'ere and demand to see a senior officer without an appointment. D'you mind tellin' me what it's regardin'?'

'I need to hand a file to him. It's on this data stick.'

'Fine. Pass it over and I'll see someone gets it.'

'No. I'm sorry. I have to hand it over personally.'

'Do you indeed?'

'Yes'.

'Right, and would you mind explain' why it's so important that you have to 'and it over personally?'

'Certainly, it contains criminal allegations against some very powerful people.'

'I see.' Constable Watts made a deliberate effort to steady herself. He was being perfectly civil, but, in her present state of mind, his steady persistence came across as stubbornness.

'Got a name 'ave we?' she snapped.

'Yes, Gareth Llewellyn.'

She paused. Llewellyn was the name the Duty Sergeant had briefed everyone to look out for.

'Wait there a moment, will you,' she commanded and hurried back to confer with him. He phoned through and spoke briefly to someone, then gave her his instructions. She stomped back to the front desk, riled that the chopsy, little upstart had got his way so easily.

'Would you like to go over to the delivery window?' she said, sourly. 'Chief Inspector Ringer will be out to collect it shortly.'

23

Al Sullivan glanced at his watch. It was eleven fifteen and he was parked opposite the main entrance to Swansea Central Police Station. He reached across and opened the glove box of Prosser's car. If there was one thing you could rely on with Prosser, it was a never-ending supply of grub; gutsy bastard. He helped himself to a pork pie and a packet of crisps. He hesitated, and then chose a can of Coke. He sat up straight and set about his afternoon snack with relish – he'd nicked his car, so he might as well nick his lunch. He grinned to himself. Perhaps when the job was over he ought to pop around and see what his wife was like!

A print out of the files Charlie had emailed to him lay on the passenger seat beside him. He'd read it through a couple of times and it was explosive stuff. It certainly explained why the heroin being brought into Swansea by the syndicate he was investigating seemed to vanish into thin air.

Normally when a consignment of drugs arrived in any city there was a flurry of clandestine activity. Phone taps produced leads as the word went around. The regular faces appeared in the pubs and clubs with gear to sell. There were always new arrivals in casualty, as users misjudged the strength of the latest gear; but not with this outfit. His team had watched them bringing the stuff in for over two years, but each time they made a run, and the undercover boys working the streets were given the nod, the trail ran cold. Frustrating wasn't the word!

The stuff was coming out of Afghanistan and Iran, via a

processing factory in Iraq, and the supply was never-ending. It then travelled through Turkey and across the Black Sea into Bulgaria, Romania and Hungary. From there the routes lay open into any part of Europe. It was a battle against expendable couriers and unbelievable corruption. Trying to cut the supply at that end was like cutting off one of the heads of that monster in Greek mythology – two more grew back in its place.

This syndicate favoured boats. The gear destined for the big English cities was coming into Lincolnshire and Norfolk from Antwerp, Amsterdam and Rotterdam, whisked across the channel at night by speedboat. The stuff bound for Wales and Ireland was being dropped offshore in floating containers around the Pembrokeshire coast by Spanish 'fishing' vessels and picked up by leisure craft tracking their modified distress signals.

Occasionally Customs took out one of the trawlers on the water, as much for morale, as for the good it did. These people were shrewd – they never tied up too much money in any one shipment. Still, it did them good not to have it all their own way.

The containers were made of foam filled fibreglass and designed to look like driftwood. The frequencies of their distress transmitters were changed every run, so once the consignment was in the water, there was virtually no chance of catching the collectors. The real problem, however, was that there was no distribution network to attack on the ground, and that nullified the powers that allowed them to seize the drugs at sea, and then mop up the distribution networks separately. The idea of importing heroin to supply the needs of an entirely closed ring of drug addicts, who never bought on the street or through known dealers, was ingenious; it completely sidestepped the grasses and undercover agents on whom the drugs intelligence agencies relied.

It was the murder of that kid off the tower block that had persuaded Maddocks to change tactics. They were no closer to cracking the case than they had been when it began. He had become convinced that the gang was being tipped off by a bent copper. He put Sullivan in charge of a high-level profiling exercise, intended to identify who in the Swansea police force might best fit the bill, and Sullivan had set to work with all the considerable powers of a Customs and Excise investigation officer at his disposal. He had worked from the rank of Inspector up, and looked at bank accounts, insurance policies, and shareholdings. He had matched lifestyles to incomes and checked career records for reprimands and anomalies. He had then looked at arrest records for any possibility of blackmail or intimidation. Finally, he had looked at known associates and friends. He had checked out memberships of clubs and societies. This was real shadow boxing. These people understood the system. If any of them were rotten, they wouldn't be advertising the fact with champagne lifestyles. He dredged and he trawled, back and forth across ground he had often covered many times before.

Gradually a name began to emerge. Chief Inspector Ringer, an ambitious career copper who hadn't quite made it to the top. He was abrasive with authority in his younger days and impatient of the promotion structure. There had been a nasty incident in the late seventies when a suspect in his custody had been hospitalised following an interrogation. Ringer had not been charged, but nor had he been entirely exonerated. In 1986 he had been interviewed regarding his relationship with certain Swansea businessmen, following a scandal concerning building contracts, but had satisfied his superiors that the people concerned were legitimate and useful informants. His finances looked clean, but, unless he was a complete fool, that was to be expected. He was a mason in Swansea's leading lodge.

Sullivan got permission to send in a team of watchers. Over the next two months they built up a picture of Ringer's friends and social contacts. The only thing that stood out was a number of meetings with a man called Preece. He was a city Councillor who ran a firm of solicitors. He was also a fellow mason. What struck Sullivan was that the meetings took place in office hours, in places that guaranteed privacy. If they weren't social encounters, what were they, and what was the big secret?

He had a dig around in Preece's background. This man had a reputation for being a real high-flier and very wealthy. The Preece's had been bastions of the Swansea legal fraternity for generations. But in this day and age why wasn't he practising in London or New York? Who knows? Maybe he liked beaches. Perhaps he enjoyed being a big fish in a small pond. As far as Sullivan could see from the outside, Preece was clean. The only thing that rang the faintest bell was that his partner, a man called Semple, had a drugs conviction from his student days. That prompted him to dig a little deeper.

Preece had not returned immediately to Swansea after graduating from Cambridge with a first class law degree in 1980. He had moved to London to become articled with a firm in which his uncle was a senior partner. However, despite the appearance of a cushy future, he had left, as soon as he was qualified, to work for the Foreign Office.

He asked Joe Prosser to take up the chase, but Joe rapidly hit the wall. Preece had spent a couple of years in Berlin at the British Embassy then returned home. Within a couple of months he had resigned from the Foreign Office altogether and moved back down to Swansea. No one would talk to Joe about the nature of Preece's German posting and it seemed odd that he had abandoned London as well as Berlin.

He was still a young man. What had happened to so tarnish his glittering prospects in the Smoke?

Sullivan took the matter up the ladder to his boss. As usual he seemed dismissive, but a week later he had stuck his head around Sullivan's door and asked what he was doing the following day.

Nothing cast in concrete.

Good. How did he fancy a trip up to London to talk to somebody about Preece's diplomatic career?

The following day, at eleven-fifteen he found himself being shown into the lounge of a converted oast-house at the end of a long, unmarked, tree-lined driveway somewhere in the heart of the Kent countryside by a taciturn young man who gave his name as Greg.

The middle-aged woman who rose to greet him in the lounge did not live in this house. Nothing about her sharp, slightly masculine, business attire fitted with the faded, chintzy surroundings and the horsy pictures on the walls. She peered at him quizzically over her half-moon, horn-rimmed glasses before she shook hands and gestured him into a seat.

'I take it Mr Sullivan's documentation is in order?' she asked the driver. He nodded and departed silently. The woman resumed her seat on the opposite side of a rather over-ornate marble coffee table. She picked up the open file she had been flicking through when Sullivan entered the room. Only now did she introduce herself.

'My name is Dr Veronica Campbell, Mr Sullivan. I am a psychologist and a senior personnel manager with M16. I gather you are making enquiries into the background for a former employee of ours, a Mr Hywel Preece.'

Sullivan nodded, trying not to look too taken aback.

'Er, yes that's right...' he managed in reply.

'Hmmn, well I will try to be of help, but I should point out that Preece only worked for the agency briefly and that was nearly twenty years ago. I'm afraid I only have his personnel file here to assist you. Perhaps it would be helpful if you were to outline the exact nature of your investigation. Naturally, anything you say will be treated with absolute discretion.'

'Naturally.' Sullivan sat for a moment, his mind racing. He had a soldier's distrust of the intelligence community and Maddocks had given him no clues about who he was meeting and how to play this. It was as if he didn't know, either. Presumably they had nothing to hide from these people about the investigation or Maddocks would have warned him. He took the plunge.

'Well, to be frank, Doctor Campbell...'

'Call me Veronica if you prefer.'

'Right, Veronica...we are, er, rather groping in the dark on this one.'

The woman sat patiently and expectantly, as if that was not an uncommon situation in her line of work.

'What I mean is, we are trying to crack a drugs ring operating in the UK. Our immediate concern is their Swansea operation. They appear to be benefiting from the help of a bent copper and we have a possible candidate. We have linked him in turn to this man Preece who, from the outside, looks like Mr Respectability himself. We are trying to build a profile that will prove or disprove our suspicions.'

She nodded now.

'I see. So you want primarily a psychological appraisal?'

'I guess you could say that.'

'Right, well I think we can provide you with that. Some of this stuff makes quite interesting reading. I'm afraid I cannot simply hand it over to you, but I can give you edited highlights.'

'I see.'

The doctor selected a small bundle of typed notes from the file.

'This goes back to our first contact with Mr Preece. He was picked up as a likely candidate in his second year at Cambridge by our vetting agency. An approach was made and he was as keen as mustard. Too hot if anything, but that was put down to youthful enthusiasm. We ran him past the usual targets – student activist groups etcetera – and he did a pretty competent job. His reports were clear and to the point though his strong right-wing political views tended to unbalance them. He obviously could only see the left as a threat to democracy. His controller notes that he was very bright, but questions his judgement.'

'Despite that reservation, he was considered worthy of further investment, partly because, if nothing else, he had outstanding capability as a lawyer. In fact, it seems that was what he was earmarked for within the agency. Over the last two decades the agency has had to interface with the mainstream to a far greater extent than was previously the case and that has entailed the up-grading of our legal and political remit.'

Sullivan nodded understandingly. Apparently, they needed lawyers.

'However, Preece appears to have seen himself operating out in the field, not stuck behind a desk,' continued the doctor. 'According to his controller, he was extremely impatient of the need to become articled and irritated by the suggestion that his legal qualifications were probably his greatest asset from the agency's point of view. During this period he joined a pistol club, the Territorial Army and took up martial arts.'

'A budding James Bond, then?'

'Yes, he appears to have had a rather romanticised view of the role of the modern intelligence officer. His case officer refers on one occasion to 'a touch of the Walter Mitty's.'

'And yet you still took him on after he qualified?'

'Mr Sullivan, he was a young, immature man, but extremely capable in his field. To be frank, that is a not uncommon profile for many people in the intelligence community...'

There was a knock at the door.

'Come!' commanded the doctor, and waited silently until the young man, Greg, had delivered a tray of sandwiches and coffee and departed. Then she continued.

'As I was saying, my line of business attracts people with all sorts of motivations and agendas. Preece's clearly seemed to fall within acceptable parameters to his selection panel.'

'I see.'

The woman was extracting more documents from the file. Sullivan found himself wondering about her inner demons. His boss could be rude and patronising when the need arose – usually several times a day – but this woman had a lecturing manner all of her own. He suddenly had the unnerving feeling that, if he questioned her conclusions, she would slap his legs for him. He suppressed a grin at the notion and leant forward to make it clear he was paying attention.

'Let me see,' she continued. 'Yes, he qualified in eighty-four and joined the Foreign Office, obviously under our auspices. The Wall was still up and Berlin was the espionage capital of the World, so we shipped him out there to see how he reacted to the buzz.'

'How did he do?'

'Bloody disaster, basically. Seems it was that judgement thing again. The old Station hands will tell you what a weird place it was in those days. Everyone out to stitch someone up. Not just the enemy – colleagues as well. Needed eyes in your arse. Preece couldn't hack it. Perhaps it was a baptism of fire, but then so's being dropped behind enemy lines, with the added risk of being shot. Anyway, he couldn't cope with eating in the same restaurants as known Stasi spies and all that stuff. The world was not black and white enough for him. His controller comments that his reporting of quite straightforward meetings became fanciful and exaggerated. After eighteen months the agency called him home for reassessment.

'And?'

'My colleagues found they had a paranoiac on their hands.'

'How on earth didn't they pick it up before?'

'Paranoia and most other psychiatric conditions are like cancer. They are often invisible and it is usually the patient that sounds the alarm. With mental illness the problem is compounded by the patient's frequent inability to recognise his own symptoms. In Preece's case he would swing from a grandiose phase, in which he was developing contacts with Europe's top spymasters, politicians and industrialists, to a persecuted phase, in which he would become withdrawn and distrustful of colleagues, even his own case officer. The condition was progressive, presumably as he began to feel increasingly out of his depth. Some of his later reports were pathetically delusional.'

'So what happened?'

'He was given therapy and sent back to Berlin to complete his tour, but he was kept out of the field. When he returned to London he was offered a desk job in the contracts department. He resigned immediately.'

'What do you make of that?'

'You want my personal opinion?'

'Sure.'

'It smacks of denial. Most of Preece's paranoia seems to have grandiose overtones. His ego and intellect are clearly strong to the point of domineering under normal circumstances – hence his rigid political views. Having recovered his centre of gravity, he would have refused to accept that he had failed. Look at his background. Everything in his upbringing, schooling and university career must have conspired to convince him that he had the golden touch. That's a lot of gilt-edged egoism on deposit. He would have taken the classic paranoiac's option and convinced himself that he was the victim of a conspiracy. You can hardly blame him – they were going on around him all the time.'

'So what sort of attitude would he harbour towards the agency?'

'Oh, bitterness without a doubt. They had failed to appreciate his talents. They hadn't given him a fair crack of the whip, etcetera, etcetera.'

'Might that have affected his attitude to the establishment or, indeed, society in general?'

The doctor paused and eyed Sullivan with something approaching respect.

'I see where you're going. Yes, it would be very easy for such an individual to project a single failure into a universal rejection – a 'misunderstood by fools' rationale, if you like.'

Al Sullivan leant forward and picked up his briefcase.

'Thank you doctor. You have been most helpful.'

Suddenly, he stopped as another question occurred to him. 'Oh, there is one other thing I would appreciate your opinion on...'

The doctor nodded encouragingly. She had found a promising pupil.

'Do you think that sense of rejection could have led to anti-social activity such as violence or crime?'

The doctor grinned and held up her hands to show there was nothing up her sleeves.

'Sorry, got me there. That's a crystal ball job. He may have settled into a stimulating job, or a loving relationship, which quite supplanted the negative emotions. The paranoid episode may have been a temporary thing brought on by circumstances that were exceptionally stressful to him. However,' she paused to give extra emphasis to the subtlety of her reasoning, 'you might ask yourself one thing...'

'And that is?'

'Why did he join up in the first place? He obviously fancied himself as a manipulator and intriguer. And then there's the gun club and the martial arts. Machiavellianism and testosterone kicking in with the mood swings of a paranoiac – now that could make for a pretty volatile personality in my book. No doubt the strong intellect would add an element of control, but it could be very ugly underneath. That, however, is of course purely hypothetical.'

'Of course, but it does help us understand quite what we might be dealing with.'

'I hope so.'

*

Sullivan roused himself as a movement caught his eye. He had been automatically checking out the steady human traffic in and out of the station for over an hour now. Suddenly, he was alert. A young man was hurrying up the road towards the entrance of the building. He was half running, half walking and he glanced back over his shoulder a couple of times. Could this be young Llewellyn, the son Charlie had told him to expect in their brief conversation earlier? He grabbed a camera and fired off a couple of rolls. He was sure now that Charlie was one of the good guys, but Maddocks was still sticking stubbornly to his suspicions, so he was duty bound to gather anything that might be evidence.

The kid reached the front door of the Police Station and pushed through almost knocking an exiting visitor aside in his haste. According to Charlie he had to deliver a memory stick to a Chief Inspector Ringer in person, so, if Sullivan knew anything about Chief Inspectors, he could expect to be kept waiting!

Rather to his disappointment the kid emerged barely five minutes later and hurried off. Perhaps it wasn't Charlie's boy after all or perhaps the arrival of the memory stick had lit a fire under Ringer's arse. Who knew? Only time would tell. Sullivan sat back and let his thoughts drift back to the investigation.

*

He had returned to Bristol somewhat encouraged by the meeting with the doctor, but he was beginning to conclude that he was chasing shadows when Charlie Llewellyn's name appeared through the blizzard of paperwork that his researchers were threatening to bury him under. Someone had dug up a rumour that Preece was having an affair. According to the source, it was none too discreet and Llewellyn was the injured party. Sullivan wondered if his luck was changing. If it was the same Charlie Llewellyn, he hadn't seen him since he vanished into the exalted company of the SAS. Even if nothing came of it on the business side, he fancied a reunion with his old pal.

He ran a check and it was the same old Charlie alright. They met for a pie and a pint in Swansea. In fact they had several pints as they reminisced. They drifted on from army days to the present. Sullivan admitted ruefully that a career in the Excise had not sat well with a stable love life. Bristol was littered with his romantic failures. How had Charlie faired?

Well had he heard what happened to Carys?

No, were they still together? He knew immediately that that was the wrong question from the look on Charlie's face. His old pal shook his head.

Carys died whilst he was out in the Gulf.

Carys? You're kidding!

'Fraid not; leukaemia. They knew she had it, but she was sure she could hang on till he got back. They had a little boy, Gareth. He was nineteen now and doing alright at college.

Christ, he was sorry. Carys was a great girl. Who would have thought...?

Charlie brushed it aside. It obviously still hurt. He hadn't chosen so well second time around, mind. He'd married a right bitch and their marriage was on the rocks. They had more irreconcilable differences than the Arabs and the Israelis. To top it all she was shagging her boss.

Jesus! That was a bit steep. What was he going to do?

Let her get on with it. Tempting as it was to give this Preece bloke a good hiding, he wasn't going to land himself in trouble over his bitch of a wife. Preece was acting as her solicitor and he was due to meet him to sort things out that morning.

Preece? Preece? Where did he know that name from?

Well, anywhere – there were hundreds in the phone book.

Oh yes, of course. What was he thinking of?

Suddenly he found himself the object of Charlie's steady gaze.

'Okay, Al, spill the beans. What are you after?

He began to bluster, but those mocking green eyes were laughing at him just like they used to. You could never hide a thing from the bugger. He cut the crap and told him about the investigation. What did he think?

Charlie thought Preece was a nasty piece of work. He'd met him once or twice and he struck him as rabidly ambitious. Calculating and unscrupulous were the words he used. Crooked? He couldn't say, but he wouldn't be surprised. He certainly came across as a ruthless bastard.

Would he keep his ear to the ground?

Sure, but he couldn't promise anything. He had a business to run and, besides, he and Juliet were splitting up and he wasn't exactly part of Preece's inner circle. They dropped the subject and returned to Memory Lane.

That was two months ago, then came the news of Charlie's suicide. At first he was stunned, but when no body was found, he began to wonder. Llewellyn was known as the Cat even before he left for the Regiment and, after he disappeared into that secret world, tales still filtered back about his indestructibility. He even dared to wonder if Charlie's disappearance was related to Preece and the case that was driving him to distraction. He had gone back over the reports of Charlie's suicide and studied the sea charts. He'd noted the Police report regarding the stolen motor bike and then returned to Swansea to talk to an undercover Drugs Squad officer called Dyer about a fight he had reported. Finally, he had persuaded Maddocks to hit the caravan.

He had warned Maddocks that Charlie would be

unimpressed by strong-arm tactics, but his boss knew better; he seemed more that a little convinced that Charlie was one of the bad guys, despite Sullivan's assurances to the contrary. Still he'd smoothed that over and engineered a sort of pact. Unfortunately, he had the nagging suspicion that Charlie had only agreed to it in order to further his own ends. Like it or not, he sensed that they were working to different agendas. He wouldn't hear from him again unless those agendas happened to coincide to Charlie's advantage.

And then, that morning, he had checked his e-mails as he was drinking his first coffee of the day and there it was. The message they had agreed on if anything turned up:

Charlie needs a chat.

Basically, Charlie had some important information and wanted to talk urgently. He deleted the message and left the office heading for the nearest payphone. Five minutes later he replaced the receiver his head spinning. If Customs wanted a piece of the action they needed a stakeout in place outside Swansea Central Police Station by eleven that morning. He rushed back to the office and called up Google Maps on his computer. He zoomed in on Swansea. The station was near the junction of Orchard Street and Alexandra Road. He couldn't see the station marked on the map, but that was normal. He glanced at his watch. Jesus Christ! It was quarter-past-nine already and he had to round up a team and get from his office in Bristol to Swansea in less than two hours! He grabbed the phone and buzzed through to his boss.

*

Sullivan's mobile phone rang. He answered it.

'Zero One.'

'Zero One, this is Zero Four. There is an unmarked Daimler pulling out of the back entrance. Could be our bunny,' said a voice in his ear.

'Roger, Zero Four. Any eyeball?'

'Affirmative, Zero One. He is passing me now, and matches his picture. We have a positive contact. I repeat, we have a positive contact.'

'Good work, Zero Four. I'll get on his back. You know the area, so switch to radio and cue the others in as required.'

Sullivan shoved the remains of his snack back into Prosser's glove box and turned the ignition key. Operation Switchback had begun.

24

Annette Preece watched in horrified fascination as young Bomber prepared to inject himself. It wasn't the sight of the injection or even the quiet desperation with which he went about it that troubled her, though that was disturbing enough. What really alarmed her was that he was about to inject vodka. What the hell would it do to him? She tried to think rationally. It was a syringe full. What was that? A pub measure? More? Obviously it would go straight into the blood stream, so the effects would be pretty instantaneous.

It had never occurred to her that people injected alcohol, but in a coldly rational way it was logical enough. That, she decided, was what was so awful about it. There was absolutely no concession to sociability or entertainment. It was a deliberate plunge into oblivion. Even at her worst, she had only used alcohol to hold an intolerable reality at bay. She had softened its edges, not blotted it out altogether. But then, she reminded herself, young Bomber wasn't just hiding from reality, he was hiding from the effects of an imminent heroin withdrawal. Part of that, he had explained, was the urge to inject himself. She had agreed to go out and buy him a bottle of vodka, never dreaming that he was planning to use it to satisfy that urge.

She watched now as he let the end of the belt fall from his mouth and fumbled to loosen it from around his arm. She hurried forward to help him as he slumped back on the pillows on the bed. For the hundredth time, she wondered what to do. The boy could not go on like this. He needed help.

Her mind went back to the conversation with Charlie when he emerged from the warehouse the second time. As he stepped forward out of the shadows, his face was as hard as granite. She guessed that something terrible had gone on inside. He did not volunteer an explanation and she did not ask for one. They got straight down to practicalities.

He advised her to drive to the station and buy two train tickets to Manchester. She should get off at Cardiff and stay in a hotel overnight. Then she should do everything she could to change her appearance, before returning to Swansea by bus the following day.

She suggested trying to get to London instead. It was a big place in which to hide and she'd live there for years. There were even old friends that she might be able to track down. Charlie shook his head. London would be very different from the place she remembered and so would be the friends. People change, particularly when they become successful. What would they say if a fugitive turned up on their doorsteps with a young heroin addict in tow?

Fugitive?

Sure. The Rent Men couldn't simply let her disappear with a witness as dangerous as Bomber. Preece was hand in glove with at least one senior police officer and would use his influence to organise a manhunt. If they caught up with her in Swansea, at least Charlie would be within striking distance. He should be able to arrange a safe evacuation for her and Bomber within a day or two. He gave her the address of a guest house on Bryn Rd. It wasn't exactly a safe house, but it belonged to the wife of a dead comrade. She was to ask for Betty Stone and tell her that the Cat had sent her. Betty would put her up, no questions asked.

He told her to sit tight until he contacted her. Stay away from any form of authority, including doctors and hospitals. She had to avoid the police at all costs. If Bomber got really desperate, drop him off at Singleton or Morriston Casualty and try and make it to London by cab, but that was the last resort. The ungodly would be watching for just such an eventuality and a heroin withdrawal was nothing compared to what those bastards would do to such potentially damaging witnesses.

She had followed his instructions and even improved on them, visiting two Cardiff hairdressers – one to have the old fashioned perm cut out of her hair, the other to have it dyed strawberry blonde. She had replaced her blouse and skirt with a cream, turtle-necked top from the market and a pair of rather trendy jeans. She had added a loose-fitting jacket over the top for warmth. A rather neat miniature rucksack and a pair of pink-tinted shades with thin black frames had combined with plenty of bangles and a large pair of earrings to complete the transformation. Thanks to the new outfit, and the weight she'd lost since giving up drinking, the stranger in the mirror looked ten years younger than Mrs Annette Preece, formerly of Derwen Fawr.

Bomber had taken some restyling. He looked more comfortable in trainers, jeans and a sweatshirt than he did in Semple's shirt and trousers. He looked less gaunt with his hair cut shorter. He seemed to approve of his new appearance and was generally quite docile. Charlie had agreed with her suggestion that she share her tranquillisers with the boy in the hope that it would make the remains of the heroin he had taken from the warehouse last longer.

That had worked throughout yesterday and this morning, but now it was gone ten o'clock in the evening of the second day and the heroin had run out. More ominously, she had heard nothing from Charlie. Annette leant forward and ran her hand soothingly across the boy's forehead. What kind of people could have done this to him she wondered? He opened his eyes and stared at her unseeingly. He had told her he was sixteen. It was terrible to see such dark hopelessness staring back from such a young face.

She had to do something. The vodka might help with his need to inject, but she couldn't imagine it would stave off the effects of the heroin withdrawal indefinitely. Besides, there was such a thing as alcohol poisoning. She paused and made herself think logically. Okay. She had no access to prescribed drugs and she didn't know anyone who did. The years of isolation had made sure of that. She didn't know how to go about stealing any, and she would not know what to steal anyway, so that was not an option.

She did, however, have money and a disguise. Furthermore, she was no longer the matronly figure of two days ago. Other people bought heroin in Swansea. Why shouldn't she? The problem was where to begin. She had no idea where drug dealers hung out. She knew pubs got raided occasionally – she'd seen it in the paper. But which pubs? She couldn't wander around pubs at random asking strangers if they had heroin for sale.

That reminded her that there was also something of a language barrier to contend with. What was the latest jargon?

Bomber always referred to heroin as 'brown', so that was one piece of terminology to cling to. 'Banging' was how he referred to injecting, so that had taken on a new meaning since her day! Other than that, he called a syringe a 'gun' and referred to withdrawing as 'clucking'. She couldn't see how she was going to need those terms to buy the stuff. Perhaps she could get by, if only she could find a dealer!

Where else apart from pubs? Night clubs! She recalled an interview on the television after a young girl died from taking an Ecstatic tablet. Ecstatic? That didn't sound right. Ecstasy, that was it. The expert they were interviewing was explaining that Ecstasy was a relatively minor problem. Heroin was now being offered cheaply to younger people, who were smoking it for fun without realising how addictive it was. Nightclubs were mentioned as a favourite haunt of dealers.

She leaned forward and grasped Bomber by the shoulder. She shook him gently, then more firmly. He opened his eyes. There was recognition in them now.

'Can you hear me?' she asked.

He nodded drowsily.

'Okay, listen. I'm going to try and get you some brown, alright?'

He nodded again.

'Fine. Now it's very important that you wait for me here. You mustn't go anywhere and you mustn't make a noise. Do you understand?'

'Yeah,' he slurred, thickly.

'Good. I'll be as quick as I can, but don't expect me back for at least a couple of hours. I'll lock the door from the outside and, if anybody tries to get in, hide under the bed and don't make a sound. Promise?'

The boy nodded again. Annette picked up her bag, checked it for her keys and money, and then let herself out.

*

The music was pumping out across the dance-floor as the synchronised lights illuminated the mass of heaving bodies. Annette sat at the bar watching the gyrating youngsters. It was all a bit more melodic in her day, not quite so hard edged and beat driven. Then she reminded herself of the Clash and the Sex Pistols, and guitars getting smashed. That was pretty hard edged! Just different sounds for different generations she decided. She tried to catch a barman's eye to order another orange juice without much success.

She noticed that a large, shaven-headed man had moved in beside her at the bar. He was wearing a short-sleeved, white, silk shirt with a logo on the pocket. He had several heavy gold chains around his neck with an obviously expensive gold watch on his wrist. Her first thought, given his pumped-up physique, was that he was a bouncer, but he was too expensively and informally dressed. He raised his hand and snapped his fingers twice. The gesture couldn't be heard above the music, but a barman hurried over immediately. The man turned to Annette and nodded at her glass. He leant forward, giving her a flash of a couple of gold fillings.

'What's that you're drinkin'?'

'Orange juice.'

'Want anything in it?'

'Nothing they sell in the bar.'

He looked at her calculatingly for a moment, letting his eyes rove over her figure before returning to her face. Annette stared back, challengingly. He turned and said something to the barman who returned later with a fresh glass of orange. He paid him, picked up the glass and handed it to her.

'So what sort of thing d'you like that they don't sell behind the bar?'

'Well generally, when I'm looking to get laid, I fancy something nice and relaxing to smoke.'

His eyebrows shot up, but otherwise he controlled his expression admirably.

'What like blow?'

Blow? Blow? What the hell was that? Avoid the question.

'Brown turns me on the most.' Annette had never heard of heroin having an aphrodisiac effect on women, but she knew that women talking about sex had an aphrodisiac effect on men. 'It makes me seem to last forever.'

The man licked his lips.

'D'you want some now?' he asked, hoarsely.

'Sure, why not? This music is pissing me off.'

The man nodded his agreement and gestured for her to follow him. Annette slipped off the bar stool, her heart pounding. Using her charms to get the heroin was one thing, but this gorilla was going to expect something in return, and she hadn't quite figured an escape plan yet. He didn't look like the sort to accept rejection gracefully.

He led her out of the main room and across the corridor

into a smaller room. It was cooler and darker with no flashing lights and the music was far more mellow. There were people sitting on sofas, chatting and drinking bottled water. Obviously the place was set aside for relaxing. Her companion showed her to a seat and went over to talk to a young woman, then he returned and sat down beside her. He patted her on the thigh.

'Maxine'll sort you out in a minute,' he announced. 'Just follow 'er to the bog.'

A couple of minutes later the woman put down her drink and stood up. She sauntered past them on the way to the door. Annette rose and followed her as she headed down the corridor and into the ladies.

A couple of girls were sitting in cubicles with the doors open. They were swigging from Bacardi Breezer bottles with their pants around their ankles, lost in their own hilarity.

'I wouldn't go in a lock-up with Maxine if I was you, luv!' shrieked one of the girls. 'Never know what you'll find in 'er magic box!'

'What's in Maxy's ming tonight, everybody?' sang the other one.

'Fuck off you twats,' responded Maxine, indifferently and motioned Annette into a cubical. She followed her in and shut the door. Rather to Annette's surprise, she hitched up her skirt and reached into her panties. She pulled out a number of small packages and inspected them closely. Annette noticed she had a severe squint, which combined with her dyed blonde hair, drawn tightly back into a top-knot, gave the impression that her eye sight ended at the tip of her nose. She selected a couple of packets and handed them over.

'E's paid for 'em,' she muttered and stuffed the others back into their hiding place.

'Hey Maxy!' came a drunken voice from the other side of the partition. 'Does shovin' all that gear up your twat make you go boss-eyed?'

There were more shrieks of laughter as Maxine let herself out, then Annette heard a thud and the sound of breaking glass. As she followed Maxine out of the toilet, one of the girls was sitting slumped forward with a pool of Bacardi Breezer and glass around her feet.

*

As they left the club, it occurred to Annette that they hadn't even exchanged names. She had bought the heroin with the promise of sex. It was as mechanical as that. It was quite likely, given that she could hardly go to the police that she was going to be held to that promise. What would be the reaction if she told him that she had lied – that the drugs were for someone that needed them desperately and here was the money for them? Here was double the money for them? Wise up. The man was expecting sex. He'd take that and probably the money as well. She'd experienced enough brutal, unfeeling sex at the hands of her husband to know what to expect. She'd better concentrate on getting away.

'The car's down here,' he announced abruptly and turned right down a poorly lit side road. He had his arm around her shoulders and there was nothing she could do to resist. She sensed he could lift her clean off the ground with one arm and carry on walking if he wanted to.

A few yards further on, they passed some council refuse bins spilling rubbish from a nearby restaurant and suddenly she found herself pinned up against a wall. She glanced wildly back the way they'd come. They were hidden from the main road by the bins. She glanced in the opposite direction and made out other figures in the shadows. This was clearly Lover's Lane for club goers. The man yanked up her top and bra in a single movement. She reached up and ran an arm around his neck.

'Hey, steady on. I thought I was going to get a smoke. What's the rush?'

'I've got business to do. I'm not sittin' around watchin' you get stoned. You can do that after. Come on. You're fuckin' gaggin' for it, so don't piss me about.'

He was fumbling with the button at the waist of her jeans and she knew at any moment he would lose patience and rip them down.

'Okay, okay, take it easy.' She reached forward with her other hand and felt for his fly. As long as he didn't turn violent, she stood a chance of controlling the situation. She tugged at his zipper.

'I'll only do it if you wear a condom,' she murmured. 'Otherwise I'll start screaming rape and fight like hell.'

'I haven't got any.'

'I have. I'll even put it on for you.' She sank down on her knees in front of him. She undid his belt and pulled down his trousers and briefs. She caressed him with one hand as she felt in her bag with the other.

'Oh yeah!' he breathed. 'Come on, babes, I wanna shag.'

Her hand closed around the sharp pointed nail scissors she had bought in Cardiff the previous day.

'Let me just do this,' she murmured. In a single movement she whipped the scissors from her bag and drove them deep into the muscle of his overdeveloped left thigh. She half expected him to scream, but he simply muttered 'Jesus fuck!' and tried to grab her by the hair. It hadn't occurred to her that he might be anaesthetised by the drugs he sold. She twisted and pulled away, leaving some hair behind. She scrabbled forward on her hands and knees; half got to her feet and stumbled down the road. She heard a bellow from behind her and glanced back. He was standing, framed in the light from the main road. She paused to watch as he threw the scissors he had yanked out of his thigh to the ground, then pulled his trousers up, turned and limped back up the road.

She adjusted her clothing and looked around to get her bearings. She realised she was shaking like a leaf. Without warning, she lurched forward and doubled over. Despite her best efforts to control herself, she was suddenly and violently sick.

*

Arnie Dyer watched with growing curiosity from his position on the other side of The Kingsway. He'd seen the transaction in the chill-out room of the club and followed the woman and Horse outside. He'd remained at a safe distance as the pair headed down the side road. He guessed what for. He'd been working undercover in the club for long enough to know why couples nipped down there. He was rather more surprised, however, when Horse emerged a couple of minutes later, limping and obviously in a foul temper. What the hell had happened? Who was she? He had to know all the regular faces on the Swansea drug scene, but she was new and from the look of it she'd run a right number on the man. Horse was not a man to mess with. He ran the petty dealers like that cockeyed slag Maxine and he was rumoured to be a senior fixer for the Rent Man gang. He didn't handle the gear himself. He'd never even been busted, at least not for drugs.

Dyer crossed the road and headed down the side road. Someone had thrown up by some bins. He lifted the lids, half expecting to find a body, but there was no sign of foul play. He hurried down the road, ignoring the groping couples in the shadows. As he emerged in the car park, he spotted her turning up another of the lanes that led back up to The Kingsway. What did he do? It was pretty dead in the club and this was a new face. Should he investigate? Al Sullivan was still drawing a blank according to their last conversation, thank God! He was on a tidy earner from the Gang and didn't need anyone rocking the boat. She was probably just a new customer and, besides, he had that skunk he'd confiscated earlier to check out. Fuck it, he'd done enough for the night!

25

Councillor Preece's black Range Rover Autobiography pulled into the unmarked entrance of the private members club where only the City's wealthiest went to lunch. As it coasted up the long drive Juliet Llewellyn turned to him.

'What's wrong?' she began.

'What d'you mean?'

'You're very tense. What's the matter?'

'It looks like your bloody husband's come back to haunt us.'

'Oh right. I thought it was all too good to be true.'

There was a pause, and then he spoke again.

'You want him dead, then?'

'Well I didn't want him back. He was a bloody liability with his drinking and bankrupt business. If he'd drowned himself, we'd have been shot of him for once and all for all no one could have pointed the finger of suspicion at us.'

There was another pause. His voice was a little more than a murmur when he spoke again.

'As far as the world's concerned, he's still dead.'

'What d'you mean?'

'Well, if you don't want him back...?' he let the question hang in the air.

'Go on,' she whispered, a note of excitement creeping into her voice.

'If you don't want him back and something happens to him now, he's not exactly going to be missed, is he?'

'What sort of thing?'

'Well I've told O'Leary to put a couple of boys on the job and make sure they finish it properly.'

'How will they do it?' Preece glanced at his mistress; her eyes were wide with excitement.

'Oh, I don't know. I stay well clear of that side of things. I expect they'll find a way to trap him somewhere well out of the way. How they'll kill him is anyone's guess, but I know they'll avoid guns because of the noise.'

'So it'll be slow?'

'I really don't know. How do you feel about your husband being killed?'

'Wet.'

*

He slipped his mobile back in his pocket, then picked up his glass of mineral water and sipped it, frowning thoughtfully. Suddenly, he spoke in a low voice.

'It seems your husband is harder to kill than Rasputin,' he remarked dryly. 'He walked into O'Leary's ambush and walked out the other side leaving one man and a Doberman dead.'

'What are you going to do?'

'I don't know. O'Leary's clearing up the bodies, but O'Connell is livid. He's trying to blame it all on you and me for pissing Llewellyn off.'

'That's crap. I warned you all that Mr Goody-Two-Shoes Llewellyn doesn't take kindly to being pushed around and wouldn't just walk away. Now Mr ex-IRA hard man O'Connell has fucked up with his strong-arm tactics, he's trying to blame us. Tell him to sort his own cock-ups out!'

'Hmmn, I might just do that, but in the meantime we need to think about protecting our own backs in case things start coming further apart...'

'Have you heard any more about the Cow?'

Preece shook his head.

'Nothing too helpful at present; Ringer's got every man he can spare on it. It appears that when she went into town the other day she visited the bank and withdrew some cash from our account. She was next seen buying a second-hand car from a backstreet garage in Brynmill and she went on a spending spree in Debenhams. It looks like she was planning to leave town.

'Good. I'm sick of the sight of her.'

'It's not as easy as that. I spoke to a contact in the Coroner's Office earlier. According to the path lab at Singleton, Semple died of a massive stroke. Given his lifestyle, that's not particularly surprising, but strokes can be induced. It's possible your husband had a hand in it. Anyway the kid's missing.'

'But we know Charlie has been too busy to be baby sitting him.'

'Exactly, so the next most likely candidate is Annette.'

Juliet paused.

'That boy would make a damn inconvenient witness if this ever came to court.'

Preece shrugged.

'Certainly, but unless she's already out of Britain, I wouldn't worry too much. Ringer's already circulated her description and she'll shortly be the target of a national kidnapping hunt.

She's going to have to come up with a hell of a story to talk her way out of that, particularly with you and me waiting in the wings to welcome her home.'

His mobile rang. He picked it up off the tablecloth and answered it.

'Preece.'

He frowned as he recognised Ringer's panicky tones.

'Hywel, listen, young Llewellyn just called in here with that package we discussed and, frankly, it's fucking bad news...'

'How do you know this line is secure?'

'I, er, don't.'

'Exactly. So get a grip will you. You know better than to ring under such circumstances. As far as Llewellyn's concerned, the files have been delivered safely to the powers that be, so we still have time to act. Bring it to the flat. I'll see you there in an hour and a half.' He cut the connection and turned to Juliet. 'That was Ringer flapping about the Llewellyn files. Christ, the man's a bloody idiot!'

He glanced around, suddenly conscious of his surroundings, but the bosses and secretaries that comprised most of the club's lunchtime trade were all wrapped up in their own affairs. The waiters stationed around the walls stood unblinking to attention, shrouded in professional discretion. Preece was still not satisfied.

'Look, this is not the place to be discussing this; we can talk more in the car on the way to the Marina. Finish that dessert.' He snapped his fingers impatiently and a waiter appeared from nowhere. 'The bill please, and right away if you want a tip!' The man hurried away.

'I like it when you get all bossy and domineering.'

'Yes, well, if we get a move on, I'll have a chance to check there are no nosy people hanging around before Ringer arrives.'

'Of course you will and still have time to fuck me hard before he does.'

26

The window of the apartment on Mannheim Quay, with its narrow-slatted blinds, was the perfect vantage point from which to observe the comings and goings around the Marina, which was precisely why Preece owned the place. Not that it was recorded anywhere that he owned it. It officially belonged to a Bermudan boat building company who used it as a business base in the UK. In practice, it was his ultimate safe house.

He was enjoying the benefits of its unique location now. He saw Ringer around the corner by Dickie's Yacht Sales on the other side of the water and walk down the quayside to cross the footbridge. He was carrying a black attaché case. Preece's gaze returned to the corner. Nothing... Nothing... Then he saw him. The man stopped dead. He obviously realised he was exposed. He glanced at his watch briefly, and then retreated. Most intriguing: he had been expecting Llewellyn, but his adversary had obviously drummed up reinforcements from somewhere.

Without taking his eyes off the corner he picked up his mobile from the coffee table and pressed the button for a programmed number. O'Leary's voice answered.

'Duke.'

'What's happening at your end?'

'Have ya seen the fella?'

'Yes. He just showed his face around the corner.'

'Right, well he turned up in a BMW. There's also an Escort with a fella and a tart in it, and a Suzuki jeep with another couple of tarts in it. They've stopped down this end by the estate agents. No, hang on there. Something's happenin'. It looks like they're pullin' out.'

'Right, they're probably planning to approach from this side of the Marina. That's fine. You pick up The Lone Ranger across the way and I'll go down to meet Ringer. We'll lose the others. You take our new chum on board the Beneteau for a chat.

Preece broke the connection. He could just make out the man peering around the corner of Dickies. Whoever he was, he was in for a nasty shock any minute now. No doubt, someone thought they were very clever trying to use this file to link Ringer to him, but they would have to come up with something a bit more original that that if they wanted to play cat and mouse with Hywel Preece.

He dropped his mobile into his jacket pocket and let himself out of the apartment. With a bit of timing he would meet Ringer precisely as he reached the front door.

*

Sullivan was feeling increasingly uncomfortable as he cruised along Trawler Road about thirty yards behind Ringer's car. There was no traffic to hide in and it was all very exposed. He had already told the rest of the team to stand down some distance back. He was just driving past some apartment blocks when, suddenly, his quarry pulled into a private parking area next to a row of small warehouses. Sullivan carried on past and parked as soon as he could. He grabbed the Nikon with the long zoom from the floor in front of the passenger seat and hurried back to where Ringer's empty car was parked. He had obviously walked through between the warehouses and the apartments. Sullivan hurried forward and spotted him about to cross a narrow footbridge.

Suddenly, he froze and looked about him. This was all wrong. He was surrounded by windows from any one of which an observer could be studying his every move. This was a far as he could go in pursuit of his quarry. He slapped his hand to his forehead, and glanced at his watch, then turned and hurried back the way he had come, hoping that the little pantomime would convince a spectator that he was just an ordinary member of the public who had forgotten something on his way into town.

Back behind the shelter of Dickies Yacht Sales, he peered around the corner of the building to get a fix on Ringer. He was walking briskly along the quay on the other side of the yacht basin. He clicked on his handset and spoke into his throat mike.

'Zero Four, come in.'

'Reading you, Zero One.'

'It's hopeless from here. I'm standing out like a slug on a tablecloth. Can you get around to the other side sharpish and take Zero Three for a smooch along the quay?'

'Roger Zero One. It's a tough job, but someone's got to do it.'

Sullivan grinned at the thought of Zero Three's indignant expression. He cut the connection and brought the camera up to eye level. He fired off a couple of shots of Ringer without zooming in, just to establish him in the context of the Marina. He was about to lower the camera when a movement caught his eye. A tall, well-dressed man was emerging from the entrance to the apartments. He zoomed the lens in on him and recognised the dark, hawkish features of Councillor Hywel Preece.

He pulled the lens back to find Ringer walking into shot. He was holding out the attaché case like a relay baton. Sullivan pressed the button and held it down to catch the whole sequence. The two men did not even pause to talk. Preece turned left towards the mouth of the Marina; Ringer turned and retraced his steps. Zero Three and Zero Four had not even arrived as Ringer disappeared into a quayside pub. Sullivan looked back along Mannheim Quay. Preece had vanished completely. With him gone, and Ringer in the pub, it seemed Sullivan was the only witness to the transfer. It could have gone better, but it was always the same with these ad-libbed jobs – too much down to luck. Still, he had the pictures that made the connection. Thanks to Charlie, he could now prove that Ringer was passing incriminating evidence back to Preece. This was the break he needed.

He turned to make his way back to Prosser's BMW and stopped dead. There were three men blocking his path. The two on the outside looked like typical night-club bouncers – shaven heads and designer jeans and black bomber jackets over heavy layers of muscle. They both had the cloudy eyes of junkies. The one on the right had his feet spread slightly apart and his hands loosely clasped in front of him, in the standard bouncer's pose. He had good reason to appear relaxed; his colleague was holding a pistol, which he was pointing steadily at Sullivan's chest.

The man in the middle was as big as the other two put together. He was one of the fattest men Sullivan had ever seen. His clothes were tent-like, out of necessity, and there were sweat rings around the armpits of his shirt. A mop of greasy hair curled down over his ears, surrounding the rolls of fat through which his piggy, blue eyes stared. Despite his unprepossessing appearance, he was clearly in charge. He was holding the copy of Charlie's file that Sullivan had left in Prosser's car, and it was he who was holding out a pudgy hand now.

'I think I'll be havin' that camera if you don't mind,' he said evenly, and there was something in his tone which made it clear that he didn't very much care whether Sullivan minded or not.

*

Sullivan had lost all track of how long they had been at sea. He vaguely knew that he had been unconscious several times, but he had no idea for how long. They just kept bringing him back around with buckets of seawater. Then it would start all over again – the relentless, agonising beating, and the despair. They were utterly calculating and professional. There were no blows to the head, groin or stomach, where a misjudged hit could kill. Instead they went to work on his legs. They smashed his kneecaps, shins and feet. After an hour he knew he would never walk again. Worse, he knew he would never get the chance. It was in their attitude and in the casual way they called each other by name. Why hide anything from a dead man?

The despair was the worst, and all the time, that bastard's reasonable, persuasive Southern Irish accent and those cold, colourless eyes.

Okay, who was he? Who did he work for? How much did

he know? They had caught him with a camera and a radio. They weren't stupid. Mr O'Leary here had watched him takin' pictures. Look, this was foolish. Why put himself through it? Just a few answers and the agony would be over.

'Go fuck yourself,' he had whispered. Perhaps his tormentors were getting impatient because that produced a flurry of kicks to the face. Then a particularly vicious blow put the lights out again. He was coughing out the seawater they had thrown over his face. His tongue told him he was missing a lot of teeth. One eye was shut completely and the other was a slit.

He didn't understand, explained the voice. There was no need for all this unpleasantness. His captors were getting seasick and irritable – they weren't going to stand for much more stubbornness. His captors turned their attention back to his legs to illustrate the point. He answered the questions.

Then the voice asked about Charlie and he had to call upon his final reserves. He had known they would get the other stuff out of him, but he had fought in the hope that, when he gave them something, they would believe he had completely cracked, because deep in the very core of his being there was one secret they were not going to get out of him. They could smash him till there was nothing left to destroy, but they were not going to get the whereabouts of Charlie Llewellyn out of him.

Where did he get the file?

It came by email.

How did he know about the delivery to the police station?

An anonymous call. This morning.

Where did he meet Llewellyn?

He hadn't met Llewellyn.

Where was Llewellyn now?

He didn't know.

A lot more pain.

Where was Llewellyn now?

He didn't know.

He still didn't know.

The man straightened up with a shrug and said, coldly, to O'Leary.

'This is a waste of my time.'

Through his one remaining slit of an eye, Al Sullivan saw the fat man rise and walk towards him. He saw him reach out an arm to steady himself on the cabin roof. The man raised a huge leg and placed a foot across Sullivan's throat. Sullivan closed his swollen eye, waiting for the man's weight to come bearing down on his windpipe, crushing the life out of him.

I didn't tell 'em Charlie, mate, he thought. It's all yours now. Don't let me down.

O'Leary transferred his thirty stone bulk to his raised leg.

27

The winos were in quite a party mood for the middle of the afternoon. Their new companion had sat down on the pavement with them and opened his carrier bag. It was full of cans of Tennents Extra and bottles of Diamond White. He'd just come ashore with two months wages in his pocket and he was looking for some butties who could speak English for a change. He turned out to be a tidy bloke, handing out fags and generally having a laugh. Loco got a bit out of order and started acting like a twat as usual, shouting at passers-by, but he was harmless enough as nutters go and serve the snobby bastards right if they felt they had to cross the road.

Preece walked quickly up the street with the collar of his coat up and the brim of his hat pulled down over his eyes. It wasn't for protection from the steady drizzle. He turned sharply into the entrance of Club Casablanca and pressed the intercom button.

'Club Casablanca?'

'Let me in quick!'

The door buzzed and he hurried through, barely nodding to Duchess O'Leary as he headed for the stairs. He climbed the wooden steps to the third floor attic and knocked three times on the door. O'Leary himself answered it. Preece brushed past him into the office. The two men were alone in the room.

'It's a bit risky meetin' here, don't ya think, chief?'

'I agree, but O'Connell's called this meeting, not me. Besides, with their agent dead, it should take them a while to get back on their feet.'

'So what happens now?'

'I don't know. I assume that's what this meeting's about.'

At that moment there were three sharp raps on the door that led out to the fire escape at the back of the building. O'Leary hurried over and opened it. O'Connell strode into the room. He was clearly livid. Gone was any veneer of urbanity. The massive head on hunched shoulders gave the impression of atavistic savagery. Despite the rage in his face and the tension in his frame, his colourless eyes remained calculating. He turned to Preece.

'I told you he was dangerous, you fucking arsehole?' he hissed.

'Who?'

'Who d'you think? Llewellyn of course.'

'But that wasn't Llewellyn we caught...'

'Of course not because Llewellyn's not stupid, but why do you think Customs are suddenly hot on our tails after all these years? Why do you think Semple's dead and things are coming apart at the seams? '

'Well, I had him checked out...'

'Oh sure you did. Don't tell me, you got that useless little cunt Semple to make a couple of phone calls.'

'Well as a matter of fact, I did. He showed me the results and Llewellyn had a seamless career in the Guards right up until the end of the Gulf war. It seemed reasonable to assume he was invalided out because of that.'

'So you jumped to the easiest conclusion, you stupid fucking prick? The Welsh Guards weren't even involved in Iraq. What did you expect his record to show? People transfer into the S.A.S under the tightest security.'

'Well I don't see why there's any need to get in such a panic about it. The man's not S.A.S now and, besides, he was invalided out.'

'No one is invalided out of the S.A.S, it's part of their code. They also conduct peacetime operations and have been used against drug smugglers.'

'So what are you trying to tell me? That Llewellyn's some kind of undercover S.A.S agent?'

'It's possible. He was trained in deep-cover surveillance.'

'How do you know?'

'Because our paths have crossed before; he's the same Llewellyn who tried to stop me selling kit to Gaddafi in the Gulf. He's been planted on us on a long-term basis, while he recovered from his Gulf War injuries.'

'Why didn't you tell me this?'

'Because I work on a need to know basis and you didn't need to know until you and Semple decided to stitch him up. I told you to kill him, but you wouldn't listen, you stupid bastard!'

Preece's dark eyes hardened.

'Don't you talk to me like that! Llewellyn's got you running scared and I don't take that kind of crap from a business partner!'

'We're not business partners anymore.'

'What d'you mean?'

'What I say. We're shutting down.'

'What, the Swansea operation?'

'No, I'm shutting down the Rent Man Gang, period; the whole fucking shooting match. I told you, if you ballsed it up, you would have to live with the consequences. That file won't put us behind bars as it stands, but Llewellyn only needs a couple more pieces of the jigsaw and he sure as hell isn't going to give up now.'

Preece stared at him.

'You're mad,' he blurted suddenly. 'You're off your bloody rocker. We can't just abandon everything we've worked for!'

'Yes we fucking can! Where's Llewellyn now? You don't know, do you? Well it wasn't his fucking ghost helping his son deliver that file to the police station. You told me that you had the situation under control. Now Semple's dead, there's a highly incriminating file doing the rounds, we're being investigated by Customs and Excise and it appears your wife is sheltering a dangerous witness!'

'What makes you say that?'

'The fact that I've got my finger on the pulse, that's what! Ringer tells me an undercover cop spotted a new face buying smack in a nightclub a couple nights ago. He followed her to an address on Bryn Road. Ringer picked it up off a routine report this morning. I sent a couple of our boys to check it out and it's definitely them. The boys are watching the place now.'

'So what do you want me to do?'

'Tidy up your end of the mess and clear out. Horse and the boys will sort the kid out. It's up to you how to deal with your wife so long as she ends up dead, preferably not in Swansea. I'm shutting the whole operation down tonight, so don't hang around once O'Leary gives you the all clear. I'd use the Dublin route if I were you and, if you get caught, you better keep your mouth shut because, if I meet you in prison you're a dead man. Do you understand me?'

Preece looked for a moment as if he was about to retort, but those eyes were burning into him. O'Leary opened the door for him with a faint grin as he spun on his heel and clattered off down the rickety staircase.

He closed the door and cleared his throat.

'What about Duchess and me, boss?'

'It's up to you. You and Duchess can stay and run this place if you like. Once we've shut down, you'll be in the clear. Anyway, listen up. Round up the two boys from yesterday and take the Beneteau out to six miles south-west of Worm's Head. I've contacted Corunna and they're sending out a consignment of uncut heroin that should be here around midday. Give the boys a hit, and then dump the bodies overboard. Phone the Rent Men and tell them to meet me at nine at the warehouse in Fforestfach. I'll off the wankers and torch the place, while you deliver the smack to the kids.'

O'Leary smirked and nodded.

'No witnesses, eh, chief?'

'That's right. No witnesses.'

O'Leary pulled out his mobile and began to phone the rent Men. He grinned as he began to arrange the party. You had to take your hat off to O'Connell, he was a cunning bastard. Pure, uncut heroin was as good as strychnine, even to junkies. They'd never know what hit 'em.

*

The winos didn't notice the tall, dark man with the hat and coat leave the Club Casablanca and stride quickly off down the street. Nor did he notice them. They were always hanging around there. A couple of them noticed their new companion muttering to himself, but so what – half the time Loco reckoned he was talking to the Archangel Gabriel and no one took any notice. If the bloke wanted to sit there on the pavement chatting to himself, with his chin tucked inside the collar of his donkey jacket, fair dos. So long as he was handing out the fags and sharing his booze, who were they to say what he should or shouldn't be doing. All those months at sea with those bloody foreigners – enough to make anyone talk to themselves, for fuck's sake.

*

Charlie's decision to sit tight was largely intuitive. His business was with O'Connell not Preece and he had as yet to even set eyes on the man. Much as he hated to watch Preece go, he had to see for himself who else might emerge from the club. There was something about Preece's furtive haste that seemed to hint at panic. They were definitely rattled. There was no way Preece would be seen entering a place like that unless something serious was up.

Charlie was trying to second guess O'Connell's next move. He was a clever bastard back in the Gulf days and the success and ingenuity of the Rent Man operation was proof he hadn't lost his touch. So, if Preece was breaking ground, it had to be for a good reason. It was unlikely to be over-confidence; O'Connell might be clinically insane but he was ultra-rational when it came to business. He would probably believe that he still had a bit of time on his side, but it was just possible that he had decided to draw stumps. The file, and Al Sullivan's involvement, were certain to have shaken him up. He had already made a fortune out of the conspiracy – why risk it all? Better to back away and live to fight another day.

It was dangerous trying to predict the reactions of this gang, but, if he had to put money on it, Charlie decided he would have to back a tactical withdrawal. In fact he could envisage a well thought out escape plan already in place. O'Connell was too experienced to imagine the racket would last forever. It would be more typical of him to plan for an endgame.

As he was coming to this conclusion, a familiar figure emerged from the front door of the Club. It was the lumbering bulk of O'Leary, the controller of the Rent Men. Again Charlie's intuition was ringing bells. From what he knew of the organisation, O'Leary was a central player. He had to know most of its innermost secrets. Charlie couldn't imagine him hauling his obese body out of the club for no good reason. It was a fair assumption that O'Connell had left instructions and the Irishman was carrying them out. Preece hadn't led him to his target as yet, perhaps O'Leary would. He decided to follow him.

He shared out the remains of the drink and cigarettes with his companions as he let O'Leary build up a head start. It soon became apparent that he was heading for the station. Charlie began praying he wasn't boarding a train. The last thing he wanted was to be drawn away from Swansea with Preece on the loose. To Charlie's relief he stopped at the taxi rank and squeezed himself into the back two seats of the first cab. The car pulled out and headed down High Street towards Castle Street.

The cab behind belonged to a different company. Charlie got into the next cab back.

'Got a name?' asked Charlie as he closed the door. The driver glanced sideways at his passenger.

'Aye, Bilko,' he replied, suspiciously.

'Right, Bilko. Well, that's twenty quid down payment for you to follow the cab that just pulled out, and I need you to stick to his arse like glue.' Charlie plonked a couple of notes down on the dashboard. Bilko's suspicions seemed to evaporate. Out on High Street, Charlie counted eight cars between the two cabs. Shit! That was too many for comfort. If anyone buggered about at the lights, they would lose them for sure. The driver read his mind.

'I can't see us makin' it across this go, mate.'

'Sure. Look, you're with the same firm, is there any chance of finding out through your controller where they're heading for?'

'Oh, Christ, mun, we can do better than that. We can track 'em on the satellite. Watch this.' He clicked on his radio. As he did so the lights changed and six cars made it through. Charlie watched O'Leary's car disappear from sight.

'Data Thirty-One to base.'

'Roger Data Thirty-One. What's up?'

'Can you give me the location of Data Ten, mate?'

'Sure, he's just approachin' the mini-roundabout at the top of Wind Street. Wait there a sec...yes, he's turning right. It looks like he's headin' for Princess Way.'

'Cheers, butt, keep an eye on 'im for me will you?'

'Roger.'

The lights were changing.

'Look, can that thing track him pretty well anywhere in Swansea?'

'Of course, no probs.'

'Okay, can you go to the bottom of Wind Street and hold? He could be headed for the Marina, or out to Derwen Fawr. If it's the first, I'll go in by Gloucester Place. If not we'll have to catch up with him.'

They had only just pulled in at the bottom of Wind Street when the controller confirmed that Data Ten had turned left onto Bathurst Street and was heading down Trawler Road.

'Jesus! That was quick!'

'That's our Smithy for you. Goes like a flyin' roller skate! Straight across is it, mate?'

As Bilko pulled across the lights and headed for Gloucester Place, Charlie felt a growing tension in the pit of his stomach. He remembered the feeling from his combat days. He couldn't help wondering, as Bilko turned into the dead end that led through to the Marina, if he was walking into a variation on the same lethal trap that Al Sullivan had walked into the day before.

*

According to Bilko, Data Ten had pulled up at the end of Trawler Road by the Marina control centre on the other side of the water. If Prosser was right, it was somewhere on that side that Sullivan had been snatched. Apparently he had radioed Prosser to say that he was pulling back because he felt exposed. Charlie let his gaze drift around the area as he tried to picture the scene. Ringer was the decoy and Sullivan was tailing him. So where would it occur to an experienced watcher that he was dangerously exposed? Anywhere inside the yacht basin, basically. It was pretty well surrounded on all four sides by tall apartment blocks. It was an elegant trap. He could imagine Preece watching from any one of those windows. Had he returned here now? He headed back along Gloucester Place to where Bilko was waiting.

'Change of plan,' he explained as he climbed back into the passenger seat. 'Drop me at the end of Cambrian Place would you, I'll go in by the yacht club.'

'A few minutes later, Charlie strolled around the corner at Mannheim Quay and looked across at the control centre. He couldn't be seen from any apartments here. Immediately, he saw O'Leary waddling across the footbridge over the Marina lock gates. He had picked up a couple of beefy companions. They were glancing around in a way that suggested they were the ones wary of watchers.

They were headed his way so he retreated to a more concealed position in the car park behind the yacht club and watched as they appeared around the corner and made for the gangway which led down to the club's moorings on the Tawe. O'Leary let them in through the security gate and the three men hurried out across the pontoons. Charlie wondered what the yacht club member's would say if they knew to what purpose Councillor Hywel Preece was paying his annual subscription.

A few minutes later an elegant, white Beneteau Antares 1080 motor cruiser crept out from amongst the forest of masts and rigging and purred off in the direction of the Tawe lock. One of the thugs was at the helm. O'Leary and the other man were in the stern. Charlie had the sickening feeling that Al Sullivan's final journey had probably followed a similar route.

Anyhow it was clear that, whatever they were up to, it did not involve him. At least not from their point of view. It did, however, force him into a decision. Did he follow them? Again, it represented a real opportunity to corner O'Leary. Sullivan had told him they were bringing the heroin in using pick-ups from fishing boats. Perhaps this was one last haul before they wound it all up? God only knew. The only way to find out was to see what they were up to.

Charlie turned his attention to practical matters. The tide wasn't high enough yet for the lock to be operating on free-flow, when both gates stood open and the traffic was simply controlled by lights. That wouldn't happen for another couple of hours. In the meantime, the gates would only be opening once every hour. The Beneteau would be long gone if they went through on different openings. However, the prospect of snuggling up to those thugs in the confined space of the lock was out of the question. O'Leary had interviewed Charlie for his job as a rent man, and he didn't come across as a man who would forget a face. If he was going to follow the boat he wasn't going to do it via the lock.

To the left of the lock ran the weir – at low tide, a thirty-foot drop down an almost vertical concrete face, with the tumbling waters of the Tawe for lubrication. But right now it wasn't a low tide. Without tide tables he couldn't be certain, but the drop shouldn't be more than a few feet – ten at the most.

His eyes followed the line of huge orange buoys that were slung across the weir entrance to prevent unwary mariners from undertaking the journey that Charlie was now contemplating. There was no way through there, unless... His gaze fixed on a point at the end of the cable nearest the lock. It was as if a buoy was missing, leaving a gap. From where he was, it looked about six feet across and a foot high. It would probably turn out to be a bit bigger close up. He made his decision.

A line of steep steps led down the river wall to the water's edge. At the bottom he was out of sight of the Marina. He pulled a roll of black bags from the inside pocket of his donkey jacket and tore a couple off. He put one inside the other for double insulation and said a little prayer to the manufacturer that they really were EXTRA STRONG. He redistributed the items hidden amongst his clothing, setting aside a small penknife and a waterproof Elastoplast. Then he stripped down to his shorts, stuffing each item of clothing into the bags.

He pulled a blade out of the penknife and took a couple of deep breaths. Then he gingerly pulled on the plastic tube that was sticking out from between his ribs. That brought the stitches that were holding the tube in place, more clearly into view. He sawed through them with the sharp blade and picked them out of the wound. Then he took a deep breath and pulled. The tube slid out, leaving a tiny slit in the skin. He covered it with the plaster and then detached the plastic bag that was taped under his arm. He dropped all the bits and pieces in the black bags and caught as much air in them as possible before tying them tightly at the top.

He gripped the bag in his left hand and lowered himself into the black waters of the river. Jesus wept! It was balls-achingly cold. He kicked hard across the twenty yard gap between the river wall and the shelter of the pontoons, keeping his head and shoulders hidden behind the floating bag. As he reached the moored boats, he glanced back in time to see the Beneteau disappearing into the lock. He needed to get a move on.

The first few inflatables were just ship-to-shore tenders with eggbeater outboards. Then he spotted it, moored between two sailboats. It was a sharp looking Avon Seasport RIB with a decent Yamaha engine stuck on the back. That would have no trouble keeping up with the motor cruiser. He followed the black bags over the side of the inflatable and untied them. He removed his wet shorts and slipped into his jeans. Despite the cold he made do with just his donkey jacket. The engine started with a throaty rumble and he cast off. He eased clear of the pontoons and gave the throttle a tweak. She leapt forward in the water. Charlie grinned. So long as she had enough juice to get where the Beneteau was going, he was in business.

He pointed the boat towards the lock and watched the gap in the line of buoys grow as he got nearer. There was plenty of width, but it was going to be a squeeze getting under the cable. He waited until the very last moment, then swung the RIB's nose away from the lock entrance and drove straight at the gap. The prow passed under the cable by inches, as Charlie closed the throttle and threw himself flat in the bottom of the boat. He jammed the tiller hard over, turning the RIB tight up against the line of buoys for concealment. He opened the throttle slightly, keeping the boat hard against the buoys until he reached what he judged to be halfway across the top of the weir. He reversed the direction of the tiller, so that the nose of the boat swung out from the buoys. He peered over the side. Ten yards ahead he could see the line of seagulls that were perched arrogantly on the lip of the weir, where the water was cascading over the drop.

He took his third deep breath of the afternoon, and jammed the throttle wide open. The Yamaha's fifty horses churned the water and sent the RIB flying forward, scattering the birds and lifting her nose. As the front of the boat reached the lip of the weir, Charlie tipped the outboard forward to lift the propeller out of the water. Then he was flying.

The nose was coming higher and higher, in ghastly slow motion, as Charlie and the Yamaha weighed down the stern. Just as Charlie was sure the boat would flip into a back somersault, it hit the water with a winding, bone rattling jolt that almost bounced him out. The impact rocked the Yamaha back and they screamed around in a crazy pirouette before Charlie had the presence of mind to close the throttle. Then everything was quiet, apart from the low rumble of the engine and the high-pitched screaming of the outraged seagulls.

28

O'Leary watched contemptuously as the boys struggled to pull the fake lump of driftwood on-board. That was the trouble with all this body-buildin' - all paddin', no power. Too scared of getting their flash, bloody clobber wet, the fuckin' nancy boys! He turned away in disgust and did yet another three hundred and sixty degree sweep of the surrounding sea with his binoculars. He paused. What was that about a hundred yards out on the seaward side and slightly astern? He couldn't see anything now, but there was a slight swell. Probably nothing to worry about. All sorts of shit was floating around in these waters. It certainly wasn't a coastguard cutter steaming across the bay towards them, which was all he gave a bugger about. Losing his patience he grabbed one of the boys and pushed him roughly out the way.

'For fucks sake, we haven't got all day, ya fuckin' quair,' he growled. He leaned over the side, grabbed the piece of rope that held the container together and yanked it out the water.

'Right,' he continued, 'now the boss says I'm to allow ya a hit by way of showin' his appreciation for the tunin' you gave that fella yesterday, though I can't think why, meself. Anyhow, it'll do to check the gear out, so get a fuckin' move on, will ya.'

'How strong is it, boss?'

'Oh, it's good stuff I'm told. About forty percent, accordin' to the man. Come on, shift your arses. I'm not hangin' around here all day.'

The two men produced flick knives. One cut through the

rope, while the other sliced through the silicone sealant that protected the contents from the seawater.

They had obviously done this before. Within seconds the lid was off, revealing rows of vacuum-packed, clear, plastic bags full of brownish powder.

'Got the spikes?' enquired one. The other nodded producing a glasses case from inside his pocket.

'Yeah. Fancy a hit?'

'Aye, tidy.'

The one with the glasses case picked up one of the bags of brown and walked forward into the cabin. He sat down, made a small slit in the bag with his flick knife and began measuring out a couple of shots of heroin. His companion joined him a couple of minutes later, as he was loosening the belt wrapped around his arm.

'Good hit?' the second man enquired, as he removed a shoe and a sock, and began searching for a vein in his foot that hadn't collapsed. He found a possible and picked up the second syringe.

'Alright,' muttered his mate, thickly. 'Jesus, it's fuckin' strong...'

His companion looked up in time to see the man's head loll forward onto his chest. He hadn't even taken the spike out of his arm! Jesus shit, there was something wrong! He grabbed him by the hair and lifted his head. His eyes were shut and he was hardly breathing. He lifted an eyelid. The pupil was pinpoint and it didn't react to the light.

In desperation he spun around to call for O'Leary's help and found the Irishman pointing a vicious looking, snub-nosed revolver at his stomach.

'Your turn,' prompted the fat man, unemotionally, nodding at the loaded syringe, which the man was still clutching as he gazed uncomprehendingly at the gun.

If realisation was slow in dawning, his reaction was fast when it did.

'You murderin' fat cunt!' he suddenly screamed, kicking out at the gun. He hurled the syringe like a dart at O'Leary's face. More by luck than judgement it hit him in the eye and he staggered back, bellowing with pain. The shaven-headed thug chopped down on the hand holding the gun and pounced on it as it hit the deck. He came up grinning nastily.

*

Charlie peered out from behind the RIB. He was back in his shorts and back in the water. He was slightly surprised that his approach had gone unchallenged, but there again, these were busy waters and small boats were lost off the back of leisure craft all the time. An empty inflatable drifting by was hardly that threatening.

He was now within ten yards of the stern of the Beneteau and the real reason for the success of his stealthy arrival was becoming apparent. There was trouble on board. One of the thugs was slumped over the helm and O'Leary had a gun on the other one. Then Charlie saw the man kick it aside and throw something in the fat man's face. O'Leary staggered back and the next thing the thug had the gun on O'Leary.

Charlie hadn't gone to this much trouble simply to lose the

key that could unlock O'Connell's plans. He pushed away from the RIB and, as the swell lifted him and the Beneteau together, he kicked to lift his shoulders clear of the water, raised the 9mm Browning Automatic, which Maddocks had so unwillingly given him, and shot the thug through the head.

As the wave passed it rocked him off balance and, despite himself, he sank back in the water. He saw O'Leary wrench something away from his face and hurl the object overboard. Then he bent down out of sight. He'd be going for the gun. Charlie felt another wave beginning to lift him, so he kicked right with the direction of it. As O'Leary hauled himself up from behind the back of the boat, brandishing the snub-nosed revolver, he was looking in the wrong place. Charlie raised the Browning, two-handed again, and shot him in the left shoulder.

The fat man spun around and collapsed out of sight. Did he still have the gun? Charlie didn't fancy having his head shot off as he climbed over the stern. He swam to the RIB and pulled himself over the side. He discarded the black bag he had held the gun in to keep it dry and trained it on the stern of the Beneteau. He gently opened the throttle to bring the boat within a few yards.

'O'Leary, can you hear me?' he shouted.

'Whaddya want?'

'Throw out the gun and I'll talk business. Otherwise, I'll call in Customs and Excise and you can't talk business with them, though I warn you, they're pretty pissed off over what you did to their boy yesterday.'

'Go fuck yourself!'

A tightly packed plastic bag flew over the side. Shit! He was disposing of the evidence. Charlie thought quickly. O'Leary had to be throwing with his good arm and holding the gun in his left hand. He had held it in his right hand when he was pointing it at the thug. With a bullet in his shoulder, his field of fire would be limited to the wrist action of his weaker hand. He would expect an attack from the stern. Another bag of heroin sailed through the air.

Charlie guided the RIB alongside the cruiser at the point where the cabin began. He grabbed the boat's handrail and crouched on the side of the inflatable. He stood up quickly, bringing the Browning to bear as he did so. O'Leary was sitting like a venomous Buddha on the plastic white deck. He was weighing another bag of heroin in his right hand. He must have caught the movement out of the corner of his eye, because he tried to swing the gun around. Charlie shot him in the wrist and vaulted into the boat. He picked up the revolver, which lay spinning on the deck. O'Leary had dropped the heroin to clasp his injured wrist. He was pale and perspiration stood out on his forehead despite the cold.

Charlie put the guns on the roof of the cabin out of reach, and then he bent over the body of the thug he had shot and went through his pockets. He found a handkerchief in his trousers and used it to pick up the bags of heroin. One by one he transferred them into the cabin, out of O'Leary's reach. Then he examined the man slumped over the helm. He had obviously died of a heroin overdose, even though the track marks on his arm suggested he was a heavy user. A terrible suspicion crossed Charlie's mind. He went back out to where O'Leary lay.

'You're shutting down the operation, aren't you?'

'Mind your own fuckin' business.'

'But it is my business. You see I've got a score to settle with you and your pals and that was before you tortured a friend of mine to death yesterday, you piece of shit.'

O'Leary hawked and spat at him. Charlie shot him though his right thigh.

'Oh look,' he remarked, 'I seem to have shot a hole in the bottom of your nice boat, as well as your leg.'

'Ya can't do that, ya bastard!'

'Can't do what? Shoot holes in your nice boat? Yes I can. Watch.' Charlie put another couple of rounds through the hull. 'Or do you mean I can't shoot holes in you? Because, if you do, you're very much mistaken.' He bent over O'Leary and pressed the gun down on his wounded thigh.

'I get the feeling,' he continued, conversationally, 'that you think I'm some kind of copper, but unfortunately for you, I'm not.'

'Who are you then?' hissed the fat man.

'Think of me as your worst bloody nightmare, the one that has come to get revenge for all those poor kids you and your scumbag friends are planning to murder with that poisonous heroin.'

'Whaddya gonna do?'

'I'm going to ask you a couple of questions and, if you don't answer them, I'm going to shoot your leg off. I reckon it'll take at least ten rounds.' For the first time Charlie saw the light of real fear in O'Leary's eyes. He pressed home the advantage.

'First, when is O'Connell planning to leave?'

'When he knows I've delivered the smack.'

'How's he going to know that?'

'I'm to phone him.'

'How does he plan to get away?'

'I dunno.'

Charlie pressed the gun harder into the roll of fat that covered O'Leary's thigh.

'I'm not asking again.'

'I don't know. Honest to God. They only ever tell you what you need to know. Please don't!'

'Did Al Sullivan beg when you smashed his knees up?'

'I dunno. I can't remember. Please!'

'When is O'Connor going to leave?'

'When he's dealt with the Rent Men.'

'When will that be?'

'He's meeting them at nine tonight.'

'Where?'

'The warehouse.'

'Why then?'

'That's when the cops know to look the other way.'

Charlie stood up. He walked forward into the cabin and pulled the loosened belt from around the dead man's arm. He knelt back down in front of O'Leary and strapped it around one of his ankles. He yanked him forward by the belt, toppling him onto his back, and dragged him to the stepladder that was fixed over the stern. He tied the belt tightly around the top rung. Given his bulk and his injuries, there was no way that the Irishman could reach to undo it. He lay like a beached whale in the deepening puddle of blood and seawater that was swilling around the bottom of the boat.

Charlie collected the handkerchief from the cabin and wiped the Browning over carefully. He pressed it into the hand of the thug he had shot. He picked up a flick knife with the handkerchief and cut a length of nylon blue rope from the painter that was coiled in the stern. He went into the cabin and pulled the dead thug away from the helm, lowering his body to the floor. He started the engines. He pushed the throttle forward to slow ahead, then spun the wheel hard to starboard and lashed it in position with the rope. The Beneteau began to chase its own tail in slow, tight circles.

He retrieved the other gun from the roof of the cabin and stepped up onto the gunwale of the boat.

'Whaddya doin', man?' gasped O'Leary.

'I reckon you've told me everything you know, so I'm off.'

'But the fuckin' boat's sinkin'!'

Charlie nodded his agreement.

'It would certainly appear to be. I'd give it two hours top end.'

'Well, for pity's sake man, ya can't leave me here like this! Have ya no mercy?'

'And what mercy would that be? The mercy you showed to Sullivan? The mercy you showed to the kids who are slowly dying in those brothels of yours to line your oversized pockets?'

'But ya said we could talk business.'

'You didn't seem particularly keen at the time, besides you have nothing that interests me now. You never know. Someone might come along in time to save your skin. That's a better deal than you ever offered your victims.'

Charlie turned and dived over the side.

*

He pulled himself aboard the RIB, which had drifted some thirty yards away from the sinking Beneteau. He dressed, and then fished his mobile phone out of one of the side pockets of his jacket. He pressed one of the programmed buttons.

'Maddocks, its Llewellyn. I've just thrown a party and I've got some clearing up for you... Yeah, that's right. Listen, there's a white Beneteau Antares 1080 circling in the sea eight to ten clicks south of Worm's Head. I can't be exact, but a chopper will spot it easily enough. Two of the guests have crashed out completely and the other one is likely to be very tired and emotional by the time you get to him. He's a bit damaged, but he's not my man... Yeah, that's right. Don't leave it too long. I reckon the boat won't last more than another couple of hours at the outside. You'll need plenty of elbow grease to clean this up. Good luck!'

He cut the connection and grinned. It would take some while for Maddocks to get airborne with a forensics team, which should leave O'Leary plenty of time to contemplate the error of his ways as the water levels rose around him.

29

Annette Preece was packing, or more accurately, she was dumping any useful items that she and Bomber had accumulated in her holdall. He was sitting, slumped in an armchair, as she worked. He had taken the last of the heroin shortly before she noticed the car and he was still fairly out of it. She went over to the window and peered through the net curtain again. The car was still there. There was a scruffy-looking individual sitting in the driver's seat and she thought she could make out a dog in the back. To her horror the man from the night club, the one they called Horse, was leaning on the roof, smoking a cigarette. Even from a distance he had a manic, violent air about him. He was making no effort to conceal the fact that he was watching the guesthouse. She felt her stomach knot with fear. It was as if he was looking straight at her.

She sat down on the bed and put her head in her hands. What the hell was she to do? There was a fire escape outside the landing window at the back of the building, but she stood no chance of getting Bomber to clamber onto it in his present condition. Mrs Stone was pleasant enough, but didn't strike her as the sort to go out of her way to be helpful. What could she say to her anyway? Excuse me I've been hiding out in your guesthouse with a young heroin addict and some thugs are waiting outside to kidnap us. If she didn't treat her like a lunatic, she'd call the police.

Her car was parked in the car park of Cardiff's main shopping centre, assuming it hadn't been stolen or impounded. Charlie had warned her that the police wouldn't take long to find it. He had advised her to dump it and take minicabs. If she was forced to head for London, she should travel from town to town, changing cabs to muddy the trail as much as possible.

The light was fading. What if she sat it out until dark then called a cab? Bomber would be in better shape for travelling by then. They could wait out of sight in the foyer of the guesthouse and, as the cab drew up, jump in and go. Who did she think she was kidding? As if those thugs outside were going to sit there and let her get away with that!

What about an ambulance? That wasn't so stupid. Would they dare to obstruct an ambulance? Bomber would be driven straight to hospital and she could explain to the ambulance men what the Rent Men had done to him. That he was in desperate danger. Hospitals had security and not even that mad-looking individual downstairs could barge in and kidnap a patient with impunity. She certainly stood a better chance of giving them the slip in a busy hospital.

They had been in hiding for four days now and, with no heroin left, Bomber would soon be needing help again. Surely Charlie had made some progress by now. If he hadn't, it was futile anyway. She and Bomber couldn't carry on like this, even without the attentions of those thugs. She knew Charlie had said that the hospital was a last resort, but what else could she do? They had tracked her down and she had nowhere left to hide. She reached for her bag. The ambulance was definitely the best bet. She pulled out her mobile phone.

That's when she heard the movement in the corridor. Don't panic! It could be a guest or a cleaner. She hurried to the door and clicked the latch on the Yale lock, and then she rushed back to the window. She looked down and froze. The driver, a tall, skinny man was standing on the pavement holding a dog on a lead. Horse was nowhere to be seen. But what left her paralysed with fear was the sight of her husband's black Range Rover parked a few yards down the road.

Even as she turned back towards the door, the handle turned and the door began to creak. She gazed in fascination, like a rabbit caught in headlights, as the lock buckled and splintered out of the flimsy frame. With barely a noise it gave way and Horse stood framed in the door. He limped forward, as if some stiffness were preventing him from walking comfortably.

'Well, well,' he leered, 'if it isn't the clever little twat from the club! Don't like payin' for our gear, eh? Come 'ere, you owes me a blow job!'

He grabbed her by the hair and forced her to his knees as he began unzipping his fly.

'What the bloody hell do you think you're doing?' snapped a voice behind him. 'Take your hands off her and deal with the boy!' Councillor Preece clearly didn't like his property being used even when he had discarded it.

Horse hesitated for a moment, frustrated by Annette for the second time, then threw her roughly aside and hobbled over to Bomber. He seized him by the hair instead, dragging him face down onto the floor. He planted a knee between his shoulder blades pinning him down. In desperation, Annette flung herself forward and threw a punch. It connected. The giant reached up, touched his lip and inspected the blood on his fingers with a look of surprise. Then he lashed out with the back of his hand, knocking her backward across the room.

'Likes the little fucker, do we, bitch?' he sneered. He reached down and gripped the boy's chin in one huge hand, clasping the back of his head with the other. As Bomber's head was dragged back his eyes were resting on her. They were clear and calm as if he knew he was about to find peace at last.

'Bye, Netty,' he whispered.

The giant laughed and twisted the boy's head brutally to one side. There was a sickening crack and Annette watched silently through a mist of tears as Bomber's head flopped back to the floor. She made no effort to resist as Preece stepped forward and dragged her to her feet. He slammed her back into the armchair Bomber had so recently occupied and picked up the bottle of vodka that the boy had injected himself with. He grabbed her by the hair and forced her head back, bringing his knee down hard across her stomach. He rammed the neck of the bottle into her mouth and upended it.

At first she fought frantically not to swallow, but then she had to, to breathe. As if from a great distance, she heard her husband giving orders.

'Throw the body down the fire escape. The police will assume he's just a junkie kid who fell and broke his neck, trying to break in. We'll set off the fire alarm and take her out in the confusion.'

She closed her eyes in despair. Annette Preece's hopes of making a stand against her tyrannical husband, and her equally tyrannical addiction, evaporated as more and more of the neat spirit hit her stomach and began to be absorbed into her bloodstream.

30

The internal phone on his desk was ringing insistently. Chief Inspector Ringer sat staring at it mesmerised. Finally he reached out a hand to answer it. He recognised the lilting tones of Duty Sergeant Betrys Dodd. Right now, not even the thought of her pneumatic knockers packed into her slightly-too-tight tunic could allay his rising sense of panic.

'Sorry to trouble you sir. I've got a gentleman out 'ere by the name of Maddocks from Customs and Excise. Says 'e wants a word. Shall I show 'im in?'

Maddocks? Maddocks? Who the hell was this? Jesus, this was all going pear-shaped and he was the one who was going to be left holding the bloody baby, he could see it now! He pulled a handkerchief out of his pocket with an unsteady hand and mopped his brow. He fought to keep his voice steady.

'Yes, fine, Sergeant. Please show him in.' the receiver rattled as he replaced it. The tranquillisers he had taken earlier didn't seem to be having much effect. How on Earth had he allowed himself to be drawn into this business in the first place? He remembered the evening that Preece had approached him at the Lodge with that fucking dossier of photographs. He should have told him to sod off then and there; called his bluff and countered with the threat of blackmail charges. But then he had too much to lose; his job, his marriage, the respect of his kids and the community. No, that was too much to risk and all for the sake of a night with the boy. Well, several nights, but then he'd had real feelings for the kid!

They'd set him up of course. He was so stupid not to see it coming, but the sudden urge to take a walk on the dark side had come out of nowhere. He'd read a report from Vice about the male prostitution scene in South Wales and found himself fantasising about it instead of studying it! He found the whole thing bewildering. He had never had such feelings before. He was a married man and a copper to boot! He tried to fall back on his profession by making it his business to take part in eradicating the problem, but this only bought him into contact with information and images that turned him on. One thing led to another and eventually he found himself knocking on a door in Penlan wearing horn-rimmed glasses and a cap pulled down to hide his face. Quite when Preece and his cronies sussed him out was anyone's guess, but they were clever. His help was generously rewarded with cash and an endless supply of kids. Once they'd hooked him they reeled him in with his own weaknesses.

Now the wheels were coming off big time. That file of Llewellyn's was dynamite, no matter what Preece said. Not everyone had ice-cold nerves like him! He'd called in earlier and announced that O'Connell was shutting it all down. That part of it at least, made sense, but they were planning to poison all those kids with uncut heroin. That O'Connell man was deranged. According to Preece he reckoned that, with no witnesses, there was nothing to worry about! What about one of the biggest serial killings in history? That was something to bloody well worry about!

There was a knock at the door.

'Come!' his voice sounded unnaturally loud.

The door opened. Sergeant Dodd ushered in a man he'd never seen before. He was rather scruffily dressed in plain clothes; typical undercover type.

'That'll be all, thank you Sergeant.'

Ringer gestured to the chair in front of his desk. The man ignored it as he strode forward. He did not waste time getting to the point:

'Chief Inspector Ringer, my name is Maddocks and I'm from Customs and Excise. I'm arresting you for aiding and abetting in the supply of Class A drugs and for aiding and abetting in the enslavement and supply of male prostitutes. I warn you that you do not have to say anything, but it may harm your defence if you do not mention, when questioned, something which you later rely on in court. Anything you do say may be given in evidence.'

The man was waving a badge in front of him, but Ringer's eyes were full of sweat and he was having trouble breathing.

'I'm not saying anything without my solicitor present,' he gasped.

'Suit yourself, but before you make that decision, you might like to know what I have to offer you.'

An offer? The man was making an offer! Could there be some way out of this?

'Go on,' he croaked.

The man sat down.

'An hour ago we picked up a motor cruiser just off the coast. On board were two corpses, a large consignment of heroin and an individual called O'Leary. According to a file that has recently come into our possession, Mr O'Leary is heavily implicated in a drugs and prostitution ring run by an associate of yours called Preece. Both men are also implicated in the murder of one of my fellow officers yesterday. O'Leary has already named you as one of the major players in this conspiracy and he hasn't finished singing yet.'

He said this with a cold matter-of-factness that was like a slap around the face. Ringer had seen countless villains confronted with their wrongdoings without ever fully grasping the sickening shock of it. He knew what it felt like now. His accuser continued remorselessly.

'Contrary to what your pal Preece may have told you, we have all the evidence to put you away for a very long time, particularly given how cooperative O'Leary is proving to be. Quite how long that is, depends on just how helpful you decide to be right now.'

Ringer pulled the handkerchief back out of his pocket and ran it over his face and around the back of his neck.

'What d'you mean?' he mumbled.

The man leant forward, almost confidentially.

'We know Preece is the brains behind this thing and we know he is planning to flee the country as soon as he believes his murderous little plan is underway. Unfortunately, he has a hostage and we don't know his escape route. So it's simple. If he gets away, you're in the frame as the mastermind and we will do everything we can to ensure the judge throws away the key. Imagine what they'll do to a bent ex-copper inside, particularly one involved in a paedophile ring. However, if you help us catch him, we'll at least make your assistance known in the right quarters. It's your choice.'

'How do I know you'll do that?'

'You don't and you don't even know that a word from us will make any difference, but compared to the alternative...' he left the sentence dangling in the air.

Ringer sat with his head bowed, automatically running the handkerchief back and forth across the back of his neck. Finally, he looked up.

'Okay, Preece keeps a Piper Navajo Chieftain at Swansea Airport. He's got a civil licence. He's never said so, but I'm sure in an emergency he'd plan to fly out.'

'Good, then I'd say it's about time you and I created a little emergency for him.'

*

Juliet watched her lover prowling up and down the living room. He was like an angry, caged animal; tense and dangerous. Christ, it made her horny! She rose to embrace him. She slid a hand around the back of his neck, pulling him down to her, while the other slid down feeling for his cock through his trousers. He tried to shove her roughly aside, but she clung on knowing resistance would arouse him.

His mobile rang. He pushed her away and snatched it out of his jacket pocket.

'Preece.'

'Hywel, it's me.'

Damn! He was expecting O'Leary and it was that bloody simpleton Ringer!

'What do you want?'

'Hywel, listen to me. The shit's hit the fan big time around here. O'Leary was caught on the Beneteau with the gear and two bodies on board. Customs have Llewellyn's file and they are commandeering all our officers and cars to go and round up the kids.'

'Where are you?'

'I'm on my car phone, not my mobile. They asked me for the file that young Llewellyn gave me and I handed it over like you said. That seemed to allay their suspicions. In fact I'm leading a team up to Mayhill to raid one of the houses, now.'

'Alright, thanks for the tip.' Preece rang off and turned to Juliet.

'Go and get Annette,' he said. 'The whole thing's coming apart at the seams. We're leaving.'

*

Charlie leant forward and broke the connection of Ringer's hands-free car phone. 'Why was it so important to mention that you were on your car phone and not you're mobile,' he asked dryly. He saw Ringer's shoulders tense.

'It just came out like that. I thought it sounded more natural,' he replied.

'I don't recall telling you to think. Still, if it was a warning, it'll only serve to create more panic.'

The car swung right onto a road lined with council houses. It shortly opened onto a patch of green signposted Llewellyn Circle.

'Keep going,' instructed Charlie. 'Llewellyn would be

appropriate, but Cadwalader's more private.' The car continued on until the road opened out at a second circle. 'Pull in here,' he said.

Ringer looked around wildly.

'What the bloody hell's going on?' he demanded. 'I've made the phone call like you said. What're we doing here?'

'Get out of the car,' replied Charlie.

'You must be bloody joking! They're animals around here. They'd rip me to pieces the moment they saw this uniform.'

'Take it off then.'

'What?'

'Take it off. If it will make you feel more at home with the locals, a less formal approach might be a good idea. After all, I expect quite a few of them are harbouring some rather nasty grudges against you. It seems silly to rub their noses in it.'

'You're not really going to leave me here?'

'I certainly am. What do I want to be driving around with a piece of shit like you for? Besides, I've got Preece to chase now he's out of the trap.'

'We had a deal'

'I'm afraid not. I lied. You can't trust anyone nowadays. Now get out.'

'You're not Maddocks; you're Llewellyn, aren't you?'

'I said get out.'

'I'm not moving.'

There was a ringing crack as Charlie slapped Ringer around the side of the head. He slipped out of the back door of the car and hauled Ringer out of the front. The man staggered drunkenly, his balance knocked out by a perforated eardrum.

Charlie marched him across onto the green. He ripped his jacket open and pulled it off his back. He did the same with his shirt.

'There, I knew the more casual look would be fine,' He remarked as he pulled the Chief Inspector's braces off his shoulders. He unbuttoned them from his trousers and used them to secure his hands behind his back. He bent down and tugged Ringer's trousers, which dropped, obligingly down to his ankles. Ringer stood shivering with fear in his vest and shorts. As Charlie stood up he realised an audience had gathered. Mostly women and children and a few old men. The Circle formed a perfect auditorium. He glanced at his watch. With Preece on the move there wasn't much time. He held his hands up for quiet.

'Ladies, please, please...' The buzz of questions died away.

'Ladies, I would just like to introduce this gentleman here. He feels his uniform may arouse some ill feeling in this neighbourhood, so I have removed it for him in order to assure him of your warmest hospitality. Ladies please give a big welcome to Chief Inspector Ringer!'

A hard looking woman with bleached hair and tattoos down her shoulders and arms stepped forward.

'Oh we knows Chief Inspector Ringer alright. Don't we girls?' There were several exclamations in the affirmative, the mildest of which was 'Bastard!' The bleached woman had moved right up to Ringer. She spat in his face, and then turned to the crowd. 'I wonder if his missus knows what it's like to be without a man for years at a time, eh girls?' She asked with a malicious grin.

'Bout time she found out I reckons.' Said another, who had

been edging forward. She turned to a boy in the crowd. 'Jackie, go fetch the carving knife for mammy, will you.'

Ringer turned to Charlie with terror in his eyes.

'Llewellyn, please, for the love of God!'

Charlie stared back, he was seeing Bomber and Al Sullivan.

'I'll phone the real Maddocks from the car to come pick you up. He should be here in half-an-hour,' he replied, coldly. 'He's all yours girls,' he added over his shoulder, as he turned and walked back to the car.

31

Al Sullivan's Audi was parked thirty yards up Derwen Fawr Road facing back towards the entrance to the Preece residence. Gareth was stretching his legs for the third time, despite what his common sense told him. This was leafy suburbia where young men sauntering about for no apparent reason would be viewed with the greatest suspicion. He was beginning to wonder if he should have obeyed his dad and gone back to the flat, but he didn't want to leave him to have all the fun! The trouble was, when he was sitting in the car, he kept imagining that Preece's silent, green Range Rover had somehow slipped out of the driveway and vanished from under his nose.

By the light of the ornamental street lamp that stood at the top of the drive, Gareth could see the vehicle still sitting there. He carried on past for ten yards in the shelter of the high walls that flanked the road, then he turned and walked back.

This was it! As he crossed the entrance to the drive again, he saw Preece escorting his wife around to the passenger door. She seemed to be very unsteady on her feet. He shoved her roughly into the back as Juliet climbed into the passenger seat. Then he was past the drive. He hurried back to the Audi and sat in the dark waiting. A minute later he saw lights coming down the drive. The Range Rover turned right, away from the Audi, heading down towards the Mumbles Road. Gareth waited until he was out of sight, then turned on his sidelights and followed.

Even if he had been going slower he wouldn't have stood a chance. As he entered the single-file stretch and rounded the first corner, he found himself staring in horror at a pair of rapidly approaching reversing lights. He didn't even have time to brake as he hit the back of the Range Rover and found himself enveloped in the Audi's airbag. He heard his door open. He was grabbed by the hair and something hard and cold was pressed into the side of his neck. A familiar, icy voice spoke.

'Get out Gareth, and don't try anything stupid. I'm beginning to find you extremely irritating.'

As Gareth squeezed out from behind the airbag, Preece grabbed him by the hair and dragged him out of the car, ramming his fist into Gareth's solar plexus. Gareth groaned and sank to his knees, doubled-over in pain. Preece grabbed him by the collar and dragged him to his feet. He shoved him towards the Range Rover and opened the back.

'Get in!' He ordered, indicating the luggage space behind the seats. Gareth curled up painfully on the floor. His captor grabbed him by the face, digging his fingers into his cheeks, forcing him to return his stare.

'It seems you're determined to interfere in my affairs, so I think it's time you made yourself useful' he snarled. 'There's a colleague of mine who could use a hostage right now with your fucking father on the rampage. By the time he's done with you, you'll wish you'd never been born!'

With that he slammed the hatchback shut.

*

Charlie breathed a gentle sigh of relief as he felt the lock turn. He dropped the picks back in his pocket and made his way cautiously forward. Suddenly, from the expanse of glass around Swansea Airport's control tower, he could see lights twinkling around Gower and the orange glow of the city in the distance. It was eight-thirty. The place was only used for domestic and recreational flying and everyone had gone home. Down below a Piper Navajo Chieftain was sitting on the apron. Preece had obviously phoned ahead and, unaware that they were aiding and abetting a fugitive from justice, the Duty Crew had obligingly parked it for him.

Charlie flicked on his torch and followed the beam around the room. They could arrive any minute. He located the controller's desk and hurried over to it. He clicked on the radio and located the placard, which showed the airport's frequencies. He extinguished the torch and walked over to where he could see the entrance to the airport's approach road. A number of sets of headlights flashed by. He saw a pair slowing down and swinging left into the turning. They rocked slightly up and down as the vehicle crossed the cattle grid, then they were sweeping up the unlit road towards the airfield. He lost them behind the building for a moment, and then the vehicle rolled out onto the apron and pulled up beside the plane's passenger door, floodlighting the scene with its headlights. It was Preece's Range Rover.

Preece got out and opened the back door. He was holding a gun. He dragged out Annette by her hair. He used it to control her like a rag doll as she staggered around drunkenly at arm's length. The cruel bastard had used drink to put an end to her resistance. He marched her roughly up to the rear door of the plane as Juliet walked around the car to join him. He handed her the gun and watched as she shoved Annette on-board, then he walked around to the pilot's door and got in.

Charlie waited a few moments and then clicked on the radio.

'Golf, Charley, Delta, come in please. Golf, Charley, Delta, are you receiving me? Over.' He imagined the reaction on board as his voice came over the cabin speaker that he had left turned on. Then Preece's voice replied.

'Is that you Llewellyn?'

'It certainly is.'

'What do you want?'

'I want Annette.'

'What do you want a drunken cow like her for?'

'Because I don't intend to let you murder her.'

'And how precisely do you intend to do that, Action Man? We'll be at twenty thousand feet above the Irish Sea in fifteen minutes and the drunken cow can't swim. What are you going to do, swim out to rescue her, tough guy?'

Charlie paused as the sneering, taunting voice sought a weakness in his armour. Preece wanted revenge for the damage Charlie had inflicted. Charlie clicked on his microphone. His voice was even.

'That won't be necessary; you're not going anywhere.'

'That's what you think, loser. I'm just sorry I can't hang around to enjoy putting a bullet in your head!'

Charlie sat back. A grin spread across his face as he watched and listened. He heard the rapid click of switches as Preece prepared for take-off, then a string off profanities as he hit the start button and nothing happened.

'What the fuck's going on...' snarled Preece as he tried again and again but got no response.

'I might be able to help you there,' Charlie cut in. 'Unfortunately for you, I took the trouble of removing the ignition cable before you arrived. That's what I meant when I said you aren't going anywhere and you're not getting it back until you release Annette.'

'Who do you think you are threatening me? Give it back, or I'll shoot the stupid cow right now and then you for good measure!'

'Oh dear, I do believe I'm hearing paranoid delusions of grandeur; not much good under pressure are you Preece? A hostage is no good to you dead. No wonder MI6 washed their hands of you.'

'Fuck off Llewellyn you pathetic prick. Can't stand the thought that I'm fucking your wife, eh? I'm not so foolish as to kill my best negotiating chip. Hand over that lead or I'll put a bullet through her kneecap and take it from there!'

'I wouldn't do that if I were you. If you weren't so chickenshit scared you'd have realised I'm offering you a way out. All I want is Annette in return for that lead, then, as far as I'm concerned you're free to go.'

There was a pause. Charlie could almost hear Preece's brain whirring as he tried to spot the catch. At last he spoke.

'Are you serious? That's it; a straight swap?'

'That's it. I'm not a policeman. I can't arrest you and I don't intend to get an innocent party killed. Give me Annette and you're free to take your chances with the law.'

'Okay, how do we do this?'

'We do it calmly and sensibly. You and Juliet bring Annette

out; I'll come down to the apron. You three stay by the plane while I walk forward and place the lead on the ground halfway between us. You leave the gun with Juliet to cover you, then walk forward with Annette. You collect your lead and hand her over to me. Both parties then walk back out of handgun range and Annette and I, for one, will be off.'

'Very ingenious Llewellyn, you've obviously done this before...'

'Yes, and I've seen people try to double-cross the system and end up dead, so don't try anything clever.'

'What's to stop you returning while I'm fitting the lead?'

'Juliet's still got a gun remember? Besides I've got other fish to fry and we're running out of time. Do you want to do this?'

There was another pause, then Preece answered.

'Okay, we're coming out.'

*

Charlie stepped out from the shadow of the control tower and walked forward into the pool of light it was casting from above. Preece, Juliet and Annette were standing by the plane. Preece handed Juliet the gun. She levelled the gun in Charlie's direction, gripping it in both hands, waiting for him to come into range. Charlie held up the lead where they could see it and began to walk forward.

He reached the middle and paused as Preece arrived, shoving Annette ahead of him. Her face was badly cut and bruised. He toyed with the idea of shooting the man then and there, but he'd promised him to Maddocks and he had no idea who'd get caught in the crossfire if Juliet cut loose. He held up the lead and spoke steadily and clearly.

'Okay Preece, let's not lose it now. Send Annette forward and I'll toss you the lead. I won't fuck around with Juliet pointing that gun at me.'

Preece's reply was gloating.

'I afraid it's not as simple as that, now you're in range, Llewellyn. You see, on our way here we happened to bump into your rather irritating offspring; quite literally as a matter of fact. We were already rather overloaded with this cow and our bags, so we took a little detour and dropped him off with my business partner for safe-keeping. A chap called Pat O'Connell; I believe you two were once very well acquainted...'

'If that bastard does anything to Gareth...'

'I believe it's a bit late for that. When we left, Pat had already given young Gareth a shot of heroin to calm him down and, if I know Pat's sexual proclivities, he'll no doubt be planning to shoot something else into him before long. I left him there half-an-hour ago and he said if he didn't hear from me within the hour to say I was safely in the air, he was going to shoot the little bastard, so you can drop that lead and that gun and piss off or I'll tell Juliet to shoot you right now; I'm not handing over any hostages to a prick like you!'

Charlie stood there, stunned. O'Connell had Gareth? His son was in the hands of his sworn enemy; the man who had tortured him for weeks for no better reason than to break him? He had to get to him. He fought to keep his gun steady as he replied.

'You'll let me go?'

'Sure, why not? You're no threat to me without that gun and that lead, and, as it stands I can only be done for manslaughter, not murder. You'll no doubt go chasing off after Gareth and get yourself killed anyway. Who am I to deprive Pat of the pleasure?'

Charlie studied Preece more closely. Despite the urbane tone, the man was sweating profusely and a nervous tic fluttered in the corner of his left eye. This was a man who enjoyed cruelty, but had no stomach for violence. He was sickened at the thought of leaving Annette in Preece's hands, but Gareth was his son and he'd got him into this.

'If you'll let me go, why not Annette?'

'Because we might still need a hostage. Now fuck off before I change my mind!'

Charlie paused a second longer, then nodded dropped the gun and lead. He turned and began to walk away.

A shot rang out and he flew forward as if hit by a giant fist. He crashed down, rolled onto his back and lay still. As Preece spun around in surprise, Juliet came striding up, her face twisted with rage.

'What the fuck d'you think you're doing you gutless moron?' she screamed. 'You were going to let him go!'

'Well, I thought it better to let Pat deal with him...buy ourselves some extra time.'

'And what if Pat didn't 'deal' with him? He's a trained fucking killer for God's sake. He wasn't going to just pop around and ask him for his son back! And, if he'd got the upper hand, the next people he'd have come looking for would be us!'

'We'd be well away by then...'

'Oh yeah? Look how many years he's spent tracking Pat down! He's like a fucking Mountie. Anyhow, I'm not wasting any more time with a faggot like you, I'm off to join Pat!'

'What d'you mean...?'

'I mean this!'

There was a crack as she pulled the trigger and Preece collapsed to the ground with a bullet through the forehead. She stared down at him for a moment and then calmly walked over to Charlie. His eyes were open and there was a trickle of blood running from the corner off his mouth. She squatted down beside him. Her tone was soothing.

'You still don't get it do you Charlie, my poor darling?'

She reached down and stroked his cheek.

'You see I've been keeping tabs on you ever since you sneaked out of Beirut and spoiled Patrick's fun. We knew you'd come after him when you found out that he'd given Gaddafi the slip and since, you and I had never met, it wasn't too difficult to get close to you and then, well... you men are all the same. I'm sorry I dumped you for Hywel; you were a good shag, but he was far more, shall we say, adventurous. Anyhow all good things come to an end, including you, so I'm afraid I'll have to love you and leave you.'

She bent down and lingeringly kissed his bloodied lips. As she pulled away she lowered the gun to point between his eyes.

*

Charlie groaned inwardly and cautiously opened his eyes. The bullet from Juliet's gun had knocked him to the ground and the puncture in his lung had reopened. He desperately fought the urge to cough as he concentrated on lying still. At least he was alive and the bullet hadn't beaten the Kevlar vest he had borrowed from Maddocks. He heard a shot and then, a moment later, Juliet's voice. He knew she was addressing him, but as if from a distance. He was deaf from gunshots and he half-recognised the remoteness of concussion.

Things began to clear a little and she came briefly into focus. It was definitely Juliet, but he couldn't hear what she was saying. She bent over him briefly then stood up. She was pointing a gun straight between his eyes, and then suddenly she was gone.

Puzzled by her disappearance he forced himself up onto his elbows. A few yards away he made out two people wrestling on the ground. It was all bizarre. They fought their way to their feet, hands locked in each other's hair. One was Juliet, and the other was Annette! Where had she come from? He couldn't figure it out, but one thing was certain, this was an unexpected chance to stop the woman who seconds before was about to kill him. He tried to get up, but his legs seemed to have no strength in them.

He peered around him and spotted Juliet's gun where it had been knocked from her hand. Painfully he stretched out an arm and tried to reach for it. His fingers pushed it another inch away as his head span and he fell back almost blacking out. He waited for his head to clear then dragged himself nearer before he tried again. This time his fingers closed around the butt of the gun.

He levered himself up onto his left elbow, ignoring the pain in his chest as he brought the gun to bear. The combatants had collapsed in a writhing heap again and there was no clear shot. Worse still, they were shifting in and out of focus and he could feel his head beginning to swim. He knew beyond a shadow of a doubt that, if Juliet got up from the fight and he was unconscious, he was a dead man and the Rent Man gang had won. In desperation he loosed off a couple of shots and passed out.

Time had passed. He had no idea how much, but he was still alive and it was still dark. He was suddenly aware that his ears were ringing with gunshots and he could smell them in the air. He hadn't been out long then. Everything was silent; was he completely deaf? He forced himself back up onto his elbows. He began coughing and spat out a lot of blood, then he looked around.

The wrestlers were lying still. Slowly, he rolled over onto his stomach then drew his knees up one at a time. He lifted his body up with his arms and crawled painfully over to them. Annette was dead. The bullet had hit her cleanly at the base of the skull and blown most of her jaw off on the way out. The realisation that it must have been one of his bullets hit him with sickening force. He gazed down at the woman who had fought so hard to reclaim her life, only to lose it trying to save young Bomber's and now his. He tried to remind himself that this was war and war cost lives, but the cliché rang hollow in his ears. He reached out a hand and gently lowered her eyelids against the cold night sky.

Juliet was alive, though white with shock and barely moving. Her left shoulder was blown open, but there was no exit wound.

Charlie guessed she had caught the deflecting bullet that killed Annette. He glanced at his watch. Only minutes had elapsed since she had shot Preece. With another effort of will he forced himself onto his feet and stood swaying for a moment, then bent down, seized Juliet by her hair and pulled her to her feet.

'You and I have got unfinished business to attend to,' he muttered.

He began dragging her unsteadily back across the tarmac towards Preece's Range Rover.

32

Charlie cut the headlights on Preece's Range Rover and turned onto the approach to the warehouse. As before the area was deserted but a Toyota Land Cruiser was parked outside the main entrance. He studied the building afresh as he allowed the vehicle to creep forward. Glimmers of light trickled out from between the occasional sheet of loose corrugated iron on the roof of the main building. He turned onto the slip road leading up to the roller shutter. He brought the car to a halt and opened the driver's door slightly, but didn't get out. He slipped the car back into first gear, gripped the wheel firmly with his left hand and rammed his foot to the floor. His head slammed back against the headrest as the vehicle shot forward and smashed through the flimsy metal door.

The car ploughed into several stacks of pallets and stalled as Charlie slashed at his airbag then shoved the door open wider and rolled out to crouch beside the car. Before the dust could clear, he scurried, bent double, across to the cover of a nest of sofas that were sitting in a display group on the edge of the central floor space. The dust floated back down to be replaced by silence and the overpowering stench of petrol. It wasn't coming from the Range Rover.

The dim yellow light of the warehouse revealed a macabre scene at the far end of the room. There was no sign of life amongst the twisted bodies on the floor. Charlie estimated at least a dozen at a glance. He checked the safety was off on the Browning, his finger taught on the trigger. He recognised the

THE RENT MAN

giant. He lay on his back, an arm outstretched, as if he had died lunging at his executioner. Even in death his face seemed contorted by a manic grin. The top of his skull was blown wide open. The skinny dog handler sat slumped against a display rack of cheap nylon carpet. In the dim, yellow light the blood stains that had spread across his Metallica T-shirt looked black. Mort had died cowering under a table in the corner. Charlie didn't recognise the rest, but he recognised the type. He had rarely seen such an unprepossessing looking bunch of thugs. They had no doubt lived as violently as they had died. He was clearly looking at the mortal remains of the Rent Man Gang.

From the look of the wounds he was up against an automatic weapon, probably silenced. In the confined space of the warehouse the noise would have been deafening otherwise. Given the aggressive nature of the victims, the killer would have needed to spray an arc of bullets, or risk being overwhelmed. Even then, the slaughter required nerves of steel. Only a psychopath like O'Connell would have had the unhesitating brutality to pull off a cold-blooded killing as extreme as this. Anyhow, he was probably still around. He hadn't gone to the trouble of soaking the room in petrol, not to torch it.

Gareth was sitting, naked and slumped over, on a kitchen chair in the middle of the neon lit room. He was clearly tied to it or he would have fallen off. He was either dead or unconscious. He was clearly positioned there to act as bait which meant O'Connell was expecting him. Charlie paused to consider his options; there were only two. He could either hide there until O'Connell got bored and flicked a lighter, or he could take the bait and show himself. He raised his hands, stood up and began to slowly walk forward. He got to within five yards of Gareth and O'Connell hadn't shot him yet! Perhaps he had already made his escape...? And perhaps bears didn't shit in the woods. This was a trap and O'Connell was having his fun.

Even as Charlie arrived at this conclusion he sensed the movement behind him. O'Connell's voice filled the unnatural stillness of the room. 'I had a feeling you'd show up Llewellyn and this is a nine mil Ingram submachine gun I'm holdin'. It'll cut you in half whichever way you drop, dive or spin, so don't even think about it. Raise your hands and throw away the gun.'

Charlie couldn't have done or thought about anything. Sweat was blurring his vision and his legs were shaking uncontrollably. He was back in the interrogation room in Baghdad, chained naked to a wall. He had just taken another fearful beating and O'Connell's pale blue, almost colourless, eyes were inches away from his face. They studied him for what seemed like an eternity and then disappeared from his field of vision. Then his tormenter spoke in that mild Irish accent.

'Well Captain. It seems that you would rather die than talk to me. I'm sure your colleagues will prove far more amenable, so let's not waste more time.'

O'Connell addressed one of the torturers.

'Put him in the cell with the rest of them tonight so they know what to expect and, if he still refuses to cooperate come the morning, take him out and shoot him.'

Charlie shook his head to try and get rid of the vision. He raised his hands and, when the voice came again, it was not a hallucination.

'Obliging of you to put your hands up, Llewellyn but I also

told you to lose the gun. Throw it in the corner. There's a good fella.'

Charlie did not even hear him as the hallucination hit again. He was remembering the look on Rotty's face as he was thrown back into the cell. If he needed to be told he was a mess, that said it all. The guards threw him down next to Billy. Pete was lying unconscious in a corner, looking like Charlie felt.

He was jerked out of the trance as a spray of bullets flew just over his head.

'If you want to live, you'll have to learn to do as you're told,' remarked his captor. 'I'm a very impatient man, Llewellyn, particularly with people who take it upon themselves to meddle in my affairs.'

The shock of the gunfire had staved off the hallucination. He turned to face O'Connell. The Irishman hadn't lied about the machine gun. Charlie tossed the gun to one side as O'Connell spoke again.

'My, my,' he breathed, 'you never learn do you?'

Charlie shrugged, so O'Connell continued.

'You can't trust anyone these days. Those bloody rag-heads swore to fucking Allah that they'd topped you and so did O'Leary and Preece. Tell me, how did you get out of Baghdad'

It seemed that O'Connell was enjoying the upper hand and, without a gun, time was all Charlie had to play for.

'The Guards were lazy. When they came for me in the morning Pete took my place. We were similar in build and both in a shit state and I don't suppose the guards cared much.'

'How touching! A sort of 'I'm Spartacus' scene. Bum boys were you?'

'No, it was just that I was the only one who could identify you from the night before. We knew you were peddling weapons to Saddam Hussein using your old IRA connections, so my unit let ourselves get captured. We were the tethered goat and you were stupid enough to show yourself'.

'Careful Llewellyn; you won't provoke me into making a mistake, only into shooting you. And keep your hands up. I'm not coming close enough to check for hidden weapons, I'll just shoot you at the first hint of a wrong move. However, since you're rather more talkative than last time we met, why don't you carry on? I know you're only trying to buy time, but I'm most intrigued as to how you've found me after all these years.'

O'Connell strolled down the room, past the corpses to a counter, never taking his eyes off Charlie. He picked up the bottle of scotch that was sitting on it, unscrewed the top and upended it without once shifting his gaze. The barrel of the gun never wavered. He replaced the bottle and wiped his mouth with the back of his hand.

'Carry on,' he ordered.

O'Connell was right. Charlie was buying time. No doubt his adversary could hold his drink, but the scotch might slow his reactions or cloud his judgement just enough. Besides, talk was cheap compared to a bullet in the head. He carried on.

'Unfortunately for you, after I escaped, Iraqi intelligence appears to have decided you were too expensive and took you off their lists of suppliers so you needed to find a new toy market. That meant you were no longer any use to MI6, who employ double-crossers, but never trust them. Your former colleagues in the IRA had fallen for your faked death, so you were in the clear.

Then in late ninety-two we heard a Middle Eastern arms dealer had made an approach to an American arms manufacturer. Saddam was desperate for some new toys and wanted to trade. The manufacturer contacted the CIA and, when Langley asked what he had to offer in return, he gave the manufacturer a detailed description of your bent war record including the phoney plane crash and your resurrection as a businessman.'

'Was his name Tabakian by any chance?'

'I believe so.'

'Hmmn, that's when I learned not to mix business with pleasure; continue.'

'There was the usual squabble over whose pigeon you were. The Brits wanted you for your IRA activities. The Yanks wanted you for supplying arms to Saddam Hussein. By the time they stopped bickering you'd flown the nest. Finally, a bit of international cooperation won the day. Vauxhall handled the paper chase through the European banks while the CIA tried to pick up your trail using their profiling experts. Appropriately enough you were caught by a shrink.'

'I've warned you once about trying to provoke me...'

'It's true. Your penchant for young boys was known to MI6 before the war, but as long as it was Arab boys, they didn't seem bothered. You appeared to be doing good work in Baghdad. The profilers picked up on this and their top shrink argued that a sexual predator like you would soon be looking for more young boys. They began checking paedophile rings. Meanwhile, Vauxhall could see your money moving across Europe. They very nearly grabbed you in Zurich, but you slipped the net. However, it must have panicked you, because you made your first contract with Semple using one of your banking aliases.'

O'Connell shrugged.

'We all make mistakes.'

'That was a bad one because, after Zurich, you stopped using personal bank accounts and the paper chase dried up. They would have lost you without that link to Semple.'

'So how come the SAS are involved?'

'The Regiment isn't involved officially. Det Eight goes back to our original Baghdad mission, but has evolved as your activities have moved from terrorism, through gun-running and into drugs and prostitution. It now includes people from all sorts of agencies.'

'And it diverts them into a personal vendetta against me.'

Charlie shrugged.

'You don't exist. Officially, MI6 and the CIA never accepted the Iraqi version of your escape. You are still missing believed dead. You don't pay tax. If you have bank accounts and passports, they're in other names.'

'Shouldn't you be trying to bring me to justice?'

'You can't try someone who doesn't exist and, if we brought you back to life, the only evidence we could produce is entirely circumstantial. Besides, as far as we are concerned you were part of the Iraqi war machine, and our mission was to destroy that. We didn't hear your name mentioned in the ceasefire so we don't see any reason to end the mission. Given what you did in the Gulf, and what you've done since, nor does anyone else.'

'It's not like Vauxhall to hand over one of their own.'

'Vauxhall agreed that you were ours from day one. They

were happy for us to clean up their mess though others showed some interest in a slice of the action for a while. Bringing your dirty washing back home, caused an argument over territory amongst the agencies. Even MI5 had a case for arguing that you had become a domestic matter and part of their remit. Rather than let the whole thing turn into a tug-of-war, our brass pointed out that I was the only person who could reliably identify you.'

'So they sent their top Sass squaddie off to track me down and murder me; me a simple Irish businessman supplying the demands of a hungry marketplace...'

'There's nothing simple about you O'Connell and I am not a squaddie. I took this job because as long as you live, innocent people will die. I don't know what made you the way you are and I don't care; someone has to stop you and if it's not me there will be others.'

O'Connell raised his eyebrows in mock alarm, then threw back his head and laughed.

'Fine, and I'll kill them too, and their stupid fuckin' sons. You're gettin' a bit long in the tooth to be playin' Action Man, what with your family to consider, aren't ya? What took you so long?'

'My health. I didn't know it when I moved to Swansea, but the Post Traumatic Stress was only just beginning to catch up with me.'

'Lost your bottle, did you?'

'Call it what you like.'

'Hmm, from the way you began shaking when you heard my voice just now, I would say you haven't exactly got it back. Stand up!'

Charlie rose, slowly.

'Killing me will leave a trail. Torching this room won't conceal my identity.'

'Have I given you any reason to think I'm particularly stupid? The petrol is meant for these morons.' O'Connell gestured towards the corpses with a nod. 'There are plenty of far more discreet places around here where your body will never be found. I'll be long gone before your chums realise you've fucked up. Turn around.'

'No. If you're going to shoot me, you'll have to look me in the face to do it.'

'Suit yourself. Erkaa ya khinzer, ya kaleb!'

Charlie collapsed instantly to his knees, at the Arabic command. He was staring down into the filthy sewer surrounded by his guards. He could hear the rats scampering around in the darkness. He began to shake so violently that his teeth were chattering and waves of nausea made his head reel. From a distance he could hear O'Connell laughing, and then the Irishman was speaking again.

'Look at you, man! You'll have to forgive me if I don't shit myself with fright. If you're the best they've got to send against me, I think I'll come out of hiding altogether!' There was more mocking laughter.

With a tremendous effort of will, Charlie lifted his head to stare at O'Connell. The strong smell of petrol was momentarily helping to overpower the visions, but he knew O'Connell could trigger them again at will.

'Wait!' he gasped.

'Wait for what?' O'Connell leant forward in mock interest.

'Go on, I'm all ears.'

'Don't you want to know where your sister is?'

'My sister, Juliet? She's with Preece...'

'No she's not. She shot him half-an-hour ago. How do you think I knew where to find you?'

'Don't talk fuckin' crap, she'd never betray me!'

'Are you sure? She told me you were rubbish in bed.'

'She did what you liar? She'd never say such a thing!'

'She said your cock was too small to satisfy a woman so she left you to your little Arab boys. She thought her prayers had been answered when you asked her to spy on me and she found herself in bed with a real man. She's in the car if she's still alive. Don't take my word for it. Go and ask her yourself.'

O'Connell had transformed. His face was puce with rage and spittle flecked his mouth. For a moment Charlie was sure he was going to pull the trigger, but he'd hit a nerve and he needed to keep the man off balance.

'Go on, what are you waiting for? She's been shot but she might be good for a farewell fuck if you're quick enough!'

'You animal, you filthy fuckin' animal! What have you done to her?'

'Nothing compared to what you used to do to her apparently, but she's got a bullet in the shoulder that needs looking at so you'd better hurry if you fancy...'

Without warning O'Connell lashed out with the butt of the gun, knocking Charlie to the ground and reopening the gash on his head.

'I'll deal with you in a minute!' he roared and stormed off towards the car.

Charlie shook his head and blinked hard to try and clear the concussion. He heard a spurt from the Ingrams. O'Connell was on the rampage and he and Gareth would be next assuming he was still alive. He reached into his trouser pocket and pulled out a lighter.

'Die you fucking bastard!' he whispered. He clicked the lighter's switch and rolled aside as the evaporated petrol caught above his head and a fireball gathered and tore around the room. As it spread it enveloped Gareth's chair and flames danced around his naked body, then Charlie hit it with his shoulder, knocking it over and smothering them. He seized the back of the chair and began crawling desperately towards the door that led into the front office as poisonous smoke filled the air and pieces of cheap plastic furniture exploded around him.

*

He was out of the smoke and flames and coughing hard despite the pain in his chest. There was too much blood to swallow, so he rolled his head to one side and let it trickle out of the corner of his mouth. His head was pounding and he could not gather his thoughts. He closed his eyes and felt the darkness rising up. Just as consciousness was about to slip away he heard a wild voice bellowing: 'Llewellyn! Llewellyn!' It was a voice that filled him with dread, though he couldn't remember exactly why. He forced himself to open his eyes again. He saw the man framed in the doorway briefly, flames leaping up behind him. He was staggering around as if he couldn't see.

From somewhere deep in Charlie's mind, a voice was telling

him he had to do something or he'd die. This man was going to kill him. He reached down and pulled up his trouser leg. He eased his only remaining weapon out of its sheath and gripped it by the blade.

Again the dreadful bellowing came and the man was back in the doorway.

'Llewellyn, you fucking bastard, you've blinded me!'

This time the man's outstretched hand found the doorframe and he advanced into the room his head cocked to one side, listening. The upper half of his face was blackened and blistered. His eyes were closed and tears streaked down his cheeks. Some sixth sense obviously told him his quarry was nearby. He squeezed the machine gun trigger, spraying the small room at waist height.

Charlie threw the knife. It hit, but not well enough. O'Connell grunted in pain and felt down to where it was sticking out of his stomach. Then he fell to his knees, swaying. His face registered surprise and pain, and then it twisted into a manic grin.

'Bad hit Llewellyn,' he sneered. 'You must be on the floor!'

The muzzle of the Ingram began to lower and Charlie closed his eyes.

33

The day Charlie disappeared it was like the Tower of fucking Babel down the Railway and no mistake!

First, in comes 'Wing Commander' bloody Morgan waving a copy of the Post about and spouting off like John the Baptist.

Had we heard?

Had we heard what?

Had we heard about the fire at that warehouse in Fforestfach?

What about it?

What about it? Burnt to the bloody ground, that's what was about it! Kids, according to the paper, the lazy little sods; good spell in the RAF was what they needed, damn 'em.

If you listened to him, you'd have thought he'd personally defeated the entire Luftwaffe single-handed, even though he'd have only been four years old at the time according to the Landlord's missus. Nobby started humming the Dam Busters tune and the silly old sod got in a huff as usual.

Jenks nicked his paper for the racing and we all had a laugh at the announcement of Chief Inspector Ringer's retirement. Good riddance to the useless bastard. Perhaps they'd get someone tidy in to clear up that bloody Rent Man Gang so people could go about their business again.

Then Jones Bach arrived and things got really interesting. According to his mate who was a porter in Morriston, they'd been ferrying in bodies all day. Seems like it was more than kids who'd set that fire because the stiffs were full of bullet holes! That got the drinks flowing as the boys wet their whistles and the speculating began in earnest. Finally, Jenks bowed to public opinion and someone borrowed the remote from the bar and switched over to the News.

It was better than if we'd declared war on Cardiff. There was that bird with the tits from BBC Wales outside Swansea Central Nick and a new bloke out in Fforestfach at the warehouse. There was a small bloody army of punters with microphones laying siege to Morriston Hospital and Doug Newton from Wales Today was down at the docks shouting questions at a man from Customs who had just found a boat full of dead bodies drifting around the Bay.

It wasn't 'til gone nine that Jenks noticed Charlie and Jacs were missing and tried their mobiles. He must have tried for the best part of an hour, but no reply. By then we were all well pissed and no one took much notice.

*

The following afternoon 'Wing Commander' bloody Morgan comes marching in with the news that there was a Dawlishes' sign up on Charlie's lawn again. Well go fetch a feather and knock us all down with it! As if we hadn't noticed! More's to the point Jenks had stopped on his way past and asked the sign boys if they knew who had told them to put it up. Turned out some posh English solicitor that no one had ever heard of had phoned up; certainly not that bastard Preece who Charlie's missus had run off with.

Not long after that, Colin and Bev came in and she couldn't wait to tell all and sundry that Jacs had missed work again

366

and the Twins weren't in school. In fact, so she'd heard, the Head Mistress had received her written resignation that very morning! The Landlord's missus pointed out that it wouldn't have gone to the head because lollipop ladies were employed by the Council, but no-one gave a shit about that. Had anyone seen Jacs in the last couple of days? No and Charlie neither.

Then they start coming in from work and the word was that the cafe up at Fairwood had been serving tea and welsh cakes to the Customs boys like they're going out of fashion. Apparently they'd shut the airport for a week while they were carrying out an 'investigation'. Course they'd all got their gobs welded shut, except when it comes to stuffing welsh cakes in them, but the fact they were up there was bound to make you wonder and Neris who cleans up at the Flying School reckons she saw that Preece's plane being taken off on the back of a low-loader. She knew it was his, because the prick was always up there polishing it.

*

That was six months ago and we haven't seen Charlie or Jacs since. There was a rumour that Jacs had taken the kids to live up near Wrexham, but her Mum isn't saying a dickie bird and no self-respecting Swansea girl would move up there, so that's died the death.

Beryl Blackwell who works down the University reckoned some coppers from London turned up and buggered of with all the records on Charlie's boy Gareth and he hasn't been seen since. She tried to find out a bit more from his tutor, but the bloke swore blind he knew nothing. Reckoned he'd probably dropped out of college and gone travelling.

'Wing Commander' bloody Morgan will still tell anyone who's soft enough to listen that he's the only one with the full S.P. thanks to a personal contact of his in Special Branch or such like, but no one around here takes any notice of his bullshit. As Charlie used to say, the only good thing about that bastard is he keeps the strangers out.

According to the paper that pompous prick Ringer is standing for Mayor now! Can you believe it? It never made the paper, but it was common knowledge that someone fitting Charlie's description left him on Mayhill with his trousers around his ankles and the ladies of Cadwaladr Circle tried to cut his nuts off with a carving knife. Fair dos, that doesn't prove anything, but no-one's going to tell anyone around here that Ex-Chief Inspector bloody Ringer wasn't connected to all the other stuff. The word is in some circles that he was even the mastermind behind the Rent man Gang, but Dai Scrap will give up shagging sheep before a bent copper gets done in Swansea.

Of course, as everybody knows, the Police investigation spread right up as far as Scotland and, for a while, it was a bit of a laugh being the centre of attention as the place where it all kicked off. The newspapers called it the Morriston Massacre, but that's only because Fforestfach and Massacre don't sound right together. After a while it got to be a pain in the arse with all those tossers from London turning up to interview us. At last we found a use for 'Wing Commander' Morgan who drove them away with his war stories. Jenks even got him some war medals from the boot sale to show the fuckers.

I still call in for an occasional pint with the boys after work, but me and the missus prefer the Commercial for an evening out these days. Trouble is the place just isn't the same anymore without those evenings with Charlie having a banter with Jacs, and Jenks, and Jones Bach, or taking the piss out of Dai Scrap's speedboat, which everyone knows came from the skip. Even the Landlord and his missus are taking a new pub in Landore, more fool them.

Of course, when I do call in, it's not long before the conversation turns to what really went on. I for one find it hard to swallow that Charlie topped himself and Jenks won't hear a word of it. Then there's the women up at Cadwaladr who've ID'd him from photos. That business at the furniture warehouse is still a mystery. The coppers reckon all the bodies were identified, and Charlie's name never got a mention. More than that, it's common knowledge that those bodies were the Rent Man Gang and Swansea's a different place now. You can't tell me it's just a coincidence that Charlie disappears and suddenly the bad guys get wiped out.

Still, he's gone, and God knows where, and it's probably for the best if he doesn't come back now anyway; not since Minister Hughes' cockerel fell off the chapel roof. It's funny, but somehow our Charlie boy never really struck me as an Architectural Sculptor, but then what's one of them when you come to think about it?

Also by
MIKE ADLAM:

The Stamford Trilogy:
Malpractice
Sharp Practice
Out of Practice

 ponymous

SHARP PRACTICE
By Mike Adlam

Released from prison and bereft of his licence to practice, philandering surgeon Tony Stamford sets about restoring his fortunes administering to the most private medical needs of Hampstead's wealthy women. However, when his past comes knocking in the guise of Detective Inspector Newcombe, he is forced to seek refuge in the bosom of Médecins Sans Frontières, the Foreign Legion of the medical profession. Spurned by them, a chance encounter leads him into the dark and labyrinth world of Lebanese Minister for the Interior, Khoury, the horrifying Syrian conflict and then into the even darker world of international arms dealer Peter Chisholm.

As always funny and dark, Sharp Practice, the second book in the Malpractice trilogy, takes the reader on an odyssey through the very darkest realms of human nature as hapless anti-hero, British surgeon Tony Stamford, finds himself yet again fighting for his very survival in war torn Syria.

'A no-holds-barred, pull-out-all-the stops, breathless tangle of a thriller full of dark comedy…A heck of a good read'
Amazon.com

'An outstanding comic novel…Tony Stamford, philandering surgeon, is a masterpiece of grotesque invention'
Bookbrowse.com

'Darkly comic, beautifully paced, the novel is crammed with an almost Dickensian sense of atmosphere and turbulence, yet blessed with the deftness of Waugh. Full of great moments, it also succeeds in being momentous'
Goodreads.com

'Brilliantly entertaining and consistently outrageous, Adlam's brand of salacious humour spills out a tidal wave of manic delight'
Metro

'Sharp Practice is…admirably plotted, full of vitality, a novel that is truly comic, and, like all true comedy, also disturbing'
Literary Journal

MALPRACTICE

By Mike Adlam

Wealthy, philandering surgeon Tony Stamford seems to have the world at his feet until an embarrassing email from a recent conquest, Katya, proves the final straw for his long-suffering wife. But is she as long-suffering as she seems, and who really is Katya? As Stamford's life begins to unravel he finds himself lost in a world of mirrors, no longer certain who he can trust and doubting the value of his very existence. Stripped of everything he once owned, he embarks on a battle for his freedom and even sanity which can only end in death.

Sharply satirical and disturbingly dark, Malpractice takes a scalpel to the vanities of the medical profession and, in doing so lays bare the deceits and cruelties to which desperate people will stoop.

'A no-holds-barred, pull-out-all-the stops, breathless tangle of a thriller full of dark comedy…A heck of a good read'
Amazon.com

'An outstanding comic novel…Tony Stamford, philandering surgeon, is a masterpiece of grotesque invention'
Bookbrowse.com

'Darkly comic, beautifully paced, the novel is crammed with an almost Dickensian sense of atmosphere and turbulence, yet blessed with the deftness of Waugh. Full of great moments, it also succeeds in being momentous'
Goodreads.com

'Brilliantly entertaining and consistently outrageous, Adlam's brand of salacious humour spills out a tidal wave of manic delight'
Metro

'Sharp Practice is…admirably plotted, full of vitality, a novel that is truly comic, and, like all true comedy, also disturbing'
Literary Journal

THE FINAL MILE

By Cal Smyth

The Final Mile is a biting social commentary of both the jobless hordes and the glitzy, gold-plated world of dirty deals and fat cat cronyism.

A man who has lost everything. Push him a little further. And he's going to fight back... Ryan Morgan is a good guy, a family man who runs his own business and lives by the rules. But when his business is liquidated, his house repossessed and his wife leaves him, Ryan starts to question the system. For years, the rich have ripped us off. It's time someone made them pay. Seeking payback, Ryan treks cross-country through a broken Britain menaced by an economic crisis. With nothing left to lose, Ryan cuts a brutally sweet swathe through the murky greed and corruption of bankers, CEOs and politicians whose skewered morals and hypocrisy have crippled a nation.

A stunning tale of morality and justice in which a simple, honest man is transformed into a killer, The Final Mile depicts a moral turnaround in the vein of TV's Breaking Bad. A story ripped from the headlines of tomorrow's newspapers.

'A resonant wish-fulfilment thriller that is cinematic and sparse genre writing at its very best. With nods to Richard Stark, Elmore Leonard and George Pelecanos, Cal Smyth has written a tale of revenge that challenges and entertains in equal measure: a blazing read that burns off the page, righteous indignation rippling through every heart-stopping moment'
Amazon.com

'Amoral, frighteningly violent and…portrays with deadpan brilliance the soul-less bankers who wheel and deal, exploit and thrive like rats in present-day Britain'
Goodreads.com

'A powerful and chilling story. The plot is convincing in every detail, the characters are entirely believable'
Metro

'Smyth's new thriller is a triumph…Suspenseful and elegant…a thoughtful, frightening story'
Literary Journal

'The Final Mile is, thankfully, fiction…it is five days since I finished reading the novel and it is still rumbling around in my head'
Bookbrowse.com

A TOUCH OF PIGSKIN

By Dai Blatchford

Piers Prideaux's promising career at an Oxford College is brought to an abrupt end following the intervention of a new master, one Sebastian Slope. It is not quite as simple as that, matters in Oxford never are. In defending himself Prideaux is directly responsible for Slope being sacked, arrested and jailed for fraud. Years later Slope returns to Oxford and it becomes clear that he is bent on revenge.

Slope is the leader of a group of dangerous men who are descended from an ancient Cornish secret society known as the Spriggans. Prideaux is forced to go on the run with his oldest best friend William Radleigh de Beaune, aka Billy Bones, an aristocrat fallen on hard times. As Slope pursues his deadly obsession anyone associated with Bones and Prideaux is in great danger.

Pigskin is a wise, quite surreal, philosophical meditation on the business of living, but with a witty and whimsical undercurrent, full of oddball characters and even odder secret societies.

'Cross Inspector Morse with Monty Python and you might get some idea of a book that, reduced to its pure essence, is a read and a half all the way… a dark and brilliant surreal thriller. Dai Blatchford has written a glittering, fantastical, cunningly contrived novel that leads the reader down a labyrinth of fear and dread. Rich with humour, character and incident'
Amazon.com

'A brilliant book, barmy and barnacled with the grotesque'
Metro

'A Touch of Pigskin is a first novel not only of tremendous promise, but also of achievement, a minor masterpiece…a mighty imagination has arrived on the scene'
Literary Journal

'A dazzling performance by Blatchford…a delightful display that marries the gusto of an international thriller with a collection of fascinating esoterica…stunning'
Bookbrowse.com

'Enthralling…there's no denying the bizarre fertility of the author's imagination: his brilliant dialogue , his wicked humour…'
The Literary Supplement

'Blatchford's the kind of writer who makes you want to nag your friends until they read him so that they share the pleasure'
Goodreads.com

www.ingramcontent.com/pod-product-compliance
Lightning Source LLC
Chambersburg PA
CBHW020837020726
47497CB00005B/1135